Lucy Score

PROTECTING WHAT'S

LUCY SCORE

Bloom books

Published by Bloom Books, an imprint of Sourcebooks
P.O. Box 4410, Naperville, Illinois 60567-4410
(630) 961-3900
sourcebooks.com

Originally self-published in 2020 by That's What She Said, Inc.

Cataloging-in-Publication data is on file with the Library of Congress.

Printed and bound in the United States of America.
VP 10 9 8 7 6 5 4 3

To first responders everywhere for standing between us and danger.

CHAPTER 1

S eriously? What's next, Chief? A cat in a tree?"
Fire Chief Lincoln Reed smirked at the rookie slumped in his passenger seat.

Skyler—better known as New Guy despite her gender— was fresh off a bachelor's in fire science from Purdue University, and like all rookies, she was restless when it came to the mundane grunt work of fire station life.

"You're breaking a cardinal rule, rook," he warned her. "Never even think the word s-l-o-w. We'll all regret it."

He checked his speed as he merged onto the highway, leaving Benevolence behind them. The V8 of his SUV, the cherry-red chief's vehicle, rumbled appreciatively as it opened up.

"I just expected there to be more action," she complained. "Instead we're running to Home Depot for extension cords."

"It can't all be four alarms and water rescues," Linc pointed out, tapping out the beat in time with the radio. He was grateful for that. Earlier in his career, he too lived for the action of a structure fire, the excitement of a crash with entrapment. But with time, experience, and considerable wisdom, Linc had grown to appreciate the other side of being a firefighter. Training and community education. Fire safety plans. Outreach. They were just as important as the calls.

Sure, the paperwork sucked. But it had a purpose. And he could appreciate that.

It was a beautiful, windows-down and sunglasses-on kind of day. Summer was butting up against the encroaching fall, daring the next season to steal its thunder.

"Oh, shit. What the hell is that?" Skyler said, pointing ahead as a shower of sparks shot up against the concrete barrier a few hundred yards ahead of them. A sea of red lights appeared as vehicles slammed on their brakes, skidding and sliding.

"Fuck," Linc muttered, slowing down and yanking the wheel hard to the right. "Hang on."

He punched the switch, and lights and sirens cut through the eerie post-crash silence. On the shoulder, he swerved around an orange construction sign and stomped the gas, flying past the stunned occupants of stopped cars.

A cloud of black smoke rose up in front of a jackknifed tractor-trailer truck. He could smell it. Burnt rubber, spilled chemicals, and fire.

"That's not good," Skyler said, already slipping out of her seat belt.

"Call it in and kill the sirens," he ordered. Slamming on the brakes, he threw the SUV in park and killed the engine.

"We've got a multivehicle collision on Highway 422, mile marker thirty-three," he heard her saying into the radio as he jumped out of the SUV. "Benevolence FD chief is on-scene."

He popped the hatch and dragged out his turnout gear. Adrenaline was his friend, keeping his movements quick and efficient. In seconds, he was geared up and heading in the direction of calls for help while he stuffed his gloves in his pockets.

"Hey, man! What can I do?" the driver of a tractor-trailer truck yelled from his cab window.

"Get some of your eighteen-wheeled pals to block traffic on both sides," Linc called back. They'd need to land the helicopter on the other side of the highway.

The guy threw him a salute.

"Get the kit," Linc yelled to Skyler when she popped out of the passenger side.

A woman, early fifties, with blood from a cut on her forehead dripping onto her bright-blue tank top, walked dazedly toward him. She looked like she'd just come from a yoga class.

That was the kicker about this job. It was a constant reminder that life could change on a dime. People never knew when their everyday lives were going to come to an unceremonious halt. When their schedules and to-do lists would be interrupted by something that changed everything.

"Ma'am, if you can walk, I need you to move to the side of the road," he said, squeezing her shoulders. "Can you do that?"

She nodded slowly.

"I got her." A man in a business suit limped toward them. His shirt was covered in whatever he'd been eating at the time of the crash.

"Take her over there, as far away as you can get from the smoke. Grab anyone else you can," Linc ordered.

He didn't wait to see if they did his bidding. There were more people, climbing out of mangled metal. Broken glass crunched under feet that hadn't intended to walk through disaster today. He reached the rear of the truck, still shouting for everyone to get clear, when the heat hit him head-on.

Two cars—a Jeep and the sedan in front of it—were smashed between the eighteen-wheeler and the center divider. The engine compartment of the Jeep was engulfed in flames.

"Oh my God. Oh my God. He just slammed into us." The girl in the Jeep, she couldn't have been more than twenty, crawled out of the back, shaking so hard her teeth chattered.

"Anyone else with you?" Linc asked.

"N-n-n-no. I couldn't stop. It happened so fast. I didn't mean to hit that car."

"Honey, I need you to get to the side of the road," he insisted.

"I should see if they're okay," she said, pointing a trembling finger at the sedan. "N-n-no one got out."

Skyler jogged up, breathless with excitement.

"Take her," Linc said. "Shock. Start triaging the others. Keep them out of the hot zone."

"On it," she said calmly. She was shaking too, but it was a different kind of physiological reaction. Adrenaline meeting preparation. "Come with me, miss."

He debated his approach to the sedan. The cab of the tractor-trailer was smashed into the barrier, blocking the access from the front. The fire made rear entry impossible.

"Only one way in," he muttered, stripping off his air tank and helmet and dragging on his gloves. He slid under the belly of the low trailer. Fluids bled over the asphalt, puddling and pooling, slipping over his gear. It was a good goddamn mess.

The heat was getting worse by the second, and he paused for a second to adjust his hood.

His heart beat steadily in his ears as he crawled out from the undercarriage.

"Someone help us!"

Linc wedged himself into the space between the sedan's rear door and the trailer. The driver was awake and panicking behind the wheel as the flames from the Jeep were licking at the trunk of the car.

There were two bystanders leaning over the concrete barrier, yanking in vain at the driver's side door. But there wasn't enough clearance.

"Fuck me," Linc muttered. Nothing was ever easy when it came to life and death.

"Help us!" The woman, tall and dark, was hanging over the barrier, a half-dozen expensive bracelets shimmering on her wrists as she pulled on the bent frame of the door. She reminded him of Wonder Woman. The man helping her was five foot nothing and couldn't have weighed more than a buck twenty-five. He had a Tweety Bird tie on. Linc would put five bucks on it being a clip-on.

"You okay, buddy?" Linc asked the driver, ducking his head into the open window of the back seat. The guy had been enjoying the same windows-down drive only moments before it all went to hell.

"My leg hurts like hell, and I'm stuck, man."

He was a big man whose bushy white mustache was turning pink thanks to a bloody nose from the airbag. Sweat matted his hair.

"We're gonna get you out of here, okay? Just hang in there," Linc promised.

There was a loud pop, and a metal projectile exploded from where the trunk had been.

"Holy shit! What was that?" Tweety Bird yelped. Wonder Woman cringed but never slowed her fruitless pulls on the door.

"Trunk hydraulic bursting," Linc said, shimmying through the back passenger side window into the back seat. The heat was a hellish inferno.

"Mister, I don't know if this is such a good idea," the driver said, his voice shaking. "I might not make it outta here, and I'd sure feel bad if you went tryin' to save me. I'm seventy-two. You've got more ahead of you than I do."

Linc gripped the man's shoulder. Sometimes firm physical contact was the quickest reassurance. "It's gonna be fine. Just do what I say, and we'll both be having cold beers tonight."

The heat in the car was unbearable, but Linc ignored it. He aligned his body to create a barrier between the encroaching fire and the driver's seat. His turnout gear would protect him and the driver, for the next few minutes at least.

"What's the game plan, fire guy?" Wonder Woman demanded as he stripped off his gloves and dug through his pockets.

"Can't take him out through the door. I need you to find fire extinguishers and someone who'll use this glass breaker," he said, pulling the tool free of his pocket. "We gotta move fast." The windshield was the worst possible egress. The glass was stronger than the windows and shatter-resistant. It would take more than a miracle to get the driver out that way.

She grabbed the glass breaker, looked at the driver, and bit her lip.

"Honey, you best get going. It's gettin' hot over here," the man said, squeezing her hand.

She squeezed right back and glanced over her shoulder. "Hey, yo! I need a hero glass breaker and a fucking fire extinguisher now! You, go scavenge," she said, giving Tweety Bird a shove before turning back to the driver and giving him a serene smile. "There's no place else I need to be. So I'm just going to hang out here with you until we get this figured out. Count me in for one of those cold beers."

Jamming his hand into another pocket, Linc produced a seat belt cutter and reached around the front seat to grip the belt. "I'm gonna cut through your belt while we work on an escape route."

"Okay," the driver wheezed.

"What's your name, sir?" Linc asked, hooking the blade of the cutter over the belt.

"Nelson," he said. "Nelson. My wife. I got her flowers," he said.

Linc gritted his teeth and tightened his grip on the seat belt as he started to saw through it. The scent of roses hit him, and he spotted the bouquet on the passenger seat. White and pink.

"It's her birthday," Nelson said weakly.

"They might be a little wilted by the time you get them to her, but you will," Linc promised.

Fuck. The angle made it nearly impossible. Instead of a clean cut, he was sawing through thread by miserly thread. Sweat was running freely, turning his gear into a damn sauna.

"I got you some guys," Wonder Woman said, her eyes tearing with the smoke. Sweat matted her hair down, sticking it to her forehead. "One of them had a glass breaker in his car."

Linc loved a prepared bystander.

"Where do you want us?" Two men appeared on the other side of the barrier. They each held up their tools.

"Climb over onto the hood," Linc ordered. "We're going through the sunroof."

"Can we get a blanket over here?" Wonder Woman shouted at the gathering crowd. "And where are my fire extinguishers? The rest of you all need to get the hell back!"

"You'd make a great incident command," Linc told her.

"Honey, I've got five kids at home. I can command the hell out of any incident."

"Listen, you all give this two minutes. If we're still not out by then, you need to get clear," Linc ordered.

"Two minutes," she repeated.

A blanket was produced and draped over Nelson's head to protect him from the glass.

Time disappeared. There was only the intensity of the heat and Linc's focus. The seat belt gave way finally, the belt cutter slipping and nicking his hand. He heard the telltale whoosh of single-use fire extinguishers, the hiss of flames. But it was still damn hot. He was still burning. The good Samaritans attacked the sunroof, and chips of glass rained down in a shower.

"Thank fucking God," he muttered, stashing the cutter back in his pocket and pulling on his gloves. It was too late. He already felt the blistering on his right hand. But what was a firefighter without a few burns to show off?

"Holy hell, Chief." Skyler's pretty face appeared in the open sunroof.

"It's about time, New Guy," Linc shouted. "Nelson, buddy, are you ready to get the hell out of here?"

The heat was beyond oppressive. His muscles felt like they were liquifying. Black smoke filled the vehicle and poured out of the open windows.

"But I'm having such a nice time," the man joked, coughing and sputtering.

Linc grinned. "Okay. On the count of three, Wonder Woman, you and I are going to heave Nelson here up and out. Rookie, you and your Good Sams are going to pull him out and get him across the barrier. And then everyone is going to run like hell. Copy?"

"Copy!" They shouted it as if they'd been training together for years instead of a fate-dealt group of strangers trying to save a life.

The back window shattered behind Linc as the flames licked closer. "Now!" he shouted.

Still using his body as a shield, he reached around to lever Nelson up out of the seat. His weight, the angle, the twisting. He felt the pop in his right shoulder and welcomed the pain as distraction from the misery of the hellish heat. They heaved and pushed and pulled together, grunting and shouting.

It sounded like labor. Like birth. The back seat was on fire. Flames were eating the upholstery, the fabric on the roof. Time was up.

And then Nelson was disappearing through the sunroof. Linc sent up a prayer of thanks as the man's loafers vanished and the distinct sound of cheers reached him over the lick and crack of the fire.

"Get out of there, Chief!" Skyler yelled, reaching down for him.

He gave her his left hand and, gasping for oxygen, let her pull him toward the air, the sunshine, the blue sky that was blotted out with thick, black smoke.

"Hang on!" Reaching down with his bad arm, Linc clutched the flowers. "Okay. Get me the fuck out of here."

"Never pegged you for a romantic," Skyler said through gritted teeth as she hauled his two hundred and fifty pounds of muscle and gear through the roof of the car.

They landed on the hood, and then she was shoving him over the barrier, and they were both falling. There was a loud pop behind them as one of the tires exploded.

Hands. What felt like a dozen of them grabbed him, pulled him up. They were surrounded by angels. Bloodied, bruised angels. Everyone crying and laughing at the same time. A girl in a softball uniform. A woman in a pencil skirt with bloody knees. A pizza delivery guy. A truck driver in a Jimmy Buffett shirt. Black. White. Rich. Poor. They came together to defy death.

Linc's shoulder sang, his knuckles throbbed. But he grabbed Skyler's arm. "Everybody move!"

There were sirens. An entire opera of them. Help was coming.

They moved as one, snaking between the stopped cars to the other shoulder of the highway. Skyler's braid was no longer neat and tidy. Black flyaways escaped from all angles, and her dark skin was smudged with soot and dirt. She grinned at him.

"Not a bad day's work, Chief," she said.

Nelson, arms draped over the shoulders of the glass-breaking golfers, limped ahead of them. Linc stole a glance over his shoulder, and just like that, the gas tank finally blew, shooting orange flames thirty feet into the air.

The flowers clutched in his hand were wilted and browning. But they'd survive, just like the man who'd bought them.

No. Not a bad day's work at all.

CHAPTER 2

On the side of the road, Linc used his left hand to apply pressure to a motorcyclist's leg wound while an EMT worked to stabilize the unconscious woman's spine.

He could feel, rather than see, the web of emergency responders as they infiltrated the chaos and began to carefully restore order. Fire crews would control and reroute traffic. Police departments would begin the painstaking investigation. EMTs and paramedics triaged and treated victims, arranging for transport to the nearest hospitals. Wreckers, an army of them, would be staging now, ready for the mop-up. More help arrived by the minute.

He could feel the environment shifting around them. Men and women in uniform brought with them a sense of calm, a perception of control.

But here on this scrap of crispy brown grass stained with blood, it was still life and death. The girl had been found fifteen feet from her crushed bike. Unconscious, unmoving.

The waterfall of sweat that had started in the car had yet to cease, though Linc had stripped out of his jacket. He was going to need six showers just to feel human again.

His shoulder throbbed. His right arm hung uselessly at his

side, flesh still pulsing with the painful burn. But every hand with medical training was a necessity right now.

Fire departments and cops converged and dispersed around them, each with their own tasks. Traffic control. Cleanup. Patient transpo.

Linc looked down at the pale, bruised face of the woman. He didn't recognize her. Had this happened in Benevolence, odds were he would have known her first name. Maybe even what street she lived on.

"Chopper coming?" he asked the EMT. The gauze he held to the victim's leg was already saturated. She wouldn't last in an ambulance.

"En route. Two minutes out."

"She the worst?" he asked. He'd only witnessed a small corner of the carnage.

The paramedic spared him a quick glance. "Sure as hell hope so."

But it was likely there were worse. The skeletal remains of minivans and sedans all around them predicted it.

No tarps yet, Linc thought grimly. But given the dozen mangled vehicle corpses, it would be a miracle if the coroner wasn't needed.

Accidents happened. People died.

But what kept him going, what kept them all going, was what else happened at every scene.

Between twisted metal and over broken glass, strangers helped strangers. Bystanders became heroes on someone else's worst day. They fetched water bottles and corralled pets. Applied pressure to wounds, lent cell phones and shoulders. They offered strangers hard hugs and whispered promises that everything would be okay.

A pretty young thing in a green dress gently cleaned blood

from an elderly man's face with a napkin while an EMT checked his vitals. The man's wife clutched his hand to her chest. Silent tears tracked down her lined face.

Linc didn't care for the hero label when others applied it to him. He was trained for this. He had years of experience. He chose this profession. But the woman, probably on her way to meet a friend for lunch, hadn't. The truck driver supporting a limping teenager and the teenage girl whispering jokes to the man on a stretcher? Those were the real heroes.

"Chopper's coming." The paramedic fastened the leg strap on the spine board. "Let's get her closer to the landing zone."

Linc gripped the board with his left hand and winced when they stood.

"Sorry, man, didn't know you were banged up," the paramedic said. "Yo! Someone with two good hands!"

"It's nothing," Linc insisted. His shoulder took exception.

"Shit, Chief. Must have been one hell of an extension cord." Brody Lighthorse, the bald, tattooed, Benevolence FD captain and Linc's best friend, appeared out of the wreckage and grabbed the end of the spine board.

"Never a dull moment," Linc shot back. He jogged alongside, still applying pressure to the leg wound while Brody and the paramedic quickly made their way through cars and casualties.

The helicopter touched down nice and neat on the westbound lane dotted line. The cargo door was already opening, and a doctor jumped out.

"What've we got, gentlemen?"

Even over the sound of the rotors, the huskiness of her voice made him forget about the ache in his shoulder. And that was before he saw those eyes. Cool, bottle green. An old scar ran under her left eye, adding an interesting asymmetry to an already arresting face.

The paramedic recited the particulars—internal bleeding, possible spine injuries—while the doctor whipped off her stethoscope. She was long-legged and sure-footed. Her short dark hair was pulled back in a messy, stubby tail. Loose, wavy strands had already escaped and framed that face. She wore red, red lipstick.

"Looks like you've got a mess on your hands," she shouted over the rotors to Linc. "Glad there's only one for me."

He opened his mouth, but words failed him.

"Real miracle, Doc," Brody called back. He tossed an elbow into Linc's side. "Cat got your tongue, Chief?"

"Let's see if we can get ourselves another one of those," she said. "Load her up."

As the flight nurse and paramedics shoved the spine board into the chopper, the doctor's gaze slid Linc's way again in cool assessment. His tongue felt two sizes too big for his mouth.

He'd never had trouble talking to women. Hell, he'd flirted outrageously with his kindergarten teacher on the first day of school.

As the flight nurse—a big, burly, bearded guy—started an IV, the doc's eyes zeroed in on Linc's limp arm. "You getting that checked out, Lefty?" she asked.

His tongue finally loosened. "You doing the checking, Doc Dreamy?" he croaked.

She paused for a second and arched an eyebrow. "Haven't heard that in a long time," she said. "Nice try, but I don't *play* doctor." With an emphasis on the word *play* and a wink, she was climbing back aboard. "Let's get this bird in the air!"

They hightailed it away from the rotors as the engine whine increased. Linc gave himself a moment to watch as the helicopter hovered off the ground, then headed off in the direction of the hospital, taking the green-eyed doctor with it.

"A distinct improvement over Doc Singh," Brody decided. The usual flight doc on-scene was short, round, and always looking for an argument over northeast sports franchises.

"Yeah," Linc agreed. *A definite improvement.*

"You got little hearts in your eyes." Brody grinned.

"I think I'm in love."

CHAPTER 3

Dr. Mackenzie O'Neil hovered over her patient as the bird lifted fast enough to tickle the floor of her stomach. Flight medicine came with its own brand of challenges, and she thrived on them. Communication with her patients en route to the trauma center was usually impossible even when they were conscious.

It was a high-stakes guessing game. A high-wire act of stabilization and being prepared for when things went to hell.

The unconscious girl before her, early twenties, good physical shape, was a mystery to be solved and saved.

Mack continued her quick, careful physical exam while Bubba, flight nurse extraordinaire, cut through the jacket and the T-shirt beneath. Bubba was just an inch and a few pounds shy of the max size limits to practice medicine in the cramped quarters of the EC145. But he was light on his feet.

"Patient's abdomen is hard as a rock. Significant bruising on the chest," Mack reported, pressing on each quadrant.

"Bleeder, Doc?" Sally chirped over the headset from her seat behind the controls. Ride Sally, or RS, as she was known to the air medicine team at Keppler Medical Center, was the best damn pilot Mack had ever had the privilege of flying with. Whisper-soft landings, lightning-fast reflexes, cool under pressure. She was also so petite, she sat on a cushion to reach the controls easier.

"Looks like it," Mack confirmed into the headset's mic.

She heard Sally relay the information to the hospital over the radio.

"Bubs, what's the BP?" Mack asked.

Bubba was the exact physical opposite of their tiny pilot. Black to her fair freckles. Burly to her waifish stature. Mack had found the opposites amusing. He still looked like the college football player he'd been while studying nursing. He shook his head. "Tanking."

"Let's push the fluids, see if we can't get her BP stabilized." Mack ran through the mental calculations. They were ten minutes out from the hospital. For now, her sole job was to get the girl there alive.

She took another listen to the chest, eyeing the monitor next to her. "Tachycardic. Decreased breath sounds on right side."

"She's hypoxic," Bubba said, reading the oximeter. "Intubate?"

She could feel the patient slipping away. "Yeah. Let's do this," she said.

They moved quickly and in tandem. This was only her third shift and fifth call in a new job in a new place, but she liked and respected her team. Bubba had no problems taking orders from a woman who wasn't afraid of giving them. And RS was happy to chauffeur them.

When they'd come in for a landing, the devastation on the highway beneath them was grimly fascinating. Mack had started her medical career flying in and out of battle, hauling injured soldiers. She'd been on choppers under fire, even survived two emergency landings. But seeing this kind of carnage on domestic soil was oddly unsettling.

From the looks of it, the eighteen-wheeler hadn't seen the construction signs and was unprepared for the slowdown, plowing into multiple vehicles and causing a chain reaction wreck.

The people on the ground hadn't been deployed to a hot zone. They didn't have military training under their belts. They were soccer dads running errands, businesswomen taking lunch breaks, teens playing hooky. Or, like the girl before her, just young women enjoying a nice summer afternoon on a motorcycle.

"ETA, RS?" she called.

"Nine minutes," came the reply.

"You ever intubated en route, Bubs?" Mack asked.

"Virgin. Be gentle with me," he said.

"She's crashing," she noted. "Stay with us, kid."

They worked quickly, speaking only when necessary. Sweat coated her brow, and her back grumbled a complaint from her hunched posture. The adrenaline hummed its familiar tune in her bloodstream. It was a siren song. One she was going to have to start resisting…eventually.

The heart monitor reading flatlined.

"Hell," she said and grimly charged the paddles while Bubba started CPR.

Life and death. She'd grown accustomed to walking that line daily. To seeing the disasters only small percentages of the human race would ever witness firsthand. A retrievalist, a flight doctor, like other first responders, was wired differently. They sought out the crises, made themselves tools. There were protocols in facing down death and gore and trauma. Protocols organized the chaos, gave the brain something to think about besides the horror of young lives slipping away.

Her hands shook, and she tightened her grip on the paddles.

"Clear."

Bubba danced back.

It still surprised her how a man of his stature could move so gracefully in the confines. Working in close quarters wasn't easy, but it did make things convenient. Everything she needed was within easy reach.

Mack positioned the paddles, sent up her superstitious prayer of "please," and shocked the hell out of the young heart in her hands.

"Got beats," Bubba yelled.

Thank you, baby Jesus.

"Let's intubate," she said. She swiped an arm over the sweat on her brow and blamed said sweat when she stood too straight and smacked her forehead—the part not covered by her helmet—on the metal shelf above the stretcher.

"Fucking A," she muttered.

The blow surprised the shake out of her hands, and she cleanly slid the tube into her patient's airway.

"Nice job, Mack," Bubba said in the headset as their patient's vitals stabilized.

They made quick work of one of the leg wounds as the hospital loomed into view, sunlight bouncing off its glass. Hundreds of cars dotted its parking lots, and people scurried in and out like ants.

Her stomach dipped again as the helicopter descended toward the rooftop helipad. The patient was stable. She'd done her job.

The trauma team, white coats flapping in the air kicked up by the rotors, waited just inside the doors.

"Good save," Bubba said, offering her a fist bump over the patient.

She returned it. "Back at you, man. Really nice work."

19

The skids touched down almost simultaneously in a slick, smooth landing. "Honey, we're home," RS sang.

Bubba released the door from inside, and Mack jumped out, ducking low. She helped the roof team unload the stretcher and filled them in on the details.

"Polytraumatic patient, female early twenties, motorcycle versus car. In shock. Intubated." She rattled off the information to the trauma team. "Lost her and brought her back. One shock."

"We got her from here, Doc," the trauma surgeon shouted with a nod. He grabbed a rail on the gurney, and together the team wheeled the nameless girl inside.

"Another day, another good karma point," RS said, joining them on the roof.

"Think she'll pull through?" Bubba asked.

"She's young and otherwise healthy. She's got a good chance," Mack predicted. She stretched her arms up and over her head.

"That her blood?" RS asked, nodding at the smear on Mack's forehead.

"Smacked my damn head on the shelf again."

"That's twice now," RS said, cracking her gum. "Third time, and we get you one of those giant bubble helmets."

Bubba joined them at the edge of the helipad and tapped the scar through his eyebrow. "At least you didn't need stitches en route," he said cheerfully.

RS checked her watch. "Looks like that's a wrap, folks. Anyone wanna grab some grub?"

Mack's first instinct was a firm no. She was bone-tired, and the shake was back in her hands. She clenched them into fists and slid them into the pockets of her flight suit. She was here for a change of scenery, a break while she figured out next steps. Fraternizing with her crew was a good thing, she reminded herself. Normal even. She was forcing herself to embrace normal.

"Yeah. Sure. Lemme grab a shower first."

"And a Band-Aid." RS smirked, tapping her own unblemished forehead.

"I'm out. Promised the little lady I'd take the kids grocery shopping tonight to give her an hour of peace," Bubba said, throwing them a salute. "Great work, Mack."

"You, too, Bubs."

"Meet you downstairs in thirty? I gotta do some postflight checks," RS said, jerking her chin toward the helicopter.

Another thing Mack appreciated about the pilot. She'd flown with pilots who focused only on preflight checklists, then walked away from the bird without a backward glance after landing. RS took her job seriously, beginning to end.

Mack headed inside and down three flights to the locker room where she indulged in a five-minute, scalding-hot shower. Her muscles loosened as she washed away the layer of dried sweat. When she was sufficiently clean, she threw the knob to cold and counted down from sixty, letting the iciness reinvigorate her brain.

She wanted a tall green tea and a sandwich with a mountain of cold cuts. She'd play a little getting to know you with RS, then head on home. Maybe unpack another box, catch up on another study or journal. Bed early. Wake early. Workout. Breakfast.

And then head into the small-town family practice—God help her—where she'd be spending the next six months of her life.

She stepped out and toweled off. Examining the cut on her forehead in the mirror, she rolled her eyes. "You were the one who wanted normal," she muttered to her reflection.

She ran a comb through her hair, gave it a blast with the hair dryer, and stepped into her civilian clothes. A glance at the clock on the wall told her she still had fifteen minutes.

For the first time, her thoughts flitted back to the firefighter on the ground.

Her brain always sifted through calls and responses in odd, dreamlike ways. Rather than replaying the action during the flight, she was thinking of the blue-eyed firefighter with the bum shoulder. He looked more like a lifeguard. Tanned, blond, easy charming grin.

A pair of nurses in scrubs wandered in and gave her a nod. The one with a short cap of silver-blond hair popped open her locker and toed off her clogs with a grateful sigh. "I hate twelves."

"They're not all bad when you get to work on Chief Sexy Pants." The other nurse, willowy and weary, flopped down on the bench. Her long, dark hair was pulled back in a sleek tail. "Hear what he did on-scene?"

"I got the broad strokes from Javier. Something about climbing into a car on fire like a sexy superhero?"

"He used that beautiful body of his to block the driver from the flames while sawing through the guy's seat belt. Dislocates his shoulder, burns his hand, but stays put. Had some Good Sams pull the man through the sunroof. Then his own rookie is hauling his fine ass up, and he stops to grab the flowers the guy got for his wife's birthday off the front seat."

"Swoon," the first nurse sighed.

"Yeah, swoon and a subluxed shoulder and third-degree burns on the hand that I hear is capable of delivering multiple orgasms within impossible windows of time."

"This guy tall, blond, gorgeous? A little on the flirty side?" Mack asked.

The first nurse looked up as she dragged on an ancient pair of gym shorts. "Yeah. Lincoln Reed. Fire chief over in Benevolence. He was first on-scene. You meet him?" she asked, eyeing the flight suit Mack was shoving into her bag.

"Briefly."

"He's downstairs in the ED. You know, if you want to check him out with two working arms," the second nurse said with a glint in her eye.

Mack chewed it over. "I might just do that."

"I'm Nellie, by the way."

"Mack. Dr. O'Neil," she said.

"The new flight doc. Nice to meet you. Great work today. Your girl is in surgery. No spine injury. I'm Sharon."

"Oh…thanks for that." She said her goodbyes and headed out into the hallway.

She wasn't used to knowing that. The after. Whether they made it or didn't. Her job as a retrievalist was to get the patient to the best resources. End of story. She'd gotten used to the not knowing. Gotten comfortable with it.

Sometimes it was better not to know.

Faces flashed before her. The ones she'd lost.

Two orderlies wandered by cracking jokes. Mack pulled herself out of her head. Nothing good came from looking back.

Going on instinct, she veered away from the parking lot and headed instead into the emergency department. It was relatively quiet here. Most of the other crash victims would have been routed through the county hospital. It was smaller but closer. The fact that Linc was here told her he hadn't wanted to add another case to the overtaxed emergency department. A point for him.

She didn't have to look hard for her flirty firefighter. There was a clump of adoring female medical personnel clustered around a trauma bay.

Chief Sexy Pants, with his broad shoulders and easy grin, took up most of the space between the vinyl curtains. The back of his left hand was bandaged, and his right arm was in a sling that she could tell he was itching to get out of. He was hooked to a bag of fluids, most likely for the dehydration that came from battling blazes.

Mack thought of the flowers, wondered if it was true. If it was, it was wildly romantic and irresponsible.

Dr. Ling, according to the fiercely frowning woman's ID badge, glanced up from the laptop. "Unless you're family, you're going to need to stay in the waiting room," she said without looking up.

"Doc Dreamy here is family. She's my future wife," Linc said.

Mack laughed and pretended not to notice the daggers the nursing staff shot in her direction. Holding up her hospital ID, she noted the disappointment that flashed across Dr. Ling's face. Mack had known doctors like Ling. Territorial, a shade aggressive. But usually very, very good at medicine. "We're old friends," Mack said. "Nice to see you again, Lefty. How's the wing?"

"Good as new thanks to the doc here."

"That's not even remotely accurate," Dr. Ling announced dryly, then reluctantly, for Mack's behalf, added, "Partial subluxation. It's back in place and needs to stay stabilized. The chief is under strict orders not to overstress the injury."

"How's our patient?" Linc asked, swinging his legs over the side of the bed and pointing at the IV in his arm. With a nod from Dr. Ling, one of the nurses jumped into action to remove it. Mack was a little disappointed when the woman didn't kiss the Band-Aid she gently smoothed over the tiny needle hole.

"Not sure," Mack said, shoving a hand in the pocket of her shorts. "Made it here in one piece. She's in surgery. No spinal. But that's all I know."

"I can find out for you, Chief," one of the younger nurses said, American as apple pie with blond curls and pretty blue eyes with lashes that were batting a mile a minute.

"I'd appreciate that, Lurlene."

Oh, she would recognize that hotshot charm anywhere, Mack thought, as Lurlene sprinted for the desk. And not so long ago, she'd have had no issues with enjoying a couple of rounds in bed with said hotshot charm. But she was turning over a new leaf.

A new, celibate, boring leaf.

Too bad there was something in those eyes that she liked, that she recognized. The slick, harmless charm. The exhaustion he was keeping tamped down.

He stood, and even the indomitable Dr. Ling took a step back to accommodate him.

Taller than she'd thought. A little broader too. But not soft. Except around the eyes.

His build reminded her of the neighbor she'd accidentally spied over her backyard fence in the early dawn hours putting himself through a punishing workout, a yellow Lab delightedly shadowing his movements.

Not a bad way to wake up.

"Feel like giving a wounded man a ride home, Doc?" Linc asked.

Mack heard the internal swooning of a half-dozen women.

"Sorry, Lefty. I've got plans."

On cue, RS poked her head around the curtain and held up her pager. "Yo, Doc. Caught another one. Next shift pilot's late. Rain check?"

Mack sent her a wave. "Happy flying, RS. Next shift."

Linc's grin broadened. "Looks like you've got time to drive me home after all."

CHAPTER 4

Linc liked the conflict he read on her bare face. Freshly showered—her hair smelled like lavender and honey—Doc Dreamy was as attractive in shorts and a worn National Guard shirt as she was in a flight suit.

"Where do you live?" she asked, chewing on that now naked lip as she gave the idea some thought.

"Little town called Benevolence. I'm sure it's on the way to wherever you're headed," he said, all charm now. The sock-in-the-gut speechless reaction he'd had to her on-scene was going to be chalked up to being distracted by his shoulder. Now that he was trussed up like a damn turkey and rehydrated, he was free to focus on those wary green eyes.

"Honey, I don't care if he lives in South Dakota." Janice the RN had twenty years on him and barely topped out at five feet even, but she returned his shameless flirting with an expertise he hoped to someday possess. "You drive our boy home and thank us later."

It was official. Janice was his favorite.

Linc's cell rang from the depths of his gym bag. Automatically he reached for it with his right hand and winced.

Doc Dreamy—he wondered if knowing her real name

would ruin any of the entertaining fantasies he'd concocted while Dr. Ling ruthlessly shoved the head of his damn humerus back into the socket—rolled her eyes.

She took the bag from him and fished out the phone.

"What's up, Lighthorse?" he said.

"Checking in. Still have both arms?" his friend asked.

"Good as new. In fact, if you're still at the scene, I can probably swing by and help with cleanup," he offered.

"No!" Dr. Ling and Doc Dreamy announced together.

Brody laughed. "Sounds like you've got some babysitters. We've got it under control. DUI, by the way. Truck driver had five doubles at a dive bar before climbing behind the wheel. Ran after the wreck, but the highway patrol found him. One dead. Seventeen injured. Six seriously."

Linc swore under his breath.

One was too many. A useless death for a selfish, bullshit reason.

"One's better than I expected," Brody said.

"Me too. Still."

"Yeah. Still. Anyway, I sent the rook to take Sunshine home. Want me to have her swing by the hospital? Give you a lift?"

Linc looked at Doc Dreamy, who was stuffing the patient care instructions he fully intended to ignore into his gym bag.

"Nah. Got it covered. Thanks for taking care of my girl," he said.

"Your girl probably ate your curtains and pissed on your toaster by now," Brody predicted.

That sounded about right. "Yeah, thanks. I'll see you tomorrow at the station."

"For light duty only," Dr. Ling yelled.

"Busted." Brody snickered. "Save your energy for the forty tons of paperwork."

They disconnected, and Doc Dreamy took Linc's phone and stuffed it in the bag. "Let's go, Lefty."

"You want to ask about my girl, don't you?"

"Nope," she said, shouldering his bag. "You ready?"

"Dr. Ling?" He extended his left hand and shook hers. "Ladies? Thanks for the superior medical care. Five stars all around."

"Happy to help," Dr. Ling said dryly.

He followed the doc out of the curtained-off bay into the bustle of the emergency department. A kid, young from the sounds of it, wailed pitifully from somewhere. A guy in the next bed held a towel soaked with blood over his forehead and stared miserably at his shoes. Nurses—at least the ones of the female persuasion—paused long enough to flash Linc a smile before sailing off to the next patient. They flirted in rotation, folding a wink or a sweet smile in with the rest of their duties.

"Chief! Wait!" Lurlene rushed up, cheeks flushed. "I just heard from the OR. Splenectomy is going well. She's expected to make it."

"Thanks, honey." Linc placed a hand on her shoulder and squeezed.

"Said she coded on the way here and the air team brought her back and intubated her. She was real lucky."

"Yeah, she was," he murmured, thinking about the devastation caused by one man and his problem. "Nice save, Doc."

Dreamy looked embarrassed. "You ready?" she asked abruptly.

His very attractive chauffeur looked like she was ready to crawl out of her skin if she had to stand there another second and accept accolades.

"I am." Linc used the exhausted and injured thing to his advantage and slung his good arm around her shoulders. She stiffened for a second and then shifted her bag and his to better handle his weight.

With the first step, he realized it wasn't a play. Weak as a fucking kitten. Hollowed out, hungry, and tired. He clenched his jaw and tried to cover his sharp intake of breath.

Her arm came around his waist. He wasn't fooling her. *Fuck.*

"Nice work today, you two," Dr. Ling said grudgingly as they made for the exit.

"Thanks. You too," his pretty doctor crutch called back.

They slowly made their way in the direction of the waiting room and paused to let a nurse leading an older woman hurry by. "Your husband's right in here, ma'am," the nurse said, pulling back the curtain to one of the first bays.

Nelson, a little worse for the wear, beamed up from his bed. His head was bandaged, as was his left arm. There were enough wires sticking out of him to reanimate Frankenstein's monster. But he was alive and smiling up at his wife like they were teenage sweethearts.

Linc felt the hitch in Dreamy's stride.

"I leave you alone for an hour and look what you get yourself into," Nelson's wife blustered. She leaned over him, brushing a shock of white hair off his forehead and kissing him ever so gently on the forehead.

"Have I got a story to tell you," Nelson said. "Here. I got you these." He pointed to the flowers a nurse had thoughtfully put in an ugly plastic ice pitcher. They were wilted and browned, and the baby's breath was singed to a crisp.

"Oh, Nelson." His wife dissolved into tears and carefully climbed into the bed next to him.

The patient glanced up and spied Linc. "Thank you," he mouthed.

Linc nodded at Nelson, then cleared his throat. Dreamy

cleared hers. Two stoic responders trying not to let their feelings show.

"Let's get out of here, Dreamy," he said softly.

They made it out the front doors and into the summer evening in silence. He was sweating from the effort of not limping and groaning and painfully aware of how badly he needed a shower. This was not his best first impression.

"You can put more weight on me," she said. "I can handle it."

"Pfft. I'm fine. This was just an excuse to put my arm around you," he said through gritted teeth.

"You've officially been upgraded from Lefty to Hotshot," Dreamy decided.

Linc glanced over his shoulder and made sure they no longer had an audience. "In that case." He leaned heavily on her. That lavender scent wafting up from her hair wreaked havoc on his senses.

"I'm parked pretty far out," she said. "Wait here, and I'll get the car."

"No way. Gotta keep moving," he countered. If he stopped and sat, he'd be asleep in seconds. And snoring on a bus bench was no way to charm a beautiful woman.

She sighed, and he knew she'd been there. "Suit yourself. Think we should exchange names?" she mused to him as they slowly, painfully made their way down the longest row of cars in the history of parking lots.

"Nah. What's the fun in that?" he said.

"Good point. To give you something to look forward to, Hotshot, my car has air-conditioned seats."

It boded well for the fresh river of sweat working its way down his back. He hoped the deluge wouldn't short out her car's electrical system.

"Almost there," she said.

He had a good amount of his body weight on her, and she was barely breathing heavy. From his grip on her shoulder, he felt the telltale flexing of well-developed muscle.

They arrived finally at a big-ass dark-blue SUV. She propped him against the fender and dumped both their bags into the hatch. "Can you get into your seat yourself, or do you need a hand?"

Linc searched for something flirty or the appropriate euphemism and came up dry. He blamed it on exhaustion and hunger.

She grinned at him, and he felt it in his gut.

"Relax, Hotshot. We're not having sex. You don't have to worry about impressing me. You're allowed to be tired."

"Why aren't we having sex?" he demanded, collapsing into the passenger seat of the spotless vehicle.

"I'm new here. I could be an axe-murdering black widow with a string of dead husbands."

He gave her a deliberate once-over, pausing on her bare left ring finger. "I'm willing to take that chance."

"Yeah, I bet you are. And if circumstances were different, if we met a few months ago, I wouldn't mind taking your very impressive body for a spin."

Linc felt just the slightest bit objectified, then decided he didn't mind one bit.

"Well, now I have to ask what happened between past Doc Dreamy and present."

"No. You don't," she said cheerfully. The engine roared to life. "Just like I'm not asking you about 'your girl.'"

"If we're not sleeping together, then we're gonna be friends. And friends tell each other everything," he said, changing tactics.

She smirked at him and shifted into reverse. "Always wanted myself a gal pal."

31

He laughed. She was sharp. And he was smart enough to find that very attractive.

His stomach interrupted his entertainment with an aggressive reminder that it was empty.

"Listen, I know you're valiantly holding out on my charm. But how do you feel about food? I don't mean to come on strong," he lied, "but I could eat your very shapely arm right now."

"Cannibalism is certainly the most interesting offer I've had today," she said, backing out of the space and steering them in the direction of the highway that paralleled the hospital's parking lot.

They rode in silence for a few minutes. Linc thought of Nelson and his wife. One minute later, he and Nelson and anyone else working on that car would have ended up as charcoal.

They'd all been extremely lucky.

They exited the highway two stops before Benevolence, and Linc thanked his lucky stars when she pulled into the cracked asphalt parking lot of a diner.

He let her help him inside more out of necessity than flirtation. They settled into a booth with a scarred stainless-steel top and shiny napkin dispenser.

"Wanna tell me about it?" she asked, signaling for the waitress. "We can swap war stories, only make ourselves sound more heroic and good-looking."

"Dreamy, look at us. People don't get more good-looking than this."

"Pfft. Listen, Hotshot, when you're as attractive as we are, try to have at least a *feigned* sense of humility. No one likes a beautiful asshole."

He grinned at her and decided it was possible that he'd finally met his match.

The server, a no-nonsense, end-of-her-shift type, arrived

and peered at them over her blue-framed reading glasses. "What'll it be, kids?"

Dreamy ordered green tea and an egg white omelet with a side of fresh fruit. Linc went for a gallon of coffee, three waters, and the meatloaf with a side of turkey sandwich.

The waitress didn't blink, but Dreamy smirked. "Must have been quite the calorie burn," she predicted.

Orders placed, they traded stories of the shift, the call, the victims.

"It was a DUI. The truck driver was shit-faced and didn't see the construction signs. He just plowed into stopped traffic," Linc told her.

Her sigh had weight to it. "If drivers' ed kids had to walk on to an accident scene, no one would ever text or drink and drive again."

He recognized it. The frustration. The fact that so many of these injuries, so many deaths, could be completely avoided. But there would always be people incapable of making the right choice. They would always hurt someone else. And he, and others like the doctor lounging across from him, would be there to pick up the pieces.

The exhaustion that pushed at his brain started to encroach. He took another hit of very good diner coffee, resisting the urge to guzzle it.

"I know what you're saying. At least every single one of those people who went home today will drive more carefully."

"The nurses in the ED were all aflutter over you saving those flowers," Dreamy said, sipping her green tea that she'd accessorized with a judicious squirt of lemon. "But it sounds like they're usually aflutter over Chief Sexy Pants."

"So you *do* know my name," he teased.

The eyebrow she arched at him was flippant.

"This your first in-flight intubation?" he asked. She seemed more comfortable talking medicine and calls than the personal. He'd use it to his advantage…when he had more energy.

"Third," she said, leaning back and draping an arm over the back of the booth.

"Not here though," he guessed. "I'd remember seeing you on-scene."

"New in town," she said.

He grinned and waited a beat or two while she refused to divulge more.

"Military before this for a few years," she said, finally giving in.

He pointed at her National Guard T-shirt. "So I guessed."

"Devastatingly handsome and wildly astute," she said, fluttering her lashes.

Their food arrived, Linc's plates taking up most of the acreage of the table, and they dove in.

He was still tired. He still hurt. But the food, the company, helped.

When the waitress slapped the check down on the table, Linc's good hand got there first. "This is our first date. I'm paying."

"No offense, but this is a terrible first date. You smell like smoke and antiseptic."

"Aphrodisiacs for first responders," he insisted.

"I'll let you pay but only as reimbursement for the chauffeur routine."

"I'll take what I can get."

She waited patiently while he fished out cash with one hand.

"Okay, Hotshot. Lead the way," Dreamy said, sliding out of the booth.

Linc played tour guide on the way into Benevolence,

pointing out the high school, the fire station, the little downtown that was much the same as it had been since he'd been born here. Change wasn't a bad thing. But there was something comforting about the sameness of his hometown.

It was going dark now, and the crickets and peepers were making the most of August's last hurrah.

While he was looking forward to his dog and his bed, he wasn't ready for his time with the dreamy doctor to come to an end.

"Turn right here." He pointed at the next road sign. "Third one on the left."

"You have *got* to be kidding me," she muttered under her breath.

"What? You've never seen an incredibly good-looking man live in a renovated gas station?" he teased.

"Something like that," she said wryly. It made him want to be in on the private joke. "Looks like someone's excited to see you." She pointed to the big front window.

Sunshine, his yellow Lab disaster, scrabbled at the glass, frantic with excitement.

"Separation anxiety. Usually she's with someone, but with the call today, a rookie brought her back. That, by the way, is my girl," he said as Sunshine's front paws got tangled up in the heavy curtains. There was a muffled crash as curtains and rod rained down. Undaunted, Sunshine danced to the door and back to the window.

"Huh. Guess I was right when I pictured you with a high-maintenance blond," she quipped.

Yeah. He was definitely looking forward to seeing her again. "Wanna come in for a nightcap? Maybe see me with a complicated brunette?"

"It's a nice offer, Hotshot. But I'm gonna pass."

"If I wanted to pursue you relentlessly, how would I do that?" he asked, his good hand on the door handle.

"I have a feeling you'll find a way," she predicted.

He certainly would. After a long, hot shower and a good night's sleep.

Linc opened the door with his left hand. "I'll see you around, Doc," he said.

"I'm sure you will."

He grabbed his bag from the back and, with a little salute, let himself in where he was promptly mauled with unconditional love.

CHAPTER 5

She knew it was still dark without opening her eyes. Her internal clock was a marvel. An annoyingly consistent marvel.

Five thirty in the morning. She considered pulling the pillow over her head and trying for another half an hour, but it was futile. The day had begun.

She kicked off what covers had survived the night and stepped over the bedspread that had been rejected. A lousy sleeper, Mack had gotten used to getting by on a few hours a night. There was too much adrenaline in her life.

The bedroom was small by most people's standards. But most people hadn't spent a good amount of time deployed to field hospitals in foreign lands. The double mattress was comfortable enough for the next six months. And when she had a spare minute, she'd probably finish unpacking her clothes.

This stopover in Benevolence, Maryland, was like another deployment. A temporary placement. A short-term job to do. Today, she'd find out exactly what she'd gotten herself into.

The floorboards creaked under her bare feet as she headed into the bathroom. It was tiny—like the rest of the house— but the landlord had managed to squeeze in enough storage in the vanity, open shelves, and sliver of a linen closet to make it usable.

Mack wrapped an elastic band around her hair, securing it in a stubby tail, and splashed cold water on her face until she felt the burn of blood flow.

Ten minutes later, she was out the door, running shoes on and muscles warm.

Late August in Maryland, she was learning, meant the fingers of summer humidity clung tight, even in the early morning hours. Turning left, she headed down the block, deciding to zigzag through a new-to-her part of town before hitting the trail by the lake.

As her feet beat out a steady rhythm on the sidewalk beneath her, her brain organized her day. Shower. Breakfast. Tea. Then her first day on the job shadowing Dr. Dunnigan in the woman's family medical practice where she would be spending four days a week until March.

Nerves danced up her spine, and she laughed out loud in the residential quiet. *Mack O'Neil, afraid of a challenge?* She was more afraid it wouldn't be enough of a challenge. Worried the quiet, small-town life would end up being worse for her health than her previous high-stress career.

Adrenal fatigue. Impending burnout. Looming exhaustion.

As a medical professional, she knew the dangers of pushing the body too hard for too long. Yet she hadn't just stepped a toe or two over that line. No. She'd run a good hundred yards in the wrong direction.

She'd always been able to temper the hard work with hard play. And when necessary, well-earned island vacations with nothing to worry about but umbrellas in drinks and sunscreen applications. But lately, she hadn't been able to play hard enough. Hadn't been able to level out.

And she was smart enough to tackle the problem now before it cost her too much.

She had the next six months to get herself together. Six months of fish oil and vegetables, meditation and sleep.

God, she hoped it wouldn't take that long.

She'd been pushing hard since forever. And now it was time to stop pushing and start…whatever the opposite of pushing was.

Glancing down at her watch, she slowed her pace to stay in the appropriate heart rate zone. Enough for a workout but not a flat-out sprint.

"Just breathe," Mack reminded herself. That was all she had to do. Breathe and rest. And hope the boredom wouldn't kill her.

She sucked in a long, slow breath, then blew it out. The concrete under her feet changed to dirt and pine needles, and she let her thoughts shake free as the trees of the woods closed around her.

Four miles, and she was back at the front door of her rental. The flower beds—hell, she had flower beds now—needed a good weeding. The lawn was a little tall, and she remembered there was a push mower in the garage that was too small to house her SUV.

She'd squeeze in some yard work later today.

She jogged up the tidy brick steps and let herself inside. The house, a cottage really, felt like something out of a storybook with its rounded front door painted cerulean to accent the daffodil-yellow siding. The door opened into the living room that took up the entire front half of the house. Yellow pine floors, cute built-ins, even a tidy brick fireplace that—were she the type—would be nice to curl up in front of with a good book on a snowy night.

But Mack wasn't the good-book-on-a-snowy-night type.

She was the type to hang out of a helicopter, transporting patients from the scenes of their snowy accidents to the nearest trauma center.

"One shift a week," she reminded herself, heading down the short hallway into the kitchen. Four days in the clinic. One day with the air team.

The kitchen could have used an update, but the creaky cabinets, painted a pale blue, had their own kind of well-used charm. There was a short L of butcher block countertop. A white fridge and stove. No dishwasher. But cooking for one didn't produce an excess of dishes.

Mack put the kettle on and then assembled the ingredients for her protein shake, her breakfast of nutritional necessity. She jammed fruits, yogurt, sprouts, and green stuff into the blender, topped it with protein powder and chia seeds, and let the appliance do its job.

She gave the kettle and blender a break and ran through a quick set of planks, push-ups, and sit-ups in the dining room next to the adorable stenciled table.

By the time she finished, the kettle was whistling, and the smoothie was as smooth as it was going to get.

She poured both into the appropriate receptacles and headed out onto the deck.

Five days in this place and spying on her sexy neighbor had easily slipped into her daily routine. Of course, that was going to have to change now that she'd given said neighbor a ride home last night.

What were the odds, she wondered. *Apparently very good in a small town.*

Chief Lincoln Reed was awake. Over the chest-high fence that divided their properties, she could see the lights were on at his place.

"Better not be working out," she whispered to herself. Just like most health issues, partial dislocations were tricky if they weren't given the rest they required.

Pot, kettle, she thought blandly.

And there he was. The big, blond beefcake came into view in the window of what appeared to be a small home gym. He had a piece of pizza in his hand.

Breakfast of champions.

He bent, giving the dog a good scruff, and then eyed the pull-up bar mounted to the wall.

"Don't you dare do it," Mack murmured into her tea.

Shirtless and slingless, Linc grabbed the bar with both hands and pulled his body up with perfect form.

The big, macho idiot. She knew the type, had spent enough of her adult life around men—and women—like that. First in med school, then the military. Now in her own backyard.

He dropped like a stone after one pull-up instead of his usual thirty and sank to the floor. The dog scooted closer until she was practically in his lap.

Reluctantly, Mack checked her watch. If she skipped meditation, she had time.

A house call would eat up the excess time between now and her first day on the job. He'd probably take it as a sign of attraction, and that didn't really bother her enough to not go.

On a sigh, she put down the tea, picked up the abominable smoothie, and headed in the direction of the shower.

CHAPTER 6

A knock on Linc's door before seven a.m. usually meant his previous night's guest had left something behind. A phone. Car keys. One time a thong.

But he'd slept alone last night and dreamed of the pretty doctor.

He dragged a T-shirt over his head, a heroic feat with one good arm, and headed toward the front door with Sunshine trotting at his heels.

He wondered if his eyes were deceiving him. There on the concrete stoop stood the woman of his dreams and fantasies. She was wearing slim navy pants and a fitted white polo, and she was carrying a bag.

"Doc Dreamy. Couldn't stop thinking about me, could you?" He leaned against the doorframe. Sunshine poked her face out between his knees.

"I couldn't stop thinking about the damage you were probably doing to yourself, Hotshot."

"Damage?" he scoffed. "I'm resting. Doctor's orders." Idly, he scratched at his shoulder and wondered where he'd put the shoulder sling. Oh yeah, the kitchen trash can.

She stepped around him and walked right into the

front room that served as a living room and man cave with the gigantic flat screen, pool table, and bar made from red metal cabinets.

"You weren't trying to work out, were you? Turn that tweak into a tear?" she chided, eyeing the neon beer sign on the wall.

Either the woman was psychic, or he'd become predictable.

"If you know so much, smarty-pants, what did I have for breakfast?"

She dumped her bag on the pool table and gave him a contemplative look. The scar under her left eye created the slightest dimple under her lid. "You look like the cold pizza for breakfast kind of guy."

Linc looked down at his dog. "Did you tattle on me?"

Sunshine's tail swished happily against the black-and-white tile floor.

Dreamy's face softened. "She's kinda cute. I see you didn't fix your curtains yet." They were still in a rumpled pile on the floor where they'd fallen the night before.

"Two-handed job," he explained.

"How are the burns?" she asked conversationally as she picked up the curtain rod and crumpled draperies.

"Not bad," he said, glancing down at his bandaged hand.

She nudged a leather ottoman over to the window and hefted the rod and curtains off the floor, leaning against his *Ms. Pac-Man* pinball machine for support before clicking the rod back into place.

"Thanks."

She stepped down onto the floor and pushed the ottoman back into place. "Figured I'd stop by and yell at you for whatever you were doing and swap out your bandages," she said.

Sunshine wiggled her way over to the doc and plopped her butt on the floor.

"She is politely requesting that you give her all your love immediately," he told her.

This could make or break their relationship. Any woman who didn't snuggle his dog and tell her she was the prettiest girl in the world was one he had to walk away from.

"Hello there. It's very nice to meet you," she said, patting Sunshine awkwardly on the head. Sunshine looked confused.

"Have you never played with a dog before?"

"Am I doing it wrong?"

"Try squishing her face in your hands and telling her she's a pretty, pretty girl," Linc suggested.

"You're a pretty, pretty girl," Dreamy said, gently holding Sunshine's face in her hands. The dog approved the effort and gave her face a welcoming slurp.

"Good job. That means she likes you."

"Likes me or wants to eat me?" she asked, still stroking the dog's silky fur.

"In the dog world, there isn't much difference."

At his voice, Sunshine remembered her unconditional love for him and galloped back to his side.

"Where can I wash my hands? I'll get you bandaged up, and you can return to your day of ignoring doctor's orders," Dreamy said, rising and brushing the dog hair off her pants.

He pointed to the doorway between the bar and the TV.

"This is definitely a bachelor pad," she said when she returned, wiping her hands on a paper towel.

"A lot of this was my grandfather's," he explained, sweeping an arm toward the shelves that displayed a collection of 1950s gas station memorabilia and firefighter-related knickknacks. "He owned it when it was a gas station and garage."

Dreamy dug through her bag and produced gauze and tape.

"Interesting," she decided. Though he noticed her

questioning look at the kegerator in the corner. His place was unapologetically him. His grandfather owned and operated the service center into the seventies. Linc bought it several years ago and started the eclectic renovation, paying homage to the building's past and his own love of firefighting history.

"Where can we do this?" she asked, then held up a hand when he opened his mouth. "I'll save us both from you suggesting the bedroom. Here is fine."

She chose the sofa. A long, low leather piece that usually held buddies for the game or whoever called next game on the table. Not one to be left out, Sunshine hopped up on the end of the couch.

They sat facing each other, and Dreamy took his bandaged hand in hers.

He'd leaned on her heavily last night to and from the car. But this time *she* was touching *him*. He liked her touch. Cool, competent. Strong, but there was a gentleness there too.

The burn on the back of his hand was angry, red, and blistered. But he'd had worse. Would have worse again.

Gently, she applied a light layer of burn cream and laid a clean piece of gauze on top.

He was sitting on his couch holding hands with a woman whose name he didn't know…yet.

Say what you would about Lincoln Reed, but the man always had a name to go with the face accompanying him home. But not this time. She'd turned down his first invitation into his home, then turned up on his doorstep with first aid supplies and window treatment skills.

"Try to keep the wound clean and moist. Rest the shoulder. Your body can only take so much," she said, wrapping another layer of sticky tape around his hand.

"Are you doubting my stamina, Dreamy?"

Sunshine wriggled down the couch to stick her head in the doctor's lap.

"I'm doubting your sanity, Hotshot." She pressed the tape flat against his hand, sealing it to his skin. "And now I'm doubting mine for coming here." But she gave Sunshine another pet, more confident now. And when his dog's tail thumped happily, Dreamy's grin was joyful. "You're a very good girl. You take good care of your daddy and don't let him do anything stupid."

Sunshine squished herself against the doctor, trying to get as close as possible to the nice lady.

"What's the rush? You could hang out here and make sure I follow doctor's orders," he offered.

"I'm going to work."

"Back on the bird?" Linc pressed. She was an enigma to be decoded.

She shook her head. "That's just for fun. Keeps me sharp. The real work starts today."

"Emergency department? Burn unit?" he teased, holding up his expertly bandaged hand.

"Worse." She winced. "Family practice."

He laughed. They were a match made in heaven, and she really had no idea.

"Did I miss something hilarious?"

He liked that she didn't seem to mind being laughed at. Didn't take herself too seriously.

"Just thinking about how much we have in common."

"Oh, really?"

"I'm fire chief here," he said. "I always wanted to be a firefighter. Was a good one too. Good enough to move up the ranks. Guess how often a chief gets to run into a burning building?"

Her smile was understanding. "About as often as a family practitioner gets to intubate a patient in a helicopter?"

"Bingo, Dreamy. You and me, friend. Two peas in a pod. So if you need some kind of distraction from the grind—"

"The still essential grind," she reminded him.

He nodded, giving her that. "Someone's got to take temperatures and write scrips."

"And someone's got to organize the guys running into the fire."

"And gals," he said with a wink and a point.

"And gals," she agreed. She sighed and took another look around the room. "Place suits you."

It had. Linc wasn't sure if that was still true. Recently, he noticed a restlessness creeping in on the contentment he'd known for so long.

"Who's that?" she asked, nodding at a photo on the wall.

"That's my sister. She lives in Sedona with her three kids. Do you have any?"

"Siblings or kids?" she clarified.

"Both. Either."

She waited a beat. One just long enough that he knew what followed was either a lie or only a small part of a complicated story.

"Nope. Neither. And on that note, I need to get to work."

He rose with her and followed her to the door, Sunshine on his heels.

"Good luck organizing all those tongue depressors, Doc."

"Have fun with all your paperwork today, Chief."

He opened the door for her and enjoyed watching her amble across the asphalt to the sidewalk.

No car, he noted. *Interesting.*

Doc Dreamy was a puzzle that begged to be solved.

CHAPTER 7

The Benevolence Fire Department was housed in a new two-story building where the faucets didn't leak, the drivers didn't have to mind the piddly four inches of clearance on the garage doors, and the furniture didn't smell like decades of firefighter farts.

They'd made the move three years ago after a lifetime of fundraising and a few generous grants.

But part of Linc still felt nostalgic for the original brick station with the garage doors that stuck, the cracked concrete floors, and the wood-paneled living quarters with their creaky, uneven floors.

"Morning," he called, strolling in through the open bay. Shift change officially happened at seven every morning, but after bigger incidents, volunteers usually came in early to get the scoop from their counterparts.

"Morning, Chief," the crew echoed.

"How's the shoulder?" Assistant Chief Kelly Wu asked, nimbly hopping down from the engine and slamming the access panel.

She cruised in at five feet six inches with jet-black hair that she kept cropped in a stylish pixie cut. It fit under her hood and helmet better that way, she said. What she lacked in long legs, she made up for in fast feet and freakish strength. At forty-five, she ran long-distance mud races for fun and got matching tattoos with her eighteen-year-old daughter.

"Right as rain," he fibbed. Sore as hell was what it was.

Sunshine raced around, greeting everyone with equal enthusiasm. She accepted Kelly's head scratch and then happily bolted for the stairs and kitchen where a variety of dog treats waited.

The garage smelled of diesel and fresh cleaners. To Linc, the scent meant new starts. No matter what the apparatus and equipment had been through the previous day, it was reset to like-new.

Two of his day shift volunteers were already going over the engines, checking the med kits and emergency lighting, while last night's crew filled them in on the accident cleanup.

Every day began with a thorough check of all equipment and vehicles. Personal gear was stowed, equipment tested, and each apparatus gone over with a fine-tooth comb.

There was something satisfying, almost meditative, about the daily check. It prepared them all both physically and mentally for anything.

"Shouldn't you be wearing a sling?" Kelly asked in her best mom voice.

"Shouldn't you be buying your kid another hamster?"

"Deflecting," she shot back. "And it's on the agenda for tonight. Still not sure how the last furry little bastard got out of that damn ball."

"You're the one who named him Houdini."

"I just hope he doesn't turn up in an air vent or something." She sighed. "Then we'll have five."

The glass windows gleamed in the morning sun. The crew

took pride in their new station. Saturday was cleaning day. It was a hell of a lot easier—and more satisfying—to clean a brand-new facility than try to scrub through the decades of sludge on twenty-year-old turd-brown carpet.

The novelty of a new facility had yet to wear off.

"Want an unofficial briefing?" she offered.

"If there's coffee involved," he yawned. He stopped himself midstretch when he felt the twinge in his shoulder.

He'd slept like a log but could have used another hour or two.

Kelly followed him up the stairs where they ducked into the kitchen.

"Morning, Chief." Zane "Stairmaster" Jones greeted him with a bagel in one hand and his gym bag in the other. The deli in town always dropped off bagels the morning after a tough incident. Yet another benefit of small-town life.

"What's up, Stairmaster?"

"Heard you tweaked your shoulder pretty good," he said. The man was short and stocky but had the endurance of a professional athlete. He'd earned the nickname for organizing the local 9/11 memorial tribute. One hundred ten floors on stair climbers in full gear at the local gym.

Linc shrugged, then regretted the motion. "It's not bad. Doctor's being overly cautious if you ask me."

"Is that the doctor who looked you over in the ED or the one you had dinner with last night?" Kelly asked, the picture of innocence.

News traveled at lightning speeds in Benevolence.

He gave her an enigmatic smile and changed the subject. "How's the 'stache race going?" he asked Zane. Some of the guys were competing in a pre-Movember facial hair growing contest.

Zane stroked a hand over the sad wisps of facial hair dotting his upper lip. "Pretty good. I mean, Harry's in the lead, but I think I'm doing all right."

"He's a hirsute bastard," Linc agreed, thinking of the thick-haired Italian volunteer. "Make sure he's not just letting his nose hair grow out."

"I think it's muscle memory. Dude shaved his decades-old 'stache off just to participate."

"I'm competing in the leg hair division," Kelly put in. She took a drink of coffee so pale it could pass for milk.

"Please. You draw on your eyebrows every day," Zane scoffed.

Kelly gave her brows a wiggle. "With a hundred bucks at stake, I'm willing to draw on a mustache."

"A hundred bucks?" Linc mused. "Maybe I need to get in on this action."

Hearing his voice, Sunshine lifted her head from where she'd buried it in the couch cushions, surfing for dropped food. She bolted off the couch and ran to his side.

"That dog loves you more than anything in this universe," Zane noted wistfully. The guy was working on six months of single and was starting to make noises about wanting to meet a nice girl and settle down.

"Speaking of action and l-o-v-e," Kelly said with a pointed look at Linc. "How was dinner with hotshot air doc?"

"It was a professional face stuffing," Linc said. He didn't kiss and tell, and he certainly didn't talk about getting shot down from kissing.

"Professional? I heard she's sixty shades of gorgeous and you practically choked on your tongue when she popped her pretty face out of the helicopter," Kelly said.

"I heard he threw out his shoulder begging her to give him the time of day," Zane said, miming falling to his knees and clasping his hands.

"I'm happy to put you both on toilet scrubbing duty for the rest of the week," Linc mused.

"Aw, Chief. Why'd you do a thing like that when we've got ourselves a rookie?" Zane asked.

"That rookie hauled my ass out of a flaming car yesterday."

"After you heroically saved a bouquet of flowers," Kelly pointed out. "For what it's worth, that would have scored points with me if I were in the market for a Hottie McHotterson guy. I can make sure the pretty doc hears about your heroism, give her a nudge about what a catch you are."

"You're off toilet duty," Linc decided.

Zane took a bite of bagel under Sunshine's watchful eyes. "The chief doesn't need our help. He's never *not* landed the girl."

Linc shoved a hand through his hair. He didn't know what this feeling was. It felt like the opposite of confidence, and he didn't much care for it. There was something about Doc Dreamy that unsettled him. Made him doubt himself. It tightened up his glib tongue, made his flirting rusty. She was a challenge, and he didn't have the best track record with challenges.

Sunshine, bored with the conversation and lack of treats, trotted down the hallway and into his office.

"Maybe we can get to that briefing, Wu?" Linc hinted.

She snatched a bagel off the tray on the table. "Be there in a minute," she promised. "You want half?"

He eyed the bagel. Thought of the piece of pizza. "Nah. Thanks."

He ambled into the chief's office. Sunshine was perched on the dog bed, looking out the sole skinny window the room offered. Her tail swished happily across the carpet at whatever held her attention outside.

Linc flopped down in the desk chair and booted up the computer. His desk was littered with hand-written notes and papers, all waiting to be compiled neatly, concisely into his daily report, the bane of his existence.

Being chief had its perks. But the avalanche of paperwork was not one of them.

"Seriously, how are you feeling?" Kelly asked. She dropped into the chair across from him and bit into her bagel, slathered with a half-inch layer of cream cheese.

"Fine," he said, opening his email program and wincing when he saw the number of unread messages.

"Chief." Her mom voice required an answer.

"Hurts like a son of a bitch. There. Happy?"

She smirked at him. "That my chief was injured on a call? Yeah, I'm ecstatic. Ass."

"That's Chief Ass to you," he groused.

"Okay, Chief Ass, let's catch up."

She walked him through the night shift and the accident cleanup. Still only one fatality.

"Crew had the usual round of cuts and bumps and bruises. Rookie had some burns from hauling your cute butt out of the car, but you got the worst of it injury-wise."

"She didn't have any gear on." He sighed. "I told her to work triage."

"Lucky for her, there was an ear, nose, and throat doc whose Mercedes got turned into a tin can. He took over triage until the EMTs got there. How'd she do on her first big call?"

Linc walked through it in his head. "Good. Kept her head. She was excited. But not in the unhinged-rodeo-clown kind of way."

"She's gonna be a good addition to the crew," Kelly predicted.

"Seems so."

"I mean, we still have to razz her."

"Of course. It's part of the process."

"Oh, since you were bumming around the emergency department yesterday, I wrote up a draft of your DR for you."

"Bless you, Wu."

"Yeah, you just remember that when I ask for the next Fourth of July off." She stood and brushed bagel crumbs off her pants. "Need anything before I head out?"

"Nope. Hoping it'll be a quiet one after yesterday. Go on home."

Kelly gave Sunshine an enthusiastic ruffle before heading out the door. "Keep that shoulder rested," she called.

"Yeah. Yeah."

She left, but Kelly was just the first one through his door for the day.

"Yo, Chief! How's the shoulder?" Hairy Harry poked his head in.

"I barely recognize you without the 'stache," Linc said. The man had had one as long as Linc could remember.

Harry brushed a hand over his stubbled lip. "Be back in no time. Sounds like you guys had quite the mess yesterday."

One of the worst things for a firefighter was missing out on the big call.

"It was ugly," Linc agreed and mentally pushed back his DR and email for another ten minutes to shoot the shit.

It was the theme of the day apparently.

His eight thirty briefing was interrupted no less than three times by neighbors "just dropping by." Most brought goodies with them, so the interruptions weren't exactly annoying. It was a sign of the kind of community they lived in. They were all involved. Everyone had stakes in everyone else's lives. An accident, a trauma, had wide-reaching effect. Like ripples in a pond.

With the day shift tucked into the upstairs conference room for classroom training on responding to calls with victims with special needs, Linc headed back to his office. His shoulder hurt. His hand burned. But his mind was working on a different problem.

One Dr. Dreamy.

She wasn't exactly resistant to his charm. She seemed to enjoy it, had even flirted back. But she'd made it clear she wasn't looking for any extracurricular excitement with him.

He found the push-pull of her interest and disinterest in him fascinating.

It had gotten him burned before in the past. The strong, interesting woman who caught his eye, made him hope hopes and think thoughts. It hadn't panned out. But he'd never stopped hoping.

He tapped out a beat on the desk with the tip of his pen, debating. He could afford a few more dents, he decided. Better to regret something he'd done than something he hadn't.

He picked up the phone and dialed.

"Yeah, hey, Gloria. How do you feel about making up one of those pretty bouquets for me?"

CHAPTER 8

D unnigan & Associates was located in a barn-red single-level building on the way out of town past the high school. The concrete ramp and steps that led to the front door of the office were clean enough to eat from. Inside, the waiting room smelled faintly of fresh paint.

The chairs were the standard kind found in family doctor waiting rooms around the country, wooden legs with mint-green cushions. A tiny table and chairs topped with coloring books and fat crayons sat in a corner next to a fish tank. Some little colorer had gotten overzealous and scribbled orange zigzags on the off-white wall.

There was a mother holding a flush-cheeked toddler on her lap. She was reading a Frog and Toad book to him.

The girl behind the front desk looked up. She had the cheerleader look. Bright eyes. Bouncy curls that went from warm brown at the roots to glossy caramel at the ends. Perfect shimmery makeup. And a beauty queen smile.

"Hi! You must be Dr. O'Neil," the girl said, rising. "I'm Tuesday, and I'm so happy to meet you."

Oh boy. A sincere cheerleader.

Well, Mack wanted different. So rather than a military

pilot nicknamed Buzz who spit tobacco out the chopper door, she now had Tuesday. This was already a significant step up.

"Hi. Yes. Tuesday." Years of dealing with unconscious patients had apparently rendered her unable to communicate with the conscious.

Nerves. It was vaguely funny that the big, bad helicopter doc was nervous about practicing a little ol' family medicine.

A woman, short, comfortably round with a close-cropped cap of jet-black hair and more eye makeup than Cruella de Vil, bustled out of a doorway. She wore unsullied white orthopedic sneakers and purple scrubs.

"Freida, Dr. O'Neil is here," Tuesday announced cheerily. Mack wondered where Tuesday had been in the pyramid foundation.

"Dr. O'Neil. Nice to meet you," Freida said, extending a hand. Her nails were short and polish-free, but she wore four jeweled rings to make up for it.

"Call me Mack," she said, remembering to make eye contact with both of her new coworkers.

"Dr. Mack then," Freida compromised. "You can follow me."

Mack didn't know where she was going or what was waiting for her. But the unknown had been a familiar comfort up to this point. She never knew exactly what she was going to find when the helicopter touched down. She'd just treat this entire experience as one small, odd emergency call.

Freida led her to the end of a hallway and down another shorter one before pausing to rap lightly on a closed door.

"Yo," was the energetic response.

Freida opened the door. "Dr. D., Dr. Mack is here."

Dr. Trish Dunnigan was unapologetically wiping powdered sugar off her coat. Mack liked her already.

She stood up, brushing the crumbs into the trash can before wiping her hand on her pants and extending it to Mack.

"Great to meet you. Welcome aboard," she said heartily. The handshake was firm and a little sugary. Dr. Dunnigan was tall and on the stocky side with a spectacular head of frizzy red curls. Her smile was confident.

"Thanks, Dr. Dunnigan. I'm happy to be here." Happy. The word echoed in Mack's head, and she briefly wondered if she really had any idea what happy felt like. *Great.* Now she had to worry about an existential crisis as well as staving off burnout.

"Call me Trish. I planned to start with pleasantries, but I've got a walk-in. If you're up for observing, we can dive in from there."

"Fine by me."

Mack left her bag, keys, and phone in Trish's office and followed her back into the waiting room.

"Hey there, Colleen. How's our little guy today?" Trish asked.

"Fever again. And that means he's back to not sleeping," the mom answered.

"And that means you aren't either, poor thing. Come on back, and we'll see what we can do."

Mack followed them into the exam room and closed the door. She arranged herself in the corner like a resident on rounds and tried to look nonthreatening.

Trish made quick work of the physical exam while the boy seemed determined to burrow back into his mother's flesh. The mother looked worn out to the point of giving up.

"Looks like Tommy's got that rhinovirus that's going around," Trish announced.

"Nothing serious. Okay," Colleen said, nodding. "Does it make me a horrible mother that I really wished for some kind of magic cold medicine to give him that would make him sleep through the night?"

Trish's laugh was one hard-hitting "Ha!" She shook her head, curls shaking. "Honey, that makes you normal."

Relief that you weren't a bad person was sometimes as much of a balm as actual medicine. Mack knew that from experience.

"Now, here's my prescription for you. We just started to get you back into good health. Tommy here has been a challenge since you first found out you were pregnant with him. No offense, kiddo. I was a challenge to my parents too. You can't parent or work or wife or whatever other verbs you've got going on when you're completely depleted.

"So. Fluids. Easily digestible meals for the little guy here. If he's not better in another two or three days, call the office. Dr. Mack here will give you a scrip for antibiotics if she thinks this thing has turned bacterial. Okay?"

Mack gave what she hoped was an encouraging smile.

"Okay." Colleen paused, bouncing Tommy on her hip. "What if he doesn't help me?"

"Your husband? If he refuses to help raise the child he had a fifty-percent hand in creating, then you leave Daddy and Tommy for two nights and get yourself a hotel room. Two nights. Not one."

Mack blinked. *The country doctor is telling her patient to leave her husband.*

"Anyone can function on one night of bad sleep," Trish continued. "But you need him to feel the pain of chronic depletion. Two nights of him not sleeping will give him a whole new perspective on the last three years for you. And if it doesn't, tell his mama on him. She'll scare him straight."

Colleen nodded, her face blank. "Hotel. His mother. Got it."

"Good. Now go on and get your lollipop at the front desk. It's all gonna be fine."

Mack watched them.

"Is that typical? To get that involved in a patient's personal life?" she asked, feeling uneasy. "I'm not qualified to give marital advice."

The doctor's guffaw could probably be heard a block away. "Welcome to small-town family medicine, Mack. You'll figure it out. I have faith in you."

"I have zero experience with patient relationships. Mine begin with most of them unconscious and end with me handing them off before they regain consciousness."

"Good! Then this will be a good learning experience for you," Trish said, patting her on the shoulder. "I'd hate for you to be bored. Just remember, we focus a lot on preventative care. We're still saving lives, just in slower motion."

This was a definite shift in gears. Mack was used to slapping on metaphorical bandages and leaving the details up to the hospital. Now, she'd be in charge of the details.

"Let's get to that tour," Trish suggested.

The tour was short. Two offices. Two exam rooms. A room with X-ray and ultrasound tech. A sunny kitchen/break room with a new fridge and an old table. There was the supply closet that housed both medical paraphernalia and office supplies. Employees parked in the back. Mack's office was Trish's office.

"Want me to clear out any of this personal crap?" Trish asked, making a sweeping gesture at the bookcase in the corner that sagged under the weight of photos of the Dunnigans' wedding day, framed certificates, and an intriguing number of bobbleheads.

Mack shook her head. "No, it's fine. You're coming back. I don't need to personalize anything."

"Still. Feel free to slap up some pictures or at least order a new desk chair. This one can be temperamental if you're not used to it." To demonstrate, Trish flopped down and leaned back. The entire seat assembly bucked backward.

Mack reached out to catch her.

"Don't worry," Trish snickered. "Hasn't thrown me yet. I'm a professional. But don't let it sneak up on you. Catch you unawares."

———

Lunch was Trish's treat. She devoured half an order of spring rolls and the lunchtime cheesesteak special. "I can feel your nutritional judgment," she said, washing a bite of cheesesteak down with a gulp of raspberry iced tea. "But I'm about to embark on a four-month world tour with my opinionated, vegetarian wife. I'll be lucky to sneak a cheeseburger once a month."

Mack smiled. There was something so *normal* about the doctor.

"Well, while you're off sneaking fast-food runs, are there any areas you need me to concentrate on in your practice?"

"I just want to know that my patients, my friends, my neighbors are in the best possible hands."

Medically speaking, they would be. But if they were all looking for a life coach, they were up shit's creek.

"I'll do my best," she promised.

"All anyone can ask. We're a small, independent practice. Practically unheard of these days. But we make it work. Insurance billing is always a bitch. But we've got people on staff. If you run into any issues, put Freida on it. She's terrifying. And Russell Robinson, your counterpart, is a truly excellent practitioner. A little hoity-toity for small town, but we love him for it. If you have any questions, go to him. He'll be in the office this afternoon."

"What are you doing with the other two months of your sabbatical?"

"Recovering. Want a spring roll?"

CHAPTER 9

While Trish took care of a sprained wrist follow-up and a case of pink eye, Mack sat behind the front desk crammed in between Tuesday and Freida so they could take turns explaining the office database.

"So here's where you update the patient visit notes," Tuesday said, pointing at the laptop screen with a fingernail the color of sparkling sand.

"Do not, repeat, *do not* write anything you don't want the patient to read, because these notes are uploaded directly to their patient portal," Freida said, her sweeping hand gesture nearly catching Mack in the right boob.

"Tell her about Mrs. Moretta," Tuesday insisted, bouncing in her seat.

Mack's interest piqued. She happened to know a Moretta or two in this town.

Freida's eye roll was extravagant and entertaining. "Mrs. Moretta, bless her heart, is a bit…"

"She likes things her way," Tuesday filled in generously. A *nice* cheerleader.

"She does not like to be told to lay off the box wine and ice cream." Freida was less generous and perhaps more realistic.

They are definitely talking about Aldo's mother, not the man's wife, Mack decided.

"Anyway, Mrs. Moretta's numbers were high. Cholesterol, sugar, weight. Dr. D tried to gently encourage her to consider some healthier options," Freida said.

Tuesday wrinkled her cute little nose. "And Mrs. Moretta was uncomfortable with the suggestion and tried to explain—"

"At the top of her lungs," Freida added.

"In an enthusiastic manner—"

"The walls shook. Children cried."

"So Mrs. Moretta goes home, and we had just rolled out the new patient portal," Tuesday continued, obviously enjoying Freida's commentary.

"An hour later, we're locking up, ready to head home for the day, and the phone rings. Guess who it is?" Freida demanded, stabbing Mack in the shoulder with a very pointy finger.

"Mrs. Moretta?"

"Yep. And she had just read Dr. D's patient notes."

Mack hid her smile. "And what did the patient notes say?"

"That the patient was belligerently determined to make poor nutritional choices."

"Mrs. Moretta took offense to the wording."

"She told Dr. D to kiss her double-wide ass."

The laugh sputtered out of Mack, and she was grateful that the waiting room was empty.

"So Dr. D had to call Mrs. D and ask her to reschedule their dinner reservations so she could go apologize to Mrs. Moretta."

"With a box of chardonnay."

"Only polite patient notes in the file. Got it," Mack said. She was getting itchy to *do* something. The patient database was as straightforward as it could get. She was ready to jump in.

Tuesday scrolled through another patient file where a note caught Mack's eye.

"Hang on. Why do you have the work schedule of this patient's next-door neighbor in the file?" Mack asked. They also had out-of-state adult children listed with occupations. There was another notation of the woman's favorite cookie.

Freida and Tuesday shared a knowing look. "The better we know our patients, the higher the level of care we can provide," Freida said with a sweeping gesture as if addressing a crowd.

"Perhaps it's not the way everyone does medicine, or should I say *business*." A man's voice carrying an obvious opinion interrupted them.

Dr. Russell Robinson was a lean, well-dressed man with dark skin, close-cropped hair, and a beauty mark–like mole on his right cheek. He wore a jaunty bow tie under his white coat and a frown.

"Dr. O'Neil." He offered his hand across the desk to Mack.

Apparently, it wasn't a pleasure to meet her.

"Dr. Robinson." She returned his firm handshake.

"Dr. Robinson is a semiretired cardiac specialist," Freida explained. "He usually works Thursdays, Fridays, and every other Saturday. But he agreed to help out extra this week and next while you get your feet wet."

"My wife is a political consultant in DC," he said, pride tinging his tone. "We divide our time between here and the city. I'm assuming you'll make an actual effort here so my presence won't be required full-time."

It wasn't a question.

"You don't get into medicine to half-ass care," Mack said firmly.

"No. But some get into medicine to play God," he mused.

"Some. Others beat around the bush instead of getting

to the point." Mack had done what was necessary to survive her childhood, but as an adult, she didn't tiptoe. If there was a problem, she walked right up to it and dealt with it.

Tuesday giggled nervously behind her.

"We don't do assembly line care here, Dr. O'Neil. Patients come first. We're about quality of life. So if you don't think you'll be able to care about our patients beyond writing a prescription or slapping on a bandage, I suggest you save us all some time and go back to emergency medicine."

"I'm here to learn how family practice works," she said coolly. "Dr. Dunnigan seems to feel that I'm capable of providing the required level of care. So if you have concerns over my abilities, I suggest you raise them with her."

"I have. Now I'm raising them with you. Do your job well, and we won't have any problems."

The man was succinct.

"Fair enough," she said.

He turned to Tuesday and Freida, his expression warming considerably. "Ladies. It's nice to see you, as always."

"Hi, Dr. Robinson," Tuesday greeted him cheerfully.

"I'll be in my office until my next appointment if you need anything," he said. He shot Mack one last warning look before disappearing down the hall.

"Sorry about that. Dr. Robinson is a little protective of the practice and our patients," Freida said. "I'm sure he'll warm up to you in no time."

"Yeah. Sure," Mack said.

"Well, this is it," Trish sighed, locking the back door behind her.

She looked fondly at the building and patted the window in a silent goodbye.

It isn't too late, Mack thought foolishly.

Maybe Trish would have second thoughts and decide to stay in Benevolence. Mack could pick up rotations in the county hospital's emergency department or say screw it and repack her barely unpacked boxes and hightail it for the next high-adrenaline job placement.

But then Trish was smiling and holding out the keys.

Mack hesitated for the briefest of seconds, then took the key ring.

"Safe travels," she said to her soon-to-be absentee boss. "Your practice and your patients are in good hands."

Mack was confident in the medicine part. She was an excellent doctor. She just wasn't sure what kind of bedside manner she could muster. Or if it would meet the judgmental Dr. Robinson's exacting standards.

"Don't worry about Russ," Trish said as if reading her mind. "He'll warm up when he realizes you're not here to hit quotas and sell kidneys on the black market."

"Don't you worry about Dr. Robinson or me or anything. We've got it covered," Mack promised.

"I know you do. And I think you're really going to end up enjoying Benevolence, Mackenzie."

Visions of the shirtless firefighter in her backyard flooded her mind. Mack felt her cheeks flush.

"I'm sure it will be a memorable six months."

CHAPTER 10

Mack headed toward home with her windows down and the radio up. She would start officially on Monday and had a fluttering of nerves over the prospect. It would be good. She would be good. Dr. Robinson's snooty reception had actually made her feel more comfortable. In her experience, every job came with its peacocking naysayers. She'd proven herself on more dangerous battlefields against tougher critics.

She'd rise to the challenge and show Robinson what she was capable of.

Mack punched the sun visor back up when she made the turn onto a tree-lined street and started thinking about dinner. And her backyard neighbor.

She'd been surprised every time his blue eyes popped into her mind during the day. A distracted doctor was a malpractice suit waiting to happen. So she'd efficiently boxed him up and set him out of her mind.

Getting involved with Linc would be a stupid move. No matter how attractive he was. Or interesting. Or heroic. Okay, so maybe she'd joined the nurses in their internal swooning over Linc saving a man and his flowers.

But.

She'd had enough casual relationships carved into her metaphorical bedpost that it was one of the areas she'd vowed to change during the next six months. No flings with sexy hotshots. A six-month cooling-off period would do her good. Help her decide what was next. What was the smart move?

A figure appeared from the mouth of the lakeside trail at a gallop. Thick dark hair. Sweaty, tattooed torso. Prosthetic leg.

Mack brought her SUV to a stop, leaned out her window, and whistled.

The runner held up a hand and then pointed to the gold ring on his finger. "Thanks. Married."

"All the good ones are," she called back.

He stopped midstride and turned to face her.

"Son of a—"

She was out of the SUV and in the sweaty, beefy arms of Aldo Moretta in two seconds flat.

"Dr. Dreamy!" he said, spinning her around in the air before dragging her in for a spine-cracking bear hug.

Joy, fast and fierce, flowed between them.

She'd been there for him on the worst day of his life. Something neither of them ever forgot.

"You said you wouldn't get here until next week," he said, crushing her against his chest, her feet still dangling above the pavement.

"Dr. Dunnigan moved up her timeline, so here I am." She didn't bother letting him know she'd been in town for a few days. She hadn't wanted to impose. Had wanted to settle into the rental and routine before she called up her old friend.

"Here you are," Aldo repeated, beaming down at her.

He had the dark hair and olive complexion of his Italian heritage coupled with the build of a Clydesdale. Everything about him screamed energy, vitality, happiness.

His amputation had barely put a hitch in his stride. His wife, the lovely Latina Gloria, had quite a bit to do with that.

"How's the hardware holding up?" she asked.

He set her neatly on her feet and danced a jig. "Pretty damn good. It keeps up with me."

"That says something." Mack shook her head, her face aching from the smile. "It's so good to see you."

He yanked her in for another hard hug. "Back at you. I'm really glad this substitution for Doc Dunnigan worked out."

"Me too." And right now, she was sincerely happy.

A horn tooted behind them. "You got yourself a new lady, Moretta?" A skinny guy in a dirty ball cap was leaning the whole way out of the driver's side window of a pickup truck that sounded like its spark plugs were rattling loose.

"Mind your business, Carl!" Aldo yelled back good-naturedly. "This isn't a lady. This is the doc who saved my life."

"Well, don't that just beat all. Wait'll I tell the wife!"

"Try not to impregnate her while you tell her," Aldo said.

Carl grinned and flipped him the bird. "Nice to meet you, Doc!" He gave another jaunty toot of the horn and then puttered off toward downtown.

"Everyone sure is friendly here," Mack observed wryly.

"Friendly and nosy. Don't be surprised if you find Georgia Rae going through your trash."

"Who's Georgia Rae?"

"Now why would I go and spoil the surprise?"

A siren chirped, catching their attention. "Aldo Moretta, unhand the pretty doctor lady and stop blocking traffic." Lincoln Reed's voice came through loud and clear thanks to the speaker on the chief's vehicle.

"I see you've already caught Lover Boy's attention," Aldo said, slinging an arm around her shoulder.

"Not officially," she deferred.

"Don't fall for anything he says. It's all a line," he teased.

"Just what I need. An interfering big brother," she quipped.

Arm in arm, they strolled over to Linc's SUV.

"Aren't you married?" Linc asked Aldo through his open window.

"Blissfully. And I need to text Gloria immediately before the town starts beating down our door with rumors that I'm making out with another woman in the middle of town," Aldo said. "So you're a fan of Doc Dreamy?"

Linc's grin was slow and just for Mack. "That explains a lot."

"Ladies' man Chief Lincoln Reed, meet Dr. Mackenzie 'Hero Is My Middle Name' O'Neil," Aldo said.

Linc held out his bandaged hand. "Real nice to meet you officially, Doc O'Neil."

Mack accepted it and pretended to ignore the flutter in her stomach when his grip tightened suggestively.

"A pleasure, Chief," she said, the picture of innocence.

"It will be," he predicted.

"Don't even start, man. She's too good for you," Aldo teased, but Mack caught the flash in Linc's eyes.

But then his grin grew degrees more charming, his gaze warmer, and she wondered if she'd imagined it.

"Watch out for this one. He's a connoisseur of the opposite sex," Aldo said, elbowing Mack. "Linc loves 'em and leaves 'em."

A hatchback drove by slower than the mom with the double stroller on the sidewalk. The driver gawked at them, and Linc gave her a lazy wave.

"You better move out before all of Benevolence is talking about your illicit affair," Linc said. "I'll see you around, Doc."

"I should stop blocking traffic," Mack said, jerking her thumb in the direction of her SUV.

"Cookout. Next week," Aldo said, pointing at her. "You can meet Gloria and the kids. I'd say tonight, but we just got back from Disney a few days ago, and we're still drowning in laundry and wondering how the kids packed an entire suitcase full of sand."

Mack shook her head and grinned. "A lot to catch up on," she said.

At least on Aldo's part. He'd been shipped home, retired from the National Guard, gotten married, and started a family. Five years ago, the only sand he'd seen had been desert. Now he went to Disney on family vacations.

But she was still doing the same thing. Her deployments were over. But wasn't this basically the same? A short-term placement.

"Sounds great," she said.

"I'll text you."

Mack waved Aldo off as he resumed his run. She felt the weight of Linc's gaze on her.

He stared out his windshield. "You know there's more to me than my dating history."

"I'm not not sleeping with you because you enjoy women," she assured him.

He turned to look at her.

"Maybe I'm not sleeping with you because of *my* dating history."

"Just get out of a long-term relationship?" he guessed.

"Opposite. If you're a ladies' man, I'm a man's lady. Men's lady? Anyway, I'm taking a break from it."

"Maybe we should both try something different. We'll just have to get married," Linc decided with a grin.

He drove off and left Mack blinking after him.

CHAPTER 11

L eah, if you stop trying to kick your brother in the nuts, maybe he won't be such a little turd to you," Linc called from his patio where he warmed up the grill for hot dogs and burgers to feed his young hostages. He'd gotten up early on his day off and had put in a full day of paperwork and maintenance work at the station by noon.

"Uncle Linc! Make her stop," Bryson screeched, his voice cracking in the middle of the whine as puberty asserted its presence.

"Why? If you stop taking her water gun and she stops kicking you, you're just gonna find something else to fight about."

Linc's oldest sister, Rebecca, found out about his day off and dumped his niece and nephew on him for a few hours because, as she put it, "If I have to listen to them scream at each other for one more second, I'm going to enter the witness relocation program."

When he pointed out that the entrance requirements involved actually witnessing something that required relocation, she'd threatened to commit the crime herself.

So he had Bryson, thirteen, and Leah, ten, to entertain and terrorize him for the afternoon.

His cell phone rang on the picnic table. "Shit. Which one of you big mouths told Aunt Christa you were here?" Both hooligans raised their hands.

News of free babysitting traveled fast in the Reed family.

"What's up, Sis?"

"How's my favorite brother?"

"Great. Busy. Heading in to the station," he lied. Leah let out a bloodcurdling scream. To silence her, he threw a water balloon that hit her in the shoulder.

"No, you're not. You're watching Becca's kids, and I'm out front with mine."

He feigned a groan. "Seriously? I'm injured. How am I supposed to break up the fights when they start to go *Hunger Games* on each other?"

His back door opened, and his sister Christa poked her head out. "Surprise!" Where Becca was tall and athletic, Christa was shorter, curvier, and abhorred anything that made her sweat. Both had the trademark Reed blond hair and dimpled chins.

Her two daughters followed her out onto the patio. Sunshine lifted her head and gave a mighty yawn before deigning to greet the new guests.

Christa made the appropriate fuss over her before the girls got their hugs in.

Bryson jogged over and initiated a complicated cousin handshake with eleven-year-old Samantha. Kinley was lugging a backpack of books.

"If they're too much for you, just turn a fire hose on them," she suggested, giving him a loud kiss on the cheek. "How's your shoulder? Where's your sling?"

"You sound like Dreamy," Linc complained.

"Who's Dreamy?" she demanded.

"Uncle Linc, are you making us hot dogs too?" Samantha asked, sniffing the air.

"That depends, Mantha. Got five bucks?"

Samantha had spent two full years railing against the "boyish" nickname Sam, adding "mantha" to the shortened moniker until she ended up as just Mantha.

She gave him a small smile. "No. But if you distract my mom, I can probably get in her purse like last time." Linc and Samantha were united in their continuing mission to drive Christa crazy.

His sister rolled her eyes and tugged Samantha's braid. "Nice try, champ. Now, Mom's gotta go crack a nice lady's back. I'll be back in an hour, two tops, if I decide to swing by the grocery store to feed you monsters later tonight. Don't burn down Uncle Linc's house."

His sister practically danced out of the backyard, ecstatic with newfound freedom. Linc didn't hold it against her. She'd gone through a shitty divorce two years ago, and he was happy to step up his uncle game to give her breaks when she needed it.

He threw four more dogs on the grill. Kinley was small, but the kid could put away hot dogs like a drunk fraternity pledge. Sunshine sighed against his shin and gave him *the look*.

He threw another hot dog on the grill.

His home was designed for a bachelor's lifestyle, which coincidentally also made it great for entertaining kids. In addition to the pool table and beer fridge, he had a freezer full of hot dogs, a server that hosted every kid's movie known to man, and an endless supply of dart guns.

"Whatcha reading, Kins?" he asked. His niece was curled up in the hammock swing he'd hung just for her from the rafter of his overhang trellis.

Kinley hated being interrupted when she was reading and reminded him of that fact with a weighty sigh for a seven-year-old before flashing the cover at him. *Common Psychological Conditions, Their Symptoms, and Diagnoses.*

Kinley, an advanced reader, had carte blanche at the local library.

"Who wants to play with knives?" he called to the three kids who were competing in some complex *Star Wars* pirate game with sticks and sound effects.

All three dropped their sticks and came running.

"You get the onion," he said, dropping it in front of Bryson. "Real men cry. Deal with it."

"I want the tomato," Leah said, expressing her desires with gimme fingers.

"Life is full of disappointments. Here's the lettuce. I want it finely chopped, not like those giant chunks you did at Fourth of July."

Samantha waited patiently and smirked when he gave her the tomato. "Thank you, Uncle Linc."

He took the tomato and replaced it with a block of cheese. "Don't be a kiss-ass."

The kids snickered. Sunshine beamed up at him and wiggled closer to Samantha, hoping for a cheese handout.

"Remember knife safety," he said, strutting behind them like a drill sergeant as the kids picked up their paring knives.

"No stabbing ourselves or anyone else," they recited.

"Good. Now slice and dice, dorks."

———

They ate grilled meat with clumsily sliced vegetables on paper plates under the sunny afternoon sky and enjoyed each other's company.

Sunshine wolfed down her hot dog and then made eyes at Kinley until she forked over a generous bite of hamburger.

"Uncle Linc, why don't you have kids?" Kinley asked out of nowhere.

"Because I haven't made any yet." His sisters were almost uncomfortably open with their kids on the baby-making process. And Linc was only just beginning to start considering the possibilities of family life. Someday. If he met the right woman.

"But you practice a lot," Bryson pointed out.

Linc riffed the bill of his nephew's cap. "Smart-ass."

"Mom says he isn't ready to settle down," Samantha insisted knowledgeably.

"Maybe your mom should mind her own beeswax," Linc said to the delight of the kids.

"Don't you want to have kids?"

"He has to find a wife or a husband first, dummy," Kinley chimed in. "Do you have a preference, Uncle Linc?"

"He doesn't have to be married," Leah said. "Our dad says you can have babies and not be married, but we should make sure we're in a solid 'nancial position before deciding."

"*Fi*nancial," Bryson corrected disdainfully. "Uncle Linc, do you make a lot of money being a fire chief?"

"No, nephew. No, I do not. But I'm expecting my bath bomb store on Etsy to take off any day now."

Four pairs of eyes pinned him with stares. Either they didn't get the joke or didn't think it was funny.

"So who's up for a dart gun war?"

They battled it out for dominion on the summer crispy lawn, Linc firing left-handed in deference to his shoulder injury and burns.

He was up against the fence, Sunshine gleefully chasing Kinley, who was using her psychology tome as a shield to head to higher ground. Bryson, Leah, and Samantha fired and shrieked in kid glee.

He heard a door slide open and close and took a peek over the fence. The cottage that backed up to his property was a rental, and he'd forgotten the landlord had signed a new lease.

He meant to only glance. Maybe throw up a friendly wave and apologize for the volume of his charges. But when he saw who it was, leaning against the railing of the small, tidy deck, he forgot everything.

"You've got to be kidding me."

She wiggled her fingers at him. "Hi, neighbor."

"The devious Dr. Dreamy."

"Is that her superhero name?" Leah wondered. Her pink sneakers scrabbled at the fence as she tried to climb up to get a better view.

"Hi," Bryson said, dropping his voice lower and hiding the dart gun behind his back. "Uncle Linc, can we spend the night?" It looked like two Reed men had a crush on the same woman.

"Take that!" Samantha crowed, raining Nerf darts down on them in a fatal torrent.

"Excuse me for a minute," Linc said to Mack and then collapsed to the grass in an epic death scene.

Bryson and Leah followed suit.

"I am the victor!" Samantha shouted, taking a victory lap around the yard.

A dart pegged her square in the forehead. "Not anymore, Mantha." Kinley smugly twirled her dart gun around her finger.

"No fair!" Samantha complained. "I didn't know you were playing!"

"It's called strategy. You should use it sometime," Kinley said in a superior tone.

"You know the rules, Mantha. Let's see the death scene. Make it Oscar-worthy," Linc called.

Samantha stomped her foot and then swept a hand to her forehead. "I feel faint! I see light. Great-Granny Mildred? Is that you?" Her knees buckled. Sunshine, concerned with the moaning, trotted over to lick her reassuringly.

But Samantha couldn't be revived. She fell forward and crawled the twenty feet to her audience. "Always remember," she rasped. "That you're all fart faces."

And with that, she left this mortal coil.

Sunshine, confused and concerned, lay down next to Samantha and licked her ear.

"Bravo!" Linc started the standing ovation and was joined by the rest of the kids and Mack.

"I didn't know you had almost an entire starting basketball team lineup," Mack teased.

"Oh, we're not his kids," Samantha said, coming back to life.

"Yeah, he can't settle down," Kinley piped up from over her book.

"He likes practicing making babies more than actually making them," Bryson said with a "what are you gonna do" shrug.

The kid had charm in spades.

"Are you single?" Leah asked Mack. "Do you like kids and hot dogs and darts and Sunshine?" Leah smooshed Sunshine's face in her hands to emphasize the dog's cuteness.

"We don't know if he likes ladies or men yet," Kinley reminded them.

"Ladies! I like ladies," Linc said emphatically. "Not that there's anything wrong with liking men or both or whatever. I like ladies, and you all can feel free to shut your traps right about now."

Mack laughed. A low, rich rasp that caught him in the chest. And Linc decided he'd be happy to be the butt of all jokes forever if he got to hear that laugh again.

"Did you guys know that your uncle got hurt?" Mack asked, stepping off the deck and wandering over to the chest-high fence.

"Mom said he saved someone's life," Samantha said, tying her long hair back in a lumpy ponytail. "I like your hair."

"Thanks." Mack smiled. "I like yours. Uncle Linc hurt his shoulder and got burnt, and he's supposed to be resting. I think you're supposed to babysit him today and make sure he doesn't do anything too strenuous."

They converged on him like lions on a fresh kill.

"Dr. Mack is just kidding. She's lying," Linc said desperately when Kinley grabbed his good arm and started dragging him toward the house. The other kids pushed from behind.

"We'll take good care of him, Dr. Mack," Bryson assured her confidently.

"I can make him supper! Do you like toast with peanut butter and chocolate chips?" Leah wanted to know.

"See if you can get him to take a nap," Mack called after them, and Linc heard that husky laugh again.

"You'll pay for this," he warned her.

"Have fun, Chief."

CHAPTER 12

Mack stripped off her exam gloves, then washed her hands again for good measure.

"A case of pink eye, Mr...." Ah, hell, what was his name? Rarely in the last several years of practicing medicine had she needed to know and remember a patient's name.

"Botham," the man supplied. She tried not to stare in medical fascination at his crusty, red, swollen left eye.

"Mr. Botham, you and...your son will be just fine," Mack promised. Dammit. She needed to figure out a mnemonic to temporarily memorize names. "I'll write a scrip for both of you. You'll start feeling and seeing better tomorrow."

"How about we get some ice cream after we swing by the pharmacy, Spence?" Mr. Botham asked his seven-year-old son.

Spencer. Right.

The kid perked up.

"I'll call in the prescriptions now. They should be ready for you shortly," Mack said, fingers stumbling over the laptop keyboard. Typing and remembering patient names hadn't been essential skills in her job until now. She'd work on both. "You should both stay home tomorrow, though, since pink eye is very contagious." *Clearly.*

"Thanks, Doc. Welcome to town," Mr. Botham said and ushered Spencer out of the exam room.

"Thank you," she called after them.

Mack's eye suddenly felt itchy, and she resisted the urge to wash her hands again. The Bothams had been the second and third cases of pink eye today. A wild first day in family medicine.

She tore off the exam table paper and gave it, the doorknobs, and chair arms a quick swipe with a Lysol wipe.

Glancing at the patient queue on the computer, she noted there were several more appointments on the calendar than there had been when she came in this morning.

She headed in the direction of the front desk. "Tuesday, is this a glitch—" Mack didn't get to finish the sentence. The waiting room was full. Nearly everybody in the room had at least one red, crusty eye. While the majority of the patients were of elementary school age, there were also quite a few itchy-eyed adults. The oldest in the room was pushing ninety by her estimation.

"Oh, shit," she said under her breath.

They were going to have to Lysol bomb the waiting room.

"Happy first day," Freida said. "We got 'em scheduled out in ten-minute windows."

"Okay," Mack sighed. "Who here is on a schedule and needs to get out of here quickly?"

About half the hands rose.

"We'll start with you all. Do the rest of you like pizza?" she asked.

The response was lethargically positive.

She reached into her pocket and produced a slim wallet. "Tuesday, call whatever pizza place we've got in town and get a couple of pies and whatever else you recommend." She tossed her credit card to the receptionist. "And, for God's sake, don't let anyone touch you."

"On it, Dr. Mack," Tuesday said cheerfully.

"We'll start with you," Mack said, pointing at a harried mother with three kids.

In three hours of emergency medicine–style efficiency, Mack had nearly cleared the waiting room. The last of the pink eyes had been seen. She'd just wrapped up a UTI, and the final patients on her list were two kids with fevers.

She snagged a piece of cold pizza from the break room and scarfed it down. She poked her head out into the waiting room and found it empty.

"Freida's getting their vitals in exam room 2," Tuesday told her. "And these came for you."

Mack blinked at the wildflower bouquet sitting on the front desk.

"They're from Chief Reed," Tuesday said, unable to contain her enthusiasm.

Mack plucked the opened card out of the blooms.

Dreamy,

I found Nemo twice yesterday, and now I can't get the *Moana* songs out of my head. Also I hate burnt toast with chocolate chips. I owe you. Good luck on your first day.

Your Very Attractive Neighbor (Linc) (Clarifying in case you noticed how swole Mr. Nabuki two houses down is)

She bit her lip to keep her face from exploding into a gossip-inducing smile.

Yeah, she definitely had a soft spot for the sexy fire chief. And that was inconvenient.

She met Freida in the hallway outside exam room 2.

"So did you retire from the military or quit?" Freida asked.

The woman had been grilling her in increments since that morning.

Where are you from originally?

Where did you go to medical school?

Ever been married?

Do you have a favorite Jonas brother?

It was all part of the small-town experience. An alternate universe.

"Declined to stay in after my last deployment," she said. "Didn't have enough years for retirement." *Or the physical and emotional stamina to survive another few years.*

"You've got the Garrisons in there. Mom Harper, almost eight-year-old Ava, and four-year-old Sadie. Spoiler alert: It's not pink eye."

"Thank God for that. Do you and Tuesday mind wiping down every surface in the waiting room before heading out?"

"Might be faster to burn it down, but we'll save the drastic measures for flu season," Freida said. "Gorgeous flowers. I didn't know you and Linc knew each other."

"We're neighbors," Mack said.

Freida's eyebrows seemed to insist on more of a disclosure. But there were patients waiting.

Mack knocked briskly on the exam room door. Garrison. Harper and Ava and…shit. She'd forgotten.

"Come in!"

"Mrs. Garrison, what can we do for you today?"

Harper Garrison was a pretty blond with big gray eyes and the kind of smile that seemed permanent…and genuine. She and Tuesday probably got along great.

Her kids were cuties. Ava was admiring her sparkly flip-flops every time she kicked her little legs up from the end of the exam table. She had dark, curly hair and big, dark eyes. There was zero family resemblance.

Sadie, however, could have been cut from the same cloth as her mother. She had fine hair so blond it was almost platinum. Her gray eyes were wary.

Harper plopped Sadie on the table next to her sister and surprised Mack with a hug.

"Oh. Uh, is this a thing? Hugging doctors?" Mack asked.

"I'm Luke Garrison's wife and Aldo's friend," Harper explained.

It clicked into place. Aldo, recovering from his amputation, had enlisted the help of his buddy's then-girlfriend. He'd ended up teaching her to run. Mack had seen the pictures from that long-ago Fourth of July 5K when Aldo Moretta had reminded the entire town—and himself—what he was made of.

"Harper. Of course. It's nice to meet you." From all accounts, Luke Garrison's wife was a ray of sunshine. It appeared the rumors were true.

"So this is Ava and Sadie," Harper said, making the introductions. She placed a loving hand on each girl's head. "This is only half of the family. The boys are healthy, thankfully. But our girls don't feel very well, do you?"

Ava shook her head, dark curls bouncing. Sadie looked at Mack like she expected the doctor to steal her soul.

"We don't feel good," Ava announced, still kicking her flip-flopped feet to a beat only an almost eight-year-old could hear.

"Mama says we can't go to school until we stop throwing up and having fevers."

"Your mom is right. How about I do a quick examination, and then we'll see what we can do to make you feel better?" Mack suggested. Her talking-to-children skills were rusty. She thought of Linc in the backyard with his nieces and nephew.

"Do you guys like dogs?" she asked, channeling Linc.

Ava told Mack all about their two dogs—Lola and Max—while Mack did a quick physical exam. Swollen glands. Fevers.

"Have you been hungry lately?"

Ava shook her head swiftly. "Nope." Sadie sat like a sphinx while Mack repeated the exam on her.

Mack slung her stethoscope over her shoulders while Ava told her how Daddy and Lola snuck a nap on the couch while Mama was weeding the garden.

"So there's a highly contagious stomach bug making the rounds," Mack began.

"Oh, hell," Harper muttered.

"Yeah," Mack said. "Keep these two quarantined and hydrated for the next forty-eight. Lots of electrolytes and broth. BRAT diet: bananas, rice, applesauce, and toast are good, bland foods to start with. The worst should be over by tomorrow, but if there's any more vomiting or diarrhea tomorrow—"

"Poop!" Ava shouted joyfully.

"Yes, poop," Mack continued with a laugh. "Call me so we can make sure they don't get dehydrated."

Harper took enthusiastic notes in a notebook she produced from her massive mom tote. "Okay. So now that you've diagnosed my kids, what are you doing Friday night?" she asked.

Mack opened her mouth and realized she didn't know what to say.

"Aldo mentioned doing a cookout, and since he and Gloria are in the middle of a backyard patio project, I volunteered to host it. Shoot. Girls, do you know if I told Daddy we were going to have a cookout?"

Ava brought a finger to her chin, the picture of deep thought.

Sadie made her first human move. "I don't fink you told Daddy. You were tawking to Aunt Gworwia on the phone, and you said 'Remind me to say somefing to Wooke.' And then Wowa got sprayed by the skunk."

Harper beamed at her daughter. "It takes her a little while to thaw, but when she does, watch out."

Sadie launched into a description of how bad "Wowa" smelled and how many baths she had.

Mack wrestled with the knee-jerk urge to wrap up the appointment. Efficiency was key in a medical practice. And she wasn't sure how comfortable she was with being invited to a patient's house. Even if the patient's husband was an ex-military acquaintance of hers.

"So we'll see you Friday night at seven, right?" Harper said brightly as she helped her daughters off the exam table.

"Um. Okay," Mack said, unable to come up with a good enough excuse to bail. Unless, of course, the kids were still sick. Then the Garrison house would be quarantined. Not that she *hoped* children would be ill to get her out of a social situation.

"I'll make you brownies, Dr. Mack," Ava announced, making Mack feel like an asshole.

"Ava here is a baking fiend," Harper explained. "Most of her treats are edible," she told Mack as she gathered her tote, keys, and daughters.

They walked together toward the lobby.

"Seven p.m. Friday. Our house. Aldo has the address. Bring a side dish or a dessert in case the brownies don't pan out."

"I like ice cream sandwiches," Sadie announced.

"See you Friday," Ava said, strutting out of the room and linking fingers with her sister. "Mama, can we have ice cream since we're sick?"

"Kiddo, if ice cream sounds good to you right now, you can absolutely have ice cream. Oh! What beautiful flowers," Harper exclaimed, spotting the arrangement on the desk.

"They're for Dr. Mack from Chief Reed," Tuesday announced cheerfully.

"Well, isn't that interesting?" Harper beamed suspiciously.

CHAPTER 13

Mack eased up to the curb in front of the big, three-story brick house. She cut the engine and grabbed the covered bowl of potato salad she'd made and the box of ice cream sandwiches she'd impulse bought at Val's Groceries. Climbing the porch steps, she admired the overflowing flower boxes and the comfortable furniture.

There was a doll facedown on a blanket and a couple of kids' bikes propped against the porch.

The whole thing screamed "Home sweet home."

A message the welcome mat reiterated word for word.

A small, friendly backyard BBQ. Who the hell was she?

Mack pressed the doorbell and waited while a chorus of barks and kids' voices exploded on the other side of the door.

The door opened, and Mack grinned when she recognized Captain Lucas Garrison. There was a boy on his back, a smiling pit bull wriggling at his feet, and a chorus of chaos behind him.

"Dr. O'Neil," he said with a grin that had never been that quick on deployment. "Welcome to chaos."

"Thanks for having me," she said.

"This is Henry, who's way too big for piggyback rides,"

Luke said as the kid choking the life out of him grinned. "And that's Lola."

"Ah, the skunked dog," Mack said, reaching down to let Lola sniff her.

Lola sniffed delicately and then unleashed her Gene Simmons tongue.

"Come on back. The rest of the crew is in the backyard."

Crew was apparently a loose term for half the town of Benevolence.

Harper and a dark-haired fashionista Mack recognized as Gloria Moretta were organizing the food table and yelling at an entire army of kids. Aldo was manning the grill with sunglasses, a cold beer, and tongs that looked beefy enough to flip a cow.

There was another couple—he was tall and blond, she a leggy brunette—canoodling around the fire pit instead of actually lighting the fire.

"Get a room if you're making us more grandkids," a woman with a silvery pixie cut called from the lawn chair where she was supervising Aldo's grilling process. The canoodling couple broke apart sheepishly.

There were dogs. Two more in addition to the now skunk-free Lola. Both non-Lolas were small. The wiry one had only had three legs, but it didn't seem to slow him down as he zoomed around the fenced-in yard. The other one was so small it looked like Lola could mistake it for a snack. But they seemed to recognize each other as peers rather than predator and snack.

"Wow," Mack said, taking in the chaos.

"You're telling me." Luke grinned. He dumped Henry in the grass and led Mack over to meet his parents, the perky Claire and the stoic Charlie. The canoodling couple, Sophie and her husband, Ty, the sheriff, introduced themselves. Sophie was pretty and vivacious in a way that made Mack think the woman had never once lacked an ounce of self-confidence. Her husband was clearly crazy about her and their two kids, who were buzzing around the backyard with the rest of the pack.

"It's nice to meet the doctor everyone's been talking about," Sophie said mischievously.

"Behave, Soph," Gloria teased, walking up and wrapping Mack into a hard hug.

People in Benevolence really seemed to enjoy inappropriately long hugs.

"I'm just saying it's awfully big of you to be so nice to the woman seen mauling your husband in the middle of the road," Sophie teased with a dimpled grin.

"Don't forget she's also gettin' flower deliveries from the fire chief," Ty added. He was Ken-doll pretty with cop-short hair and the kind of easy smile that made public service a little easier. "Word is she's a man-eater." He winked.

Mack laughed. "Rawr."

"Welcome to Benevolence, where everyone knows your business, and if they don't, they'll make something more interesting up," Sophie said. "I bartend at Remo's, so I pick up all the gossip folks are dropping."

An argument involving several of the kids broke out near the swing set.

"Who had first tears at ten after seven?" Harper called from the food table.

"Me!" a short, round, loud woman who could only be Mrs. Ina Moretta shouted.

"Ina gets the pot," Charlie said, consulting a handwritten paper while parents jumped into the fray.

Another dog, this one blond and fluffy, bulleted past Mack. It looked suspiciously like...oh, hell.

"Sunshine!" The kids who weren't fighting or crying chorused gleefully.

"Well, well. If it isn't my favorite neighbor and gal pal. We could have carpooled." Fire Chief Lincoln Reed, in a well-worn Benevolence FD T-shirt and shorts that couldn't help but call attention to his muscled thighs, strolled her way. He had on a ball cap that added to his boyish charm. Mack purposely ignored the little pitter-patter of attraction she felt in her chest.

"I didn't know you'd be here," she said casually.

He stepped up to her, and they turned to survey the backyard festivities, his shoulder brushing hers. He was so *big*, so solid. He took up so much room.

"You look real pretty, Dreamy."

"Uh, thanks," Mack said, running a hand through her short hair. She'd let it air dry. But she had slapped on a coat of toenail polish and her new favorite red gloss that Tuesday assured her was "totally complimentary" to her skin tone. "So I thought this was just a small family thing."

Linc's grin was underwear incinerating. "It is. It's just we've got big families around here. You and I are the only two unrelateds."

Sunshine, suddenly needing to touch base with her father, came bulleting over to them. She flopped down on Linc's feet and stared up at him expectantly.

"Belly rub time," he said, sinking down to pat Sunshine's exposed belly. The dog vibrated in ecstasy until he stopped. Then she looked up at Mack.

"Why is she looking at me like that?"

"Well, she either wants your potato salad or her belly rubbed."

Mack sank down next to him and tentatively poked

Sunshine in the stomach. The dog wriggled back and forth on her back, making grunting noises. "What does that mean?"

"Means she likes it. She likes you."

Lola barreled over to see what the fuss was, and Mack took a break from Sunshine's silky fur to give the pit bull's short hair a stroke.

"You're a natural," Linc said, giving Lola's side a good thump.

The little gray wad of fluff bounced their way and started yapping, making sure to stay just out of arm's reach.

"Bitsy, shut up!" Sophie and Ty yelled together.

"Sunshine, attack!" Linc teased.

"Harper!" Luke barked. "You forget to tell me about an addition to the guest list?" He shot Linc a dirty look.

Harper hurried over, beaming. She appeared to be immune to Luke's scowl. "Linc! I'm so glad you could make it. Don't mind Luke," she said to Mack. "He hates Linc."

"I don't *hate* him," Luke grumbled. "I just don't like him."

"Well, that's definite progress," Linc said. He held up a platter. "I made a fruit tray. Where do you want it?"

A guy with thighs like that, with a smile like that, showing up with a homemade fruit tray? Mack felt her sexual interest emerge from hibernation.

Harper swooned over the artful display and carried it and Mack's potato salad and ice cream sandwiches over to the food table.

"Kiss-ass," Luke muttered to Linc. But he held his hand out.

"Asshole," Linc said, amicably shaking his hand.

"Ignore them." Gloria enveloped Mack in another breezy hug. She wore a flowy red top over high-waisted shorts. Her sandals wrapped around her ankle in multicolor threads. "It's so good to see you, Mackenzie."

"Hi, Dr. Mack," Ava shouted from the top of the swing set in the corner of the yard.

"Hiiiiiii!" Sadie sprinted at Mack and threw her body into the doctor's legs.

Mack leaned down to gingerly hug the kid.

"Up!" Sadie said gleefully, and Mack felt rather heroic as she hefted the girl onto her hip.

Sadie smashed her face against Mack's cheek. "Muah! Okay, your turn!" She reached for Linc, and Mack gratefully handed her over. She had delivered a baby once and had done a pediatric rotation in med school. That was the sum total of her kid experience.

Linc, showing off his prowess with small humans, tossed the little girl in the air. She giggled and the sound drew the attention of the rest of the kids.

"Me next!"

"No, *me*!"

Gloria grinned and tugged Mack in the direction of the grill and her husband. "I love it when Linc is at these things. He's a built-in babysitter. Kids adore him."

"I saw him with his nieces and nephew last weekend. He appears to be a natural," Mack said.

"He certainly taught me a few things." Gloria grinned.

Aldo ditched the tongs and picked up his beer. "How was your first week on the front lines of small-town health care?"

"Well, I didn't know pink eye could spread that quickly," Mack joked.

"Dreamy, get you a drink?" Linc called from the cooler.

She gave him a thumbs-up, and he handed one of the kids a beer and directed her toward Mack.

"Dreamy, hmm?" Gloria said. "I heard our handsome fire chief sent you flowers this week."

"He was being funny," Mack insisted.

"Nothing says hilarious like a bouquet of wildflowers."

It clicked then. Gloria managed the floral shop in town. "And you made the arrangement."

Her smile was quick. "Guilty as charged. Linc swung by to personally sign the card, you know."

Both women skimmed their gazes over the man who was grazing at the food table and keeping up an animated discussion with Sadie.

It didn't mean anything. They were flirting. Flirts flirted.

"Well, thank you both for making me feel so welcome," Mack said lamely. *God*, her small talk was rusty.

"We'll have you feeling smothered in no time," Aldo predicted.

"How's the firm doing?" she asked him.

"Good. Swamped. We're bringing on another engineer. This bridge project turned out to be a massive undertaking." As he talked, he draped his arm around Gloria's slim shoulders. It was a casual gesture, one Mack wasn't sure if he was conscious of. His wife curled into him as if she had always belonged in his arms.

It was…sweet. Romantic. Beautiful to see a man who'd sacrificed so much finally be rewarded. And what the hell was in this beer? A love potion?

"Daddy!" The tiniest Vietnamese toddler raced over to Aldo, heedless of the giant smoking grill behind him. She threw herself at the man with the confidence of a little girl who knew that her dad would always catch her.

"There's my girl," Aldo said, swinging her up on his hip and giving her a noisy kiss between her lopsided, black pigtails. "Lucia, say hello to Dr. Mack."

"Hi! Do you like dinosaurs or ponies better?" Lucia demanded.

"Hi. Um, dinosaurs?" Mack answered.

Lucia gave an approving nod. "Good. Me too. Daddy, can I have a snack?"

"Listen here, snack weasel," Gloria said, tickling her daughter under the arms and then transferring her to her own hip. "Dinner is in fifteen minutes. You may not have a snack, but you will eat every bite of your delicious dinner, and you'll say thank you to everyone who made the food."

Lucia's brow furrowed. "Okay. *Then* I can have a snack?"

Mack smothered a laugh.

Aldo watched his wife and daughter wander off, still arguing. "Ain't life something?"

"This side of five years, and I was hauling your ass across the desert in a helicopter," Mack mused. "And now here you are."

"And now here we are," he said. "Come meet the newest member of the family."

She followed him across the yard to where the stocky woman was bellowing sweet sentiments into a wide-eyed baby's face.

"You are just the cutest little baby in the whole wide world," Mrs. Moretta shouted.

"Ma! Avery's not deaf. You're piercing her eardrums," Aldo said, sweeping the baby out of his mother's grip.

"I'm not piercing her eardrums! She loves when I talk to her!"

"Ma, this is Mackenzie O'Neil. I believe you screamed at her on the phone once."

Mrs. Moretta gave Mack a formidable stare. "You the one who saved this dumbass's life?"

"Uh. One of them," Mack said.

The woman wrapped her in what apparently was the Moretta family back-breaking hug. "You're okay by me, Doc."

"Ma, please stop strangling her," Aldo said, trying to wedge his way between them.

Reluctantly, Mrs. Moretta released Mack from her death grip. "You're a good girl, honey," the woman said at an almost conversational level.

"Now that you can breathe, this is our daughter Avery," Aldo said, holding up the round-cheeked baby. She had Aldo's complexion, Gloria's eyes, and, so far, she hadn't demonstrated Mrs. Moretta's vocal cords. But Mack wasn't ruling out the possibility.

The baby gave her a toothless, drooly grin, and Mack felt a funny, mushy sensation in her chest.

"Want to hold her?" Aldo offered.

Mack's hands rose at the same time as she shook her head. "Oh no. That's okay. I don't really know how—"

"Let a pro show you," Linc said, muscling his way into the conversation. "Hey, pretty girl!"

The baby's eyes widened, and after a moment of contemplation, she giggled and held out her chubby arms to him.

Aldo expertly transferred Avery into Linc's arms. The baby looked up at him in awe. She reached up to touch his jaw with a drool-covered fist. Linc pretended to eat her hand, and Mack felt light-headed.

It was as if she'd hit the very last snooze on her biological clock. But she wasn't a husband and babies type of woman. She wasn't sure exactly what type of woman she was, but it was a thousand percent not a mommy.

She took a long pull on her beer.

Harper danced into their circle and gave Avery a smooch on her round cheek. "I'm so glad you all could come over tonight. We've been so busy with back to school that I almost forgot what socializing was like."

"Well, you'll get to socialize with someone very special," Mrs. Moretta shouted mysteriously.

Harper's face lit up. "Tell me everything, Mrs. Moretta."

"Well, his name is Ricky, and we met on an app. He's fifty-four, and his profile says he's an entrepreneur."

"That's code for unemployed, Ma. And you can't just invite a boyfriend no one's met to a family get-together," Aldo complained.

"Why the hell not? James did!" Mrs. Moretta pointed accusingly in the direction of the man walking through the gate in the fence.

He looked like Luke, and the way Sophie hug-tackled him told Mack he was definitely family.

Behind him, another man stood tentatively in the open gate, holding a covered dish.

"They came!" Harper clasped her hands together. "I'm so excited!"

"I'm gonna get a closer look." Mrs. Moretta barreled across the yard with Harper on her heels.

Claire and Charlie rose from their pile of grandkids and started toward the newcomers too.

"Small town gossip update. That's James, Luke and Sophie's brother. After years of serially dating women, he realized he was very, very gay," Aldo said.

Linc pointed the baby in the direction of the couple. "Do you see that nice, handsome guy with Uncle James, Aves? That's Manny, and it's the first time Uncle James has brought a boy home to meet the family, so be nice and try not to barf on him."

Mack watched as Harper gave James and then Manny welcoming hugs. Claire and Sophie each took one of Manny's arms and led him in the direction of the beer cooler while James and his dad, Charlie, hugged it out.

"Moretta, dogs are done," Luke called from the grill.

"Duty calls."

"He forgot his baby," Mack said.

"Time for your crash course in baby holding," Linc announced. "Now, Avery here is three months old. So she prefers to be up so she can see what's going on," he said, demonstrating.

"It's fine. Really. I don't need to hold her."

But he was depositing the wiggly bundle in her arms, and she was holding on tight.

"If I drop her, I'm blaming you," she hissed.

Avery apparently thought that was hilarious. Her giggle was belly deep and ridiculously charming.

"Oh, you're very cute," Mack told her. Avery beamed up at her and made a humming noise.

"See? You're a natural," Linc said, leaning in to make faces over Mack's shoulder.

She could smell his shower gel, his deodorant. She could feel the heat that pumped off his body. It felt...close. Intimate. And entirely inappropriate for all her new goals.

She turned and took a step back to put a little distance between them. "How's the shoulder?" she asked abruptly.

He circled his arm slowly. "Still a little tender. How are you at massage?" he asked wolfishly.

"About as good as I am at holding babies."

"That good, huh? Maybe you can sneak over the fence sometime and—"

Mack whirled around. "Not in front of the baby!"

CHAPTER 14

It was a study in normal. Parents, couples, families. All enjoying a Friday night with the people they loved the most. Mack felt an odd, decades-old ache at the unfamiliarity of it all.

"What do you think? Wanna give it a go?" Once again, Linc appeared at her side. It kept happening, one of them drawn into the other's orbit in this backyard.

"Give what a go?"

"Marriage. Kids. Backyard BBQs on a Friday night with half the town in attendance. I've got the day off Wednesday. We could swing by the justice of the peace."

She knew he was flirting. But there was something intoxicating about him being so close, so focused on her.

"Yeah, I don't think I have those genes," she sighed. "I can barely recognize healthy family dynamics, let alone live them."

"You'd figure it out," he said with confidence. "I'd help."

"I appreciate your faith in me. But this is like a foreign language to me." She lifted her beer. "They make it look easy."

"That's because you're seeing the end result of years of blood, sweat, and tears."

"Aldo definitely deserves a happily ever after," she said, remembering in a flash his ashen face, covered in dirt and blood. The way he clung to the hand of her other patient, cracking jokes, while she grimly kept him from bleeding out.

"They all do, Dreamy. Just like you."

"I've got too many skeletons," she said lightly. There were too many dents and dings between childhood and here. Reminders that there were no guarantees.

"Did you know that Gloria was in an abusive relationship that almost got her killed?" He said it calmly, as if he were discussing the weather. "Or that Harper lost her parents and grew up in foster care? She put a foster parent in prison for abuse when she was twelve. Got a broken arm and ribs for putting herself between a monster and another kid. And then there's Garrison."

"No love lost between you two," she observed.

Linc grinned. "He always thinks I'm trying to steal his women."

"He's got good taste." She watched Harper ruffle her oldest's hair while she perched on Luke's knee and said something that made her father-in-law laugh. Harper was happy. Down deep, in-the-bone happy.

"Always has. He was married before. High school sweetheart. Lost her in a car accident the day he came home from deployment. She was on her way to pick him up." There was a tone present in Linc's voice that she couldn't quite identify.

"Jesus." She took a long pull on her beer.

"They make it look easy. But it sure as hell isn't. It's work. Hard work. But you're not afraid of a little manual labor, Dreamy. You'll do fine."

She cleared her throat, surprised at the emotion she found there. "Your approach is all wrong, Hotshot," she complained, trying to lighten the mood.

"Educate me."

"You can't come at me all flirty about weddings and babies.

I'm a short-term, no-strings kind of woman. No messy endings that no one saw coming. No long-term commitments. No fuss. That"—she pointed at the campfire where couples canoodled and kids begged to roast the bag of marshmallows they found— "is not for me. Now, if you wanted to make real progress with me, you'd promise me no-holds-barred, stringless sex and a drama-free parting when one or both of us is ready to move on."

She returned his grin. Like recognizing like.

Linc held up his hands. "I'm just laying it out there for you, Dreamy. We're two of a kind. Peas in a pod. We can practically read each other's minds. Why wouldn't we want to settle down and show the rest of this town what happily ever after looks like?"

The fire chief was an expert-level flirt.

Mack sighed theatrically. "I guess I'm going to need a new pair of shoes."

"Okaaaay. Maybe I'm not reading your mind all the time yet."

She stepped in a little closer, testing the proximity.

"I just keep trampling hearts and getting heart juice all over my shoes. Looks like you're lining yourself up to be my next victim."

Linc's laugh was a loud, appreciative rumble.

"What are you two talking about over there?" Claire wondered.

"Pizza," they said together.

"Peas in a pod, Dreamy," Linc said under his breath. "Peas in a pod."

———

The kids were fed and then sent off to a corner of the yard with a blow-up projector screen and a movie, leaving the adults to eat and chat. Meals were plated, drinks poured, seats taken.

In what Mack thought of as an interesting twist of fate, a latecomer arrived: Joni, Luke's first wife's mother. And with her, her long-time boyfriend Frank, a grizzled foreman with Luke's construction company.

Linc was one of the first to greet Joni, and Mack was surprised by the tight hug they exchanged. They had no link that she could identify. In fact, the woman had no real link to the family either. Her daughter, Karen, had died years ago. Yet here she was, chitchatting with Ina Moretta and Claire while the kids called her Aunt Joni.

The only negative undercurrent Mack could pick up on was Luke's dislike of Linc. And even that felt more like habit.

"What's with the salad fest, Garrison?" Linc asked from where he crowded Mack on her left. Broad shoulders, beefy thighs.

The host was staring morosely at his plate of vegetables. "Lost a bet," he groused.

"Five years ago," Harper interjected at his side. "He's been putting off the consequences until this week. But he officially used up his last free pass, and now he must pay." A dimple winked to life in her cheek.

"I'm wasting away, Harp," Luke complained, but his hand was gentle as it threaded through his wife's hair.

"You're probably dropping your cholesterol by twenty points," she teased, cuddling into his side.

"I can't believe you're making me do the whole week," he said, staring longingly at the chicken on his mother's plate.

Claire made a show of savoring her forkful. "Aldo, this chicken is *fabulous*," she said with a wicked smile. "I've never tasted anything so delicious."

"Mean, Mom. Mean," Luke complained.

"Mom! Dad called Gram mean," Robbie, the oldest, teased

as he strolled by to refill his plate. He was sixteen, and the adults had been razzing him about a girlfriend and his learner's permit.

"I heard," Harper said, reaching a hand out for her son.

"He's so grounded," Henry piped up, trailing his big brother to the food.

"Are the kids behaving?" Harper whispered to Robbie.

"Yeah, they're fine. But Lucia bribed Henry to bring her another brownie."

"Make it a very small one, please." Gloria sighed and rolled her eyes.

"You know, if you weren't such an amazing baker, Lu and I wouldn't be sugar monsters," Aldo added.

"I didn't make the brownies," Gloria pointed out with a laugh. "Our daughter did."

"She learned it from watching you," Aldo insisted, pressing a kiss to the top of Gloria's head.

"I'm sure Avery will take after you in overhead squats," she teased, bouncing said daughter on her lap.

"At least I can still eat dessert," Luke sighed dramatically from the head of the table.

"Well, we could always go double or nothing," Harper mused.

Luke's eyes narrowed. "Now what?"

Harper shot a pointed look at Mack and then Linc. "What do you think, Luke? Care to bet against me again?"

He followed her gaze, then winced. "You're wrong. She's too smart for him."

"Care to wager?" Harper said, cocky now.

Luke gave Mack another look and then narrowed his eyes at Linc.

"No."

"Good, smart man," she said, patting him on the thigh. "Now eat your veggies."

He went back to his sad salad.

"Do I want to know what that was about?" Mack asked Gloria.

She grinned. "Luke told Harper she was full of crap when she said Aldo had a crush on me. He said if Aldo and I ever got together, he'd go vegetarian."

"Never doubt your wife's genius and your best friend's heart," Aldo said, holding his plate of chicken under Luke's nose.

"Luke is lucky I'm the benevolent goddess I am and only sentenced him to a week," Harper said airily.

"Change of subject! So how's work going in small-town America, Mack?" Luke asked.

"Quieter than I'm used to," she said.

"It's got to be a heck of a change of pace for you," Joni ventured.

"It is." Mack nodded. "But I think it's going to be good for me. I'm still flying shifts with the hospital's air med team on my days off."

"Still, it's a tough transition," Aldo said.

He and Luke would know.

Both men had made the transition from active combat to quiet home life multiple times. To go from life and death to running errands in the span of a few days was dizzying. It was why Mack was happy to keep the air shifts. One foot in and one foot out.

"The thin blue line," Linc said.

The adults all nodded, and Mack realized they were all profoundly aware of what first responders and members of the military did to protect their normal, everyday lives. Right now, they were a cop, a fire chief, and three members of the military surrounded by people who loved them. The people whose lives had been forever changed by those career choices, those callings.

They understood, accepted, and appreciated the sacrifices. And for the first time, Mack wondered if there was hope for her after all. If there was a possibility that a Friday night BBQ with friends and family could be in her future.

"You know what sucks?" Luke said. "Hummus."

CHAPTER 15

A nd then my father-in-law moved in, so now every Monday night is lasagna night because it's my mother-in-law's recipe. For once in my life, I'd just like to have what I want for dinner, you know?"

It was a rhetorical "you know." Mack had learned from the four previous "you knows" that Ellen, a redheaded, slightly overweight mother of two with borderline blood pressure, had dropped during the first five minutes of her appointment.

Mack didn't bother responding this time. It didn't feel right carrying on a conversation while she was examining the woman's cervix. Awkward conversations and Pap smears. Another exciting day in the life of Mack O'Neil.

"And then there's Barry and his freakin' socks on the floor next to the hamper. I mean for fuck's sake, Barry—sorry—you can lift the toilet lid and leave it up, but you can't lift the damn hamper lid?"

"Little pinch," Mack said, collecting the cells from the cervical wall.

Her patient winced but kept up the one-sided conversation.

Mack tucked the sample in the collection jar and screwed on the top.

"Are your periods regular?" she asked, ticking down the standard list of gynecological exam questions.

"They're fine. I'm just stressed. But who isn't? Ha. I mean, it could be worse. There could be two Barrys."

"Any new medical developments in your family history?" Mack asked, sliding the speculum out of what her patient had referred to as her lady cave.

Ellen breathed a sigh of relief and scooted away from the edge of the exam table. "Not unless you count my mom passing out from her blood pressure meds."

"We should talk about your blood pressure," Mack said, glancing at the measurements Freida had taken earlier. They were high.

"Dr. Dunnigan is giving me until the end of the year to lower it lifestyle-wise. If it's not lower by Christmas, she's putting me on a prescription. I hate prescriptions, you know? Just one more thing to remember and worry about."

When Ellen pushed her hand through her hair, Mack caught a whiff of cigarette smoke.

"You know, cigarette smoking isn't the best of stress relievers."

"Oh, ha. I don't smoke," Ellen said, looking shifty-eyed.

Secret smoker, Mack typed in her notes. At least unconscious patients couldn't lie to you.

"Good. Because with borderline blood pressure, all that stress, and you being on oral contraceptives, you'd be cruising for a stroke."

Ellen was uncharacteristically silent.

"So no smoking then?" Mack pressed.

Her patient shook her head. "Nope. No smoking."

Mack's eye twitched. Being lied to was a pet peeve. Being lied to by someone who was so wrapped up in their fabricated version of reality took her right back to childhood. But Ellen wasn't Mack's mother, she reminded herself.

"We're all done here, Ellen. You can get dressed and check out at the front desk," she said. She forced a smile and left the room.

The nice thing about being a doctor was that there was never enough time for moping. Mack didn't have to come to terms with her annoying feelings about her past because her present was too busy.

She passed Russell in the hallway as he ducked out of the supply closet and headed in the direction of the break room.

He gave her a curt nod that she didn't bother returning. They had a tentative, unfriendly truce, and she was comfortable with that.

Exam room 2 held a grandfather and grandson duo, the younger of whom was enthusiastically vomiting into the trash can.

"It's okay, Tyrone. You're not in trouble," the grandfather, Leroy, promised, mopping the boy's brow with a damp paper towel when he looked up wide-eyed at Mack like he'd gotten caught.

She flashed them both a sympathetic smile and checked the chart. "Hi there, Tyrone. How are you feeling?" *Stupid question.*

"Do you feel good enough to sit on the table, bud?" his grandfather asked.

Tyrone nodded wearily and, with Leroy's help, climbed up on the exam table.

He was average height and weight for an eight-year-old. But unlike the average eight-year-old, he was dressed like a mini grandpa in shorts, a T-shirt, and suspenders. Mack couldn't decide if it was adorable or creepy.

"I'm going to look you over real quick, okay?"

The boy nodded again. "Okay," he rasped.

During the physical exam, Leroy kept up a running patter of conversation. His daughter was a single mom, and he and Tyrone were close. The school nurse called him when Tyrone threw up at school.

The boy's lymph nodes were swollen, and he had a decently high fever.

She took out her scope. "Let's take a look at your throat, buddy. Can you open wide and say 'ah'?"

Tyrone did as he was told.

The poor kid's tonsils were covered in white goop and red spots.

"It looks like strep throat," she told the grandpa, reaching for a swab.

"What does strep throat look like?" Tyrone asked in a rasp.

"There's white junk and red spots all over your tonsils."

"Cool!"

"The test is fast, and we can do it here. If it comes back positive—which it will—I've got a prescription for antibiotics with Tyrone's name on it."

"When will he start feeling better?" Leroy asked.

"Once he starts the course of antibiotics, he should start feeling better within a day or two. Lots of fluids will help the antibiotics work to flush out the bacteria. You can give him acetaminophen for the pain."

"Am I contagious?" the kid asked.

"Yes, you are. But after twenty-four hours on the medicine, you won't be. I need you to 'ah' again while I swab your throat, okay? I promise I'll be quick."

She made quick work of it, in and out with the swab before the boy could gag.

"So you like gross things, Tyrone?" she asked.

"Yeah!"

"Want me to take a picture of your throat?" she offered. "Then you can show everyone what it looks like before the medicine starts working." And not breathe on anyone while doing so.

"That would be so cool."

She snapped a shot with the grandfather's cell phone.

"That was smart," Leroy said while Tyrone admired the photographic evidence of his strep throat. "Now, he won't try to show everyone the real thing."

Mack smiled. Maybe she was getting the hang of this country doctor thing.

———

It wasn't a twelve-hour shift in the emergency department or a trauma call, but a day in family practice was still exhausting.

She stirred the reheated soup she hadn't had a chance to eat the first time around when a walk-in with medication side effects showed up.

Russell had been busy too, though he'd seen fewer patients than she had. She kept an eye on the numbers and felt like she'd won there.

She turned the page in the medical journal, keeping an ear out for any trouble in the waiting room.

But the trouble was coming to her. Russell stalked into the break room, his white coat billowing out behind him.

He slapped a handful of printouts down on the table in front of her. "What is the first line in the patient notes on Ellen Kowalski?"

Warily, Mack picked up the paper. "Ask patient if she's reconsidered taking anxiety medication."

Shit.

"I missed the notes section. I'll give her a call at home—"

"Now, read the first line of Tyrone Mahoney's notes."

"I get it. I forgot to check the patient notes. It won't happen again."

"Engage Leroy Mahoney in conversation about his surgery, including blood thinner use," Russell read from the paper over his reading glasses.

"Why is that even in a kid's chart?" she asked, growing irritated with the shaming performance.

He slid the paper to her again. "Because Leroy will do anything to avoid going to the doctor. He'll take his grandson, but he cancels almost every appointment we've made for him since his hip surgery. We use his grandson's appointments to check up on him. *Especially* since he stopped refilling his blood thinners."

She read the file and sighed. "I'll fix this," she promised.

"There shouldn't be anything for you to fix. How difficult is it to take thirty seconds to read the notes, *Dr. O'Neil*? Carelessness costs people's lives. And this is why I'm here in Benevolence on my day off instead of admiring my wife in an evening gown on our way to a fundraiser."

Mack pushed back from the table and rose.

"Look, *Dr. Robinson*, I get that you're pissed off that you're here instead of enjoying appetizers and tuxedos with your wife, but the situation is what it is. And if you can't *educate* me on how to be good enough to not need a babysitter, there's no point in being pissed off at me. Because you may not tolerate doctors who practice differently than you, but I don't tolerate deliberate disrespect. I made a mistake, and I'll fix it. I won't make it again. And you're just going to have to deal with it."

Abandoning her once-again cold soup, Mack brushed past him—ignoring the gapes of Freida, Tuesday, and the two patients in the waiting room—and stormed into her office and shut the door. Seconds later, she heard Dr. Robinson's door slam.

"Well, *that* was fun," she said dryly to no one. Her stomach growled. "Dammit."

She sat down behind the desk and picked up the phone, then let out a girly squeak when the chair tipped backward without warning.

"Dammit," she muttered again under her breath. She put down the phone and picked up a sticky note.

Buy new fucking desk chair.

Carefully, she wheeled herself back in and picked up the phone again.

"Hey, Tuesday, would you mind bringing my soup in here when you get a chance?"

Finally, the last patient was seen, the last chart updated, the office locked up for the day. There was nothing between her and the sirloin she planned to grill tonight and the glass of red wine she'd earned. Mack dug for her keys in her bag and headed in the direction of her SUV.

Unfortunately, it appeared that Russell had parked his snazzy luxury sedan next to her vehicle. He was leaning against the hood, arms crossed over his crisp blue shirt. His polka-dot bow tie made him look more approachable than her experience dictated.

Mack wondered how quickly word would spread in Benevolence if the two town doctors got into a fistfight in the office parking lot.

"Dr. O'Neil."

She let out a soft sigh. *Fine.* One grumpy, aggressive

obstacle. She'd personally hold it against him if he kept her from her steak and wine dreams. "Dr. Robinson."

"I made a point in there today, and unfortunately in doing so, I also made a scene."

"Yes. You did," she said easily.

"For that, I apologize. I know I'm coming across as a hard-ass. It's not that I doubt your capabilities. I just don't trust you. Yet."

Honesty, even brutal, was better in Mack's mind than polite lies.

"That's fair. But it would be easier for both of us if you gave me an actual chance here. This *is* very different from what I've been doing. But I want to be here. And I want to provide the best level of care that I can. But I can't do that if you're making scenes about my shortcomings in front of our patients."

"I understand, and I apologize for being unprofessional."

"Accepted. And I'm sorry for missing the notes. I'm used to unconscious patients teetering between life and death, not having medical records and family histories at my fingertips. I won't miss it again."

"Good."

"Okay." She reached for her keys again.

"Are you confident in your ability to build a rapport with our patients?" he asked, recrossing his arms.

She took a breath. Honesty. "No. I'm not."

He nodded, accepting her statement. "Then that's what we'll focus on."

"Okay. Thanks."

"Have a good night, Dr. O'Neil," he said, straightening from the hood of his car. "Oh, and make sure you reach out to Ellen and Leroy this week."

The steak and wine could wait, she supposed.

CHAPTER 16

Ellen wasn't interested in coming back to the office for a chat, but she was amenable to happy hour at Remo's, a rustic-looking bar with a full parking lot on a Wednesday night.

Early, Mack took a spot at the back of the lot and answered a few emails on her phone. A couple of friends from the service. A headhunter wanting to know what her plans were after this stint in small-town America.

She stowed her phone and keys in her small clutch and headed in the direction of the front door. The porch was skinny, the cedar-shake shingles had seen better days, but the exterior was remarkably clean for a bar.

Inside, the clamor of neighbors catching up warred with an undistinguishable country song on the jukebox in the corner. It smelled like hot wings and beer.

She spotted Ellen waving from the bar to the left of the sea of crowded tables. Intrepid servers wound their way through the mess, hauling pitchers of beer and baskets of fried deliciousness.

"Hey, Mackenzie," Sophie, Luke's sister, greeted her from behind the bar. She was dressed in a form-fitting Remo's polo. Her hair was up in a spunky side ponytail that bounced as she spun a bottle of vodka in one hand. She sent a cheerful wink to a patron in overalls and a John Deere hat who was eighty if he was a day. "What brings you out tonight?"

"Girls' night," Ellen said, cheerfully sucking on the straw of a frozen pink concoction.

Or girls' medical ambush, more accurately. Mack felt a stab of guilt for not being clearer on the phone. She just couldn't seem to get this patient relationship thing down. She hated failing.

Sophie poured the vodka into a shaker. "It's half-priced wing night, and onion rings are on special too. What'll it be, Doc?"

Mack perused the shelves on the wall behind the striking bartender and spotted an okay merlot. She ordered a glass, watching as Sophie simultaneously poured two beers on tap while reaching for a wineglass.

It was a thing to behold, someone in their element. And right now, Mack felt a little too sensitive about being a fish out of water. She picked up her wine as soon as Sophie set it in front of her.

"I know I should go with a salad. But I have a soft spot for Remo's hot wings," Ellen said, staring mournfully at the menu.

Dutifully, Mack opened hers. "How about we split the garden salad and an order of wings?"

Ellen brightened, further driving the guilt knife into Mack's chest. "That would be amazing!"

"There's some tables on the patio," Sophie said, nodding toward the doors as she trayed up a flight of beers at the service bar. "I'll have your food brought out if you want to enjoy some fresh air."

"Perfect!" Ellen bounced off her stool, carting her fishbowl-sized drink.

Mack took her wine and followed her new gal pal, who was trying not to whack anyone in the head with her oversize mom tote.

Ellen chose a table in the middle of the patio whereas Mack would have preferred the one in the corner. But her new pal seemed to enjoy being around people.

"Thank you so much for this," Ellen said, sighing happily. "Do you hear that?"

Mack looked around them. The low buzz of conversation, the tinny sound of music coming from the crappy outdoor speakers mounted on the building. "Hear what?"

"No one asking me to do *anything*. No mom or wife or daughter-in-law, you know? Just me."

"When's the last time you had a girls' night?" Mack asked, wondering if she'd ever had one.

"Do baby showers count?"

Mack wasn't a socializing expert, but even *she* knew the answer to that one. "They do not."

"So I heard Lincoln Reed sent you flowers," Ellen said, leaning in and taking another slurp of pink alcohol.

And *this* was why Mack didn't do girls' nights.

"It was just a joke." *Mostly.*

"Our Chief Reed doesn't joke about women," Ellen said knowledgeably.

"He does have a reputation," Mack agreed.

Ellen waved her comment away. "That's mostly just good fun. He's not a misogynistic womanizer. He just loves women and dates them, serially and monogamously without any intentions to settle down. I mean, who can blame him? I settled down, and look at my life. I've got two kids who don't listen to me, a husband who thinks I'm a laundry service, and my minivan smells like sports equipment and feet." She leaned in conspiratorially. "Sometimes I wish I would have kept right on dating Linc."

It was Mack's turn to lean in. "You dated Linc?"

This was insider information she wasn't sure she wanted.

Ellen fluffed her shoulder-length auburn hair. "It was ten years and twenty-nine pounds ago. We went out a few times before I met Barry. He's got a way with women. You know?"

"He certainly does." A reluctant smile tugged at the corners of Mack's mouth. "Why did you stop seeing each other?" Great. Now she was prying into a patient's personal life. Benevolence was rubbing off on her already.

Was she going to start asking trauma patients what their tattoos meant now?

Ellen shrugged. "Why does anyone stop seeing a beautiful firefighter?"

"Ah. The schedule," Mack guessed. She understood that to "normal" people, the on-call shifts, long hours, and physical danger didn't make a lot of sense. But she also knew exactly why some were called to those professions.

"Life-and-death jobs aren't exactly conducive to family life," Ellen agreed. "I was ready for kids and a house and a husband who would be around on weekends. Linc's first love is his job. It was as amicable as splits get. I still get to wink at him in the produce department every once in a while."

It sounded a lot like Mack's splits. Easy. No strings. No harm, no foul.

"Has he ever been serious about anyone?" Mack asked.

Ellen shook her head with a giggle. "Linc doesn't have a serious bone in his body. He's fun. You know? If he's sending you flowers, you should go for it. No one has ever regretted a fling with Chief Sexy Pants."

Fun.

Would it really hurt Mack to have a little fun while she was in town? Maybe not. But it would go against her new code. The New Mackenzie O'Neil was too busy finding herself and being admirably healthy to fall into bed with handsome acquaintances.

The New Mackenzie O'Neil was a real buzzkill.

Ellen's phone rang shrilly from inside her purse. "Ugh. That's Barry. Hang on. What do you want, Bare?"

Mack watched Ellen's eyes roll dramatically.

"No. I did *not* tell him that he could have cake for dinner. Don't let him play you. You're better than that, Barry." *No, he's not*, she mouthed.

Mack snickered.

Sophie swung out onto the patio, her hands full with their food. The patron who held the door watched her admiringly.

"Another round, ladies?" she asked, setting the salad, wings, plates, and napkins on the table.

Ellen nodded vehemently. "Calm down. Just make him nuggets and call it a night."

Mack looked at her glass. "Sure."

Sophie whirled away with their order and headed back inside.

"Ugh. Yes. I'll go to the grocery store on my way home. But can you try to remember this stuff when I'm actually making my list next time? Make my life just a little bit easier for once? Hello? Hello?" Annoyance crackling off her, Ellen shoved her phone back in her bag. "He hung up on me. Can you believe that?"

Mack wasn't sure if she could or not.

"This is why I'm so stressed. I can't even get ten minutes to myself without someone needing something." Ellen reached into her bag and produced a pack of cigarettes.

Mack cleared her throat.

"Oh, hell. Okay, fine. I lied. I'm stressed out."

"Okay. So tell me about it," Mack said, sliding half the salad onto a plate.

They ate wings and speared vinaigrette-tossed lettuce

while Ellen talked and Mack listened. She was getting a clearer picture. One she'd missed in the office because she'd been in a hurry to move on to the next appointment.

"Have you thought about anxiety meds?" Mack asked when Ellen seemed to have emptied out her stress tank.

"Thought about and rejected," Ellen said cheerfully. "I'm cautious about what I put in my body."

"Don't take this the wrong way. I'm saying this as a friend and not a doctor. But are you really?" Mack looked pointedly at the wings, the cigarettes, the second fishbowl-sized margarita.

Ellen winced. "Don't I deserve to have a vice or two… or three?"

"What you deserve is to feel good, to be healthy. Stress isn't good for anyone."

"What am I supposed to do? Sell a kid and get a divorce?"

Mack looked around them to make sure no one else was listening. "I am definitely *not* saying that. What I am saying is you have options. You can make some lifestyle changes, or you can consider prescriptions, or both. You don't have to keep feeling like this. But you will if you keep doing what you're doing."

"Lifestyle like eating healthy and exercising? You sound like Dr. Dunnigan and Dr. Robinson, you know?" Ellen groaned.

"It doesn't have to be torture," Mack said. "What did you like to do before you had kids?"

Her dinner partner shrugged, looking morose. "I don't know. Going on bar crawls and eating tacos at one in the morning?"

Mack laughed. "Anything else?"

Ellen's face brightened. "You know what I used to love to do?"

"What?"

"Swim."

"Really? That's a great sport," Mack said. "Why did you stop?"

"I started hating how I looked in a bathing suit."

Honesty. Mack could work with that.

"Here's what I propose. You take a month. Find a place to swim. Try a little harder on the food. Grab some 'me time' for yourself every single day no matter what. And for God's sake, kick the cigarettes. We'll meet back up and see how you're feeling. Then we can go from there."

"Another girls' night?" Ellen was so excited that Mack felt an odd mixture of flattered, happy, and inexplicably sad for them both.

Mack shrugged. "Yeah. Sure."

Ellen bit her lip. "Do you really think I can do this?"

"Of course you can. Look at everything else you already do. You're raising kids, running a family, working, dealing with a husband and a father-in-law. You're already doing the hard stuff. This is easier."

Ellen was nodding. "I never really thought about it like that."

"You're just replacing bad coping habits with good ones."

"Ooh! We can be accountability partners," Ellen squealed, clapping her hands. "What do you want to work on?"

"Oh. Uh. Meditation? I guess." Mack congratulated herself on not saying, "Talking myself out of sleeping with Linc."

"That sounds amazing. Meditation is so, like, enlightened," Ellen said to the interior of her purse. Her hands and face disappeared.

"Yeah. Sure."

"Aha!" She triumphantly produced a notebook and a pencil decorated with teeth marks. "Okay. We're writing these down.

Oprah says if you're going to set goals, they have to be measurable and specific."

Well, if Oprah said so…

Ellen neatly scratched out her goals on the pad and pushed it across the table to Mack.

> 1. Swim or walk five days a week.
> 2. Have a salad for lunch every day.
> 3. Quit pork rinds.

"This doesn't say anything about smoking," Mack pointed out.

"That's the pork rinds. In case Barry or the kids find the list. I fib to them too."

"Fair enough."

"Now add yours," Ellen ordered. "We'll make it official. Can I have one last cigar—"

"No," Mack said firmly as she wrote: *Meditate 10 minutes a day.*

"Party pooper."

Mack snickered and picked up a buffalo wing. "To accountability," she said.

Ellen helped herself to another wing and tapped it to Mack's. "To the sexy firefighter who's headed this way."

CHAPTER 17

Linc had stopped in for a beer and some wings and instead found his sexy, reticent neighbor enjoying dinner with one of his old girlfriends.

"Ladies," he said, strolling across the patio. "A little birdie bartender told me you were out here."

It was getting closer to dusk. A server bustled out behind him to turn on the patio heaters and plug in the overhead string lights.

"We were just talking about you." Ellen beamed up at him. "Pull up a chair, Chief."

He bent and gave her a peck on the cheek, then did as he was told. "All good, I hope. How are Barry and the kids?"

While Ellen filled him in on all the family news, Mack studiously avoided eye contact with him. But when his knee pressed against hers under the small table, she didn't make any effort to move away from him.

"How was your day off?" Ellen asked, finally taking a breath.

He pulled his attention away from the feel of Mack's leg.

"Good. Took Sunshine for a hike. She's at my sister's now." He couldn't stop looking at Mack. There was something about her that pulled him in. A magnetism, a pull, an orbit.

This wasn't a normal, easy crush. There was a real hunger here. He'd felt it at the cookout last Friday when he'd seen the longing in her eyes as she observed the Garrison and Moretta clans.

"How was your day, Doc?" he asked.

When she finally looked at him, it was both a relief and a rush. Those cool green eyes held secrets he wanted to unravel one by one. He wanted to know how she got the scar under her eye. He wanted to know what her skin felt like under his hands. How he'd feel when he watched her lips part as he slid inside her.

Time slowed down when she looked at him. And his baser instincts were ringing a four-alarm bell.

He shifted in his seat, mindful of the hard-on that roared to life. Unfortunately, that pushed his leg more firmly into hers. If simple under-the-table leg rubbing was pushing his buttons, he had a serious control problem.

"Fine," she said finally.

The way she said it told him it was a deliberate brush-off. What secrets would she share while he worshipped her body?

Fuck. He was going to have to turn off his water heater to get through having her in his backyard yet still untouchable.

He became aware of Ellen looking back and forth between them like she was observing a Wimbledon match.

She noticed him noticing and nodded pointedly in Mack's direction. "Dr. Mack, you're not seeing anyone, are you?" she asked innocently.

"Uh, no," Mack said with suspicion.

"You know, Linc here is a real catch," Ellen said.

"So I've heard," Mack said dryly.

"It's true," Linc said, snagging a cherry tomato off her plate. "You'd be doing yourself a disservice by not at least going out with me once."

"Linc is *the best* at first dates. You know?"

He grinned at Ellen. This was, in his opinion, one of the best things about life in Benevolence. Even his old girlfriends were invested in his happiness.

"Uh-oh," Ellen said, sending him a conspiratorial wink. "I think Barry's calling me again. I should probably be getting home. Here, Linc. You can finish my drink."

She stood up and heaved her giant purse onto her shoulder. It probably weighed nearly as much as his turnout gear, Linc guessed.

"I don't hear your phone," Mack said.

"Oh, I put it on vibrate." Ellen shook her bag. "There it goes again. Thanks for girls' night, Dr. Mack. I'll see you next month."

"She did not just get a phone call," Mack said, watching her go.

Linc picked up Ellen's abandoned margarita, took a sip, and winced. "I think she was subtly trying to give us some alone time."

"Are all your old girlfriends this happy to fix you up with new ones?"

He thought about it and reached for a wing.

Mack slapped his hand away. "Mine."

Grinning, he helped himself to the last one on Ellen's plate. "Maybe not all of them. But a strong majority."

"What was your ugliest breakup?" she asked.

"Uh-uh, Dreamy. That's first date conversation."

She polished off the wing while studying him.

"Why isn't this a date?" she asked. "There's food. Alcohol. We're having a conversation. I'm valiantly trying to resist your flirtatious charm." She ticked off the dating requirements on her fingers as she licked the hot sauce from them.

Linc was fairly certain he'd never been more turned on in his entire life. He picked up his beer to give his hands something to do besides ease the ache in his monster hard-on or reach out and touch Dr. Dreamy.

"This is the flirtation leading up to the first date," he explained. "A Lincoln Reed first date isn't a spontaneous run-in. A Lincoln Reed first date is a carefully curated experience designed for maximum enjoyment."

She laughed loud and long and got impossibly prettier.

"Now I'm really curious," she told him, cupping her chin in her hand.

"There's only one way to find out what it's like to date me," he said, lifting his beer at her. "All you have to do is say yes."

Her sigh was long. "I want you to know that I'm tempted. Very tempted. But."

The word hung in the air between them. He wondered if she knew she was leaning into him, that her leg was pressing against his.

"But?" he prodded.

"That's not why I'm here."

"Why are you here?" he asked.

"I need a change of pace."

Need, not want, he noted.

"Tell me?"

She paused and took a sip of her wine.

"You know the feel of a big call? When you're in the middle of it, and it's life and death and you're on autopilot, getting it done?"

He nodded. "Yeah. The buzz. That shot of adrenaline, and you're, like, outside time."

"Exactly. I like it. No, that's not true. I *crave* it," she admitted, running an index finger around the mouth of her wineglass.

"We all do to some extent."

"True. But for me, it's a problem."

He nodded, waiting.

"My hands started shaking," she admitted. "Then I stopped sleeping."

"Burnout."

"Burnout. Adrenal fatigue. Worse, those highs were the only time I felt anything."

He took a chance and reached for her hand. She didn't pull away but sat there considering their intertwined fingers.

And damn did it feel natural.

"What makes you feel numb, Dreamy?"

She shook her head. "Uh-uh. That's first date conversation."

Hell. He was going to fall hard for this woman, and it was going to hurt.

"Okay," he said. "So burnout comes knocking, and you decide a lifestyle overhaul is necessary."

"And here I am." She gestured with her free hand. "Goodbye, Afghanistan. Hello, Benevolence."

"Trading hot-zone trauma medicine for small-town country doctoring," he summarized.

"Bingo. I couldn't even stick it out a few more years for retirement. I processed out."

He tightened his grip on her hand. "And that pisses you off."

She shot him a small, rueful smile that had him staring at her lips again. "Yes, it does."

"And you're more pissed that you couldn't hold up. You didn't quit because it was your idea. You had to quit."

He watched her suck her bottom lip into her mouth.

"It's okay," he told her. "You can tell me what I had for breakfast today if you want to."

"Microwave breakfast burrito," she said. "It's less fun now that you know I can see into your place."

"Speaking of less fun. Those curtains on your bedroom window are awfully thick."

"Room darkening so I can sleep past dawn."

"Do you?"

"Nope. Zero five thirty on the dot."

The music on the speakers changed to a slow country number.

"Why fight it?" he asked, pulling her to her feet.

"What are we doing?"

"We're gonna dance."

"No one else is dancing," she said, looking around the patio.

"I'm going to explain my idea to you, but it works better if we're dancing."

"Do small-town girls really fall for this shit?" Mack demanded.

He tugged her into his arms. "Big-city doctors too."

She cocked an eyebrow but let him draw her closer. "Apparently."

"Get a room, Chief!" The same skinny guy in a dirty ball cap from the car on the street last week hooted from a table full of similarly suited softball players.

"Get a vasectomy, Carl," Linc shot back with a grin.

Carl and his tablemates dissolved into laughter.

"Now, back to my idea."

"If this idea involves us getting naked together, I'm still interested, but it's still not going to happen," she said.

"Hear me out," he insisted.

She rolled those meadow-green eyes. "Fine. I'm listening."

"I'm gonna write you a prescription."

"Hands off my prescription pad, buddy."

"A Chief Sexy Pants prescription," he corrected.

"And what will this prescription entail? Orgasms?"

He pretended to consider the idea. "Those would certainly fall under the umbrella of this protocol. I'm ordering you to have fun."

"Fun?" She said it as if it were a cuss word.

"Yeah. You know, like doing things that make you smile and laugh for no good reason?" he prodded.

She frowned up at him. "You're joking, right?"

"I'm deadly serious," he insisted. "I'm volunteering to be your fun coach."

"This whole town is really weird," she mused.

He squeezed her tighter. "Pay attention, Dreamy. This is a once-in-a-lifetime offer."

"Okay. I'll bite. What does a fun coach do?"

"You mean besides handing out orgasms?" She gave him a withering look, and he grinned. "Remember to save that look for our kids. If the girls take after you, they'll be handfuls."

She purposely stepped on his foot.

In retaliation, he dipped her backward until her body arched toward the ground.

"Is this fun? I can't tell," she said snarkily.

"Honey, we're dancing under a starlit sky on a Wednesday night with a bunch of people looking at us like we're crazy. This is fun." He swept her back up.

"Well, I mean, if this is the best you've got," she teased.

"Ah, Dreamy. You just keep making me fall harder and harder for you."

She held his face in both hands and peered into his eyes.

"What are you doing?"

"Trying to check your pupil dilation."

"I don't have a head trauma." *Just a blood-flow issue.*

"Just making sure."

They swayed together, moving seamlessly into the next song. Another couple joined them between the tables. Then another, until most of the occupants on the patio were dancing to Alabama Shakes.

Sophie poked her head out the door. "What the hell is going on out here? You having a prom? Does anyone need another round?"

"Yes!" the entire patio shouted.

Mack shook her head. "I don't fit in here."

There was more to the statement than a moment of doubt. And Linc was going to get to the bottom of it. Very carefully.

"You feel just fine to me," he said, drawing her an inch closer.

"You make it very difficult to resist you."

"Why deprive us both?" he insisted and then felt lighter when she laughed. "Dreamy, you don't have to try so hard."

"If the next words out of your mouth are 'go with the flow,' I might murder you right here," she warned him.

"Just consider my offer. That's all I'm asking. I'll literally show you a good time."

She snorted. "That's the worst line ever. I expected more from you."

"I'm off my game. I've got a beautiful woman in my arms and a lot of dark fantasies in my head."

She bit her lip. "I'm not going to ask you about those fantasies," she announced.

"I'll write 'em down for you. Maybe draw some illustrations."

Her watch vibrated against his shoulder. "I should go," she said.

"Got a hot date?"

"It's my get ready for bed alert. I'm trying to be healthy and make good choices, remember?"

"I'll walk you to your car," he offered.

"Why? Does the crime rate skyrocket in the parking lot after dark?" she teased.

"You'd be surprised."

They paid their bills and said goodbye to Sophie before heading outside.

"Feel free to be overcome with gratitude," he said, opening her car door for her.

"If I swoon, I have ammonia inhalants in my med bag," she said with a slow smile designed to devastate.

Linc wasn't one to back down from a challenge or a guaranteed disaster. "I really want to kiss you right now, Mackenzie."

She cocked her head, considering. "You're just going to keep chipping away at my defenses until there's nothing left but rubble, aren't you?"

He boxed her in with his arms, careful not to touch her.

"That's the plan."

He watched her make the decision and reveled in it when she slowly, deliberately slid her arms around his neck. "It's working," she said on a sigh before pressing her lips to his. She tasted of wine and hot sauce and lust.

His hands tightened on the doorframe, still not touching her anywhere but that wild and wonderful mouth.

She wasn't delicate or dainty. She didn't need to be coaxed. No, Mackenzie dove into the kiss like jumping off a cliff. With an aggressive surrender that drove him mad.

And she gave him permission for more when she sagged against him, when she pressed that long, lean body against his. Then and only then did he finally let himself touch her.

That mouth, sharp and sarcastic, worked its magic against

his as she tasted him and let him savor her. Her teeth scraped over his bottom lip, and the world went black.

A surprise. The continual surprise of Dr. Mackenzie O'Neil.

His hands fit her waist, her hips, her back. Seeking out new curves with the intent to memorize. Crushing her to him, he heard and felt the sexy vibration of a whimper when she sidled up to his erection.

"Oh, boy. Okay." She slid her hands between them and pressed lightly against his chest. Enough to stop, not enough to part.

Her lips were swollen and rosy. Her hair that he didn't remember shoving his hand into was a disheveled tangle. Those high cheekbones wore the faint blush of excitement. And her eyes danced with arousal.

No regrets.

"That's going to give me a lot to think about," she said, pushing him back a millimeter.

He could still taste her on his lips.

"The offer still stands, Dreamy." He reached down and clasped her hand. Those green eyes, so serious now, watched as he lifted it to his mouth.

"No strings? No expectations? No complications?" she asked.

"No-expectations, monogamous fun," he said.

She gave him a nod and slid behind the wheel. "Why not platonic fun?"

"Honey, I think that kiss already answered that question."

She looked ahead through the windshield. "I'll think about your offer."

So would he. He shut the door for her and tapped the roof with a hand that seconds before had coasted over her body.

Mack drove off, leaving him watching her go.

"This is gonna get complicated," he sighed to himself.

CHAPTER 18

Mack let herself in the back door of the clinic. She'd slept like crap last night. Every time she closed her eyes, she felt Linc's mouth on hers and then spent the next several minutes fantasizing about having it everywhere else.

She'd snap out of it, long enough to carefully weigh every pro and con of letting him get past first base. Then, as soon as her eyes closed again, the delicious cycle started fresh.

She hoped to God the man had at least suffered through a cold shower.

"Good morning, Dr. O'Neil." Russell, wearing a violet Oxford shirt and eggplant tie under his white coat, greeted her at the front desk. His cognac-colored loafers gleamed under the sharp pleat of his trousers. He nudged a to-go cup in her direction. "Green tea with lemon."

Tuesday and Freida exchanged smug looks. The friendly balance of the office had been restored.

"Thank you. Good morning," she said, accepting the cup. "How was everyone's night?"

Small talk. *See?* She could do this. She could push aside dirty, naked thoughts about a sexy firefighter. She could dust off social skills.

"I hit up a cycling class and then grabbed smoothies with my brother so he could tell me about his new boyfriend who he met at the gym. Then my boyfriend and I had a nice, quiet night in," Tuesday said perkily.

Mack felt relatively certain that "quiet night in" was the girl's code for Netflix and chill.

"My husband did the laundry. That beautiful, beautiful man," Freida said dreamily and shot them all spirit fingers.

Okay. So Tuesday and Freida got laid. Fine. People in relationships had sex.

"My wife surprised me by coming home early for a long weekend," Russell said. His tone was light, friendly even, but Mack saw the residual gleam of tasteful, polished, married sex in his brown eyes.

Dammit.

She imagined a tumbleweed rolling through her vagina.

She'd already weighed the options and judged that cooling off her sex life for a while was essential to her New Mack plan. Now all she could think of was Linc. And his mouth. And those tattoos on his chest and biceps. And how she could see that V on his torso when his shorts rode low.

"How about you, Dr. Mack?" Russell asked.

She opened her mouth, ready with the usual "Not much," and then realized she had done something.

"I met Ellen at Remo's for dinner and drinks." She felt it was a good idea to leave out the fact that she'd slow danced with and then kissed the fire chief. There was probably a line of sharing too much too soon.

Russell raised his eyebrows in approval. "How nice. I happened to run into Ellen this morning at the YMCA pool."

Surprised by the fierce surge of delight, Mack forced herself to take a slow sip of her tea. "Good for her," she said. It was stupid to be excited that a patient had taken her advice for one day. The odds were Ellen would be microwaving potato skins and yelling at her husband by seven p.m. But, God, it still felt *good*. It still felt like a win.

"Dr. Mack, I thought you'd like to sit in on an appointment or two with me today so you can get to know some of our patients a little better," Russell suggested.

"I'd like that," she said, surprised even more by the fact that she meant it.

————

Russell's bedside manner differed from Trish Dunnigan's. He was smooth, urbane. His conversation made patients feel like they were attending a fancy cocktail party. He wasn't their friend, but he was their confidant.

Mack perused patient histories and listened while he talked to Mr. Lewis about retirement, amusement park road trips with the grandkids, and, inevitably, cholesterol and fitness.

"I'm busy. I've got a lot going on," Mr. Lewis insisted. He was a round, cheerful guy with tattoos down both forearms and a quick, infectious laugh.

She noted that he'd been treated for depression a few years ago. She also noted that Russell's exam included a subtle patter of questions that seemed innocent but were designed to tease apart the current mental state.

There was no, "Any side effects from your depression meds?" But there were questions about his wife—she'd recently decided they needed more quality time, and he had to choose between ballroom dance or cooking classes—and about his sleep, how he was feeling about being out of the workforce after a forty-year career.

He was a jokester. He'd send Mack a wink at the end of every punch line, like she was the audience.

They joked back and forth, with Mr. Lewis teasing Russell about his less-than-stellar racquetball performance at a local tournament.

"At least I'm trying to get my ass out there," Russell said, crossing his arms and leaning back against the exam room cabinet. "When's the last time you even hit the links?"

"Been about six weeks. My elbow's been bugging me," the patient confessed, rubbing a hand over his right elbow.

"Excuses, excuses. Let's have a look," Russell said, scooting forward on the stool. He examined the joint and ran Mr. Lewis through a few motions. "This has all the hallmarks of good old-fashioned tennis elbow."

"Tennis?" The patient gave a derisive snort. "I'm a golfer! You sure this guy has a medical degree?" he asked Mack.

"Golfer's elbow then."

"I just figured it was sore."

"For six weeks? Come on, man." Russell snorted. "Look. You just retired. I want these to be the best years of your life. We're getting old, man. Things are going to start aching. We're going to make weird noises getting out of chairs. But if something starts hurting, don't stop using it. Come see me or Dr. O'Neil."

"I hate to make a fuss," Mr. Lewis complained, again rubbing a big palm over his elbow.

"Taking care of yourself isn't making a fuss," Mack said. "It's smart. And you seem like a smart guy."

"Well, I didn't go to no medical school," he cackled. "But I did okay."

———

In the break room, Russell expertly dug into a colorful sushi roll with his chopsticks, both of which he'd packed. "So let's debrief."

They'd seen three patients together that morning. He'd taken the lead on two of them. She'd fumbled through getting-to-know-you icebreakers during a case of bronchitis with a side of high cholesterol that wasn't being taken seriously.

Mack speared a piece of crisp lettuce with her fork. "You have a history. Even possibly friends."

He nodded, waited.

"You balance the repertoire with authority. But you're respectful about digging into personal details. 'How's your wife? You've been married how many years now?'" she repeated. "You were testing out his mental state with innocent questions while still giving him an opening to bring up any topics he needed to discuss."

"A fair assessment," he announced, wiping his mouth on a linen napkin that he'd produced from his lunch bag. "Now, your turn."

She winced.

"You can intubate a patient in midair, but ask you to discuss the weather or TV and you freeze up," he told her.

She bit off a sigh. "A fair assessment."

"It's something to be improved, not embarrassed about."

"I shouldn't be this bad at something."

Russell placed his chopsticks just so in the folded napkin.

"There's no shame in not knowing how to do something. There's no shame in learning and trying. Shame never works as a motivator."

She wanted to argue. Shame had been a constant motivating factor in her life. She'd worked hard to distance herself from the things that needed distancing, to prove herself over and over again to be good enough.

"By all accounts, Mackenzie, you are one of the most technically proficient doctors this county has ever seen. That's a huge compliment. But it doesn't excuse you from having to learn how to relate to patients. We both know you can be a hell of a lot more than just a competent set of hands in an emergency."

She wasn't so sure she knew that.

He waited a beat.

"I'm processing," she said. "I suppose your theory means that shame doesn't work on patients either."

He clapped his hands—manicured nails, smooth palms—together. "Exactly."

"I can't get Leroy Mahoney to return my calls," she said. She thought of the messages she'd left. An urgent medical matter, she'd said. So it wasn't necessarily calling him out for being negligent with his health, but it wasn't a friendly open approach either.

"His grandson plays Little League in the park by the high school a couple of nights a week. He'll be there."

The personal touch. Ugh.

She wished she'd picked up a few extra air shifts with the hospital. At least there she didn't have to chase patients down for routine information. There she was in charge, in her element. Confident.

"Things happen for a reason, Mackenzie," Russell insisted. "You're here for a reason."

Yeah, to babysit patients and kiss firefighters.

"I guess we'll see," she said.

"Now, tell me about slow dancing with the fire chief at Remo's last night."

Mack's fork hit the table.

Freida and Tuesday poked their heads into the doorway. "About time you asked her," Freida said.

CHAPTER 19

The chopper rose smoothly into the early evening air at Sally's behest, and Mack's stomach gave its customary dip. Nerves and excitement hummed in her veins. Things had been too quiet the past few days, giving her entirely too much time to think about *that kiss*.

Which led to her thinking about all the other things that kiss could lead to. Which led to her making the effort to dig her vibrator out of a moving box.

A good trauma patient was exactly what she needed to clear her head and stop thinking about Chief Reed…and his very talented mouth. And his equally impressive cock.

But now she had a life to save. Female. Midtwenties. Backroad altercation with a tree. Head trauma. They'd be there in two minutes, landing in a cow pasture with permission from the farmer.

While her fingers worked their way through supplies and equipment—checking and double-checking—Mack let her mind settle. It ran through scenarios and protocols. Training, education, and experience molded together into instinct.

Here, eighteen hundred feet in the air, she was confident in her abilities and herself. Much more so than in the little exam room staring down a case of sinusitis and getting-to-know-yous.

"EMTs say there's some trouble on the ground. Belligerent, drunk passenger. They're trying to get the patient on a spine board," Sally warned matter-of-factly through the headset.

Mack glanced at Bubba. His hulking frame was crammed in the corner, triple-checking the plasma inventory. "You ever work as a bouncer, Bubba?" she asked him.

"Always wanted to."

"This might be your chance if the guys on the ground need a hand."

"Yippie-ki-yay."

———

They were on the ground less than a minute later in a grassy green pasture. The land's inhabitants, a dozen cows, crowded against the pretty-as-a-picture white fence several hundred yards away from the flying invader.

Mack could see the rescue vehicles and mangled wreckage of a pickup truck wrapped around the stalwart base of an oak tree on the other side of the country road.

"Let's give 'em a hand," she said, grabbing her med kit.

She and Bubba climbed down and ran low across the grass. They took the four feet of fence in stride. Mack scrambled over it like she was back in basic training. Bubba hopped it like a cowboy. Together, they made a beeline for the crowd of paramedics crouched around a prone victim.

Almost every accident scene had the same players. The fire department was there working on cleanup. Witnesses, most likely the farmer's family, clustered around a big, dusty truck in the field near the scene. A handful of other spectators out for an evening cruise were pulled off on the side of the road watching. A police cruiser was just pulling up to the scene.

And there was Linc. He was in gear and set up as incident command, throwing her a smug smile and a little salute.

She nodded her acknowledgment and elbowed her way into the circle. They were up against a low guardrail. On the other side, the road gave way to a steep, ten-foot drop-off down to a creek.

"What have we got, guys?"

"Female. Twenty-five. Head versus steering wheel. Unconscious. Possible neck and spine injuries. Witnesses say the idiot pulled her out of the car."

"Fuck." Mack was succinct.

"Yep," the female paramedic on her right agreed.

"Get off my girlfriend!" The man, still practically a kid, was stinking drunk...and quite possibly high on something. He was missing a canine tooth and had inch-wide holes in his earlobes. His ball cap had seen better days fifteen years ago. Skinny and mean.

Mack had dealt with enough of his type to know that addressing him wasn't worth it.

He tried to push his way into the circle, but Bubba hauled him back out. One of Linc's crew stepped in to help.

"Stay over there, man. The sheriff needs a word," Bubba said, pointing at Sheriff Ty Adler as the man approached.

"Fuck!" the drunk screamed, unhinged. "Fuck me!"

Mack ignored him. They ran through the patient's vitals while stemming the flow of blood from her head wound. She had blond hair turning pink at the roots.

Mack picked up pieces of the story while assessing injuries. Fighting with drunk boyfriend. Boyfriend grabbed the wheel and put them head-on into the tree. No airbags.

Another avoidable disaster. That pissed her off.

"Let's get her on the board, guys. We gotta get her out of here. On three," Mack ordered.

"I'm tellin' ya. Leave 'er alone!" Skinny screeched.

"I'm gonna need you to calm down, son," the sheriff insisted.

Mack slipped around to the patient's other side, putting her back to the guardrail.

"One. Two. Three." In unison, they team lifted the girl and slid her carefully onto the board.

"Strap her in tight. We've got to get her over that fence," she instructed.

With their patient snuggly braced and strapped, they lifted her, a chorus of cohesive strangers bound together by purpose.

"Incoming!" One of the EMTs at the head of the board shouted a warning.

Skinny had broken away from Ty and raged at them, shouting nonsense as he charged. Mack wanted to get in his way. To tell him he was the reason his girlfriend was strapped down and unconscious. But her skills were required here. She didn't have the luxury of acting on that snap of temper.

And then that skinny dumbass made another big mistake.

Pointy elbows flying, he shoved his way between Mack and the EMT in front of her. "Katelyn, baby! Tell 'em it's not my fault! Tell 'em you were driving!"

"Get the fuck away from my patient," Mack snapped, baring her teeth.

She saw it coming. His pointy fucking fist hurled with more enthusiasm than finesse. But she was holding the litter. The asshole caught her in the cheek, and it sang.

"Goddammit. Get your guy under control!" Bubba hollered from the other side of the board.

Ty, holding his jaw, was jogging toward them, hand on his weapon. But Linc was going to beat him there, and that man had murder in those beautiful baby blues.

Mack bodychecked Skinny with her shoulder and hip. "Move!"

Completely in-fucking-sane, the kid grabbed her by the collar, causing the litter to lurch. It only served to enrage her.

"Get her to the bird," Mack yelled and let go of the board. She turned around, dodged another poorly thrown punch, and shoved the guy back a step.

"Back the fuck off! You're the only thing keeping me from treating your girlfriend right now!"

But he kept coming.

Great. She was going to have to punch the motherfucker. That was going to be a hell of a lot of paperwork on everyone's part.

"Calm the hell down, kid," Ty said. He was close enough now that Mack could see the beginnings of a bruise blooming on his jaw. A sucker punch.

"Fuck off!"

Linc was coming full steam like a freight train. But he was too late. The guy grabbed her by the shoulders and pushed her hard. She would have been fine had it not been for the med bag behind her.

Her feet caught it, and she fell back, catching the guardrail on the backs of her thighs. And then she was tumbling over it.

"Mack!" She heard Linc calling for her.

She remembered to tuck, and that was the best she managed as her body hurled itself backward down the embankment.

Creek. Creek. Creek.

She skidded to a halt, fingers digging into the vegetation, stopping eight inches from the water. *That would have been hard to live down.*

She lay there for a full second, and her line of sight gave her the perfect angle to see Linc's angry fist connect with the idiot's jaw.

The kid went down and didn't get back up.

"You all right, Doc?" Linc jogged down the short embankment. He ran his hands over her legs and arms.

"Fine," she muttered, brushing dirt and leaves off her flight suit. "I'm fine. I gotta get in the air."

"Dreamy, that was a hell of a fall. You sure you didn't hit your head?"

"Tuck and roll, Hotshot. How's the dumbass?"

"Much quieter now."

He helped her to her feet and didn't miss it when she winced.

The lightning strike of pain in her ankle caught her by surprise. The fact that it was her bad ankle only pissed her off more. "Fuck," she hissed.

"Leg? Ankle?" He slipped an arm around her waist.

"It's fine. Just a tweak. If you pick me up right now, I swear to God I will murder you."

"Got it. Stoic support only," he said, taking her waist.

"Need a hand?" someone called out.

A paramedic, another firefighter, and the sheriff himself helped haul them both back up to the road. Skinny was cuffed and slumped against the wheel of the police cruiser. Mack could make out the team loading the patient aboard.

"I gotta go," she insisted. But she gave Linc's arm a hard squeeze.

"You better call me, Dreamy!"

She threw a wave of acknowledgment over her shoulder and jog-limped toward the waiting bird.

Climbing aboard in considerable pain, she slammed the headset over her ears. "Let's rock and roll, RS."

With her focus on the patient, she didn't notice Linc watching the chopper until it disappeared.

———

144

Linc: Status update?

Linc: Hotshot paging Dr. Dreamy.

Linc: At least tell me if you made it back to the hospital or if you crash-landed in a pasture full of goats.

Mack: Made it back. TBI for the patient.

Linc: Fuck.

Mack: My sentiments.

Linc: How are you? You were limping pretty good.

Mack: Fine.

Linc: Stop talking my ear off, Doc.

Mack: It's nothing serious. Just getting checked out in the ED.

Linc: Text me when you get home.

Mack: I won't be up for company.

Linc: Understood. Just want to make sure you're home safe.

Mack: Home now.

Linc: Sweet dreams, Dreamy. Text if you need anything.

CHAPTER 20

Linc rapped lightly on the bright-blue cottage door. Sunshine's tail swished expectantly against his leg. It was early. Before seven a.m. But he knew she was up.

He heard a slow *clump clump clump* approaching from the other side of the door and flashed the peephole his most charming grin.

The door didn't open.

"Open up, Dreamy. I know you're in there."

There was another beat of silence. Sunshine, tired of waiting for adoration, jumped and planted her paws against the sidelight window to announce her presence.

Linc considered it a point in Mack's favor when she opened the door for his dog.

There was a frown on her pretty face and a walking boot on her left foot.

"Nothing serious, huh?" he asked.

Sunshine happily trotted inside and disappeared.

"What do you want?" Mack asked grumpily.

She had a good bruise on her cheek from that skinny asshole's fist that made Linc wish he'd done a hell of a lot more than knock a tooth out. A bandage peeked out from under the sleeve of her sweatshirt. He imagined her clothing hid a multitude of bruises and scrapes.

"I came to join the party," he said, brushing past her.

"What party?"

"Your pity party."

He hefted the grocery tote.

"I'm not having a pity party," she insisted.

The whole place screamed cute little grandma. The couch that Sunshine had already made herself at home on was a faded buttercup yellow with embroidered throw pillows. The built-ins in the living room were crammed with paperbacks and ceramic knickknacks. The TV was entirely too small for the space, and the stand that held it was stenciled with violets.

He'd bet money there was a cookie jar in the kitchen and lace doilies on at least one piece of furniture upstairs. Nothing in the room reflected the sexy, heroic doctor who had taken up residence.

"What's the verdict, Doc?" he asked, crossing the living room and stepping into the minuscule kitchen. He plopped his bag of goodies on the counter.

He heard the uneven clumping follow him into the room.

"Linc," she sighed out his name in a way that brought bedroom fantasies to mind. "What are you doing in my house?"

He nudged her down in one of the two chairs at the table barely big enough to hold one dinner plate. "I'm bein' neighborly. It's a small-town, nice-person thing." When she didn't spring back up out of the chair, he knew she was tired. "Heard you're out of commission."

Glumly, she rested her chin on her hand. "Avulsion fracture. Ankle. I'm officially grounded. I can't fly with the boot."

Hurt, frustrated, and bored. He got it.

He pulled the box of green tea out of the bag and filled the electric kettle with water.

"That sucks," he said succinctly and plugged in the kettle.

"What sucks is that girl's traumatic brain injury," she said, bubbling over with frustration. "No one has good taste in men at that age, and yet she's paying the price. They don't know if she'll ever wake up, let alone resume a normal life. And now *I* know that *they* don't know because everyone in this damn town knows every damn thing."

She pushed out of the chair to limp and pace in the confined space.

"And it's all because some stupid son of a bitch made some really bad fucking choices," she said.

Because he got it, because he knew, Linc hooked his fingers in the neck of her hoodie and reeled her in. She remained rigid until his arms wrapped around her. It was like she'd given herself permission to melt for just a moment.

"I'm sorry the price of his dumbass decisions were hers and yours to pay," he said. "And I'm really fucking pissed that I didn't do more."

"I heard you knocked a tooth out of his mouth," she reminded him.

"Not enough for putting hands on my favorite trauma doc."

She sighed against him. Her face fit just right between his neck and chest. "You're a really good hugger."

"One of my many skills. You should see me—"

"If you say anything about that very impressive cock and ruin this moment, I'll add you to my pissed-off-at list."

The kettle beeped an alert.

"I was going to say, you should see me make a cup of tea." He gave her another squeeze and indulged himself by dropping a kiss on top of her dark hair.

"This doesn't mean we're going to have sex."

He guided her back to her chair. "Let's take a wait-and-see attitude on that particular point for now."

Mack's green eyes twinkled. "You don't find my podiatric apparatus an incredible turn-on?"

"Dreamy, everything about you is an incredible turn-on. Even your misplaced willpower." He turned back to the counter. Mostly to focus on making her tea. But partly because seeing her like this, vulnerable, sad, made him want to swoop in superhero-style and fix every damn thing for her.

He was already overstepping.

"One last item on the pity party agenda," she said. "I hate that I'm feeling sorry for myself when I know *I'll* be back to normal in no time. That girl won't, and I should be grateful."

Hell. Was there nothing about this woman he didn't like?

"Acknowledge," he said, setting the mug in front of her.

She snorted. "What the hell does that mean?"

"It means I've got nothing to add, but I hear you."

She swirled the tea bag around and studied him in silence.

Sunshine, sensing the potential for human attention, trotted into the room.

She stopped, then sat expectantly in front of Mack.

"Hi," Mack said to the dog.

Sunshine took it as an invitation and put her front paws on Mack's knees.

"Here," he said, producing a baggie of doggie treats.

"What are those?" she asked.

"They're t-r-e-a-t-s."

Sunshine trembled in delirium.

"Can she spell?"

"Apparently," he assessed.

"Is she having a seizure?"

"No. She just really likes t-r-e-a-t-s. You might as well give her one and earn her undying love and affection. One now. You can save the rest for later."

"Why do I need treats for your dog later?" she asked in suspicion.

She was getting her feet back under her, latching on to the distraction and setting the self-pity aside. Just as he'd diabolically planned.

"Because I'm leaving her to babysit you," he informed her cheerfully. To add her two cents, Sunshine gave an excited yip.

"This is payback for your nieces and nephews, isn't it?"

He held up his palms, the picture of innocence. "You're actually doing me a huge favor. It's wax-the-apparatus day, and she gets in the way, trying to bite all the rags."

"You're making that up."

He was indeed.

"I'm truly heartbroken that you would think that. Devastated, Dreamy."

Her lips quirked, then flattened again. "Linc. I can't watch your dog. I don't know how to watch a dog." As she said it, she stroked gentle hands over Sunshine's ears.

"It's easy," he promised, slipping the salad mix and chicken breasts into the fridge. "She'll tell you what she wants when she wants it."

"I don't speak dog."

Sunshine nosed the bag of treats, reminding Mackenzie they were there. Dutifully, she took a treat from the bag and gingerly held it out to the dog. Quivering, Sunshine deftly took the treat. With her treasure secure, she ran into the living room, hurled herself onto the couch, circled three times, and flopped down with a happy sigh.

Mack laughed despite herself.

"You'll learn," he said.

"Is that cookie dough?" she asked, watching him stash a package in the fridge.

"Oatmeal raisin and chocolate chip. I wasn't sure what kind of a cookie girl you are, and I'm partial to oatmeal raisin. Figured you could make us dessert since I'm making dinner tonight."

"That's awfully presumptuous," she observed.

"It's the least I can do since you're watching my girl today."

Groceries stashed, he pulled out the other chair at her doll-sized table and sat.

He reached a hand out to cup her chin, angling her face to see the bruising better.

"I'm sorry I wasn't faster," he said.

"It's not your job to protect me," she reminded him.

"I think if we tag team the responsibility, we'll do better." He caged her knees between his hands.

She sighed. "I can't with the full-court press today, Hotshot."

"Because you're feeling frustrated and vulnerable and pissed off that some dumb fuck made shitty choices that are rippling out into consequences that never should have happened. That girl should be heading into work today, not breathing through a tube. You shouldn't be laid up in a boot, suddenly available for dog watching. His mother will lose her son to prison because he couldn't be responsible for himself. And it was all preventable."

The tension sagged out of her shoulders.

"How do you get over it?" she asked.

"I don't. But I also don't forget the good." He reached into his back pocket and produced a card. "This is why we do what we do."

She took it, opened it. "A wedding invite?" Her face softened as she read the note inside. "You're walking the bride down the aisle?"

He took the invite, tucked it back in his pocket. His own

151

treasure, he supposed. "She was my first save. I was a rookie, fresh out of college. House fire on Christmas Eve. She was ten years old and trapped on the second floor with a big-ass family cat that she saved." He picked up Mack's mug and sampled the tea. Wincing, he slid it back to her. "Her parents and her brother were out. Her mom begged us to find her. We weren't sure if we would in time. It was a big house. Her brother told us to look in the upstairs TV room."

He still remembered it. Seeing that face peep out from the corner, skinny arms wrapped around a pissed-off cat. He wasn't sure who was protecting who.

"She made me take the cat to the window first," Linc remembered. "She wouldn't come near me until he was safe."

He remembered it. The weight of the yowling tomcat in his arms as he handed him out the window to the can man who was on the ladder.

The house was fully engulfed inside, yet the Christmas lights lining the gutters remained lit. Hotter than hell despite the frigid December temperatures outside.

"Okay, let's go," she'd said to him, coughing but smiling at him when he returned to her on the floor.

"I stayed in touch with her, with the family, over the years. You don't forget your first," he said with a shrug. "Her dad died a few years back."

"And she asked you to walk her down the aisle," Mack said.

"Yeah. I could use a wedding date."

"Damn it, Linc!"

He grinned.

"You're the literal worst."

"We could be town sweethearts," he mused.

"As appealing as that sounds, you know I'm not looking for romance or any more small-town attention."

"About that. You're going to have visitors today."

"You mean besides the four-legged variety?"

"The casserole-bearing kind. The 'just checking in' kind."

She looked horrified at the idea. "Why?"

"Because you put yourself between a patient and a criminal and got roughed up for your trouble. Because you're a hero, Doc."

She picked up his hand, and he tried hard not to think about how good the physical contact felt. "I'm not the only one who took some damage," she said, examining his bruised and split knuckles.

"No one messes with my girl."

She shot him *the look* but didn't bother arguing with him this time.

Progress. Hard-fought progress.

"Listen," he said, rising. "I've gotta go. Shift change at seven. Text me if you need anything. I'll be back to make you dinner and take Sunny off your hands." He dropped a kiss on the top of her head, liking how natural it felt.

"You could have just asked me," she called after him.

"You would have said no," he called back. "Be a good girl for the doc, Sunshine."

CHAPTER 21

W hat? What do you want?" Mack asked Sunshine while she unloaded the contents of the dog-sitting bag onto the dining room table. Treats. Dog food. Water and food dishes. A leash and some harness thing that looked like it would fit a Clydesdale. And a note. With—even in her grumpy, pity-party state—pretty amusing stick figure drawings.

The dog scooched closer and closer until she was attached to her leg and whimpered hopefully.

"Are you hungry? Because according to this note from your father, you already had breakfast, and you don't get dinner until seven." She showed Sunshine the paper.

Sunshine immediately took a bite out of it.

"Hey! I don't think that's good for you. Spit it out."

Sunshine swallowed, then made a horking noise and deposited what was essentially a spitball on the blue woven rug next to Mack's boot.

"Good girl," she said dryly.

The dog's tail swished across the floor in a windshield wiper rhythm.

Mack read the last item on Linc's note.

She likes to eat paper. Don't let her.

Once again, Sunshine scooted up against her.

"Do you have to go to the bathroom?" That probably wasn't dog language. "Do you need to urinate outside?"

Sunshine gazed at her adoringly.

"I can't take you for a—hang on." She scanned the note. *Yep.* Walk was another spelling-only word. "W-a-l-k. You may not have noticed, but I've got a broken ankle. It's not conducive to walking—"

The dog gave a joyful bark and danced on her hind legs. *Well, hell.* She'd done it now. Gotten the fluffy, sweet dog excited.

Mack didn't have the heart to disappoint her. Besides, she was already going stir-crazy.

"Okay, fine. But it's going to be very short and very slow. Got it?" Sunshine was too busy pirouetting around the kitchen like the world's clumsiest, most excited ballerina.

Her ankle throbbed in protest, but Mack managed to limp down the front steps to the walkway with Sunshine prancing happily on her hot-pink leash. It was a beautiful day, and that only added to her bad mood. She should have been up in the air today. She could have gone for a run. Could have been mowing the damn swatch of lawn that already needed it again. And there were weeds in the front flower bed that hadn't been there on her last day off.

"How are you at landscaping?" she asked the dog. But Sunshine was too busy peeing on the tall grass.

They made it halfway around the block with Mack limping, Sunshine sashaying. A pleasantly soft, round woman in a pink and purple muumuu that somehow looked actually stylish called a greeting from her front porch.

"Yoo-hoo! Is that little Miss Sunshine?"

Sunshine shoved her face over the thigh-high fence and wriggled with excitement. Everything made this dog happy. Everything was an adventure.

"It is," Mack called back.

The woman heaved herself out of her rocking chair and bustled down the front steps of her porch. "And you're that doctor lady who got herself hurt by that dumbass last night. I heard it was bath salts and booze. He always was a no-good, no-account asshole. I hear his mama refused to post his bail, and he's gonna be rotting away in jail for a long, long time."

The woman was very well-informed.

She reached the fence and pulled out a treat from a hidden muumuu pocket. "Now, who's the best girl in the whole world?" she asked.

Sunshine's butt hit the sidewalk, and the rest of her quivered in delight.

Mack wondered when the last time was that she'd been that happy. Quite possibly never.

"Here you go, sweet girl." The nice lady handed over the treat, and Sunshine took it with a surprising daintiness. "I'm Mrs. Valerie Washington. And you're Dr. Mack." She dressed and spoke like she was in her late seventies, but there wasn't a line that Mack could pick out on the woman's beaming mahogany face.

"I am," she said. "I'm dog sitting for Chief Reed today."

"That's a smart move on his part," Mrs. Washington decided. "If he can't get you to go out with him based on his charm alone, you'll fall for Sunshine here. I'm gonna pop over this afternoon and bring you some cookies fresh baked and all the fixings for a good Tom Collins because, honey, if anyone deserves a drink, it's you. I gotta get to my weightlifting class. But I'll see you later."

"Bye? Thanks?" Mack raised a hand in a wave as Mrs. Washington bebopped back into her house.

"Does everyone just give you what you want?" Mack asked the dog. Sunshine shot her a smug look.

They made the arduous return to Mack's house. Her ankle, foot, and calf were now screaming obscenities at her. Her hips, back, and shoulders were also reminding her that she'd taken a header down an embankment.

She was so distracted she almost tripped over Captain Brody Lighthorse, who was kneeling in the flower bed that paralleled her walkway.

"What the—"

Sunshine exploded into delirium.

"There's my Sunny girl!" Brody shucked off his gloves and gave the dog a full-body scruff.

There were firefighters all over her lawn. One, a young woman, presumably the rookie, was energetically push-mowing the grass. Another, an older, rounder man, was on a stepladder cleaning the first-floor windows.

Two more were weeding the front flower beds, and yet another was greasing the hinges on the storm door that squealed like a banshee every time it opened.

Someone had brought a wireless speaker that was blaring eighties pop. They all bopped to the beat in varying degrees of dancing prowess.

"What's all this?" she asked.

Brody rose. His shaved head gleamed in the midmorning sunshine. He had tattoos, intricate tribal designs, down both forearms. His teeth were blindingly white against copper-toned skin. "The BFD—Benevolence Fire Department, also Big Fucking Deal—thought we'd lend a hand to a sister. Sorry you're out of action for a while. That sucks."

It did suck.

"Thanks. But you don't have to."

He shrugged and reached for the gloves again. "There's nothing 'have to' about it. You put yourself between a dumb fuck and a patient. You're good people. Plus, there's no way in hell you're going to be up for mowing the lawn anytime soon."

He wasn't wrong.

Still, she preferred to mope in solitude. Now, she had a dog that was sniffing the butt of a firefighter with a lopsided mustache and a yard full of half the town's fire department.

"Thanks," she said again. Then remembered her manners. "Do you guys want something to drink?" She could do tap water. Or maybe some iced green tea.

"Nope. We brought our own cooler. Now, we just need you to go on inside, elevate that foot, and prepare to be waited on."

"I don't need the fire department to wait on me," she insisted.

"We're the yard and maintenance crew. The waiting-on crew comes later. You might want to grab a nap to mentally prepare or at least start drinking now."

She thought about the Tom Collins Mrs. Washington promised her.

"I don't nap," Mack told him.

He grinned. "Suit yourself."

She turned toward the house, then paused again. "I'm being rude. I'm tired. Everything hurts. And I'm feeling sorry for myself. I'm sorry for being a dick," she said.

"You earned it. You go on and feel any damn way you want. Just think of us as Santa's elves. We'll be out of your hair in no time."

"Thanks for all this," she said. "Really."

"My wife and girls made Amish cinnamon bread. It's on your table."

Mack paused again to make small talk with Skyler Robinson, the rookie and Dr. Russell Robinson's daughter. Then she openly admired the gleaming windows and squeal-less front door before finally limping inside.

She flopped down on the couch. Sunshine, having greeted all her friends, climbed up next to her. Maybe a nap wasn't such a terrible idea.

It was her last thought before the buzz of the doorbell woke her. Sunshine hurled herself off the couch and threw herself at the front door, yelping enthusiastically.

"Vicious guard dog, huh?" Mack dragged her aching self to the door and opened it.

Two women, both near carbon copies of the other, grinned at her. Blond, pretty, dimpled chins. They bore a striking resemblance to—

"Hi! I'm Christa. This is Jillian. We're Linc's sisters."

Uh-oh.

Sunshine greeted them and generously accepted their pets and compliments.

"Hi, I'm Gwiffin." A very small Asian kid poked his head between the women. He was missing a front tooth. "This is my brother Mikey. He's not supposed to be here 'cause he's usually in school. But Mom said we couldn't leave him at home."

Mikey was a few years older than Griffin—unless it really was Gwiffin. He was a little Latino stud muffin with thick, curly hair, a fake tattoo on his skinny bicep, and brown eyes that looked like they might be able to charm anyone into anything. Except today they were painfully bloodshot.

He sneezed three times in rapid succession.

"It's allergies. I swear. Not anything infectious," Christa, the slightly taller of the two, insisted. "Now, let's see where I can set this up." She patted the large folding table leaning against her leg.

"What's happening?" Mack asked, stepping back as the party entered.

"Well, Chris here is a chiropractor. We heard you took a pretty good tumble, so you're probably pretty jacked up," Jillian said, surveying the living room. "Meanwhile, I have no special skills. So while you're being adjusted, I'm going to fix you lunch and do whatever else needs doing. Laundry? I'm great at laundry. And I'll grill you on what the hell to do with Mr. Sneezy Pants over there. His seasonal allergies are getting worse every year."

Mack opened her mouth, but no one was listening. Christa set up the table, a fancy portable chiropractic thing in the middle of the living room. "Bag, nephew," she said, snapping her fingers at Griffin.

With a grunt, the kid hefted a big black bag into his aunt's hand.

"Good work. Now, turn on Dr. Mack's TV and go find your brother a box of tissues."

On cue, Mikey wiped his nose on the back of his hand.

"Hop up here, Dr. Mack. You can tell me all about your intentions with my brother while I see what we're working with."

Groggy from the nap, not her sharpest thanks to the pain, Mack thought about arguing and then gave up. She flopped facedown on the table and prayed for it all to be over and everyone to be gone.

"Whew," Christa said. "I thought you might be one of those doctors who calls chiropractic hippie woo-woo garbage."

Mack gave a weak laugh. "Not saying I am, but at this point, I can't feel any worse. So have at it."

She heard Jillian washing dishes in the kitchen, heard

the kids squabble over what show to watch. The tip-tap of Sunshine's toenails on the hardwood.

Christa's hands pressed down on her low back, and Mack groaned.

"My brother seems to be smitten with you," Christa said, moving her hands methodically over Mack's back and hips.

"Smitten?" Jillian called from the kitchen. "Is that a new interrogation technique? Old-ladying up your language?"

"Shut up, Jillybean."

"Mom! Aunt Chris said shut up," Griffin yelled.

"I heard. Bad Aunt Chris!"

"Back to the interrogation," Christa insisted. "Deep breath in."

Mack barely had a chance to draw a breath when Linc's sister pressed her hipbones firmly into the table.

She felt the resistance, was convinced she was going to snap in half, and then breathed a huge sigh of relief when something gave way with an audible pop.

"Better?"

"Yeah," Mack whimpered. "Much."

"Good." Christa worked her way up the spine. "Linc is one-of-a-kind, you know. He's got a reputation."

"I don't mind a reputation," Mack admitted. "I'm just not looking for any"—*crack*—"thing right now," she gasped.

"Just because you're not looking doesn't mean you can't find something," Christa said cheerfully.

"It's true," Jillian said, poking her head into the room. "I wasn't looking for Vijay when I stumbled into that karaoke bar ten years ago, and look at us now. Three boys, an aquarium full of goldfish, and no time to ourselves."

That did not sound like the life for Mack. That sounded like a dozen disasters waiting to happen every day.

"Not that you'd need to go that route with Linc," Christa said, working her thumbs between Mack's shoulder blades.

"Gah," Mack whimpered.

"He's the greatest guy. You can trust us. We've known him since he was born," Jillian said knowledgeably. "I think you two would be very happy together."

"I don't think one kiss means happily ever after," Mack gritted out.

"Oooooh! A kiss! Tell us more," Christa squealed.

The boys passive-aggressively turned up the TV volume.

"Turn it down," Jillian yelled. "I wanna hear about the kiss!"

Mack politely declined to share any sordid details. But she did begin to wonder why it had been only one kiss. He hadn't kissed her this morning before he abandoned his dog with her.

"It was worth a shot," Christa said, working her way through all the kinks in Mack's back.

After her adjustments and a lunch of chicken corn soup and half a turkey sandwich prepared by Jillian, Mack felt almost human again. Or at least human enough to give the sniffly Mikey a quick exam.

"He's old enough that you could look into allergy shots," she told Jillian.

"Shots?" Mikey's bloodshot brown eyes widened.

"Are you afraid of needles?" Mack asked him.

He shrugged a bony shoulder, the picture of eight-year-old nonchalance. "They're no big deal."

"Well, if they did bother you," she continued, "I could tell you a trick so it's not so scary."

"What kind of trick?"

She reached over and pinched him lightly on the arm. "Feel that?"

"Ow. Yeah."

"Okay. This time, take a deep breath."

He inhaled skeptically.

"Good. Now hold it for a second. And then blow it out really hard."

On the kid's exuberant exhale, she pinched him again.

"Hey! That didn't hurt as much," he said.

"That's the trick. A really big breath out, and your body is focusing more on the breath than the teeny tiny poke."

"Pinch me next, Dr. Mack," Griffin insisted. She felt pretty good about it.

———

Half an hour later, a grateful Mack with a folded load of laundry, sparkling kitchen, and pee-breaked Sunshine waved Linc's sisters off. She hadn't even made it back to the couch when there was another knock at the door.

Aldo and Gloria grinned at her from the front steps.

"Hey, buddy! How's it going?"

"Shouldn't you two be at work?" Mack asked wearily.

"We decided to forego our weekly scheduled afternoon delight to pop in and see how you're doing," Aldo said.

Gloria elbowed him. "Not everyone needs to know about our sex life, Moretta."

"Oh good! It's a party!" Mrs. Washington called out, hauling a grocery bag up the walk.

It was barely one p.m. And it was already the longest day of Mack's life.

CHAPTER 22

Linc gave the incident report a cursory final glance before hitting Submit.

How some yahoo managed to get his big toe stuck in a motel bathtub faucet was another one of life's great mysteries.

Checking the time, he noted he could squeeze in another hour of paperwork before heading out. Or he could cut that to thirty minutes and check in with the crew downstairs for the remainder.

The latter sounded like a much better plan. He pulled up the department calendar to refresh his memory on the maintenance and training for the rest of the month.

Brody strolled in without knocking and planted himself on the narrow, rock-hard couch that squatted against one wall. "Tanker's on E. Wanna ride shotgun on a gas run?"

"Hell yeah," Linc said, gratefully pushing away from the computer.

He followed his captain downstairs into the bay. It was spotless thanks to several slow days. They'd trained hard on forcible entries and coordinated attack drills this week and then resealed the concrete floor. The apparatus all gleamed under a fresh coat of wax.

There was an almost tangible crackling in the air. Firefighters going stir-crazy. Sure, there were the usual calls. The faulty alarm at the high school—twice—a few lift assists with EMS, the now infamous odor investigation on Pine Avenue that turned out to be a faulty bathroom exhaust fan and a whole lot of tacos. Then there was the ferret in the tree that required rescue. Par for the course in a small town.

But historically, the longer the station went without a big call, the weirder his crew got. It was already happening, Linc noted, when he spotted a group of his volunteers sitting around a kid's wading pool trying to flip quarters into floating cups. The men participating were sporting varying stages of facial hair. The women—well, he wasn't close enough to tell, but in solidarity, most of them had committed to not shaving their legs.

The weird and wonderful camaraderie of a fire company.

"Hey, Chief" Al, a fifteen-year volunteer and driver engineer, gave him a wave.

"What happened to your 'stache, Al?" Linc asked.

The man stroked a hand over what was now only half of a sparse mustache.

"Lost a bet. Had to shave half of it." He grinned. Betting and losing bets was a way of life in the BFD. Since making chief, Linc steered clear of the betting. Though he distinctly remembered the last one he'd lost. He'd had to dye his hair blue and call himself Papa Smurf.

"How'd Rocco take that?" Two years ago, Al had married his long-time boyfriend in a ceremony attended by the entire department. The happy couple was whisked away from the reception on the back of a ladder truck in an impromptu Benevolence parade. Linc had been prepared for flak from the city and was fully intending to cover the cost of gas on his own dime when the mayor showed up with a wedding gift and her congratulations for the happy couple.

"Rocco threatened to shave off the other half if it doesn't look better by his niece's quinceañera. I think the motivation will make it grow back faster," Al said optimistically.

Linc climbed up to ride shotgun in the boxy tanker truck. Brody pulled the behemoth out of the bay doors and made a wide, slow turn onto the road. Two thousand gallons of water sloshed behind them in the tank, ready and waiting to be put to good use.

"Your doc isn't used to people being nice to her," Brody said without preamble.

"Don't I know it," Linc said, sliding on a pair of sunglasses.

"Can't help but wonder what that's all about," Brody mused. "She ever say where she got that scar?"

Linc shook his head, shot his buddy a glance. "You think they're related?"

"Got a feeling," Brody said, patting a hand over his heart.

Linc did too.

"She's pretty tight-lipped on where she's from."

"You could ask," Brody suggested. "Seein' as how you two are spending time slow dancing at Remo's and all."

Linc smirked. His friend knew how to time the delivery of good gossip.

"I could. But that doesn't mean she'd answer." He'd put money on that.

"The strong, silent type," his friend sighed. He eased the tanker around a corner, waved to a pack of kids, home from school and desperate to play, in a front yard.

"On the money."

"You could look her up. Run a background."

"And ruin the fun of playing getting-to-know-you?" Linc

hated to admit that he'd had the same thought. But he dismissed it after envisioning her righteously pissed-off response to the invasion of privacy.

It was better to be patient. To earn her confidence.

"Haven't heard of you hitting the singles' nights anywhere lately," Brody mused, making a wide turn into the service station and tooting the horn.

"Haven't been interested lately."

Brody's grin was broad. "It's about damn time. The doc might need some convincing."

"I'm a persuasive guy," Linc said confidently.

———

"Honey, I'm home," Linc called through the no-longer-squeaky screen door of Mack's house. It was what could be dubbed an autumn night. The air was cooler, with an edge of crispness to it. Every cottage window was wide open, inviting the evening breeze inside.

Sunshine ran a celebratory lap around the living room before launching herself at the door.

"Don't take it too seriously," Mack said, limping over to open it for him. "She did the same thing after I came back from the bathroom."

"How's my beautiful girl?" he asked, ruffling Sunshine's fur with one hand.

"I'd be better if people stopped showing up at my house," Mack answered with a quirk of her lips.

"Long day of socializing?" he asked, noting that despite the complaint, she seemed happier than she'd been this morning.

She jerked a thumb over her shoulder at the coffee table where three gift bags and a fruit platter waited. "You have no idea."

"I grew up here," he countered. "I can imagine."

"You'd think I cured cancer with one arm tied behind my back," she said, limping out of his way as he came inside. "I was just doing my job."

"And they're grateful for that, Dreamy. So am I." He produced the riotous bouquet of wildflowers from behind his back with a flourish.

She sighed, and he knew he'd hit on a weakness. There wasn't much about Mackenzie O'Neil that said soft and romantic. But the woman appreciated flowers.

"You're giving our neighbors the wrong idea," she complained.

"I'm hoping I'm giving you the right idea. Besides, I figured the ones from your first day at work had to be potpourri by now."

She rolled her eyes but buried her face in the blooms.

"That's both thoughtful and unnecessary. Just like you sending a team of firefighters to handle my yard maintenance."

"You're welcome," he said with a wicked grin.

"Thank you," she said dryly.

He sniffed the air. "Someone's been playing Betty Crocker."

"Betty Crocker and Betty Ford," she said, nodding at the pitcher on the butcher block. "Tom Collins courtesy of Mrs. Washington."

"God bless small towns," he said reverently. "How about you pour a couple of those Tom Collinses and sit your ass on the deck while I grill? We'll talk about our days like a nice married couple."

"The worst, Reed. You're the worst."

But they did just that. Linc put the flowers in water and brought throw pillows from the couch to elevate Mack's foot on a chair. And while he grilled marinated chicken and Sunshine romped around the backyard trying to catch bugs, they compared their days.

"Seven firefighters, Christa and Jillian—your sisters pumped me for information on whether we're dating—Gloria and Aldo with pie that we can eat with the cookies, Mrs. Washington with the much-appreciated alcohol supplies, Harper and Sophie with ice cream to eat with the pie. My new pal Ellen came by with a health-conscious fruit tray and a couple of Blu-rays to keep me entertained. And Tuesday, Freida, and Russell popped by on their lunch break to tell me they're giving me tomorrow off too." She ticked them all off on her fingers and tried to look annoyed.

But he could tell it had touched her. Annoyed her, sure. But also touched her.

They enjoyed huge, grilled-to-perfection chicken salads and a second Tom Collins for them both...because why not?

"What kind of pie is it?" Linc asked. Gloria Moretta's reputation as a sinful angel in the kitchen was well earned.

"Apple with one of those fancy lattice crusts," she said.

"I'll warm up the pie," he volunteered.

"I'll get the ice cream."

He helped her out of the chair, and because the humans were abandoning her, Sunshine raced across the yard and beat them both to the back door.

"How did it go with my girl today?" he asked.

He noted the fond look Mack sent the dog as Sunshine shoved her face in the opening, forcing the door open wider.

"She was good company. She's a little on the needy side," Mack said. "But I didn't mind having her around. I think I'm starting to speak dog." In response, Sunshine plopped down, blocking the entrance, and stared lovingly up at the pretty doctor.

Mack and I are going to get married and have babies and yellow Labs everywhere, Linc decided.

"Move it, pretty girl," he said, nudging the dog out of their way.

He caught the wince on Mack's face when she shifted her weight. He pointed her in the direction of the tiny kitchen table and planted her in the chair. Doctors were the worst patients. She'd probably spent half the day on her feet.

"I'm tired of resting."

"Yeah, well, that broken bone isn't gonna heal itself with you walking half marathons on it, now is it?"

"No one likes a know-it-all," she complained.

"I'll bring you the ingredients. You plate the dessert. Points for presentation," he told her.

He found the pie in the fridge, bowls in the cabinet by the sink, and the ice cream in the otherwise empty freezer.

"Take one last look at this perfection before I massacre it into slices," he said, holding the pie up. They admired it for a full three seconds.

"Okay, I'm ready for the massacre," Mack decided.

The doorbell rang halfway through the second stab of the knife. When Mack merely groaned and slumped in her chair, Linc went to see who it was. Sunshine, he noted, stayed with Mack…and the pie.

Sheriff Ty Adler, in uniform, squad car in Mack's driveway, took off his hat.

"Bein' neighborly?" he asked Linc with a grin.

"Bein' sheriffy?" Linc shot back.

"Wish it were a social call. Is the lady of the house around, or are you just breaking in to sniff her undies while she's out?"

"Please tell me that's not from an actual call," Linc begged.

"You'd be surprised."

"If you're here to tell us that asshole is going to jail for a long, long time, then you're just in time for pie and ice cream."

"It might be a topic of discussion," Ty mused, rubbing the bruise on his jaw.

"Come on back. Mack, we've got company of the law enforcement officer type." At the closing of the screen door, Sunshine gave up her vigil and trotted into the living room for a proper greeting.

Linc led dog and man into Mack's kitchen and pulled another bowl out of the cabinet.

"Dr. O'Neil," Ty said formally.

"It's Mack," she said. "Have a seat."

He took the chair across from her and glanced down at the pie. "Looks like another crime's been committed. Who the hell murdered this poor, beautiful thing? And if it was you, Doc, remind me not to let you do any surgery on me."

"Still eats the same," Linc said, scooping a third clump of pie into a bowl. "Warmed up?" he asked.

"Is there any other way?" Ty wondered.

Linc microwaved while Ty ran through Mack's statement she'd given in the emergency department while the grumpy Dr. Ling had examined her X-rays.

"So we've got Mick Kersh for a couple of charges relating to the crash, but he wasn't driving, and without witnesses inside the car, a decent public defender can poke holes in his high-as-a-kite crime scene confession."

"That's not enough. That girl isn't waking up anytime soon. And if she does, she'll never be back to what she was before she got in that car with him," Mack said.

"That's why I'm here. I know that girl and her family. And this isn't enough for them either. If you're comfortable pressing charges, we've got a felony for assault with injury against a law enforcement officer."

"Absolutely," Mack said without hesitation. Linc put a bowl of pie and ice cream garnished with a cookie in front of her.

"Before you commit, the boy's got family. Family who don't necessarily care about what really happened or what crimes were committed. His dad, Jethro, has been popped a time or two for drunk and disorderly. A few domestic calls that never went anywhere. His uncle Abner did a nickel for possession and distribution. Both insisted to anyone who'd listen that they were set up."

"I'm not afraid of retaliation," she said.

Though Linc noted she put her spoon down when she said it.

"You should be on the lookout too, Chief," Ty said, shifting his attention to Linc. "They're making noises about you assaulting their boy."

"I was defending a fellow LEO. No one on-scene will say one shot to the face was excessive use of force in that particular instance. I'd welcome a conversation with the Kershes right about now."

"I need you both to be aware, be vigilant."

"But you need me to press charges and testify?" Mack clarified.

"I do."

She pulled out her phone from the pocket of her shorts. "I had the ED take pictures of my injuries when I went in." She flipped through her photos, and Linc felt the return of his blood-boiling anger. He wished he would have had the opportunity to do more than knock out a tooth the fucker probably wouldn't even miss.

Sunshine, sensing his mood, trotted over and leaned into him.

"Where's my pie, Chief?" Ty demanded, business concluded.

CHAPTER 23

The clink of the bat brought half the crowd to its feet. Little Anton's legs were a blur as he careened toward first base. He was the runt of the team, but the kid could hit like a player twice his size.

"Nice single, Anton!" Linc clapped along with the rest of the crowd from the dugout where he and head coach Luke Garrison wrangled the rest of the Benevolence Spider Pigs.

"You're blocking my view of the plate, *Coach*," Luke complained to Linc.

"Maybe you should move then, *Coach*," Linc suggested.

"Maybe *you* should move," Luke countered.

"Are you guys fighting again?" Linc's nephew Brandon asked from his perch on top of the water cooler. "You're not supposed to fight in front of us, remember?"

"We're not fighting, Bran," Linc lied.

"Yeah, we're practically BFFs," Luke growled.

Brandon remained unconvinced.

"Would I punch Coach Luke in the arm like this if we were fighting?" Linc asked, socking his frenemy in the bicep harder than necessary.

"Ow. And would I put your uncle in a headlock like this if we were fighting?"

They scuffled until the umpire strolled over. "You boys done causing a spectacle, or do I need to eject you again?" she asked pleasantly.

Linc gave Luke one last shove and beamed at her. "We're good. Scout's honor."

She shook her head in resignation. "Why don't you find an assistant coach you actually like?" she asked Luke.

"He's an asshole," Luke said. "But he knows the game, and he keeps the kids from ganging up on me."

Linc pretended to wipe away a tear. "That's the nicest thing you've ever said to me, buddy."

Luke shot him a covert middle finger.

"Opposite ends of the dugout, or I'm telling both your mothers," the ump ordered before returning to the plate.

Obediently, the coaches retired to their respective spaces, and the game resumed.

While the catcher scrambled after a foul ball, Sunshine perked up from the dugout and ran to the fence.

Linc spotted Mack limping toward the bleachers in sexy workout shorts to accommodate the unwieldy boot and a National Guard hoodie.

She paused to pet Sunshine through the chain link and then looked in his direction. Her sunglasses prevented him from seeing those eyes, that scar. But he felt the warmth of her gaze nonetheless. He jogged over to collect his dog, say hi to his girl.

"Didn't know you were a fan, Dreamy."

She held up the loaded hot dog that Sunshine was eyeing pathetically. "I'm a fan of ballpark food and getting the hell out of my house." Less than forty-eight hours since her injury, and she was already climbing the walls.

"And the assistant coach. Don't forget that you're a fan of him too." He grinned.

Her lips quirked. "Yeah. He's okay. Thanks again for dinner last night."

"You should let me make you breakfast sometime."

"Yo, Coach. Are you gonna pay attention to the game or not?" Luke called.

Dreamy grinned. "Someone's in trouble," she sang.

"If you wait for me after the game, I'll take you for ice cream," Linc offered. He didn't mention that they'd also be taking an entire team of preteen baseball players with them.

"Between this injury and you feeding me, I'm going to lose all fitness."

"One piece of pie and one little ice cream cone won't kill you. Besides, you're welcome to use the gym at my place any time you want. I'll spot you."

"Yeah, I bet you will," she said. "Looks like you're needed on the field, Coach."

Linc turned and saw a pile of boys between second and third base. He couldn't tell if they were fighting or celebrating.

He gave her a grin and jogged off toward the melee.

Later in the game, he searched the crowd for her and found her on the first bleacher sitting next to Tyrone's grandfather. They looked as though they were deep in conversation when a fly ball cleared the fence.

"Yo, Mack!" he called out the warning.

But it was unnecessary.

She snatched it out of the air bare-handed a foot from Leroy Mahoney's face without bobbling the remains of her hot dog. The grin she sent him when she threw it back was pure sin.

"Do *not* get any ideas there," Luke said, appearing beside him to burst his bubble.

"I think we've already established that we're not the kind of buddies who give each other dating advice," Linc warned him. He was bracing for it. The you're-not-good-enough-for-her talk.

"Look, man," Luke said, surprising Linc with his earnestness. "I know shadows when I see shadows. She's got shit to work out before she's relationship material. Don't get your hopes up."

Linc was touched. "Wait a second. Hang on. Are you trying to protect my feelings?"

Luke shrugged. "Don't make this weird. I'm just saying there's something going on there, and if she doesn't deal with shit, things will go south fast."

The man spoke from personal experience. Linc recalled their entertaining and dramatic fight years earlier in the grocery store's beverage cooler.

Luke had almost lost Harper and had to work hard to earn her back.

"I'm more comfortable with you hating my guts," Linc admitted.

"Yeah. Me too. Let's go back to that."

CHAPTER 24

Leroy Mahoney was a big man in a freebie T-shirt and denim shorts held up by suspenders. He wore blinding white sneakers with slightly dingier white socks hiked to his knees. Every time he stood up to cheer, diet soda sloshed over the rim of his plastic cup.

"Hey there, Leroy," Mack said. She pretended not to notice the guilty look he shot in her direction.

"Oh. Hello there, Dr. Mack." His mustache twitched. "I'm, uh, sorry about not returning your calls. Tyrone keeps me pretty busy and, uh, my phone is lost."

On cue, a cheery polka ringtone sounded from inside his pocket.

"I think it's in your shorts," she said helpfully.

He chuckled nervously and fished the phone out. He hit the Ignore button, which she knew was exactly what he'd been doing to her calls.

She sank down on the metal bleacher next to him and couldn't quite contain the sigh that escaped when she took the weight off her foot.

He glanced down at her boot. "Sorry to hear about you getting hurt and all," he said.

"Thanks," she said, now the self-conscious one. "How's Tyrone feeling?" she said, changing the subject.

"Couple days of rest, four viewings of *The Princess Bride*, and he's back to normal. Just like you said."

"Good." She nodded at the kid with grass stains on his knees. "So he plays left field?"

Leroy beamed, radiating proud grandpa vibes, and Mack, for just a split second, wondered what it would have been like to have a Grandpa Leroy in her life.

"He's really progressing. He's a natural just like his Pop-Pop."

"You played?" she asked, biding her time with a bite of hot dog.

He surged to his feet along with the crowd around them at a pop-up into left field. "Get it, Tyrone!"

Mack stayed on her butt to save her ankle for the arduous limp back to the parking lot.

The man's grandson trotted across the green of the outfield, screwing up his face in concentration. The ball hit his mitt and—thankfully—stayed put.

"Out!" the ump yelled over the celebrating crowd.

Leroy danced a surprisingly spry boogie. "That's my boy!" He turned back to her and gave her a hearty high five, then continued down the whole row.

The Spider Pigs skipped off the field, whooping their delight.

Her gaze skimmed to the blond, muscular coach high-fiving kids left and right.

She felt a foreign, female kind of satisfaction watching Linc with the team, then immediately dislodged the feeling. She was *not* the type of woman who would swoon imagining a gorgeous hunk of man holding a baby in his strong arms. She was more likely to be impressed by nice, neat stitches closing a wound or technical form on an overhead squat.

Or the very important ability to efficiently deliver sexual satisfaction.

When she let herself think about it, Mack was sure Linc could deliver on all those fronts.

Hell. Not having sex with the man was only making her think about having sex with him more. It was the classic forbidden fruit.

Her phone vibrated.

It was a text from Ellen, including a selfie in a swim cap.

Ellen: Five swims in toward the new me. I hate kale. But I can tolerate arugula. And I haven't murdered anyone in my house yet! How's the meditation going? I found an app that might help!

Mack decided to respond later…after she'd meditated. Just as she was pocketing her phone, it buzzed again.

Andrea: Kenzie, your direct deposit STILL isn't here, and my rent is due! I'd think you'd be more responsible than this.

One day late.

One fucking day late because some dumbass broke her foot.

She shouldn't be responsible for Andrea. The woman was an adult. Mack knew her guilt was misplaced. But it was so much easier to transfer the money every month than to have the conversation. To take that stand. Because she knew once she did, it would be her final one.

Calmly, Mack squelched the urge to hurl her phone into

the trash can in front of them. She pushed aside the knee-jerk emotional fallout that texts like these always brought. She had more pressing matters to deal with.

She cleared her throat. "You know, Leroy. It's been a while since you've had a checkup," she said, dragging her attention back to her purpose when he sat back down.

He sighed heavily. "You sound like Dr. Dunnigan. She put you up to this before she left?"

"We should schedule a checkup. You haven't been seen in almost two years. Not since your hip surgery. The surgeon made a note that you skipped out on the last follow-up."

Leroy mentioned something about Dr. Tattletale under his breath.

"We just want you to be healthy," she pressed. "You've got Tyrone here depending on you. I want to keep you healthy enough to throw a ball with him for a long time. But I can't do that without seeing you for a physical. We don't even know if you're still on your blood thinners."

"I'm not," he told her. The droop in his shoulders made her feel bad for taking the shine off Tyrone's athletic prowess. "I'm overweight," he said. "I'm old. I don't need anyone else telling me that." His lips pressed in a firm, unyielding line under the white of his mustache.

"Who told you that?" It certainly didn't sound like something Trish or Russell would say.

"The surgeon. He told me it was a waste of time doing the surgery on me if I wasn't going to get off my ass and get healthier."

"Ouch." Mack sympathized. There was that shame again. And instead of motivating him to do better, the shame had made Leroy retreat from the subject entirely. Russell was right. Some doctors didn't care about their patients as people. But she wasn't going to be one of them. "Look, you're in good shape. You have to be to keep up with an eight-year-old. And not all doctors are…"

He looked left and right, then whispered, "Assholes?"

"Exactly."

He still didn't look convinced.

"I'm here to help you figure out how to stay healthy and well for years to come. That surgery might have thrown you for a loop. I know it was a long, complicated recovery, and your surgeon sounds like a jackass. But moving forward, you and I can be proactive to keep something like that from happening again."

"I can't *not* be here for him. Tyrone needs me. His mom needs me."

And Leroy needed them.

"Then we start with a physical," she said firmly. She pulled up the scheduling app on her phone. "How does next Tuesday look?"

Mack limped her way toward the parking lot, feeling like she'd had her own victory on top of the Benevolence Spider Pigs' win. He'd pushed her back to Halloween with a litany of excuses, but she'd nailed Leroy down for a physical and blood work. She'd also added the friendly threat that she'd show up on his doorstep with her medical bag if he bailed on her.

"Hey there, Doc." Georgia Rae, in a powder-blue sweater set embroidered with sparkly threaded flowers, waved from the concession stand.

"Dr. Mack." Skinny Carl, the man with a lot of opinions *and* children, nodded at her. He had a baby in one arm and a toddler on a leash tied to his belt.

Mack waved back and quickened her pace toward the parking lot.

After she'd locked down Leroy's appointment, she'd given a foot rash a cursory glance and chatted with a mother of five who suggested Mack consider hosting a community flu shot clinic.

An idea tickled at the back of her mind. She tucked it away to mull over later.

"Skipping out on us, Dreamy?"

She turned and saw Sunshine bolting toward her in a blur of tail and tongue. Linc followed. His greeting was slightly more tempered than the dog's, but she still picked up on his enthusiasm in the slightly lecherous look he shot her legs.

A pack of kids in grass-stained uniforms and a collection of skin tones and missing teeth closed around them. "Coach Chief Linc, are we going for ice cream? Are we?"

The kids were as excited as Sunshine was.

"If I can convince Dr. Mack here to go with us."

They turned their sad, puppy-kid eyes on her. Sunshine added weight with her own.

"Please, Dr. Mack? Please?" A boy with goggles over his glasses and a runny nose clasped his hands under his chin.

A lanky youngster with a cute Afro peeking out from under his hat cocked his head and shot her a confident wink. A future heartbreaker in the making.

"Please?"

Lincoln Reed did *not* play fair.

She telegraphed him a look that said exactly that.

He sent her a cocky wink. The man's confidence was a force of nature. And she found it appealing.

The ghost of that text message floated through her mind and doused the playfulness that was arising in her. She'd never outrun the shadows of her past. And Linc, with his sisters and his nieces and nephews, came from a warm, solid family history.

It wasn't just a mismatch. It was a catastrophe. She had no idea how to be a productive partner in a healthy adult relationship.

She felt sick and sad, as if the toxicity of her past was leaking through her pores to taint the present.

Something wet and fluffy nudged her hand, and she looked down at Sunshine, who beamed up at her with unconditional doggy love.

"See, Dr. Mack? Even Sunny wants ice cream," one of the very smart, manipulative boys pointed out.

She managed a weak smile. But when she looked up, Linc's eyes were blazing into her as if he could see beneath this veneer of a competent adult. As if he could see the ugliness beneath her skin.

"Please, Dreamy?" he asked sweetly.

She couldn't do anything about her past or its effect on the now. But she could say yes to ice cream and steal a tiny moment of fun. Even if it didn't really belong to her.

"I guess we're going for ice cream," she said with forced brightness.

"Yes!" The ice cream celebration was as big as the one for the game.

"Hey, can we ride with you, Dr. Mack?" asked a dark-haired boy with dreamy brown eyes and a Gatorade stain on his jersey.

As a baffled Mack loaded up six baseball players—whose parents inexplicably trusted her with their kids' lives—Linc pulled up next to her with Sunshine hanging out of the passenger window of his truck. The grin he sent her went straight to her gut.

She wished things could be different. Because she would love a side of big, blond, handsome trouble.

CHAPTER 25

Linc watched as Mack powered through another set of chest flies on his weight bench, her walking boot propped up on a crate he'd liberated from his garage. She was a week out from her injury, and once the small-town charm of being looked in on and catered to had worn off, she was going as stir-crazy as his crew at the station.

In a week, they'd responded to four fender benders, three false alarms, and a cat stuck in a drainpipe. They'd completed every training scheduled, a new, boring record. Mack had spent the week pushing paper and wheeling herself around non-life-threatening illnesses and injuries at the clinic on a stool while her health care coworkers kept eagle eyes on her to make sure she wasn't overdoing it.

But he was picking up on something that ran deeper than just impatience. There was something brewing beneath Mack's very attractive surface. It felt like a dark cloud of thick, black smoke that hung over them, between them, obscuring his view.

She blew out a breath at the top, then lowered the dumbbells slowly.

"I meditated today. For fifteen freaking minutes," she complained.

"That's not a good thing?" he asked, gritting his teeth and working his way through triceps dips on the rack.

She sat up, let the weights drop to the floor. "I had fifteen freaking minutes to spare because I've got nothing else to do. I've read every medical journal I'd banked for the last six months. Caught up on all the podcasts I follow. I don't have any yard work to do because your guys mowed for me again yesterday—thank you again, by the way. I can't run. I can't take air shifts. All I can do is stare at those daffodil-yellow walls and write prescriptions for UTIs and hay fever."

"Yeah, yeah. Quit whining. My guys are in the home stretch of their hair-growing challenge," Linc complained. "Al lost another bet and had to shave off one of his eyebrows. The women are measuring leg hair. The guys are looking like the cops from *Super Troopers* only less well-groomed."

She stood and he dropped from the bars, facing each other in the tight space, sweating, frustrated.

He was tired of waiting. Tired of not kissing her. Linc moved in. His hands settled on her hips, and he watched the sparks fly in those eyes. *My favorite shade of green*, he decided.

His body reacted to hers immediately, cock springing to life, pulse kicking up. Every sense was heightened because he was touching Mackenzie O'Neil. He felt like he was walking into a fire.

She was nervous. The pulse at the base of that slim neck fluttered away, and he longed to brush his mouth against it. But his focus was on her mouth. She favored red lipstick. He wanted to see it smeared. To have her step out from behind those barriers long enough to ruin those perfect red lines.

Messing up the outward perfection of Dr. Dreamy was his new mission in life.

"I'm gonna kiss you now," he stated.

Heavy lids lowered over those eyes as her focus locked on to his mouth. He wondered if she knew she was nodding. Taking his time, he slid his hands all the way up her sides to her shoulders, that delicate neck, and cupped her face.

Romance was not dead. It was a living, breathing thing in the room.

He paused in his approach, a breath away from those red, red lips. Her breathing was ragged, and he noticed his was too. They stood that way, breathing the same air. Feeling the pulse of desire as it awakened like a dragon between them.

She broke first. And he thanked the gods in the heavens when those lips crashed into his. She kissed him like she needed it, needed *him*, to survive. There was no gentle brush, no savoring. This was a devouring. She pivoted and slammed him against the wall. One hand shot into his hair and tugged hard. She shoved her other hand under his shirt and touched his bare, sweaty skin.

His hard-on was in danger of rupturing when she shimmied up against him. Vision going gray, he spun them again so her back was to the wall. For a moment, they each grappled for the upper hand, then decided it didn't matter since they were both ravaging the other.

He slid a big hand under her shirt and cupped one perfect breast.

Obligingly, she yanked her tank over her head and threw it over his shoulder.

"God bless America," he breathed before diving back into the kiss.

She snickered into his mouth. "Is that the swoony firefighter version of dirty talk?"

"Baby, I want to take my cock out and shove you to your knees. I want to put my hands on this wall and fuck your mouth until your eyes water. When I'm done with you, I want eye makeup and lipstick everywhere."

Her eyes widened. Then she smiled. A sharp, shark-like grin.

"That's better," she whispered and shoved her hand into his shorts.

He was going to die on his feet with a beautiful woman gripping his cock. Linc hoped they'd put that on his tombstone.

"For the love of God, woman, slow down."

"Nope." She brushed her thumb over the unfairly sensitive head of his dick that was leaking like a fucking sieve. "I want to see you on your knees, looking up at me while you taste me."

Yep. Dead.

"I think I've been waiting my whole life for you." His confession on a groan, a breath, a prayer ruined everything.

Just like that, the fearless flight physician lost her nerve. He felt her stiffen up, muscles going to concrete, spine tensing to steel.

Her hand released him, the waistband of his shorts snapping back in an insult to his erection. He winced but didn't move.

"What's wrong?" he asked.

"Nothing," she said, trying to wriggle out of his arms. "I just don't feel like doing this right now."

"You're afraid." He stated the truth, simply and without malice.

She reacted as if he'd struck her. A button pushed.

Mack's lip curled in a sneer. But he saw it. That glimmer of fear in those green eyes. The shadows accentuated the scar.

"I am not afraid."

She enunciated each word crisply. And he wondered if she thought that would make it true.

"We're both attracted to each other. Both unattached. Both interested. But something's holding you back, and I think that something is fear."

"You start spewing things like that, and it's a real mood killer, Hotshot."

He could feel the connection they had, their bodies pressed against each other, heartbeats racing. He wasn't misreading signs, making things up. She *wanted* him. He *craved* her. But that black smoke made an impenetrable wall between them.

"What's wrong with being honest, Dreamy?"

"Back off, Hotshot," she said, shoving a hand between them.

Understanding fear, he gave her space. He took a seat on the weight bench she'd vacated. He wasn't running from this.

"Talk to me, Mackenzie. Tell me what this is about."

"What do you want to hear?" she demanded, picking her shirt up off the floor.

He mourned the loss of her streamlined raspberry sports bra. That view of the stomach he wanted to lick, to bite, to jet his release on, to lay his head on.

"I thought I'd made that clear. I want you."

"In what capacity? A quick fuck? A long-term girlfriend? Because I'm neither of those things." Her words were sharp, hard.

"Tell me what *you* want, Mackenzie."

"I asked you first."

Fine. Truth. "First, I want to see that lipstick smeared on your mouth, my mouth, my cock, and any damn where else you want to kiss me. Nothing's off-limits for you, Dreamy. Then I want to feel you come around me. I want to be holding you when you let go. I want to go off with you. After that, I want to eat ice cream in bed with you. Then I figured we'd date for enough time to convince you that fate brought you here exactly when we both needed it. We'll have a wedding. Probably a big one because the whole station is gonna want to be there and you've seen the size of my family. Sunshine can be our flower dog. We'll live a long, happy life together. How do you feel about kids? I wouldn't mind a couple. But I'd rather have you."

She sagged against the wall, blew out a swift breath. "I'm only here for six months," she argued.

"That's your plan. Plans can change."

"That's what people say when it's someone else's plan."

"Baby, I'm just asking you to be open to the possibility."

"The possibility of what? Fucking you and one of us discarding the other after a few weeks? Or giving up the career I've had my eye on since I was six years old and becoming a small-town wife?"

He wasn't sure which outcome scared her more. "Fine. We'll move. Anywhere your career takes you. Me and Sunshine will be there."

"Linc." Her voice broke. "We haven't even had sex, and you're planning a future."

"We can remedy that soon enough." His dick pulsed its agreement. "But I'd rather talk to you first. What's got you so riled, Mackenzie?"

"Riled?" She paced in front of him.

Irritation crackled off her. Irritation and that fear again.

"You pressuring me is not attractive."

He felt his own spine stiffen. *So they were both button pushers.* "I'm not pressuring you. I didn't shove your hand down my pants. I didn't take your shirt off."

Flustered now, he saw. Her cheeks were flushed, eyes glassy.

"Just because you're used to getting in a woman's pants doesn't mean you're getting in mine," she said.

"What the hell is this, Mack?" Now he was getting mad.

"I'm saying your confidence doesn't mean I have to fuck you."

"You're damn right it doesn't. Now, tell me what this is

189

really about. Because I'm not ashamed of how I live my life. How I treat the people in it."

"You bounce from woman to woman, never getting too close. Now, you're claiming that I'm 'different' and I'm 'special' and I need to give up everything so I can be different and special for you."

Linc's hands closed into fists on his knees. "I'm gonna give you a pass on that one. Because you're pissed off and scared. But don't put *your* shit on me. I've been nothing but honest with you."

"Are you saying I haven't been honest with you?"

"I'm saying you aren't being honest with yourself. You're scared because you feel something. I feel it too. But the difference is I'm up for the adventure. I'm not interested in hiding from it. Maybe you're more comfortable with being numb?"

She threw her hands up in the air. "I can't believe I almost—"

"What?" he asked, standing. "Let yourself feel something real? Be not completely in control for once in your life?"

"Fuck off, Linc."

"Back at you, Dreamy," he said, brushing past her to the door. "You can let yourself out."

He'd deny her the fight she was itching for. The reason she could use to back away. Call it quits. Hide.

He wanted to stay in the gym. To pound his mad out on the heavy bag. He hated that even after she'd dug her claws into him, after she'd taken a direct shot, he was still hard for her. He still wanted her. Desperately.

But he was just the affable good guy with no real feelings. Or the man-whore.

The front door closed with an almost slam.

She left, her lipstick still intact. But his heart wasn't.

CHAPTER 26

Mack limped into her place under a full head of steam. The evening hobble around the block had done little to calm her temper.

"How *dare* he," she said to her empty living room. She stormed into the kitchen, intending to make a cup of tea. But as was now her habit, she looked out the window. Linc was still in his gym. He was shirtless now. Even from this distance, she could see the sweat glisten on that perfect body. He threw a vicious uppercut into the bag with a rage she felt echo in her bones. She turned her back on the scene.

"Making assumptions. Calling me a control freak and a coward."

He hadn't. Exactly. Not in those words. But he'd *implied* it.

"He has no right to judge me," she muttered to herself and opened the refrigerator.

There was an open bottle of white wine on the door. She filled a glass almost to the rim.

She was agitated. With the boot, she couldn't run. She couldn't work out the way she was used to. That was it.

Or maybe it was the fact that he spoke the truth.

The tiny voice in her head was unwelcome. And annoying.

"I decide who I want to sleep with and when," she said aloud.

She'd *wanted* to sleep with *him*. She'd *wanted* to straddle him on a weight bench and ride him, chests pressed, sweat mingling, breath coming hard.

But she'd thought of her shadows. Of the scars. And had changed her mind.

She closed her eyes. She hadn't changed her mind. She'd chickened out.

She spared another glance out the window. He was still boxing. Brutal. Violent.

Mad she could respect.

He hadn't unleashed that on her. He hadn't risen to the bait of a fight. And in doing so, he'd won.

"What is wrong with me?" She glanced down, realized she didn't have a fluffy yellow Lab waiting to hear her confessional. She was alone. As always.

Mack took the wine into the living room and turned on the TV. If she couldn't run the mad out of her system, maybe she could binge-watch it away.

But all she saw was the hurt in Linc's eyes. The way he absorbed the blow she'd thrown. He'd been honest and real. She'd been the one to hide behind her defenses and take potshots.

Why?

Because the damn fire chief was right. She was scared. Shaking in her air cast scared.

He made her want things she had no business wanting. He made her feel things she had no business feeling. Lincoln Reed was nothing but a charming, built, sexy deviation from her plan. She wasn't wrong for ending things before they got started.

But she'd done it badly. She'd hurt him needlessly. Worse, she'd accused him of pressuring her.

When had she turned into such a damn coward?

"Fuck."

She turned off the TV, left the wine on the coffee table, and limped her way upstairs.

She took a long, hot shower, hoping to wash away some of the self-loathing. Some of the icy fear that collected in her belly. Closing her eyes under the spray, she let herself think about his hands on her, his mouth. The dirty talk mixed with the sweet.

She wanted Lincoln Reed. And for some reason, that scared the ever-living shit out of her.

Shifting her weight carefully on her good foot, she reached for the shampoo and for the reasons why she was too gutless to let the man into her bed.

She loved a good fling. The rush of it. The comfort in knowing exactly what the expectations—or lack thereof—were. *Linc had made his expectations clear,* she thought.

The man wanted too much, asked too much of her.

But he wasn't guilty of anything other than being honest with her.

Dammit. She was going to have to apologize to him.

It was the maddening thing about being an adult. She wanted to hold on to her righteous mad, not be faced with her own shortcomings, her own responsibility in the problem.

Being a responsible adult sucked. She could almost see the appeal of her mother's choices. No sense of responsibility or empathy. Andrea—Auhn-DREE-ah, never Andrea—O'Neil Leyva Mann or whatever her name was now was capable and happy to look out for only one person in this life. It didn't matter how many husbands or boyfriends she had, how many children she had. Nothing came before Andrea's wants and needs. Nothing was satisfied before her own addictions.

The water was starting to go cold. And so were the fingers

around her heart with thoughts of her mother. Still unsettled, Mack got out and toweled off. She ran a comb through her hair, so tired she just wanted to go to bed. But the thought of aggressive bedhead in the office tomorrow had her reluctantly reaching for the hair dryer.

Hair dry, head aching, heart dented, she wriggled back into the boot—doctor's orders—and half-heartedly clomped into the bedroom.

She turned on the bedside lamp and petulantly let the towel drop. It sat for a full two seconds before she decided she'd be more pissed at herself in the morning for leaving a wet towel on the floor and tossed it over the door to dry.

Biting her lip, she gave in to her curiosity and looked out the bedroom window. His lights were on upstairs. He was probably getting ready for bed too. Alone.

Hadn't she spent enough time alone?

Could two people enter into an agreement wanting different things? Was there some sort of tenuous middle ground they could agree on?

Strings, commitments. That was what Linc was after for reasons she couldn't fathom. She'd had no use for them, always assuming that someday, when she landed where she was going to stay, strings and commitments would follow in a natural progression.

She saw movement in his bedroom. A big, muscled arm and then the rest of—

Dear God. The man was *naked*.

She was naked.

They were staring at each other through panes of glass and an uncrossable swatch of green grass. The fence between them was both a physical and metaphorical boundary.

Chief Reed in all his naked splendor was breathtaking. The

body of a gladiator. That broad inked chest. Those hefty biceps and big hands. Thick muscled thighs. And between them…

"Yeah, I definitely need to apologize," she muttered. The numbness of the shower dissolved as a wave of heat warmed her cheeks.

He watched her neutrally, coolly. She was too far away to see the clench of his jaw, the stirring of the half-ready cock. But she felt the push and pull of anger, hurt, and a want that just might be willing to forgive anything.

She craved that body. Could picture it over her, in her, under her. Her knees trembled, and she opened her lips to say something, anything to him.

But he was drawing the curtains closed, leaving her all alone again.

————

That night, Mack dreamt. Dark, shadowy dreams that squeezed at her heart, made her blood run cold.

The room. That hot, stuffy room. With the disintegrating Kermit-green carpet. The twin mattress on the floor and the soft pink blanket. Her constant companion through moves and new men Mom said to call Uncle. It was the only thing in this place that gave her any comfort.

The cheap door might as well have been a steel vault. Her little hands couldn't break the lock. So dark. She was going to be in trouble when Mom came home and saw that she'd used the corner of her tiny room as a toilet. She'd had no choice. It wasn't her fault.

But things like choice and fault didn't matter to Mom.

The window. Painted shut. It had taken hours, maybe even an entire day. She wasn't sure. But she'd methodically pried it open with the open door of a Matchbox car. The ground was so far below. But the air felt so good on her face. It dried the tears and felt like the biggest of victories.

Could she jump? She was scared. Was the ground worse than that hot, stuffy room? Worse than no food and being alone?

Then the scene was shifting. She wasn't alone. Linc was on the ground.

"I'll catch you," he promised.

She trusted him. She believed him. She was falling.

There was a face on a stark white sheet that was slowly turning red. *His* face. The face of a dead man. The one she'd killed.

Mack woke, gasping desperately for air.

She swung her legs over the side of the bed, clumsily kicking the bedrail with her boot.

She held a hand over her scar. The phantom sensation of pain made her skin feel clammy. It was just after four. And there was no way she was going back to sleep.

Two and a half hours of unpacking every remaining moving box and carefully stacking all the cardboard neatly in the garage that was too small to house her SUV later, Mack picked up her phone and dialed.

Violet answered chipperly. "Nguyen residence, Violet speaking."

"Hey, Vi. It's Mack."

She managed to sound both amused and annoyed at the same time. "I *know* it's you."

"I didn't think your mom and dad's landline had caller ID," Mack said.

"It doesn't. But that doesn't mean I don't recognize your voice. Jeez, Mack. Sometimes I think you think you're a stranger."

The easy, almost sisterly banter soothed Mack's soul. She

settled onto the kitchen chair and propped her foot up on the table. "How's the school year going so far? Any trouble with that shithead from last year?"

"Oh. My. God. So get this. I show up on the first day of school ready to just lay it out and be serious with her like you told me, right?"

"Right."

"So I get there, and I'm all ready to be all calm and sh—stuff. Tell her she's no longer welcome to be disrespectful toward me or anyone else. And one of Lynnetta's minions walks by and she's all 'Did you hear about Lynnetta?' and I'm like 'No,' and she's like, 'Lynnetta got caught bullying some loser eighth-grader online over the summer, and her parents were so pissed they shipped her off to some boarding school for mean girls.'"

"No way," Mack said, knowing the required response.

"That's *exactly* what I said. So new year, no Lynnetta, and tenth grade is basically the best year of my life," Violet said.

"That's amazing."

"I know, right? Oh, hang on. I need to grab breakfast before school. Want to talk to Mom?"

"Yeah, that would be great," Mack said.

"Hey, come home sometime before you become an actual stranger, okay?" Violet said. She didn't wait for a reply. "Moooooom! It's Mack!"

"Mack!" The joy and surprise in Dottie Nguyen's voice made Mack feel both guilty and relieved.

"Hey, Dottie."

"I was just thinking about you. How's Benevolence? How are you adapting to small-town doctoring? Do people call you 'doc'?"

Of course Dottie would remember the name of the town Mack had mentioned in passing when she'd told the Nguyens she was relocating. The woman's care and attention to detail were in stark contrast to Mack's mother's self-centered existence.

"As a matter of fact, they do call me 'doc,'" she laughed.

"When can we come visit?" Dottie demanded.

She meant it too.

Mack's heart clenched just a little. She'd always been grateful—painfully, pathetically so—for Dottie and Winston Nguyen (comically known as Win-Win) and the ten weeks she'd had with them as a child. Strangers who'd immediately proved to be far more stable than any blood relative Mack had known. They'd all cried when she left. She'd spent years after wishing it could have been longer. When she'd turned eighteen, she'd found Dottie on Facebook and sent her a message. "You probably don't remember me, but…"

Dottie had remembered. And she'd been overjoyed then too. Had peppered her with questions about how she was and what she was doing. And when Mack had confessed her desire to go into medicine, Winston, a thin, energetic podiatrist with an entire catalog of terrible foot jokes, had counseled her on premed programs. They'd offered to help her pay for college. She hadn't accepted. It was a point of pride to do it all on her own. But the memory of that earnest offer still made the stalwart Mack just a little teary-eyed.

"Vi just asked me when I was coming to visit you guys." Violet had been the foster kid Dottie and Winston *could* keep. Mack had been both overjoyed for them and profoundly sad that it hadn't been her. But the decision hadn't been in the Nguyens' hands any more than it had been in her own.

"No reason not to do both," Dottie insisted. "What are you doing for Thanksgiving?"

Mack laughed, feeling her chest loosen. "I haven't even picked up candy for trick-or-treaters yet."

"I know you, Mackenzie. If I don't nail you down and make you put the date in your calendar, it will never happen. We'll come to you for Thanksgiving," Dottie decided.

Mack felt a tickle of panic. "My place is the size of a dollhouse."

"We'll get a hotel room."

"I don't know how to cook a Thanksgiving feast, and I might be on call."

"Win will use us as sous chefs. And I know darn well that town of yours has an urgent care that will be open on Thanksgiving. And if you *do* get called to the clinic, we'll hold dinner for you. But you are expressly forbidden from taking a flight shift that day. Got it?"

"Yeah, about that," Mack said, studying the ugly boot on her foot. "I can't take any air med shifts until I'm out of the walking boot."

There was a beat of silence, and then, "Why are you in a walking boot, Mackenzie?" Dottie shrieked.

Mack filled her in with a toned-down version.

"What kind of town is this? Was he on meth? Are you living in a meth hub?" Dottie demanded.

Mack laughed. "No. I promise. It's actually a very nice town. And that's kind of why I was calling. There's a guy."

Another pause during which she could hear Dottie tear open a single-serve bag of chips, her one and only vice. "Tell me *everything*. But be prepared to circle back to the broken ankle thing so I can guilt-trip you about not telling us the moment it happened. We care about you, Mackenzie O'Neil."

"I know. And thanks. And I'm sorry."

"Good. Now spill it."

CHAPTER 27

G ood morning, Mackenzie." Russell clapped his palms together enthusiastically. "Guess what you get to do today?"

She was already exhausted and barely in the door of her office. She was not ready for enthusiasm of any sort.

The boot was pissing her off more than usual today. Hell, everything was. Everything was unsettled and would remain so until she hashed things out with Linc. But she needed to plan out her apology. Carefully structure it. Give him a couple of days to cool off. She needed at least two or three days. Maybe put together an outline and then work her way up to a Venn diagram?

She wasn't a groveler. But she'd been an asshole, and he deserved a real apology.

"What do I get to do today?"

Gingerly, she lowered herself into the chair she'd yet to replace. It was a matter of principle now. She was determined to wait out the chair's life span. It couldn't hang on much longer. It gave a terrifying clunking noise and dropped her three inches. But the chair remained intact, and she remained upright.

Russell watched her chair drama with amusement. "You

and Freida get to go to the fire station for firefighter physicals today," he said with a big, toothy grin.

Shit.

"I don't think that's a great idea," she hedged.

"Oh, it's not really a choice," he said, dropping into the chair in front of her desk and steepling his fingers. "You see, the physician who does the physicals has to examine close to forty patients. Burly, farting firefighters who don't take kindly when you point out that they are in danger of failing the physical requirements of their service."

"Your daughter is one of those burly, farting firefighters," she reminded him. "And what requirements?"

"So is your man friend," he said with a knowing tilt of his head. "Benevolence monitors the physical fitness of its firefighters annually. The station has its own tests of aerobic capacity, grip strength, endurance. That kind of thing. But they are also required to submit to a physical exam every year."

Double shit.

"Linc isn't feeling very friendly toward me right now," she said.

"Care to talk about it?" Russell offered.

He meant it, she realized. And there was something both comforting and dismaying about that.

"I'd rather let it fester a while," she told him.

"Don't let it fester too loudly," he warned. "Freida will sense it and latch on."

"Sense what?" Freida appeared in the door wearing scrubs with little firefighters and dalmatians on them.

"Nice scrubs," Mack said.

"Bought 'em special for today. I love firefighter physical day! When are we leaving? What will I sense?"

The Benevolence Fire Department was a large, two-story building that took up half a block on the south side of town. Three huge garage bays, all of them open to the crisp fall breeze, held gleaming trucks—apparatus—ready and waiting to be called up for duty.

The floors, a polished concrete, looked clean enough to eat from. There was a wall of cherry-red metal lockers stocked with personal protection equipment. The space smelled like diesel and oil and polish.

"Hey, Doc." Assistant Chief Kelly Wu was a sharp, take-charge kind of woman who wasn't afraid to get her hands dirty. As demonstrated by the engine grease she was wiping off on a rag.

"Nice to see you, Kelly," Mack said, glancing around but not seeing Linc. Her stomach tickled like it did on her way to a call. Nerves and excitement. The fight had raised her adrenaline, and she wondered if the apology would do the same.

"Same place as usual?" Freida asked, patting her med bag.

"You got it. They put the screens up so you can go back and forth between exam rooms," Kelly said, nodding toward the stairs.

He was probably up there. Was he still mad? Was he still thinking about what an ass she'd made of herself? Had he given up on her? Was he even now turning his attention to some other less frustrating woman? Maybe one of the nurses from the ED.

Russell was right, she thought with a wince. *Shame doesn't help.*

She'd fucked up. Now she'd own up to it. And if he wasn't interested in getting naked with her now, it was his loss. She was excellent in bed.

"You all want some help with the bags?" Kelly offered.

"No thanks," Mack said, adjusting her grip on her own. "We've got 'em."

Freida looked disappointed. "You're still going to make them take their shirts off though, right?" she whispered as they mounted the steps.

The stairway opened up into a common room with a kitchen shoved into the corner and a semicircle of recliners facing a billboard-size TV. In another section, there was a pool table and a couple of couches and tables. Squished between the TV area and the pool area was a folding table in front of two makeshift exam spaces that looked more like blanket forts.

"Doc, Freida." Brody Lighthorse approached from the hallway, a cup of coffee in his hand.

"That better be black, and you all better be fasted for the blood draw," Mack said, eyeing the mug.

"Not our first rodeo. And just so you know, everyone's already bitching about being hungry." There was just the slightest edge to his tone. But Mack had been programmed from birth to pick up on subtle cues.

"Let's do the blood draws first, then circle back to the physicals," she decided.

"Good enough," he said. He gave her a long, quiet look.

It gave her the distinct impression that Linc may have mentioned her asshole snit fit from the night before. They probably all knew. That familiar, ugly shame curled again in her belly.

"I'll round up the guys," he said and disappeared down the stairs. Mack ignored the bad vibes, the nerves, and helped Freida set up the blood draw station. A minute later, Brody's voice crackled through the speakers in the building.

"BFD crew, please report to the second floor for physicals."

She could hear the groans from all corners of the building.

It was going to be a hell of a day.

Linc, Mack noted, purposely got into Freida's line for his blood draw. But he was too polite to completely avoid her.

"Nice to see you, Doc," he said. His tone was light, friendly even. But it was missing that undercurrent of "you know you want me." The intimacy that had been there since the first conversation had been snuffed out. By something she'd done.

"Ow!" The short, stocky firefighter with what looked like a well-waxed handlebar mustache whimpered when she jabbed the needle into the vein.

"Don't be such a wuss," Skyler, Russell's daughter, snorted at him from the other end of the table.

"I'm not a wuss! You're a wuss." He pouted, then twirled the end of his mustache.

"Children," Mack threatened calmly.

"Sorry, Doc."

Linc disappeared shortly after his needle stick, and Mack moved on to the physical exams. "I hope you all are wearing underwear today because I'll need you to strip down once you're behind the screens. Got it?"

"Why wait?" One of the burly, potentially farty firefighters yanked his T-shirt over his head and whirled it around with the enthusiasm, if not the skill, of an exotic dancer. Catcalls and cheers rang out. Within thirty seconds, the first dozen patients had stripped down to their unmentionables. Some smart-ass started blaring "Pony" by Ginuwine. It was raining articles of clothing.

Zane and Skyler were bumping butts to the beat. One of the larger, older firefighters was using his discarded pants as butt floss. A younger volunteer jumped onto the pool table and started doing push-ups while a couple other guys and Freida threw dollar bills at him.

It was the most ridiculous, entertaining thing she'd ever witnessed on the clock.

"Try not to get your heart rates too jacked up," Mack yelled over the music. A firefighter with half a mustache and only one eyebrow sauntered her way, crooking his finger at her.

She shook her head, but he was insistent, pulling her into a limping tango.

"I love firefighter physical day," Freida shouted, switching over to five-dollar bills.

———

Mack was good and tired by the time Chief Reed strolled into her exam room. They'd thoughtfully provided one of the mechanic's wheeled stools for her to scoot around, saving her from limping back and forth between exam spaces. But after thirty-two physicals, she was burnt, hungry, and grumpy.

"We don't have any green tea, but you're welcome to the coffee," he said, jerking his thumb in the direction of the kitchen.

Even cool and detached, Linc was still polite. And it made her feel like a steaming shit sandwich.

"Thanks. I'm almost done," she said. "Have a seat."

He pulled his T-shirt over his head in that one-handed move that hot guys all seemed to have mastered and took the chair next to her.

Her mouth went dry. And her carefully crafted apology vanished from her brain.

She was muscle drunk.

"We'll start with temperature and blood pressure," she croaked, then cleared her throat. He held out an arm for the cuff. She secured it around his bicep, trying hard not to touch bare skin or stare too long at his naked torso.

When the thermometer was in place between his delicious lips, she swallowed back nerves and took the plunge.

"I owe you an apology."

"No shit, Sherlock," he muttered around the thermometer.

"No talking. Last night, I was frustrated with…well, a lot of things. I took it out on you, and that was unfair. I'm sorry. I deliberately pushed your buttons and tried to make you feel bad. And that's embarrassingly immature."

She took the reading from the BP monitor and recorded it on her laptop.

"You've been nothing but patient and kind, and I've sent you about a hundred mixed signals," she admitted. "I came here with a plan, and that plan didn't include you. But it also didn't include this." She tapped the boot.

"Can I say something?" he mumbled.

"No. It'll screw up your temperature. Anyway, I don't have an example of a healthy relationship. It's not an excuse for me being an unmitigated ass last night," she said. "I should know better. But I have baggage. My mother. Let's leave it at she wasn't equipped to care for children. I grew up never knowing what I was coming home to. The happy sober mom. The drunk needy one. Or to half-packed boxes because we were being evicted or she'd met a new Uncle So-and-So who was going to play the white knight for all of us."

The thermometer beeped. But neither made a move to remove it.

"I've never done relationships. I don't know what a healthy one looks like. How it works. I'm scared shitless of failing. I came here to get myself back on track. But you're so damn tempting. And now I'm not sure I want to or even can stick to my guns. Last night…" She paused, blew out a breath. "I didn't like what I saw in the mirror. So maybe my plan needs adjusting."

He took the thermometer out of his mouth, handed it to her.

"Now can I say something?" he asked. Those blue eyes were unreadable.

The alarm went off inside the building. It vibrated down to her bones.

"It's a big one, boys and girls," Zane crowed, sprinting for the stairs. "Bring your A game."

Linc's jaw clenched as he dragged on his shirt.

"We'll talk," he said.

She nodded. "Go. I'll take Sunshine home with me."

His eyes softened just a bit, and he nodded. "Thanks, Doc."

Then he was gone.

CHAPTER 28

It was a bastard of a blaze in a small apartment building on the north side of town. It started on the third floor and was being a real bitch about it.

The heat it pumped off made it necessary to move the command vehicle and incident command back half a block.

It was a hot one. Neighbors, dozens of them, who lined up behind the barricades were already sweating. They'd evacuated the nearby buildings as a precaution. Traffic was rerouted, and his team was inside searching each apartment. The crew from Baylorsville was on standby to lend a hand or cover any other calls coming in.

But for now, Linc's crew had it under control.

A textbook response.

Most of the residents were accounted for. But there was still a family that lived on the third floor that no one had heard from.

The can man, or woman in this case, radioed down. "Command. Can man. I'm opening this bitch up. She's a hot one, Chief."

"Copy that, Lucille. Need any help up there?"

"Nah," she called back. "Don't want to catch any of those fine 'staches on fire. Can man out."

"Roger that. Keep me posted."

He directed one of the hose teams around the back of the building where the can man was opening up the roof. "Let's drown her," he told them. "Command to search and rescue. Wu, CAN report."

There was static and then the calm voice of his assistant chief. "We cleared two units on the third floor. But I'm not trusting the ceiling to hold up for the two on the east side. Heavy smoke. Lot of flame toward the stairs. No sprinklers. It's eating fast. Plus the fire escapes on the back are a joke."

"I'll send a team up the ladder on the east side," Linc promised. "Mind your head. Lucille is opening up the rear west corner."

Wu was silent for a beat. "Chief, we're hearing a dog barking. Gonna do another sweep."

A gangly volunteer jogged up. "Chief. One of the residents says she thinks someone's home in that last unit east side. Family's got an elderly mother-in-law living with them and a big-ass dog."

"I need a ladder team on the east side third floor," Linc radioed.

There was a rumble from inside the building that he felt under his feet on the street.

"Someone tell me what the fuck that was," he called.

"Fuck. Chief. The stairs just went. We're all fine, mostly, but we're still on the third west side. No way out," Kelly reported in.

"Hang tight, Wu. We're coming to get you."

Linc waved over one of the volunteers and shrugged into his turnout coat. Sam was a twenty-five-year veteran with the department and, thanks to a bum knee, was relegated to nonrescue work.

"What's up, Chief?"

"Got a team trapped on the third west side, possible minor injuries. And a potential entrapment on third east. Call second alarm. Get the Baylorsville company in here," Linc ordered, handing the man the radio's handset. "We need a ladder team over to the west side now."

It was protocol. Firefighters got rescued first. Otherwise, no one got rescued. But he trusted his team, and he was another able body already geared up.

He dodged the ladder truck as it maneuvered itself around the building and saw Skyler wave to the driver from the open third-floor window.

Linc jogged back to the engine and grabbed his SCBA. He threw the bottle on and was on the move in a second. Still strapping on the tank, he caught up to his second engine. The weight of it felt familiar, reassuring.

"We getting you up to the third?" the driver guessed.

"Yeah. Possible entrapment."

He didn't see quite as much action as he once had. Being chief carried other responsibilities. But when he got the chance, he took it.

The call for the second alarm went out over the radio. "Dispatch from Chestnut Street Command, take me to the second alarm," Sam said.

The fire escape in the back was a definite no-go. Supports were rusted through, and it had pulled completely out of the brick on the third floor.

A scant minute later, the engine crew had the ladder propped against the front of the building away from the flames. He climbed carefully, steadily up three floors to the unit's large front window. He felt the sway of the ladder as a man climbed behind him.

"This is chief to command. About to VES third floor unit

east side. Visibility limited." The smoke was already thick as fog inside. And it was the smoke that posed the real danger.

"Be careful up there," came Sam's cautionary warning over the radio.

Linc heard it then. Faintly over the crackle of flames, more sirens. The bark of a dog.

Training and experience were his guides. Vent. Enter. Search. He slipped the breaker from his pocket and, with a sharp blow, shattered the glass.

"Anyone here?" he shouted into the room as he cleared the window frame. Smoke billowed out the window, obscuring his vision. But there was the bark of a dog again. More insistent. More helpless.

"Chief Reed entering the structure third floor east side for search and rescue," he said into the radio.

He dropped over the sill and hunched down. It was a small, boxy living room with a cheap sofa that was a minute or two from going up in flames. Those beautiful red and orange licks teased their way through the far wall, entering the apartment like ghosts from hell.

Training dictated that responders clear rooms on their hands and knees, keeping their heads out of the noxious smoke. But when the opportunity allowed, Linc stayed on his feet, moving and clearing faster.

The bark was a lonely howl now from the back of the apartment.

"Front room clear," he said for the benefit of the firefighter at the top of the ladder.

He picked his way over worn carpet into a kitchen. It was hot enough that the linoleum was peeling. The smoke was even thicker here. If there was anyone or anything alive inside, they were living on borrowed time.

He listened to the radio chatter. His search and rescue crew was out, safe and switching to hose lines. The rest of the apartments in the building had been cleared. More units were stacking up on the scene.

The bedrooms, three of them, bumped off a skinny hallway. He kicked open the first door and swept quickly. One double bed. A crib. Both empty. Thank fuck. He checked the closet and under the bed before moving back into the hallway. The second bedroom was empty as well. He gave the third door a shove, dropping to his knees now. Inside, he found a wet towel on the floor. It had provided a seam to block the smoke until he'd opened the door.

Visibility was almost nil as the smoke rushed him.

The flames were eating at the wall, licking at the neatly made bed. He saw the body under the window, the dog lying next to it, and crawled forward.

The dog's tail wagged slowly. The body was a woman. Elderly, frail. Unconscious. With his gloves, he couldn't tell if there was a pulse, and there was no time to check.

"Hey there, buddy. Let's get you two out of here," Linc said through his mask.

"Command to BFD chief." His radio crackled. "Can man's reporting the roof is gonna go any second now. Get the hell out of there."

"Copy that. Found two victims. One unconscious woman, one large dog. Third floor. Back bedroom. Extracting now."

"Copy that. Holding for you at the window."

The flames were coming for them. Hypnotic flares, sensual snakes of orange and red. The black was closing in. The black and the heat. He could hear the monster's roar through all his protective layers.

Sweat, every drop of water in his body, was being pushed

through his pores. There was a rumble and roar. He felt the floor shake under him and prayed the ceiling in this little room would hold just another minute or so.

"What the fuck was that?" Linc yelled.

The dog gave a pitiful whimper and crawled closer to him.

"Anyone have eyes on that?" Sam called.

"Engine 21 to Command. Ceiling in front room of east unit collapsed."

And just like that, Linc was trapped in a burning apartment with someone's grandmother and a dog that only had a minute or two left to live.

"There's a window in the back bedroom. Get me the ladder!" he yelled into the radio.

"Copy that, Chief."

He got to his feet and hooked his gloved hands under the woman's armpits. She was a tiny thing, and pulling her the short distance to the window took little effort. The dog belly crawled after them, its whimper barely audible above the snarl of the fire. They were in the belly of the beast, and it was only a matter of time before the roof rained down, crushing them.

Linc braced the woman against him and shoved at the window, relieved when it budged an inch and then two. Air. He couldn't feel it or smell it through his mask. But it was there.

His breath was coming in pants, and he carefully slowed it to manage his air.

"In place. Window is stuck," he reported.

The dog gratefully shoved his nose through the crack for a moment before turning his devoted attention back to the limp and lifeless woman in Linc's grasp. Back and forth, he went to breathe and then to lick.

It felt like hours, and as those precious seconds ticked by, Linc lost all visibility again. Clouds of smoke, an entire sky's worth, filled the room, black and hot. And in another minute, there wouldn't be a life left to rescue.

He used his body to shield woman and dog from the flames that were closing in around them.

There was a rumble of engine, and he could just make out the ladder truck easing into place, half in the alley and half in the grass, its ladder extending toward him.

Linc shoved his hand out the window and waved.

The dull thud of a ladder hitting the brick was the sound of salvation.

As was the tap on the glass. The dog barked again.

"Extraction team in position. Window's stuck. Chief, might want to get back. I'm gonna bust the glass."

"Do it," he said, curling himself over his charges as the glass broke behind him and shards rained down on them all. He felt, rather than heard, the dog's pathetic whimper. "Gonna be okay, buddy," he promised. "Just hang in there."

Smoke poured through the window frame now. But he could see Zane's big, gloved hands and then the rest of him as he climbed into the room.

"Good timing, Stairmaster."

"I like to make an entrance."

Linc all but shoved the woman at him. Zane held the victim by the arms while another firefighter got her legs. And then they were gone. Disappearing onto the ladder in the rush of smoke.

"Your turn, buddy," Linc said, crouching down to find the dog. "Try not to bite me, okay? I'll forgive you if you do because this is scary shit, but it'll just slow us both down." There was no graceful way to do it. He moved by feel, kneeling down and shoving his helmeted head under the dog's belly. "I'm gonna wear you like Granny Lily's shawl, but you're getting out of here," he promised.

The dog gave a groan and shifted listlessly on his shoulders.

"Steady now," Linc said as he backed out the window, feeling for the rungs through gloves and boots. "Just another second."

He found the first rung and the second. And just as he swung out of the window and onto the ladder, the ceiling inside came crashing down.

Halle-fucking-lujah.

"Roof's going," he gasped into the radio as he climbed as quickly as he could under seventy pounds of limp dog. "Get us out of here."

Debris rained down on them as the ladder swung away from the building.

"Thank fuck," he sighed. The dog licked his mask.

"Real pretty scarf you got there, Chief," Zane called from just beneath him on the ladder.

Back on the ground, a paramedic found a pulse on the woman and had an oxygen mask strapped to her before Linc made it off the truck. Zane, still in his mask, helped him heft the dog off his shoulders onto a blanket on the ground.

He was weak. His fur was badly singed. And there was a nasty cut on one of his pads. But he looked up at Linc and wagged his tail. Linc dragged off the helmet and mask and took a deep breath.

"Here." Khalil, the six foot six ex-point guard for Benevolence's high school basketball team, handed Linc an oxygen mask.

He shook his head. "I don't need it."

"No, but your friend here could use some."

Together, they gently slipped the mask over the grateful dog's nose.

"Good boy," Linc said. "You saved Grandma."

The dog's tail tapped lightly as his eyes closed. Linc swore the dog was smiling.

CHAPTER 29

The late-night rain pelted the windows of the cottage. It was past her bedtime, but Mack wasn't inclined to admit that she felt compelled to wait up until she saw the lights come on at Linc's.

As a first responder herself, she had a unique perspective. She knew exactly how much training and protocol went into responding to an emergency. She was also acutely aware of all the ways a routine call could go sideways.

She turned the page in her novel—because she had time for fiction now—and adjusted the pillow under her boot again.

Sunshine snored contentedly, her fluffy head resting on Mack's shin. If she was going to do more dog sitting, she'd need a bigger couch.

She caught a glimpse of light from the backyard and craned her neck.

"Your daddy might be home," she told the dog. But Sunshine was too busy dreaming of rabbits and vanilla ice cream to respond.

Carefully, Mack eased her leg out from under the dog's head, replacing it with a pillow. She limped quietly into the kitchen and spied the lights on at Linc's.

"Good," she whispered.

The soft knock on the back door startled her. There on the other side of the glass was Lincoln Reed.

Illuminated by the lonely porch light, he was filthy. Ash and dirt streaked his face and forearms. Rain soaked his T-shirt through to the skin beneath. Those blue eyes burned brighter than any flame.

Mack knew what would happen if she opened the door. He knew it too. A frisson of understanding passed between them through the glass.

Her heart thudded in her chest. The familiar tendril of adrenaline awoke in her belly like a sleeping dragon.

She wanted *this*. She wanted *him*.

She reached for the handle and slowly slid the door open. Another pause. Another beat as they eyed each other, the attraction so palpable, she wondered how she ever thought she could ignore it.

"Send me home, Dreamy," he rasped.

In this moment, there was nothing she wanted more than this man's hands on her.

She shook her head. And it didn't take any more than that. Linc stepped inside. Into her space, into her arms.

He smelled of smoke and rain. His skin was wet and hot beneath her eager palms as she roamed his arms, his shoulders, his back. She felt the energy crackling off him, recognized the adrenaline of a call that couldn't be slept off.

There were other ways to burn it off, to ride that wave until the blood was cool again.

Carefully, he pulled the door shut behind him. Then his mouth was closing over hers.

Teeth and tongues tangled. Lips bruised. His hands slipped under the hem of her T-shirt to rest on the bare skin of her waist, thumbs skimming just under her breasts. She breathed him in, tasted him.

She let him lead as he backed her farther into the kitchen.

He lifted her onto the counter. Rain pattered steadily on the window above the sink.

"Linc."

"Don't change your mind. Please, Dreamy."

She cupped his face in her hands. "I'm not changing my mind. I just like saying your name while your hands are on me."

He dropped his forehead to hers. "Jesus. You level me."

"Hoping you plan on returning the favor," she said, nipping at his jaw.

He growled low in his throat and shoved a hand into her hair, gripping it tight.

She saw the clench of his jaw, the flutter of his pulse in his neck, as he carefully loosened his grip.

"You don't have to be gentle, Hotshot. I'm not some fragile flower."

"No, you're not," he said. His fingers tightened on her hair again, testing her. He guided her head back and took her mouth.

The fierceness of his desire sent her own heart galloping.

She ran her hands up his chest and dug her nails into his shoulder. His muscles tensed and bunched under her touch. His palms worshipped her skin, stroking over the flat of her stomach, the subtle dips of her waist and hips, and finally, finally the curves of her breasts.

Thank God she hadn't bothered with a bra tonight. If she had, she still wouldn't know exactly what it felt like when her nipples hardened against Linc's rough calluses.

Her head fell back, knocking smartly against a baby-blue cabinet door.

"Are you okay?"

But she was too busy reeling him in, tightening her legs around his hips so she could feel him.

"Hallelujah for sweatpants," she moaned when that thick shaft those pants didn't even try to contain notched against her clit.

Big, hard, and impossible to resist, just like the rest of him.

The ache that started between her legs before he touched her intensified to an empty throbbing.

Now she knew want. Desire. Lust. Need.

Everything before was a faded black-and-white photo. But Linc's body pressing hers against cabinet and counter was in full, high-definition color.

This was what had been missing.

He was who had been missing.

The magnitude of her train of thought, the tsunami of physical sensation, overwhelmed her. Terrified her to the bone. *This* felt like life and death. And that only made her more excited.

She reached between them and dragged the waistband of his sweats down. His cock sprang free triumphantly.

And those blue eyes bored into hers as she closed her fingers around his shaft. She stroked up and down and reveled in the shudder that rolled through his body, the moisture that leaked from the blunt crown.

He *wanted* her. *Craved* her. She knew it in her bones. And knowing was powerful.

Boldly, she slid her other hand into his pants and cupped his balls.

"Dreamy, if you don't stop looking at me like that or touching me like that, this is gonna be a real disappointment for us both," he said, gritting out the words.

"Make me."

His nostrils flared at the challenge, and she thought it was the sexiest thing she'd seen. At least until he slid his hands down to her hips and yanked her tight against him. She stroked him again, harder this time, taunting him. The head of his hard-on was pinned between them. The fabric of her shorts was saturated. Every time she stroked him, he was nudging up against her hungry clit.

With impatience, Linc grabbed her shorts and pulled.

She was so fucking glad she'd shaved her legs.

"Fuck me, Mackenzie," he breathed, skimming his hands up her bare thighs to her hips.

"That's the plan." Her breath was coming in quick draws already. She reached for him again, but he stopped her, pinning her hands to the cabinet behind her.

They both looked down. His veined cock strained toward her aching, empty pussy. Her muscles clenched and closed over nothing, anticipating what it would be like to be filled by him.

"I need a condom," he said.

He licked two fingers like they were a popsicle, and Mack nearly blacked out watching him slide them into her wet flesh.

"You came over here all hot and bothered and didn't bring one?" Her voice was shaking with need. Two fingers felt damn good.

"I didn't want to presume." Slowly, with the patience of a saint, he pulled his fingers out of her.

"Presume the fuck away, Hotshot." She ended on a hiss when he drove them back into her and flexed.

Any numbness she had carried with her thawed, then simmered.

"I need to be inside you. Feel you tighten on me, squeeze me."

On command, her walls spasmed around those skilled fingers.

"I want to know what it feels like when you come on me, Mackenzie. I need to know."

She didn't know how he could have so damn much to say while her body was ripping apart at the seams. He kept talking, kept pumping his fingers into her, and her body welcomed it, begged for it.

"I want to watch you come. I want to *make* you come. I want to see you when you're feeling nothing but good."

She wanted to touch him too. To do what he was doing to her. Make him feel out of control. But her hands, her fingers, gripped the edge of the counter convulsively. She was going to come on her kitchen counter without that fine cock making it past her opening.

It seemed wrong.

But wrong didn't stop the orgasm that was building in her.

It lifted her like the crest of a wave. Up and up she went, and then she detonated.

"Fuck. Yes, Mackenzie. Ride my hand, baby," Linc crooned to her. He forced her knees up higher, wider. Drove his fingers into her harder. And she closed around him, clamping onto him in beautiful, agonizing surrender.

"Linc," she gasped, trying to pull her soul back into her body.

"Now I really need a fucking condom."

"Upstairs. Bedroom," she said, slumping against his chest. The thunder of his heartbeat calmed her. She'd come apart on him, and he wasn't immune.

"Let's go, Dreamy. I've got plans to experience more of those orgasms of yours."

He wrapped her legs around his waist and dragged her off the counter.

She clung to him, knowing it was almost certain that her

legs wouldn't support her. "Don't wake Sunny. She's asleep on the couch."

The big firefighter, carting an adult woman, danced up the stairs in ninja-like silence.

"That was impressive," she whispered.

"I'm extremely motivated," he said, shoving open a door.

"Bathroom," she snickered.

"You could give me some directions here."

"I already had an orgasm," she said smugly.

"Dreamy, you don't want that to be your only one tonight."

"Point taken. Next door on the right."

They fell on the bed, where Mack reveled in the feel of his big body stretched out over hers. They fit like puzzle pieces reunited. He was hot and hard, every inch of him. It made her feel soft and delicate in comparison.

"I need to touch you," she hissed, shoving a hand between their bodies and palming him through the soft cotton of his pants. The head of his cock had once again fought and won the battle for freedom. It was the most erotic thing she'd ever seen in her life. "I fucking love sweatpants."

He thrust eagerly against her hand. "I'll wear them every fucking day if it gets you off."

She dragged the waistband down, down, down. Until his glorious dick sprang all the way free.

"I want to taste you," she said.

"Not this time. This time, it's gotta be fast and hard. You should find something to hang on to."

She gripped his shaft tighter.

"Funny." He dipped his head to her breast and sucked the nipple into his mouth. When his teeth closed over the sensitive peak, she hissed. Remembering that she had the upper hand, she gave his erection a rough stroke.

There was too much here. Too much to feel. Too much sensation electrifying her nerves, reporting scrambled messages to her brain.

"I want top," she demanded. Needed it. Needed the control before she lost her damn mind.

"Just make it fast and hard, Dreamy. Ride my cock until we both come."

He rolled, their legs a tangle with covers, half-discarded pants, and that damn walking boot. Sprawled over his body, Mack reached for the condom in the nightstand and shredded the wrapper. Her hands were shaking when she reached for him. He noticed and steadied her. Together, in a sinful moment of intimacy, they rolled the condom onto his thick shaft.

She felt the pulse of his blood beneath the surface. Knew he wanted it as much as she did.

And took her rightful place on his cock.

"Watch," she ordered, notching the blunt crown in place. "Watch."

She took an inch of him. Just enough to have sweat dotting his brow, his jaw clenching. It was too much and not enough. He stared down at where they were joined.

One inch of beautiful, dirty pleasure.

"I still don't know if I can give you more than this," she whispered.

His eyes bored into hers. "I'll take whatever you can give me, Mackenzie."

That was all she could ask for.

His fingers flexed into her hips hard enough to leave prints. But she was in control. Knowing he watched her, she slid down, taking more and more of him in one slow, smooth move. Linc bowed up from the bed as the last inch found its way inside her. She could feel him filling her, feel him almost in her belly.

She gave a teasing rock of her hips.

"I'm seeing stars, Dreamy."

The sweet again sprinkled in with the dirty. Was there anything sexier than that?

"You haven't seen anything yet," she promised and began to move. Rocking slowly at first, then steadily building speed. The thick slide of him in and out, veins and ridges, impossibly smooth, hot skin. He was custom-made to fuck her.

Linc ran his hands over her torso, pausing to pay special attention to her breasts.

"Get down here," he commanded.

She complied, folding over him as he wrapped one strong arm around her. It felt so good to be this close to him. Safe and wild all at once.

He used his other hand to cup her breast and bring it to his mouth. The pleasure of his mouth on her, his cock in her, gave her no way to stop and think. And no way to stop and think.

She was a mass of sensation. On a quest for pleasure.

He picked up the pace, hammering into her. Her thighs quivered, and those delicate inner muscles trembled. He wasn't kidding about more orgasms. He was about to fuck a second one out of her.

He murmured dark and dirty things against her breasts while sucking and kissing.

She gave herself over to the frenzied rhythm, forgetting about the need for control. Now she required something else. Something that was blooming in her belly like a nuclear explosion.

He grunted softly against the flesh of her breast, her nipple growing impossibly harder in his mouth.

She opened her legs wider, letting him pummel into her, his hips thrusting in an incessant rhythm.

It was starting. She could feel it drawing up from her toes, burning everything in its path.

She spasmed around his dick, and he growled. "That's right, Mackenzie."

He said her name as he drove her relentlessly toward an orgasm.

"Do you want more?" he asked, his voice gravelly.

"What more is there?" She ended on a cry as her body balanced on the precipice. The abyss. All she had to do was fall. But...

Linc's finger found her ass, slipped into the cleft, and pressed against her.

"No one's ever made me want like this before," he ground out.

"God," she hissed.

"Hang on to me, Dreamy. I've got you."

His finger slid into her at the same time as a particularly masterful thrust grazed some pleasure button deep inside her. His tongue laved her nipple.

They both exploded together.

He went rigid under her, teeth gritted, jaw clenched, pouring himself into the condom while Mack closed around him like a fist. And they came like that, rocking and shuddering, trembling as their releases ripped through their bodies, decimating them.

CHAPTER 30

Mack whistled as she let herself in through the back door of the clinic.

She was early, the first one to arrive, which was fine with her. She dropped the skinny vanilla latte and the Earl Grey with extra cream at the front desk for Tuesday and Freida. The cappuccino went on Russell's organized desk.

She took her own green tea into her office and flicked on the lights.

Since she was alone, she cranked the volume on the elderly computer speakers and played the song she'd woken up with in her head.

Warbling along with Freddie Mercury to "Somebody to Love," she collapsed into the chair, delighted at the variety of sore muscles making themselves known to her.

She'd had sex. Amazing sex. With a guy she really liked. And she'd woken up, crammed into her own bed on filthy ash-streaked sheets, between man and dog. They'd worked out together. Weights, push-ups, sit-ups. And over breakfast, Linc had filled her in on the call last night.

It felt…nice. She felt *happy*. The slate had been cleared. The playing field was even.

Linc knew she wasn't looking for permanent. She knew he was. They were at cross-purposes and honest about it. They could make this work. Whatever this was.

Of course, she was going to have to be careful to keep her distance. She definitely couldn't see him two nights in a row. That would send the wrong message. Stay in control, and everyone could have a good time.

It was going to be a very good day.

The chair had feelings about her positivity. It tipped abruptly. There was no time to catch herself as she pitched backward, her feet flipping up over her head as she and the chair landed hard.

She stared up at her walking boot and ceiling. And started to laugh.

They found her like that.

"Is she drunk?" Freida asked from the doorway.

"The beverages. The music. The laughing. She's not drunk," Tuesday insisted. "Dr. Mack got laid."

"Up we go," Russell said, pulling Mack to her feet.

She stumbled over her walking boot. "I swear I'm not drunk."

"Look at her face," Tuesday said in a gleeful mock whisper. "She's so smug and satisfied. So dewy."

"Had to be Chief Reed," Freida predicted. "Nice to know you two made up."

"Good for you," Russell said, beaming at her.

"I'm very uncomfortable right now," Mack said.

"Honey, you should be after a night with Chief Reed." Freida was in full-on spirit fingers mode.

"Go easy on her, ladies," Russell insisted. "Mackenzie is new to this kind of dysfunctional workplace intimacy."

Mack laughed. She'd bonded fiercely with her crew on the

227

bird that had crash-landed in the dirt and dust in the middle of the damn desert in Afghanistan. And she'd spent most of her career surrounded by soldiers who'd never heard the phrase "don't kiss and tell." But this was something different.

"We're just happy for you," Tuesday promised. She had her hair woven into some complex side-part braid thing that looked like it had walked off a Pinterest board. "And thank you for the latte."

"Heard that fire was a doozy last night. But no fatalities, thanks to your man friend," Freida mused.

"Maybe think about ordering a new chair?" Russell suggested as he herded Freida and Tuesday out her door. "And thank you for the coffee."

Left alone with Freddie Mercury, Mack kicked the chair before righting it. She weighed her options and then sat gingerly, avoiding the backrest while she reviewed the appointments scheduled for today.

———

Six-year-old Dalton McDowell presented with a fever that had started earlier in the week and spiked overnight.

"We took him to urgent care on Tuesday night," his mother, a harried woman in a misbuttoned white cardigan, explained. "They said it was most likely strep and gave us a prescription, but he's not getting any better. And last night he threw up."

The poor kid was shivering in his little hoodie. "Let's take a look. Dalton, buddy, do you have any pain?"

His eyes were red, she noted.

He shrugged listlessly. "I threw up a lot," he said.

"Have you been hungry?"

He shrugged again.

"He doesn't have his usual appetite. He hasn't asked for a snack in days," Mrs. McDowell reported.

"Let's check your temperature, okay?"

He nodded and sat slump shouldered while Mack slid the thermometer in his mouth. She turned to the laptop and made a few notes. "Has he been around anyone else with similar symptoms?"

"I haven't heard about anything going around school, and I would. The parents in his class are pretty tight, and when one of them gets the stomach bug, we all prepare for it."

Mack skimmed the patient record and caught the note at the very bottom. *Interesting.*

"Have you guys been camping lately?" she asked, turning back to the boy.

Dalton's mom smiled through her anxiety. "This weekend. All five of us in one tent. We went hiking, didn't we, bud?"

He nodded, and the thermometer beeped.

104.2.

Mack felt the quiet revving of her brain as it made a tentative connection. That last medical journal that she'd restlessly skimmed before she picked up the novel last night.

"I know you're probably pretty cold, but I need to take a look at your arms and your feet. So can we take your sweatshirt and shoes off for a minute? You can put them right back on," she promised.

"I guess," he said, his voice barely a whisper.

"This is so unlike him," his mom said in a low voice. "I'm worried it's something serious."

Together, she and Mrs. McDowell pulled off the sweatshirt, sneakers, and socks.

He shivered as Mack skimmed her hands over the boy's arms and turned his palms up to look at them. She did the same with his feet.

No rash.

"Do you remember getting bitten by anything while you were camping?" she asked him, handing him back his sweatshirt. Rather than putting it on, Dalton used it as a blanket and lay down on the exam table.

"We all had some mosquito bites," Mrs. McDowell reported. "We forgot the bug spray the first night and had to send Dad home for it, didn't we?" She shifted her attention back to Mack. "You don't think this is some kind of West Nile, do you?"

"I'm thinking it might be tick-borne," Mack said, pulling an adult gown out of the cabinet and draping it over the boy. He drew it around him like a cape.

"Like Lyme disease?" the mother asked, wide-eyed.

"Mrs. McDowell, have you heard of Rocky Mountain spotted fever?"

"Rocky Mountain what?"

"Rocky Mountain spotted fever. It's a bacterial infection caused by a tick bite. It's rare but on the rise. Most people who get it don't even remember getting bitten. Most people also present with a rash."

"Dalton doesn't have a rash."

"There's a small percentage of patients who don't get it, and that makes it much harder to diagnose. But I'm betting one of those bites wasn't a mosquito. Your son is very sick."

Mrs. McDowell wrapped her arms around her son as if she could protect him from the bacteria that swam through his system. "Oh, God. What do we do?"

"You did the right thing bringing him in," Mack said, standing up. "We're going to start a course of oral antibiotics right now, and then I'm sending you over to the emergency department. I want Dalton monitored. Okay?"

"Is he going to be okay?" Mrs. McDowell asked.

"If I have anything to say about it, he will be."

Mack didn't feel good about making Mrs. McDowell drive herself, so she put mother and son in her SUV, swung by the pharmacy, poured the first dose into the boy's mouth herself, and sped to Keppler Medical Center's emergency department, calling the ED on her way in.

When she pulled up in front of the doors, Dr. Ling was standing by with her white coat flapping in the breeze and a pair of orderlies ready with a stretcher. Mrs. McDowell paled.

"You want them taking this seriously," Mack said, squeezing her hand. "This is a good thing. Freida called your husband, and he's on his way. Your mom will get the kids off the bus."

Glassy-eyed, Mrs. McDowell nodded and climbed out. She hurried along behind the stretcher that held her little boy.

Mack parked the car and went inside.

CHAPTER 31

By the time Mack got back to the office, it was late afternoon, and Dalton McDowell was going to be just fine. Rocky Mountain spotted fever wouldn't be confirmed by the lab tests for a while, but Dr. Ling—after a quick internet search—agreed with the diagnosis.

They pushed doxycycline into the kid, and Mack stayed with Mrs. McDowell until her husband sprinted into the emergency department still in his septic-tank-cleaning jumpsuit. While the staff was all for supporting small businesses, the smell was overwhelming, and Dr. Ling forced him to change into a set of scrubs.

Mack frowned when she pulled into the clinic's parking lot and found it empty.

They hadn't had any appointments after three today, but there was always work to do. She parked and walked up to the back door. While digging for her keys, the paper taped to the window caught her eye. It was a terrible sketch of a fake prescription.

Patient Name: Mackenzie O'Neil
    Take one early Friday closing and meet the team at Remo's for celebratory drinks.
    Refills: As many as needed.

She laughed and peeled the paper off the glass.

Shaking her head, she folded it neatly and stowed it in her bag. It was a good day. But that didn't mean she should kick off early. There was work and…

Why the hell not? It was a beautiful fall Friday afternoon, and she'd made a great save.

She'd earned a little fun, dammit.

She pulled out her phone and dialed before she could remind herself that she wasn't going to see him tonight. Just because she was inviting him out didn't mean she had to spend the night with him. Inconsistency was the key to a good fling. It kept the expectations low.

"Dreamy." Linc's voice was like honey.

"Doing anything important, Hotshot?" she asked.

"Nothing that can't be finished later."

"Feel like meeting me for a celebratory drink at Remo's?"

"Absolutely. Give me ten. What are we celebrating?"

She bit her lip, then grinned. "Friday."

He chuckled softly. "I'll meet you there."

She felt a warm rush of something good flood through her. "Can't wait."

———

Dunnigan & Associates had commandeered half of Remo's otherwise empty bar. It was still early. But her crew made up for the lack of numbers with noise level. When Mack walked in the door, they cheered.

"Come get your on-the-house round, Dr. Mack," Sophie called from behind the bar.

"What is all this?" Mack asked, limping up to the bar and sliding onto the stool they'd saved for her. She pointed to a new IPA on draft.

"You saved a life today," Tuesday said, clapping her hands. She had a tall, skinny glass of what Mack assumed was some sort of low-carb alcohol in front of her.

"You're a hero!" Freida said, hefting up her frozen margarita.

"To Dr. O'Neil, lifesaver," Russell said, holding up his red wine.

Sophie slid Mack's beer to her. Reluctantly, she raised it. "To Friday afternoons."

"Cheers!"

"We looked it up after you left," Tuesday bubbled.

"I'd never even heard of it," Freida added.

"People *die* from this. Especially when they don't present with the rash. How did you know?" Tuesday squeaked.

"I remembered it from a medical journal article. Cases are on the rise. Global warming. More ticks. Sometimes there's no rash."

Freida thumped her on the back. "This was almost better than firefighter physical day."

Tuesday gasped. "OMG. I just realized. You're like that grumpy, mean doctor on that old show. He walked with a limp too!"

Mack guessed it was at least her second low-carb alcoholic beverage. "Unlike House, I'm not addicted to Vicodin. Just to make that clear."

Tuesday thought that was hilarious and nearly fell off her stool.

"Congratulations, Doc," Sophie said, sliding her a food menu. "Better get some bar food in Tuesday before she goes for round three."

They ordered quesadillas and french fries. Because why not?

While Tuesday and Freida hurried off to attack the jukebox, Russell slid over to the stool next to her.

"I would have missed it," he admitted. "If that boy had walked into my exam room instead of yours, he might not have made it through the weekend."

Mack pushed the thought aside. "It's not a big deal," she said. They were doctors. It was what they were trained for.

"It's the biggest deal for that family. Remember that," he said.

She nodded. "I remembered to check the patient notes. They're big into camping. Camping equals bug bites."

"I'm very proud of you, Mackenzie," he said.

She didn't want it to matter. Didn't think it should matter. But it did anyway. She felt it again, that brightness in her chest. "Thanks, Russell."

"It looks like someone else thinks pretty highly of you," he said, tilting his glass in the direction of the door.

Lincoln Reed in well-worn jeans and a tight gray T-shirt strolled her way with his eyes on her and that charming little smirk on his face.

Thunk thunk.

Her heart got in on the excitement with an uneven limp. *Just leftover hormones*, she told herself. *Nothing complicated.*

"Hey there, Dreamy," Linc said.

She expected him to take the empty stool next to her, but instead he walked right up to her and slid his hands up her jaw and into her hair. He laid a kiss on her that stole her breath and her train of thought.

"Woo! Is it just me or is it gettin' hot in here?" Sophie called from the other end of the bar, where she fanned herself with a menu.

It was definitely not just Sophie.

The kiss left Mack flush-cheeked and speechless for a beat.

"Hey," she breathed finally when her words returned.

"Oooooh," Freida crooned, sloshing margarita over the rim of her glass.

Linc grinned, and Mack felt her mouth following his lead.

"How was your day?" he asked.

"Dr. Mack saved a life today," Sophie said, sliding a beer at Linc.

He held his glass up to Mack's. "Congratulations."

"Chief Reed here saved two lives last night," Mack countered.

"Well, don't I just have myself a bar full of heroes today?" Sophie said cheerfully.

"All in a day's work, little lady," Linc said with an exaggerated wink.

But it was. Their job was to preserve life. And now there were three souls that would live to see the weekend. It gave Mack a little tingle of satisfaction. Of pride.

She'd saved lives before. Many of them. But proximity made this one different. She'd see Dalton at the grocery store or on the ball field. She'd run into his parents at the Italian place. And they'd all be connected. Forever.

Linc, not even trying to be subtle about it, dragged her stool closer, positioning it and her between his muscular thighs.

"You look happy," he said.

She gave a shrug and picked up her beer. "It was a good day."

"And last night?"

She playfully gave him a scan that started at those pretty blue eyes and traveled south to the distinctive bulge in his jeans. "Last night was pretty okay too."

He pinched her, and she laughed.

There was a small scrape on his jawline. "What happened here?" she asked, tapping a finger next to the abrasion. "You didn't have that last night." Her inner thighs would have noticed it.

He captured her hand in his. "A manly injury incurred from being manly."

"Uh-huh. You could have just said you fell off the toilet," she teased.

"You're beautiful when you're hilarious."

"So where's our girl?" she asked, changing the subject.

"Sunny is entertaining my sister Rebecca's family tonight. She has a little crush on my brother-in-law."

"She has a crush on everyone."

"Love is love, Dreamy."

The door to the bar opened, and a blue-collar crew flush with fresh paychecks ambled in, talking shit and ribbing each other.

They were followed by a thirsty group of dental hygienists.

The jukebox song clunked off and the next started.

Tuesday and Freida whooped and jumped off their stools at the first twangy bars of the song.

"Come on, Dr. Mack! Let's dance," Tuesday said, grabbing Mack's wrists and pulling.

"What the hell is this?" she asked as they dragged her toward the space in front of the empty stage that apparently served as a dance floor.

"'Down to the Honkytonk!' Dare you to not love it," Freida said.

"What's a Honkytonk?"

"Just listen to the song and follow us," Tuesday insisted firmly.

The song had caught the attention of a few of the other patrons.

More joined them, lining up on the wood floor facing the door.

"I only have one good foot," Mack reminded them.

Linc set his beer down on the bar and joined her. "Just follow my lead, Doc."

"You dance?"

But her question and his answer were lost in a coordinated heel stomp. And all questions were gone as Mack tried to mimic the line's shuffle forward.

Tuesday called out the steps—at least that was what Mack assumed a step pivot cross and a turning jazz box were—and the small crowd followed.

It was a catchy song, Mack had to admit when everyone around started singing along.

Linc made whatever this line dance was look sexy as hell, thumbs hooked into his front pockets, his scarred boots moving to the beat.

Sophie bopped out from behind the bar, joined by one of the cooks from the kitchen, and seamlessly jumped into the front line.

Mack considered it a victory when she managed to clap along with everyone else at the appropriate moment.

When the song came to the line about Sheila and the effects of tequila, the entire bar hooted, including the four firefighters who'd just walked in.

By the end of the song, there wasn't an inch left on the dance floor, and there was a very patient three-deep line at the bar.

Sophie hustled off to man the bar. "Everyone gets a discount if your first drink is a draft," she yelled.

When Mack made a move to head back to the bar, Linc stopped her with a hand on her arm.

"One more," he insisted.

"One more what?"

"Dance."

The song was slow, and Mack was relieved that all she had to do was step into Linc's arms. There was no complicated choreography here. Just an appreciation of the fine male form that was here to celebrate with her. Two bodies that were getting acquainted. Simple. Sweet.

She caught a whiff of something manly.

"You smell like sawdust and…" She leaned in and took another whiff. "Paint?"

"Imagine that," he said, spinning her out slowly and then drawing her back. "How's your ankle holding up?"

"Not gonna lie, I don't think I'd be any better at that line dancing with two good feet."

"I like just about everything about you, Dreamy."

She bit her lip coyly. She couldn't help herself. "I kinda like you too, Hotshot."

"My place tonight?" he asked huskily.

"Yeah."

He grinned. "Good. My bed's bigger."

He pushed her out again. And every time he pulled her back into his arms, she felt the flutter in her belly. It felt a little something like joy.

Russell appeared next to her with a stunning woman on his arm who looked fancy even in jeans and a cashmere sweater.

"Dr. O'Neil, my wife, Denise. Denise, Mackenzie O'Neil."

"I've heard a lot," Denise said with a warm smile. She offered a hand with a large, tasteful diamond on it.

"I can only imagine," Mack said, shaking her hand.

"Chief Reed, how's our daughter doing under your care?" Denise asked. There was nothing veiled about the question. Her message was clear: Take care of my daughter. Or else.

"Skyler is a great addition to the department. Cool under pressure," Linc said.

Denise nudged her husband. "She gets that from me."

"Although her rookie toilet-scrubbing skills leave something to be desired."

"And she gets that from me," Russell said.

"We'll talk later," Denise promised. "First, I'm going to dance with this handsome doctor."

The Robinsons moved off to their own corner of the dance floor, and Mack was once again in Linc's arms. The song was about not being fooled by love songs and the trappings of romance. She could relate.

She looked up, found Linc watching her. There was a softness in his eyes that belayed the confident smirk that lived on his talented lips.

Her knees gave out. Just a bit. And only because she'd somehow forgotten how to keep her joints stable, she told herself.

"Need a break?" he asked, misreading her embarrassing half swoon as injury-related.

"Yes." *And another beer.*

CHAPTER 32

The mood was festive in Remo's as if everyone were celebrating something that night. Linc's crew filled him in on their calls. Calls as in multiple.

They'd responded to a missing person report, a toddler locked in a car, and a garden shed fire that had spread to a farmer's dry pasture. All three calls were successful. And just like that, his department's drought was officially over.

He fired off a text to Aldo when Mrs. Moretta stormed the bar with another new boyfriend. He was a tall Black man with shoulders so broad Linc wondered if his sport coat was tailor-made. "He played for the Steelers in the eighties," Mrs. Moretta bellowed to anyone who would listen.

> **Linc:** Your mama's here with your new daddy.
> **Aldo:** He's too good for her. I'm going to ask him to adopt me when he comes to his senses and runs screaming back to Pittsburgh.

Georgia Rae, requisite small-town gossip, was celebrating the birth of her seventh grandchild and quizzed both Linc and Mack for a good twenty minutes on their most recent heroics.

He could tell Mack was thanking the baby Jesus for HIPAA laws that protected her from most of the inquisition.

The appetizers were devoured, and actual dinners were ordered. Mack switched from beer to water, and Linc did the same. They debated who was going to be more hungover the following day: Tuesday or Linc's lieutenant, Zane Jones. The guy brewed his own beer but had been goaded into switching over to shots of Fireball with Tuesday.

"Good thing neither of them work tomorrow," Mack pointed out.

"We'll still drive an engine past his apartment and blow the sirens," Linc told her cheerfully.

"Mean."

"But funny."

Sheriff Ty, out of uniform, meandered through the door around eight and laid a baby-making kiss on Sophie when she leaned across the bar to greet him.

"Evening," Ty said to Linc and Mack once his tongue was back in his own mouth.

"Sheriff," Mack said.

"We're filing charges tomorrow," Ty said, cutting to the chase. "Just givin' y'all a heads-up."

"Appreciate it."

"If anyone makes their displeasure known, you tell me."

"Will do."

Linc gave Ty a not-so-subtle nod in the direction of the men's room and then excused himself.

Ty met him in front of the urinals, leaving a respectable amount of space between them.

"You expecting trouble?" Linc asked, unzipping his jeans and trying not to piss on himself with his half hard-on thanks to those big green eyes and smart mouth at the bar.

Ty sighed. "I wouldn't put it past them. The Kershes aren't known for being logical or taking responsibility for themselves."

"You just expecting Mack and that girl's family to fend for themselves then?"

Ty broke urinal man code to give him an "are you stupid?" look. "I am not. And fuck you for thinking that I would. I've got regular patrols going past both houses for the next week or two to keep an eye on things."

"Eyes on your own paper, Sheriff," Linc told him. "What about the clinic?"

"That too. It would help if a trusted neighbor maybe insisted on a basic alarm system, some new locks," Ty mused.

He'd install them himself, Linc decided, zipping back up. Mack had handled herself in war zones and through every imaginable emergency situation. However, she hadn't yet dealt with an ignorant redneck family hell-bent on revenge. It was a different beast and required a different kind of vigilance.

He returned to the bar, finding their dinners had arrived.

"Did you two cowboys have fun man-talking about how to protect the poor, frail womenfolk?" Mack asked, batting her lashes at him over her chicken salad.

"You're in a walking boot. You can't outrun a threat," he started.

"What makes you think I'd run away?" she shot back.

This was why he'd done what he'd done today. And why he'd be perusing new door locks tonight.

"Let's argue about this tonight when we're naked," he said.

"Sex fighting? Hmm. I like it," she mused.

Sophie came out from behind the bar.

"Hey there, beautiful," Ty said, sliding an arm around her shoulder and pulling her into his side.

She sparkled up at him. "Guess who just got kicked off the

bar early and doesn't have any kids tonight because my parents are keeping them overnight?"

"Does she also have two thumbs, and can she do that weirdly wonderful thing with her tongue?" he asked.

Laughing, Sophie threw her arms around his neck. "Let's dance, Sheriff."

"Yes, ma'am!"

Linc watched them go, a feeling settling over him like a blanket. He wanted that. The wife. The partner. The history of old pain and inside jokes and good memories. He wanted the whole package.

And Dr. Mackenzie O'Neil was the first woman in his life who he could picture having it all with.

He brushed a finger over the scrape on his jaw he'd earned that morning. Yeah, he was in for a bumpy ride.

They called it a night, and Linc insisted on following her home.

"I'm coming over to your house. You don't have to shadow me," Mack complained.

"Maybe I want to see if Gloria dropped off any more pies?"

"Or you think you're going to find a Kersh lurking in my closet?"

"Nah. Your closet's too small. I was thinking maybe the basement."

"I was in the military, Linc. I know how to defend myself," she said dryly.

"Me wanting to make sure you don't *have* to defend yourself in no way implies that I don't think you *can* handle yourself. If you had two good feet, I'd feel sorry for someone who tried to hide in your basement."

That seemed to appease her.

He parked on the street and walked to the door with her.

"You're being ridiculous," she complained.

"I prefer to think of it as chivalrous and charming."

She let them in and switched on the living room lights.

"I'm coming back here tonight," she insisted, stowing her purse and her med bag precisely by the front door.

There were better ways around resistance than butting heads. And Linc could be very persuasive when he wanted to be.

"You say that now," he said, prowling into the dining room, then poking his head into the kitchen. "But when you get into that big, luxurious bed, when you see the body jets in the shower, you're going to cry. And then I'm going to feel sorry for you. And I hate feeling sorry for beautiful doctors."

"Body jets, you say?" She raised an interested eyebrow.

"Pack a contingency bag. There's no pressure to use it. But then you'll have it if you succumb to the charms of my very comfortable mattress."

"This better be one hell of a mattress or I'm going to be very disappointed."

"Dreamy, I don't oversell anything in the bedroom."

"In that case, we'd better hydrate. Want a water?" she offered over her shoulder as she headed for the fridge.

He waited for it and wasn't disappointed when he heard her gasp of outrage.

"You cut a hole in my fence!"

"My fence actually," he said, joining her in the kitchen. "And it's a gate. It makes sneaking into your bed or you sneaking into mine more convenient. Besides, now I can mow your yard without driving around the block."

There were several emotions flickering in rotation on that lovely face, most of them varying shades of annoyance.

"I'm concerned that there's something wrong with you that goes far beyond my medical expertise," she told him finally.

"Full disclosure. I fell on my face jumping that stupid fucking fence this morning. Landed in a shrub." He stroked a hand over the scrape on his jaw. "Felt like I needed to solve the problem with a chainsaw."

Mack laughed.

CHAPTER 33

The man was not lying about his bed.

Nor his shower.

She'd helped herself to the latter last night after two athletic rounds of very satisfying sex. They'd forgotten to fight. But she'd beaten him in number of orgasms and considered it a win.

As for the bed, it was a big, beautiful dream. The king mattress took up most of the space in the loft. Soft enough to gently hug any sore body parts but firm enough that she didn't feel like she was being swallowed by a cloud.

The sheets were good quality and clean. And there were pillows. Many, many pillows. They were a decadence she'd forgotten about in her years of deployments or bunking in tiny air ambulance lounges. But she remembered now. Pressing her face into the one Linc's head had vacated, she sighed.

Spending the night wasn't her plan. But the man singing Beyoncé in the shower had proven to be far more convincing than she'd given him credit for.

Mack stretched as the rising sun lightened the room.

The room was spartan, which her orderly sensibilities appreciated. There was a nondescript dresser on the wall facing the bed and a pair of matching nightstands. Two baskets of clean, folded laundry were stacked in the corner.

She helped herself to a BFD hooded sweatshirt and tiptoed downstairs so as not to disturb the amusing rendition of "Irreplaceable."

The concrete floors were chilly under her bare feet. She found a Keurig on the counter and was pleasantly surprised to find a box of green tea K-Cups sitting next to it. There was also a mug that seemed suspiciously new.

World's Okayest Trauma Doctor.

She snorted and powered up the coffee maker.

While she waited for it to warm up, she snooped. The kitchen was barely bigger than her own. One wall of cabinets and countertop. Simple gray cabinets. White counter. She opened the cabinet next to the stove.

Apparently, she hadn't been the only one to snoop. An unopened container of her preferred protein powder sat on the shelf next to Linc's bulk tub of manly firefighter muscle-producing stuff. She found acceptable smoothie ingredients in the fridge and freezer and went to work on making a double.

By the time Linc came downstairs, dressed in his BFD polo and cargo pants and now whistling what sounded like a Hall and Oates ballad, she had two protein smoothies ready to go.

He was unfairly gorgeous. Sexy. Cute. Looking at Chief Reed was rapidly becoming a favored pastime.

"I like this," he said, spinning his cap around backward so he could kiss her unimpeded.

"What? The little woman barefoot in the kitchen?" she teased when she drew back, surprised that her body could get that revved that fast from a little morning peck.

He pinched her bare ass under the sweatshirt.

"Smart-ass. You wearing nothing but my sweatshirt with your hair all messed up and your eyes all dreamy."

"Shut up. They are not all dreamy."

"Wish I could stay and prove you wrong," he said, picking up the smoothie and giving it a testing taste. "Mmm. A hot doctor in my sweatshirt and a healthy breakfast. I might just save all the lives today."

"You better." She glanced at the clock on the wall, a mechanical machination of cogs and gears. "You're heading out early."

"Gotta pick up Sunshine from my sister's. Bec's not a morning person on her days off." He grinned.

"I can pick her up," she offered. She'd be home most of the day anyway. It wouldn't hurt to have some fluffy company.

Linc's face lightened.

"Don't read anything into it," she said defensively. "I like your dog. I'm off today. I can pick her up at a reasonable hour. This is *not* a marriage proposal."

He glanced down at his watch and then back up at her with a wicked grin. "That saves me fifteen minutes that I could use to do something else."

"Like what?" she asked with suspicion.

He slid down her body to kneel on the floor in front of her.

"Oh. *That*," she said breathlessly.

Those big, calloused palms slid up the outsides of her thighs until they caught the hem of the sweatshirt. The soft material bunched as he shoved it to her waist.

Stepping her feet wider, Mack complimented herself on being so accommodating and respectful of Linc's truly excellent morning routine.

"I dreamed about fucking you with my tongue last night," he said, his breath hot on her bare skin.

She watched in fascination as he pressed his mouth to the

apex of her thighs, blue eyes on her as he did so. The whimper clawed its way free from her throat when his tongue, that goddamn talented tongue, darted out and slipped into her cleft.

"I can't get enough of your flavor." As if to demonstrate, he sank two fingers into her. She spread wider for him and watched as he pulled out and then sucked them into his mouth. Her knees quaked, and he took notice.

"Get on the floor and spread your legs for me, Dreamy."

"What's with you and kitchens?" she murmured even as she complied.

"It's you in kitchens and any other fucking room." He groaned as she opened for him.

"Is this floor clean?" she asked.

"Clean enough to eat off of." And with that he dipped his head between her legs and made her head spin. His tongue was relentless in its attack on her clit. His fingers—were there three now?—pumped into her, stretching that channel to its limits. And oh, did Mack like it.

She couldn't brace her left foot with the walking boot. But it didn't matter anymore because he was looping her legs over his shoulders. He was devouring her.

"Watch me lick you, Mackenzie. Watch me."

Lifting her head, their eyes connected. Her abs flexed hard as those overused inner muscles gave their first flutters.

"Baby, I feel that," he groaned reverently. He was on his stomach, his hips grinding into the unyielding concrete. "Squeeze my fingers."

She clamped down on him, gritting her teeth at the change in sensation. It was like forcing her orgasm from probably to definitely.

He went back to torturing her with his tongue as he thrust into her.

She couldn't stop watching him as he fucked her with mouth and fingers. "Linc!"

He growled in response.

Bucking her hips, she ground into his mouth, begging for everything he could give her.

"Goddammit. I love how greedy you are for me. How you ride my face because you can't help it."

She was going to come. Or die. Or both.

"Don't you fucking hold back, Dreamy."

She didn't. She couldn't. He tore the orgasm from her and didn't let up as she spiraled back down while every muscle clenched and released in a beautiful, gut-wrenching climax.

Her head hit the floor with a dull thud. Her legs were jelly, her blood thrumming through her body as even now aftershocks milked Linc's fingers.

He groaned like he was in pain.

"Give me your cock," she said breathlessly.

"I have to leave in five minutes, Dreamy."

"I only need four," she said, sliding out from under him. "Get up."

They traded positions, she on her knees in front of him. He watched with a primal male pride when she knelt before him and loosened his belt. She freed him from his pants and delighted in the heavy thickness of his shaft.

He pulled his shirt up, tucking it under his chin to watch her as she opened her mouth.

"Fuck," he groaned.

She held his gaze while she took the tip into her mouth. Hot, hard, smooth. She used her hands, her tongue, her teeth to work his entire shaft. Now it was *his* knees that quaked as she traced veins with the tip of her tongue. When she teased the wet slit on the underside of his crown, he hissed.

Aware of the time, she quit playing and attacked him with slick, tight strokes. When she brought him to the back of her throat and held him there, he let out a string of unintelligible dirty words.

"I wish this was your sweet pussy. That I was buried inside you." He let out a pained groan, and Mack tasted the beginning of his release.

She hummed her approval and tightened her hand on the base of his shaft.

Mindlessly, he shoved his hands into her hair and gripped. He fucked into her mouth in jerky, shallow thrusts.

"I wish I was coming in your cunt, baby."

But he wasn't. He was coming in her mouth.

The force, the volume of it, the rawness of his release made Mack's eyes water. She felt powerful, invincible as she watched him tip his head back, the cords on his neck standing out. *She* did this to him. *She* made him feel this way.

His shout was triumphant as he emptied himself into her.

A few more seconds, a few more jerky thrusts, and he slid to the floor next to her.

She watched in fascination as that incredible specimen gave one last jerk, one last pump of come that leaked onto the ridges of his abs.

"Holy shit, Dreamy."

"And look at that. You've got a whole minute to spare," she said.

"Evil temptress. I'm gonna need it just to get my legs back under me. Dinner tonight?"

She should say no. They'd spent the last two nights together already. It was sending the wrong message.

"Let me see what I have planned," she said evasively.

"I'm gonna need an IV to rehydrate," he decided, coming to his feet. He reached down and helped her up.

"I know someone who can help with that," she said and pointed to her mug.

His grin was boyish, and once again, she felt that uneven lurch in her chest. She should probably see about getting an EKG.

Linc hastily pulled up his pants. "Thanks for taking Sunshine today." He kissed her, hard on the mouth and soft on top of the head, before grabbing his smoothie and heading toward the door.

She laughed when he stumbled in the doorway.

"I'm light-headed."

"Don't forget to zip your fly, Hotshot," she told him.

"Don't forget to report any suspicious basement lurkers," he said, then sobered. "I mean it, Mackenzie. If you see anything that doesn't sit right with you, call Ty and then call me."

She gave him a salute. "Yes, sir!"

Back to playful, he sent her an exaggerated wink. "Dinner tonight," he called over his shoulder. "And don't forget to meditate!"

About thirty seconds after the front door closed, Mack's phone buzzed on the counter.

———

Linc: Thanks again. For Sunny. And the bj.

Mack: Don't be weird.

Linc: Feel free to stay and take another shower. Wi-Fi password is 4AlarmFire. Move in if you want or wait for me to do the heavy lifting.

Mack: I see blow jobs damage brain cells.

CHAPTER 34

Linc's sister Rebecca—another replica of the Reed DNA—had been more subtle in her "What are your intentions with my brother?" interrogation. Dressed in pajamas and a robe and clutching a cup of coffee, she invited Mack inside her neat and tidy two-story.

With Mack's exit cut off, Bec quizzed her on how long she planned to stay in town and if she was enjoying small-town doctoring, all while telling her kids to turn the TV down and reminding her husband to take the car in for an oil change.

Mack brought Sunshine back to her place, and they spent the rest of the morning working in the flower beds in the backyard, because apparently weeding once was not enough. While Sunshine ran back and forth between the yards, bringing Mack every dog toy and stick she could find, Mack gave the open gate a few contemplative looks, still not sure what to think of it.

Presumptuous. Yes. Convenient. Also yes.

He was already systematically pushing back on her claims that she didn't want anything serious or complicated. Which meant she was going to have to push back harder. Maybe after dinner tonight. After all, she had his dog. Obviously, she'd have to see him at some point.

Yes. *Tomorrow* she'd set firmer boundaries.

After lunch and an afternoon meditation, she took Sunshine for ice cream and laughed at the metronomic tick of the dog's tail as she wolfed down a small dish of vanilla.

It was after three. And ice cream had been her one and only "fun" idea. The clinic was closed now, so there was no point stopping in unless it was to fall out of her chair again.

Maybe fixing dinner would be fun?

So she loaded Sunshine into her SUV and headed to the grocery store.

"I'm so lame," she complained to the dog in the passenger seat as she steered toward home with steaks and veggies to grill. "I can't even come up with something spontaneous besides ice cream and grocery shopping."

Sunshine looked at her and blinked.

"No. A nap is *not* spontaneous fun."

She was still trying to explain her predicament to the dog when she pulled in the driveway without noticing the rusty pickup parked on the street.

Sunshine gave a warning *boof* at the slam of a car door. Mack looked up as she unloaded the bags from the hatch.

He was tall, reed-thin in a way that suggested poor life choices. Early fifties if she had to guess. He walked like he had a purpose.

"You Doc O'Neil?" he said. His teeth were yellowed, fingers and T-shirt dirty. There was a nasty, swollen bump swelling on his right forearm. He smelled vaguely of motor oil.

"That's right," she said, dropping the bags at her feet to free her hands.

"My nephew goes to jail, it's on you," he said and spat on the grass next to the driveway.

"Your nephew is already in jail. And it's on him."

"He didn't do nothing wrong."

Sunshine gave another *boof*.

"He put his girlfriend in the ICU and broke my ankle," she said.

She wasn't worried about him in a physical fight. She was more than capable of taking on someone bigger and stronger. But if he had a weapon, well, she'd rather know it sooner than later.

"My kind don't like it when people stick their noses in our business."

"Are you armed, Mr. Kersh?"

He snorted and ignored the question. "The kid was high. He can't be responsible for his actions while he's on that shit."

She sighed heavily. "We're all responsible for our own actions, Mr. Kersh. Your nephew is an adult. He made choices. Bad ones. Maybe this will be a turning point for him."

His laugh had no humor in it and ended in a hacking cough. She noticed that his left hand rubbed gently at the bump on his right.

"It weren't no turning point for me," he said. "It ain't gonna do him any more good."

"I'm not dropping the charges, Mr. Kersh. And if you care about your nephew at all, you'll let the legal system do its job. Your nephew's best shot at a better life is taking his lumps and doing the time. He can get clean in prison, take classes, learn a trade. If that girl lives, he'll be out before you know it."

"You can't come after my family and not expect to hear from us," he said with an almost mournful sigh. She wondered if his heart wasn't in the warning.

"I'm not coming after you. I'm playing by the rules. How long have you had that boil?" she asked.

"Huh?"

She pointed at his arm, and he covered the lump with his other hand.

"It's a boil, an abscess. Have you had it looked at?"

"No. Only had it a couple of weeks."

His answer was short but carried a message. He didn't appear to trust the medical community any more than he did law enforcement.

"Look, if you're not here to rough me up and you don't have any weapons on you, I can take a look at it inside."

He looked confused. And nonthreatening, she decided.

Sunshine seemed to agree. She'd given up her guard dog stance and was rolling on her back on the grass.

Mack held up her hands. "I'm a doctor. That looks painful. I can help."

"I'm not armed," he said, still holding his arm. "But I'm not paying no hospital bills."

"Your fee is to hear me out when I say I'm not dropping the charges. I hold no ill will toward your nephew." That wasn't exactly true. She still wished she'd had the chance to knock a tooth out of his mouth herself. "But he did this, and he needs to pay for his mistakes."

"I disagree."

"As long as we can agree to disagree, you can help me carry these bags inside, and I'll take a look at your arm."

She took two bags and let herself and Sunshine inside. She smirked when she heard the front door open again.

He stood silently in the doorway of the kitchen, holding the rest of her bags.

"You can put them on the counter and have a seat at the table," she said. She turned on the overhead light and opened her med kit on the table. She unpacked alcohol swabs, gauze, saline, tape, a scalpel, and a syringe onto the table.

"Now hold on there," he said, watery blue eyes going wide at the scalpel and needle.

"Don't worry," she told him. "I'm a professional."

"Never knew a lady doctor before," he mused.

"What do you do for a living, Mr. Kersh?"

"I work at Shorty's garage. The other side of town."

There was pride in his voice.

"Really?" Mack asked. She pulled on gloves before opening an absorbent pad and placing it on the table under his arm.

"Shorty started me with tire rotations, oil changes. Easy stuff. Last week, I dropped a new engine in a Jeep, and I'm certified to do state inspections."

"I need an oil change, like five thousand miles ago," she said, gently prodding the swollen tender skin. It was red and hot to the touch.

"You really shouldn't let it go that long," Kersh chided her.

"If I bring my truck in, will you promise not to dump sugar in the gas tank?"

"Let's see how this here boil goes first."

She chuckled. "That's fair. Okay. So what I'm going to do is swab the skin down with alcohol. I'll give you a little shot of numbing stuff. Then I'm going to use the scalpel to make an incision. You won't feel a thing."

"I don't need no sissy drugs."

"That's what all the big, manly guys say before they start swearing and crying," she said cheerfully. She swiped an alcohol pad over the area and uncapped the syringe. "Little pinch."

He looked away when she inserted the needle and made her think of a little kid trying to be brave. Wincing, he took in a breath through his teeth. Sunshine, sweet, innocent soul that she was, put her head on Kersh's knee.

He glanced down at her. "That's a pretty dog," he said.

Sunshine's tail thumped happily.

"She sure is," Mack agreed. "There," she said, withdrawing the needle and dumping it in a sharps box.

He breathed a sigh of relief.

"Have you had a fever?" she asked, tearing the packaging off the scalpel.

"Dunno."

"An abscess is a bacterial infection. I have to open it up and drain it. Then I'll wrap it up nice and clean and give you some antibiotics that you will promise to take exactly as prescribed. You don't want to half-ass it and end up losing a chunk of your arm."

"No, ma'am."

She got up and ran a dish towel under hot water, then placed it over the abscess. "We'll give it a minute for the numbing to work. Do you want some water?"

"Okay," he said. "Thank you."

She filled two glasses, setting one in front of him.

"All right. Let's see what we've got, Mr. Kersh."

"It's Abner," he said softly.

It was a big ol' pocket of nasty, and Mack was glad the man had chosen today to threaten her. She drained the pus carefully, then flushed the wound thoroughly with saline. "That's got to feel ten times better already," she guessed.

"Seems to," he said grudgingly.

She gave it another flushing, then coated the wound with antibacterial cream before snugly bandaging it up.

She was just affixing the last piece of tape when a knock on her screen door startled them both.

"Benevolence PD. Open up!"

Kersh tensed, and Sunshine made a mad, barking dash for the new arrival.

"Door's open," Mack called out. "Don't worry," she told her patient quietly.

"Dr. O'Neil?"

"Back in the kitchen."

The deputy, dark eyebrows knit together in a frown, entered. Her black hair was pulled sleek and tight in a stub of a ponytail. "Dr. O'Neil, I'm Deputy Tahir. I observed a suspicious vehicle in front of your residence."

Mack watched the deputy take in the stash of bloody gauze, the scalpel. Her kitchen did resemble a bit of a crime scene.

"Nothing suspicious, Deputy," she said brightly. "Just having a look at my patient's arm."

The deputy's radio squawked something that Mack couldn't make out. When the woman turned around to respond to the call, Mack pulled out a small bottle from her bag. "Mr. Kersh, this is doxycycline, an antibiotic. It'll get you started, and I'll send in a prescription to the pharmacy for the full course. Which you will take exactly as prescribed."

He looked warily back and forth between her and the deputy.

"Okay?" Mack said.

Kersh looked down at his neatly bandaged arm. "Can I work?"

"Of course. Just mind the wound for a couple of days. Don't dump motor oil in it. Let me print out some wound care instructions for you. The main thing is to keep it clean."

The deputy finished her radio conversation and followed Mack into the living room.

"Dr. O'Neil, I need to ask you a few questions."

"Uh-huh," Mack said, opening her laptop and downloading the clinic's wound care flyer. She hit Print, and the tiny printer she'd stuffed onto a shelf in the built-in between a ceramic frog and a framed lace doily spit out the papers.

"Do you feel unsafe?" the deputy asked.

"I feel perfectly safe. I wouldn't have invited him inside otherwise."

"The sheriff isn't happy."

Her radio squawked again, and Deputy Tahir's lips quirked. "According to dispatch, Chief Reed isn't happy either."

Shit.

"Understood."

Mack grabbed the papers and returned to the kitchen. "Okay. Here's your instructions. If you have any questions or have trouble changing the dressing, you know where to find me. Your prescription is ready at the pharmacy over on Main."

He looked down at his bandaged arm, then back at her. When he rose, he held out his hand.

"Thank you."

"You're welcome," she said, shaking it.

"Agree to disagree?"

She nodded. "Yeah." She followed him to the front door. "Abner, sometimes family loyalty means letting your family figure things out for themselves."

He paused and looked at her and then the deputy. "Maybe so. But even if you convince some of us, it don't mean you'll convince all of us."

Deputy Tahir didn't like that. But Mack took it for what it was. Not a threat but a warning.

"I understand."

He started down the walk, the paper and a baggie of gauze and tape in one hand. He stopped and called out, "Don't forget to bring your car in for that oil change."

Abner pulled away from her house and made it around the

corner before the BFD chief's vehicle came to a screaming stop in her driveway. The very pissed-off Linc didn't bother turning off the engine or closing the door. He was too busy storming toward her.

"You might need those handcuffs," Mack warned the deputy.

"Honey, you better believe it."

"What in the hell were you thinking?" he demanded, rushing her.

"I was thinking the man was no threat and he had a wound that needed to be cleaned."

Linc spun away from her and took a cleansing breath. Then another.

"Linc?"

He held up a finger over his shoulder. "Need a minute or I'm gonna say something stupid that you'll hold against me."

She understood and appreciated the restraint.

"I'll wait," she said quietly.

Deputy Tahir rolled her eyes at their antics.

Linc turned around and pressed his palms together in front of his chest. "Mackenzie."

"Yes?"

"I would really appreciate it if you would walk me through your decision-making when it comes to bringing a Kersh into your house and letting him threaten you."

There was a tic in his jaw that fascinated her, and he sounded as if he was being strangled.

"I'm sorry for worrying you," she began. His face softened a degree. "But it's not your place—"

He was back to hard and angry and was shaking his head.

"Uh-uh. Nope. You don't get to tell me that I don't get to worry about you. I care about you, Dreamy."

"Imma just wait outside," the deputy decided. "Come on, Sunny. You can hang out with me and sniff the flowers."

Tahir and Sunshine stepped outside and closed the front door behind them.

"I know you want to pretend that it's just you. That you're in this alone. That whatever we're exploring together doesn't matter. But we both know that's not reality. You will not be careless. And you won't take stupid risks," he said, his voice low.

Mack took a step forward so they were toe-to-toe. "Fine," she growled. "And *you* will not assume that I'm being careless or taking stupid risks. You will trust me to take care of my own damn self."

"Fine. And you'll allow me to back you up if you ever need it."

"Okay. Whatever."

"Good."

"Great."

"Awesome." He hugged her to him hard. "Be safe, Dreamy. I'm just getting to know you."

Her heart began a tumble-dry setting in her chest.

"He wasn't a threat," she insisted. "Sunshine liked him. And if anything, he's just warning me about the rest of his family."

Linc made a grumble noise that said he wasn't inclined to agree.

"I patched up an abscess for him, and I'm taking my car to his garage for an oil change. And I'm not stupid, Linc."

"No, you're not," he said, tilting her chin up. "Still scared me."

"I'm sorry for scaring you. Thank you for not using the lights and sirens."

"I'm sorry for possibly coming close to maybe almost overreacting."

CHAPTER 35

L inc?" Mackenzie O'Neil calling his name had rapidly become one of his favorite things on this earth.

"In the garage," he yelled over the music.

They'd taken to letting themselves in and out of each other's houses via the back door.

"What. Is. This?" she asked, stopping in the doorway.

He patted the gleaming red fender with the rag. "This is Betsy." Betsy was an antique engine with an open-air cab and a wooden ladder. All lovingly restored with his own two hands. He'd bought her on eBay from a private seller in New York and had road-tripped with Brody to bring her home.

The restoration had taken him five years in bits and pieces and obsessive part hunting. But there was something about bringing a piece of history back to life that appealed to him. Of honoring where he came from.

"I can't believe you have a fire truck in your garage."

"I can't believe you've never been in my garage. You should do a better job snooping on me now that we're having sex."

"I've been through your nightstand, your medicine cabinet, and the magazines you keep in the bathroom. By the way, *Popular Science*, Hotshot?"

"Garages are where guys always hide the good stuff," he said, standing and laying a playful kiss on her.

"Have you been in mine?" she asked, still eyeing Betsy.

He snorted. "Dreamy, I'm a guy. I've been in your garage to check for fire hazards, your basement to look for bugs, rodents, and bad guys. I even stuck my head in the attic crawl space."

"What were you looking for up there?"

"Dead bodies," he deadpanned. "Almost got my ass stuck in that tiny guest closet."

She laughed. She'd been doing more of that lately. It was all part of his diabolical plan to keep her here permanently.

"Well, speaking of garages. I was wondering if you had time to help me with something?" she said.

Asking for help with anything was a monumental task for Dreamy.

He wiped his hands on the rag and threw it on the workbench. "Name it, and it's yours."

"First, I need you to not freak out and go all manly man on me."

"Uh-huh," he said, putting his hands on his hips.

"I need you to help me drop off my SUV at Shorty's Garage for an oil change."

"Uh-huh," he said again. Counting backward from ten.

She was watching him closely. "You're not happy," she observed.

"I'm not," he agreed evenly. "But I *am* choosing to trust your judgment."

She beamed up at him and made him feel like a hero.

"Thank you, Chief Sexy Pants."

"Let me get Betsy out of the garage, and I'll be ready to go."

"You're driving *that*?" she asked, green eyes wide.

"Don't talk about Betsy that way," he said, finding his discarded sweatshirt and pulling it on over his head.

"What I meant to say is, is Betsy road legal?"

He patted her vintage license plate. "She sure is. I usually fill her up with kids for the Fourth of July parade. She loves the attention."

"You're a heck of a guy, Lincoln Reed."

He followed her to the garage and waited while she dropped her keys in the overnight box. When she climbed in next to him, Sunshine firmly between them, he handed her a sweatshirt and cranked the heat.

"It's not that long of a ride home," she insisted.

"I'm taking my favorite girls for a leisurely drive. You got a problem with that, Dreamy?"

She grinned and ducked into the oversized BFD sweatshirt. "Nope. I've got time."

———

The next day, Linc carved out some time of his own. He wasn't "overstepping boundaries." He was doing his girlfriend a thoughtful favor by picking up her SUV for her. If he happened to have words with one of the mechanics at the garage, well, then so be it.

"Thanks for giving me a ride," he told Kelly as she swung into the garage's parking lot. It looked like it was a busy day for Shorty and his crew. Vehicles were on lifts inside open garage bays, and more were stacked in the parking lot waiting for their tire rotations, oil changes, and noise checks.

"Happy to make sure you don't get arrested," she said, parking and unclasping her seat belt.

"You don't have to come in with me," he argued.

"You asked me to drive you. Not Brody," she said simply.

It was true. Brody would have let Linc stir the pot and waited on the sidelines until punches were thrown. Then he'd jump in. Kelly Wu and her mom vibes would ensure that bloodshed would be kept to a minimum.

"I have to talk to him," Linc insisted.

"Yes, you do," she agreed, walking with him toward the door.

"Just keep me on this side of stupid, okay?"

"Will do. What in the hell is that?"

Kelly went from calm, cool, and collected to coldly furious in the blink of an eye.

Linc followed her gaze to Mack's SUV parked next to the building. A team of nervous-looking garage employees stood by with scrubbing implements while the sheriff and Deputy Tahir took pictures.

"HORE" was clumsily sprayed across the hood in white, drippy spray paint.

"Hore? Ohhhhh. Shit," Kelly said.

But Linc was already crossing the parking lot.

"Kersh!" he snapped.

A skinny man with a fresh bandage on his arm and a giant sponge in one hand looked up, eyes widening.

Kelly grabbed onto the back of Linc's shirt as he plowed forward.

"Easy, cowboy," she said, digging her heels into the asphalt.

It slowed him down, but it didn't stop him.

Abner Kersh held up his hands. "I didn't have nothing to do with this," he insisted. "It was like this when we got in this morning."

Linc grabbed the man by the front of his coveralls. "Who did this?"

"Calm down, Chief," Ty ordered, stepping between them. "Abner was the one who called it in."

"I wouldn't do this," Abner said adamantly. "I swear I wouldn't. Shorty, you gotta believe me," he said to his boss, a short, round man with thick, dark hair and a blue bandanna.

Linc wasn't sure if the man was more afraid of him or his boss.

"I know, Ab," Shorty said, laying a hand on his shoulder. "I'll vouch for him, Chief. He's one of my best. He wouldn't jeopardize his job like that. Plus, the guy knows how to spell."

"I do. There's a *w*," Abner said, nodding fiercely.

Linc forced himself to relax. But Kelly, knowing him as well as she did, maintained a grip on his shirt.

"Me 'n' the doc have an understanding. It wasn't me," Abner said more calmly.

Linc believed him, and wouldn't Mackenzie get a kick out of that? But there were still questions to be answered. "Then who was it?" he demanded.

Abner looked at his feet. "Dunno."

Ty shot Linc a look. They all knew who. Abner's brother, Jethro, was an illiterate asshole who carried grudges for years at a time. He'd thrown punches over offenses committed twenty years ago.

"If your brother is responsible, we'll find out," Deputy Tahir said.

"I don't know who did it," Abner said in a less-than-convincing tone. He fidgeted with the bandage on his arm. "But maybe some of us noticed a can of spray paint behind the dumpster. Maybe it's evidence." He shrugged and stared down at the cracked asphalt.

"I didn't let anyone touch it in case there were fingerprints," Shorty said, leading the way.

Linc and Abner stayed where they were, facing each other.

"You convey a message to your family," Linc said. "Dr. O'Neil is off-limits."

"Understood. And speaking hypothetical and all, I'd imagine she won't have any more trouble from anyone," Abner said cagily.

"Good," Linc said.

Abner scratched at the back of his neck. "The doc seems like a nice lady."

"She's also terrifying. So if anyone is stupid enough to come after her, they'll have to deal with me, and if they get through me, Mackenzie will put them down," Linc said stonily.

"Message received." Abner nodded.

Kelly sighed. "Okay. Pissing contest complete. Is that shit going to come off the paint?"

Abner turned his attention back to the SUV. "Looks like water-based. We'll have it scrubbed down in no time."

"You can wash it and wax it too," Linc said.

"Yep."

Ty finished up with the pictures and bagged up the discarded can of spray paint.

And while the garage employees tackled the spray paint, Linc stayed where he was, staring at his girlfriend's defaced vehicle.

"Don't even think about not telling her," Kelly sang.

Linc growled and pulled out his phone.

CHAPTER 36

A week passed and then another after the vandalism at the garage with no other trouble from the Kersh family. The fingerprints on the can had pointed at Jethro, who loudly and drunkenly denied any involvement and then took a swing at Deputy Tahir, who had happily put the man on his ass. Charges were pending.

Mack wasn't worried.

Linc had gone overboard by changing all her locks. He'd made noise about contacting the landlord to replace the rickety sliding glass door on her deck and installing a video surveillance system. Mack had put her foot down on both.

October was showing off this year with brilliant oranges, russet reds, and sunny yellows. The weather was cool and crisp. Mack had allowed Sophie, Gloria, and Harper to talk her into a half-day shopping excursion to stock up on warmer clothes.

She didn't *need* four new sweaters, even if they were as soft as Sunshine's fur. Or the dress that would look really good once she was out of that damn boot.

Her plan to keep Linc at a distance failed just about every night that he wasn't working the B shift. When he was working nights, she kept Sunshine. She'd even brought the dog into the clinic a few times, where Sunshine worked her loving magic on sick or nervous patients.

Her ankle was healing nicely—who said doctors were terrible patients?—and the orthopedist was confident she'd be boot-free in November.

Fall was a season of change. Of new beginnings and ends of eras.

She wasn't sure which one of those Lincoln Reed was. But both possibilities made her nervous. He'd taken her and Sunshine canoeing on the lake and for slow, meandering drives through the countryside to see the leaves. They bought apple cider at roadside stands and posed for pictures with a three-hundred-pound pumpkin.

She helped man the registration table at the fire department's chili cookoff and went to the Morettas' backyard renovation unveiling. Under autumn sunshine and falling leaves, they'd all enjoyed Gloria's mother's enchiladas. Mrs. Moretta was still seeing the football player who had yet to get a word in edgewise but didn't seem to mind.

At work, Mack had had to send her first patient to an oncologist, another to a cardiologist, and physically shared their worry.

She'd stitched up a high school football player. And after a long conversation about self-respect, the right to say no at any time, and how a baby could derail college plans, she prescribed birth control pills to a very excited seventeen-year-old whose mother gave Mack a brave, watery smile in the waiting room.

She stayed busy, but the ratio of work-busy to personal-busy had shifted dramatically. She still wasn't on rotation for air shifts and had three days a week to do whatever she felt like. She was cooking on occasion now and working out in Linc's gym several days a week. She missed running, but the weight training had its own benefits. Namely, watching shirtless, sweaty Linc manhandle huge weight plates.

Meditation was still...not easy. But she stuck it out. Especially after Ellen reported in on her twentieth swim with a beaming, soggy selfie.

Everything was going well. And that too made her itchy. Because things never stayed that way.

Mack's invitation to Benevolence Elementary's First Responder Day was a pleasant surprise. To wow the kids, first responders competed for the most dramatic entry. The police went in with sirens and lights, sliding to stops in the parking lot below the field where the whole school gathered.

The fire trucks roared in and made a show of setting hose lines and climbing ladders.

But Mack's team beat them all.

It was her first time back in the air since the walking boot, and it felt like coming home.

The helicopter skimmed over the treetops, nose tilted. It swooped dramatically low when the field opened up beneath them, and Mack watched the kids waving excitedly, saw the teachers and staff wrangling everyone well away from the landing zone.

RS did a tight, showy three-sixty before setting down dead center on the school's soccer field.

"Way to stick the landing," Bubba said.

RS gave the all clear, and Mack and Bubba unhooked the radio lines and stepped out of the helicopter.

"I feel like we're slow-motion hero walking," Bubba whispered as they strolled—and limped—toward the crowd of elementary schoolers.

"We should take our helmets off and give them a hair toss," Mack suggested.

A familiar voice carried to them courtesy of a bullhorn. "Dr. Mack, you're stepping on my entrance," Linc teased from his department's command vehicle.

The kids had the chance to tour all the vehicles, igniting dozens of career ideas in bright young minds. They tried on helmets and stretched out fire hoses. They sat in the pilot's seat of the helicopter and the driver's seat of a squad car. They played victim and EMT.

Ava Garrison charged up and gave Mack a hug before running back to her little cluster of friends. A few of her other patients called greetings. "Hi, Dr. Mack!"

A long-legged girl with a cute gap between her teeth and braids popped up next to her. "Hi. I'm Samantha. We met before in my uncle's backyard."

"Right. You're Chief Reed's niece," Mack said, recalling the water battle and ensuing death scene.

"And you're his girlfriend," Samantha stated.

"Uh. Well, we haven't really discussed labels, and—"

"Don't freak out." The girl blew out a puff of breath that lifted her bangs off her forehead. "I'm not here about that. I have other business."

"Okay. Why don't we step into my office?" Mack said, gesturing to the helicopter.

They climbed inside. "So I thought I wanted to be a coroner or a mortician," Samantha said, swinging her legs from her perch on the stretcher.

Kids.

"Uh-huh."

Samantha gave her a cool look. "I know it seems weird. But everyone dies. It's job security."

Mack blinked and wasn't sure if it was weirder that an eleven-year-old would consider being a mortician or that the deciding factor was job security.

"That's true."

"But everyone also gets sick or hurt," Samantha said.

"Also true."

"So maybe I want to be a doctor and work with live people. I mean, flying around in a helicopter is pretty cool, and you get to save lives and stuff like Uncle Chief Linc."

"You have time to decide," Mack pointed out.

"Not much. If I want to be a doctor, that means a good premed program and already knowing what med school I want before I graduate high school. And let's face it, dissecting amphibians in biology or learning about hand-washing in health class isn't preparation."

The kid had done her research. Mack made a mental note to talk to Linc about talking to his sister about parental controls on internet searches.

"When did you decide that you wanted to be a doctor?" the girl asked.

Mack cleared her throat as the image popped into her head, crystal clear as if it had happened yesterday. "I was six."

"See," Samantha said in indignation. "I'm already five years behind!"

"Six is too early for anyone to decide what they want to do. You have plenty of time to decide and figure out school."

"How did you know at six?" Samantha asked, twirling the end of one braid. "Were you one of those genius kids? Did you finish med school at eighteen?"

"What? No! I broke my ankle and had to go to the hospital. The doctor was nice to me, and he made my leg stop hurting."

Samantha looked down. "He obviously wasn't very good if you're still in a cast."

"It's a walking boot, and this is a different injury," Mack said, suddenly feeling defensive.

"Same ankle?"

Smart-ass.

"Yes. Same ankle."

"It probably didn't heal correctly."

"I doubt it was the doctor's fault."

"How did you break it?"

"I jumped out of a second-story window." Mack regretted it as soon as the words were out of her mouth, but Samantha was unfazed.

"Is that how you got that cool scar too?"

Mack gritted her teeth. "No."

Hell, the kid could teach her mom and aunts a few things about interrogations.

"Are you torturing my lady friend, Mantha?"

Linc, merciful rescuer, poked his head into the helicopter bay.

"Did you know that Dr. Mack jumped out of a second-story window and broke her leg when she was six and that's how she decided to be a doctor?"

Mack pretended to be too busy refastening a harness buckle to make eye contact.

"Is that so?" he said lightly.

"But it's not how she got her scar. She wouldn't tell me that," Samantha continued.

"Mantha!"

Mack had to laugh at the dad-like admonition in Linc's tone.

"What?" the girl asked in exasperation.

"People don't have to tell you every damn thing, kid," he told her.

"Don't you think this world would be a better place if people were honest about stuff?"

"No." Linc and Mack answered together and then shared a grin.

Samantha rolled her eyes. "You guys are so weird."

"Yeah, yeah," Linc said, grabbing his niece under the arms and plucking her off the stretcher. "Now, get out of here so I can kiss this pretty doctor in privacy."

———

They managed one very thorough kiss before being summoned inside. With the students—and adults—thoroughly worn out, they all trooped into the school's assembly room. It smelled like glue sticks and ravioli.

Mack laughed with the rest of the crowd as the firefighters donned their gear—in a speed competition, of course—and then did the floss dance on the stage. Judging by the gleeful faces surrounding her, she guessed that if one of these kids ever came face-to-face with a firefighter during an emergency, they'd feel joy, not fear. It was a smart, entertaining move.

And she had to admit, *her* firefighter definitely had some nice moves.

After the dancing, the school principal invited all the first responders onto the stage for a Q and A session with the kids.

The students asked Linc if he had a dalmatian. To their glee, he introduced them to Sunshine, who went nosing through the auditorium looking for treats.

They asked Sheriff Adler about catching bad guys and if he'd ever been in a car chase.

They wanted to know how tall Bubba was and if Sally would fly them home.

A kid with thick glasses and an Iron Man T-shirt raised his

hand. "Dr. Mack, I told my dad I wanted to be a doctor, but he said it's too much responsibility because it's life and death and that I should be an accountant or something that doesn't have to keep people alive. So did you ever kill someone?"

The teacher holding the microphone for the kid snatched it away, hissing an "inappropriate" at him while the older kids in the crowd let out an "ooooh!"

The kid shrugged and watched Mack expectantly.

She opened her mouth, but nothing came out.

Faces flashed through her mind in rapid-fire. It wasn't her life she was watching but the ends of others. She'd lost some en route. Some she'd been too late getting to. A few had lost the fight after she'd gotten them to the hospital. And her first had died with his blood on her hands in an emergency department before she'd even finished med school.

That night, she'd lost a patient and become one in the span of minutes.

Under their own power, her fingers brushed over that scar as if she could still feel her own blood. Her hand was shaking.

Linc made a grab for the microphone the principal held. "To answer your question, Tony Stark, we all do everything we can to save every life. Sometimes we can't. But most of the time we do. That's why it's important for all of you"—he pointed to the students—"to know what to do in an emergency."

"What do we do?" a tiny first grader piped up from the first row. Her hair was pulled back in a ponytail made of dozens of tiny braids.

"Seat belts," Linc said into the mic. "Say it with me, gang."

"Seat belts," they parroted.

"Fire escape plans," he continued. "Smoke detectors. Pull over for emergency vehicles when you're on the road. Learn CPR and first aid."

The crowd of kids repeated every word as if they were committing them to memory. And Mack hoped they were. Carelessness hurt people.

"Every one of you is a future hero," Linc told them. "You just need to know what to do when there's an emergency."

He handed the microphone back to the principal and returned to his seat next to Mack.

"You're my hero," she whispered.

"About time you admit it," he said, resting his arm on the back of her chair and letting his fingers stroke her neck.

CHAPTER 37

Linc walked Mack outside after the assembly. "You don't have to ride back in the bird," he told her. "I can drive you to get your car."

He didn't like how pale she'd gone at the kid's question or how her hands had trembled. Secrets. She was keeping them.

"You're working," she reminded him.

"I'm the chief. What's the point of being the boss if I can't chauffeur my girlfriend around in a million-dollar vehicle?"

"Cute. But no. I'm helping with inventory back at the base for a couple of hours."

"You okay?" he asked.

She nodded and took a breath. "Yeah. Kids just stir up all kinds of things."

"That's not vague or anything," he said pointedly.

She stopped and faced him. "Speaking of kids. You're a fraud, Hotshot."

She was deflecting. But he'd allow it…for now. "What are you talking about?"

"You're not the flirty party boy whittling his bedposts down to dust that you pretend to be."

"How many of those shitty Hawaiian punches did you have, Doc?"

"Four. And don't change the subject. I saw you in there. I saw you with all those kids. You're a dad in training. You've got family man written all over you."

"Do not." He shoved up the sleeve of his shirt and showed her a tattoo. "I have BFD written all over me."

She shook her head. "I see you, Lincoln Reed. You might play at being a player. But I *see* you."

They stood there, looking at each other for a long moment. He wanted to make a joke, say something flirtatious. But just like the first time he'd laid eyes on her, he was tongue-tied and uncertain.

She didn't want what he wanted, he reminded himself. He was only opening himself up to a good ass kicking when she moved on. And it was going to hurt more because she was the only one who saw him, really saw him.

"You're going to be a great dad someday," Mack said softly.

He still didn't have any words when she rose on tiptoe and pressed a kiss to his cheek.

"Thanks for the rescue in there," she said. And with that, she turned and hobbled toward the helicopter.

———

Ty was waiting for him in the parking lot, leaning against the hood of the command vehicle.

"Any more trouble with the Kershes?" Ty asked.

"Huh? Oh. No." Linc scrubbed a hand over his jaw.

"Other trouble?"

"Are women anything but?" Linc asked.

"She got pretty rattled up there," Ty agreed.

"She told my niece she decided to be a doctor when she was six and jumped out of a two-story window. Broke her ankle."

"Jumped," Ty repeated.

Linc nodded.

"She's into adrenaline, sure. But…"

"There's no way Mackenzie O'Neil would jump out of a window for fun," Ty finished for him.

"Exactly."

"That how she got the scar?"

Linc felt his mouth quirk. "Not according to Mantha's interrogation. Mack wouldn't say how she got it, only that it wasn't related to the fall."

"You ever tried asking her?"

Linc shook his head. "Nah. Figured I'd just be patient. She'll tell me her story when she's ready."

"That sounds good and well-intentioned and all," Ty said. "But you sure you're not dragging your feet on the whole intimacy thing?"

"Oh, we're intimate all right," Linc said.

Ty drilled a finger into his chest. "That right there, Mr. Fun and Flirty Man Boy. You might say you're ready for the real thing. But if you aren't having the hard conversations now, when do you think you'll get around to it?"

"What are you trying to say, Sheriff?"

"You're holding back. Just waiting for her to pack up and leave."

"She *is* packing up and leaving," Linc argued. "What do you want me to do about it?"

"Heart can't get trampled on if it's still locked up in your chest," Ty told him. "Maybe it's time you put it out there."

"Christ. What the hell did they put in those Hawaiian punches?"

"Go on and make your jokes, my friend. But the only way

you'll earn some very patient woman's heart someday is by getting real vulnerable."

Linc blinked at his friend.

"What?" Ty shrugged. "Soph got Oprah's new book. It's pretty good."

"You're saying you didn't land Sophie Garrison by being a big shot in high school and then picking a career with a uniform that emphasizes your ass and your authority?" Linc asked.

Ty looked over his shoulder at his ass. "It really does look good in these pants, doesn't it?"

"Damn right it does, brother."

"And to answer your question, hell no. Soph wasn't falling for any of that big-shot routine. We broke up. She wanted to spread her wings. It wasn't until I got real and told her that she was the only girl for me, and if she couldn't commit, well, I'd be heartbroken, and I'd always miss her. But I would move on."

"Oh, come on. You're saying that shit worked?" Linc demanded.

Ty shoved his wedding band in Linc's face. "That and one hell of a romantic proposal. Also, periodically knocking her up and putting away the laundry go pretty far too. And only saying no to every sixth or seventh thing she asks me to do."

Now it was Ty making jokes. But Linc knew the man, knew just how much he loved and valued his wife. What a unit they made together.

"I hear what you and Oprah are saying," he told Ty. "But the doc's made it clear. She's only here temporarily."

"And you're too chickenshit to ask her to stay for real. You probably go around making jokes about weddings and babies. But in that charming, professional flirt way," Ty said, doing a reasonable impression of Linc flexing biceps and winking at what he could only guess were invisible ladies.

The truth fucking hurt.

"I'm not agreeing with the chickenshit moniker," Linc insisted.

"But?"

"But you might have a vaguely, sort of, almost-but-not-quite-accurate point. Also, I only wink with my right eye, so your impression needs work."

He demonstrated, and Ty staggered back. "Damn. It was like I heard a *ding* when you did that."

"Keep practicing," Linc told him.

———

Linc and his crew headed back to the station and spent the next few hours on easy calls. He was up to his eyeballs in a grant proposal when his phone signaled an incoming video call.

"Jilly," he said.

"How's my favorite brother?"

"No."

"I haven't even asked. You could at least do me the courtesy of letting me ask the question before you say no."

"Fine," he grumbled.

"Can I drop the boys off at the station?"

"No."

"Before you say no—"

"I already did. Twice."

"Listen. You know how they've been asking for a dog?"

Linc pinched the bridge of his nose. His sisters knew exactly what buttons to push. "Don't go there, Jillian." She absolutely would use his love of dogs against him.

"So I reached out to the rescue where you got Sunshine."

Ah, shit. He was going to end up with his nephews running around the station like lunatics.

"This isn't fair. This is a fire station, not a day care."

"They have the perfect dog," she plowed on. "He's six. He loves kids. And the poor guy has never lived in a home before. His previous owner had him tied to a stake—"

"I hate you. Bring the boys by, but I'm putting them to work," he warned.

"You're the best," Jillian chirped.

———

Brandon, Mikey, and Griffin were part of what looked like a very young United Nations delegation. Jillian was a blond-haired, blue-eyed volleyball player who'd fallen head over heels for a pharmacy major from the Philippines with a passion for cycling and hot wings. They had Brandon, the oldest, who got his hair from his father and just about everything else from the Reed side of the family. Then Jilly and Vijay were bitten by the adoption bug, and in the years after added Mikey to the family from a Venezuelan orphanage and Griffin from foster care.

"Uncle Chief Linc," Griffin said, power walking over to where Linc leaned against the engine. The kid was always in a dignified hurry.

"Hey, Griff. How's it going?"

"Uncle Chief Linc, is Mom abandoning us?" Brandon asked with a worried frown.

Griffin rolled his eyes while Mikey, hands in the pockets of his track pants, strolled around the engine, inspecting it.

Brandon had recently slept at the house of a friend who wasn't as well supervised as Brandon was used to. They'd watched a horror movie about kids whose parents abandoned them after selling them to a traveling circus. He'd been sleeping on the floor outside his parents' bedroom for the past week.

The dog will help, Linc predicted.

"I don't think so," he said, ruffling his nephew's thick, dark hair. "I think she's just running an errand."

"If she does abandon us, will you come live with us and Dad?" Brandon asked earnestly.

"Absolutely," Linc promised. "Five bachelor guys in a house living it up?"

"Is bachelor when all the ladies show up to live with you and you have to pick the prettiest one or the one that yells and cries all the time?" Mikey wanted to know.

Another unsupervised victim of television. He couldn't wait to tell Jillian.

"That's a different kind," Linc assured him.

His nephews lined up in front of him and waited expectantly. "So?" Brandon asked.

"So what?"

"Are you going to feed us or something?"

"Better. I'm putting you to work first. You have to earn those grilled cheeses." He pointed out the open bay door where the ladder truck sat outside on the asphalt.

"What kind of work?" Mikey asked suspiciously.

Linc picked up the buckets and sponges he'd stashed on a workbench. "You're washing my ladder truck."

Someday, Linc thought as he watched the boys battle over the hand line, his nephews wouldn't be ecstatic about washing the bottom two feet of the fire department's apparatus. Someday, they wouldn't be excited about visiting him. They'd be too busy with school and sports and girls—or boys. So he'd hang on to these moments now while he had them before they were gone.

He'd hang on, and he'd wish, he'd hope, that Mackenzie O'Neil would take a chance on him and give them both a shot at this.

CHAPTER 38

She'd gone and done it now. She'd officially lost her damn mind, Mack decided as she hauled the final load from the grocery store into the kitchen. There were bags everywhere. Food everywhere. And because the food couldn't be served out of shopping totes or store packaging, she'd had to buy serving dishes, bowls, paper plates, utensils.

Then there'd been the issue of where to sit. She couldn't very well have a dozen people over and cram them around her four-person dining room table. Though really, who could have known they'd all say yes on such short notice?

So she'd bought a picnic table and a couple of folding lawn chairs from Bob's Fine Furnishings. The table was due for delivery in ten minutes.

"What if they all have to go to the bathroom at the same time?" Mack groaned to herself as she unloaded ten tons of produce for the fruit and vegetable trays she thought would be nice to snack on.

She froze. *What if no one shows up?*

Leaving everything where it was—would the kids even like those little cups of ice cream anyway?—she hurried out the back door and across the yard to the gate.

She knocked on Linc's back door.

It was open. He never locked it, and sometimes she let herself in. But in her self-induced panic, she was rooted to the spot. She stopped knocking when Sunshine bounded up to the glass, followed quickly by a bewildered-looking Linc.

He opened the door with a grin.

"I made a terrible mistake. I had a good day. The weather was nice. Then some evil force took over my body and started inviting people over for a cookout. Tonight. At my place. You're invited, of course. I should have led with that. Anyway, I don't know what to do. I have a kitchen full of food, and what if no one shows up or they all have to go to the bathroom at the same time and there's a line? Do I have enough beer? What about wine? Do kids like ice cream cups?"

He stopped her by gripping her shoulders and laying a hard kiss on her mouth.

When he pulled back, Mack's brain was quiet again.

"Dreamy?"

"Yeah?"

"What do you need?"

"Help?"

He was a natural. Within five minutes, he'd unpacked all the groceries and triaged them into prep order. While she oversaw the table delivery, Linc appeared with a large plastic tote marked "PAR-TAY" and began unloading supplies.

She sliced fruit and vegetables, and he threw chicken breasts into bags of marinade.

"We'll keep the food inside. That way, everyone can sit on the deck or at the picnic table since it's a nice night," he told her as he manhandled two large coolers onto her deck. "Beer in this one. Water and soda and kids' drinks in this one."

"I don't have any kids' drinks," she groaned.

"Dreamy, I've got thirty-seven thousand nieces and nephews. I've got kids' drinks," he promised.

"I'll pay you back," she said.

He climbed the steps and put his hands on her hips. "You're breathtaking when you're Dr. O'Neil on the scene. You're beautiful when you're trying to line dance. But this frazzled, wide-eyed woman who just wants her friends to have a good time is downright adorable."

"Shut up." She let out a long breath and gave in, wrapping her arms around his neck and pressing her face into his chest for just a minute. He was so steady. So good.

Sunshine trotted inside with a face full of dirt and what looked like the better portion of a tree stump in her mouth.

"Shit," Linc said, releasing Mack.

The dog dropped the muddy chunk of wood on the floor and wagged her tail expectantly. She was covered in dirt and mud from nose to tail.

Paw prints and smears covered the black-and-white checkered tile.

"I'll clean it up," he promised, looking at his watch. "I swear."

Mack started to laugh and couldn't stop. Sunshine took the humor as a compliment and jumped up on Mack, placing two perfect muddy paw prints on her breasts.

"Sunshine!" Linc grabbed the dog by the collar. "It's not a party if a dog doesn't need a bath during it," he promised Mack as he hauled the mud monster out the back door.

"Then this is going to be a hell of a party," she predicted, surveying the disastrous kitchen.

While she scrubbed the floor, he made a run for the ice she'd forgotten and came back with ingredients for some secret recipe dip and more flowers. Grocery store flowers.

"Figured you were due for some new ones," he said, shoving the bouquet of yellow and orange and red blooms in a vase. He dropped a kiss on the top of her head. "I'll fire up the grill and get the drinks on ice. Then I'll show you my secret buffalo chicken dip recipe."

She stopped in the middle of scrubbing and stared up at the flowers.

Sunshine mournfully pressed her still-muddy nose against the sliding glass door, tail wagging hopefully. Mack smelled hot grill and heard the music that Linc was playing through a wireless speaker. She wouldn't have thought of music. She hadn't known how much she enjoyed fresh flowers. She'd had no clue how much she'd love a—mostly—good dog. And she hadn't been prepared for a hotshot neighbor with tattoos and a charming grin.

Her heart did an odd roll.

"Oh boy," she whispered, slapping a hand to her chest.

So *this* was what it was like. There was no point fighting it. She'd gone and fallen in love with Lincoln Reed.

———

Mack was still reeling an hour and a half later when her backyard was full of people. Music, a mix of pop and country, poured from the speaker. The smell of grilled meat and citronella candles wafted on the evening breeze. Someone somewhere was burning leaves.

Ellen showed up with a large Caesar salad and a six-pack of skinny spiked seltzers. Aldo and Gloria brought the girls and two pecan pies. Luke and Harper were sans kids thanks to

Luke's brother, James, and his boyfriend offering up a sleepover. They showed up with hot dog and hamburger buns and their dogs, who romped with Sunshine and made begging eyes at anyone manning the grill. Harper was sporting a fresh hickey peeking out from the neck of her sweater, and Luke had a self-satisfied grin permanently affixed to his face.

Freida and her husband brought potato salad and shrimp and arrived midargument about whether a time-share in Cabo was a good move. Russell and Denise appeared with two bottles of very nice wine and truffle mac and cheese and weighed in on the time-share debate. Tuesday would have come, but she and her boyfriend were in Pennsylvania for the weekend for a ten-mile mud run.

Everyone loaded up plates and carried on conversations. *Work. Food. Kids. Football. Medicine.*

It was exactly what she'd envisioned, and she couldn't quite believe that it was happening in her own backyard. She'd gone overboard. Mack could see that now while she enjoyed a quiet glass of wine on the deck steps. There was way too much food. The picnic table, while a nice addition to the backyard, hadn't been as urgent as she thought as her guests had shown up with their own chairs. She'd be eating fresh fruits and veggies for at least the next five days. And there was no way one three-year-old was going to eat two dozen ice cream cups. But it was still perfect.

She was watching what had turned out to be quite the successful party when Aldo's three-year-old, Lucia, skipped over to her. Her sweet, round cheeks bore the evidence of the ice cream Mack had second-guessed, and her lips were stained red from Linc's juice boxes.

"Hi!" Lucia said.

"Hi."

"I fell down and hit my face running when I wasn't 'sposta," the little girl said, pointing to a scrape on her jaw.

"Ouch," Mack said.

"How did you get your boo-boo?" Lucia asked, poking the scar under Mack's eye.

Mack moved back an inch or two so as not to lose the eye. "Oh, that happened a long time ago."

"Was it on accident or purpose?" Lucia asked. "Mama says sometimes when people get hurt, it's not on accident. But that they can still be okay."

Mack was losing control of the conversation. "Uh, I guess it was on purpose."

Lucia put her chubby little fists on her hips. "It's not okay for people to hurt other people," she lectured.

"No, it's not," Mack agreed. "But I'm okay now."

"My mama's okay now too," Lucia said with an emphatic nod. "Sometimes I kiss her old boo-boos to make sure they still don't hurt."

"That's very nice of you," Mack told her, feeling her throat tighten painfully.

Lucia leaned in and pressed a sloppy kiss to Mack's eye. "Dere. Now yours won't hurt anymore either."

Bewildered, Mack watched the little girl skip off until the image blurred behind hot tears she blinked away.

She felt a hand on her shoulder and jolted.

Linc sat next to her, and bath-fresh Sunshine burrowed under Mack's arm on the other side. He didn't say anything.

"Just got something in my eye," she fibbed.

He stroked a hand down her back, and she wanted to tell him. To blurt out the words that bubbled up and demanded to be set free. She had feelings. So many of them now that she didn't know what to do with them all.

Instead, she leaned her head on Linc's shoulder and decided to just feel it all for a while before making any rash decisions.

CHAPTER 39

Linc argued baseball with Luke and kept an eye on Mack as she joined in the conversation with Denise and Freida across the yard.

He felt a tug on the hem of his sweatshirt. "Chief Wink! Can I draw you a picture?" Lucia asked, peering up at him with those big, beautiful Vietnamese eyes.

"I'd love a picture," he told her.

"Den I need some paper," she informed him.

"I brought crayons and four coloring books," Gloria said, appearing behind her daughter. "But she's insisting on paper."

"Lemme ask Dreamy," Linc said, pretending not to see the look Gloria and Luke exchanged. If everyone was surprised by his relationship with Mackenzie, they might as well hurry up and get over it.

He inserted himself into the girl talk as they debated whether Harper should run for Benevolence mayor the following year.

"Do you have some paper a three-year-old could commandeer?" he asked.

Mack smiled up at him in a new, soft, dreamy kind of way that made him want to kick everyone out and kiss her for the rest of the night.

"Sure," she said. "There's a notebook in the living room on the shelf by the fireplace."

"Thanks." He did kiss her then. He couldn't help himself. He left her with Freida and Denise's chorus of "oooh" and headed into the house, all three dogs on his heels. "Behave yourselves," he warned them.

He found the notebook, a sketch pad actually, on top of a stack of medical journals and flipped it open. The charcoal portrait surprised and intrigued him. It was a young woman with laughing eyes and thick, black hair that kinked and curled in a celebratory riot around her face. He turned the page and found another portrait, a man with a buzz cut and lines around his eyes and the mouth that was pressed in a firm, flat line. He wore a uniform decorated with a load of military experience.

"Not that one," Mack said, breathlessly hurrying into the room. "I forgot. The notebook's on the end table."

"Mackenzie, these are amazing."

She looked like she was about to be sick.

"What's wrong? What is it?" he asked, closing the sketchbook.

She bit her lip and picked up a spiral-bound notebook next to the couch. "They're my dead," she said finally.

"Patients you've lost," he clarified, with the hope that the woman he was head over heels for wasn't confessing to being a serial killer.

She nodded.

Linc was relieved. "They're really good."

Her shrug was jerky. "Thanks. I picked it up after First Responder Day. I used to sketch when I was a teenager. I thought if I got them down on paper that maybe I wouldn't have to carry them all around with me anymore."

He got it. He carried his own shadows with him. All first responders did, and sometimes the load got too heavy.

"Who was she?" he asked, opening to the first sketch again.

"I don't really know much about most of them," she said, staring down at the woman on the page. "She was the last one I lost in Afghanistan. She was a medic and a translator and got caught in some crossfire. I knew she wasn't going to make it back to the base. But instead of sitting there and holding her hand, I gave her plasma and worked on her injuries. I knew she wasn't going to survive. Her heart stopped five minutes out and never restarted. And I didn't know her name or who she was thinking about when she slipped away. I just knew that her blood pressure was too low and her heart had stopped."

"That's what you're trained to do," he reminded her.

"But it wasn't what she needed. My medic on that flight, he leaned down and whispered in her ear the whole time. I thought I was annoyed that he wasn't getting me what I needed fast enough because he was too busy trying to make this connection to this person who wasn't going to make it. And that sounds horrible," she confessed. "But I was mad at myself for not being able to offer that kind of comfort. I could fill her up with pain meds. But he was the reason she died with this little smile on her lips. He promised her he'd tell her mom that she was the best mom in the world. And I only did what I was trained to do."

"Did he tell her?" Linc asked.

"Probably. I don't know. After that flight, I decided it was time to be done. To do something else. My deployment was up. And I decided I wasn't going back."

His doctor always seemed to be moving forward, never looking back.

"And here you are," he said. He wanted to flip through the pages and study the faces she'd drawn.

"With a backyard full of people and a house full of dogs," Mack said, cracking a hint of a smile as Lola flopped on her back on the couch, legs in the air.

Sunshine was busy chewing on a squeak toy shaped like a taco that Mack bought for her. Max was biting Sunshine's fluffy tail.

She was a miracle, he decided. A walking, talking, scarred, beautiful miracle, and he was only just beginning to scratch the surface.

"I feel like the more I get to know you, the more I want you around, Mackenzie." It wasn't exactly a confession of love or a demand for forever. But it was something.

She let out a steadying breath. "I maybe don't hate the idea of sticking around," she said.

They were standing with the coffee table between them and a whole lifetime of unspoken words. But for now it was enough.

The back door slid open. "Mack, where's your diaper changing station, and do you have any tarps and biohazard suits?" Aldo asked, holding Avery at arm's length. The baby smelled like sewage and was belly laughing.

CHAPTER 40

On a chilly Sunday just before Halloween, Sunshine's presence was requested at Jillian's so she could teach their dog how to stop eating throw pillows, socks, and loaves of bread he counter surfed for. Linc invited Mack along for the ride.

They watched together from the truck as Sunshine plowed full steam ahead through the open front door, and Jillian gave them a harried wave.

"Don't corrupt our girl," Linc called out the window of his truck.

"Oh, shit," Mack snickered. They watched through the big front window as Sunshine, followed by the new dog, Beefcake, hurled themselves onto the back of the sofa. They could hear the crash as the curtains and curtain rod fell to the floor.

"Yep. Teaching Beefcake everything she knows," Linc said, throwing the truck in reverse and peeling out of the driveway.

"Shouldn't we go back and help?" Mack asked, still laughing.

"Hell no. Up for a little detour?" he asked, taking her hand.

"I'm all yours," she said.

He wondered if she noticed the easy routine they'd settled into. How sharing a bed and a dog seemed second nature now.

"Good. Let's take a field trip."

The old fire station sat on a skinny lot on the far end of Main Street. There were two stories on one side and a long, low bump-out on the other. Paint peeled from the garage doors. The windows were dirty enough to obscure the view inside. But the brick, the roof, the bones of the building held up as they had for all the decades the building had been in service.

"Wow," Mack said when Linc let them in through the side door.

Under the layer of mustiness that all old buildings had, it still smelled vaguely of diesel fuel inside. The concrete floors were stained from decades of use. The exposed brick in the main garage was a restorer's dream, though the hideous green wood paneling in the community room and on the second floor left much to be desired.

"This was my home away from home when I was a kid," Linc told her as they strolled over old oil stains and ducked under cobwebs.

The place held a host of memories for him, ghosts of times and people past. Of childhood dreams and young adult experience. He'd ridden to his first call out of this very bay. He'd scrambled around trying to collect "exhaust samples" in sandwich bags while the rest of the crew laughed. He'd celebrated his first save, mourned his first loss. All within these walls.

"There's a pole," Mack said with delight.

"Had to stop using it after one of the LTs landed bad and fractured his tibia," he recalled. "I started visiting my uncle here when I was five or six. The guys would let me try on their helmets and climb around the engine. One time, I sat on my uncle's lap while he pulled the truck out of the garage. I got to turn on the lights."

"And you were hooked," she said.

"Yeah. It was never going to be anything but fire for me."

She nodded, getting it. Getting him.

"I had my prom pictures taken here," he told her, pointing at a spot by the big doors.

"Who did you take to prom?" she asked with a smile.

"No one. I had a date, but she changed her mind."

"Who turns down Lincoln Reed?" she teased.

"Karen Whitwood."

"And what happened to this Karen Aucker?"

"She became Karen Garrison, and a few years later, she died in a car accident." He kept his tone even. But that didn't make the feelings go away. "Let me show you the upstairs."

He turned, not wanting Mack to see the sadness.

She followed him up the creaky staircase to the second floor. Here carpet frayed, and more of that hideous paneling bowed off the walls. He paused in front of one of the windows that looked out over Main Street and the town that held all his memories.

"I'm sorry," Mack said. Her hand settled on his shoulder. "I'd heard that Luke didn't like you because you'd asked his wife out."

He sighed. "We were all just kids. Luke wanted the military and for Karen to go to college. Karen wanted to get married. They broke up over it, and maybe I thought I had a shot."

"You liked her," she filled in.

He had. A lot.

"She was pretty and smart. Hardheaded, like someone else I know," he said, shooting Mack a look. "Anyway, when I heard they broke up, I waited a respectful twenty-four hours before showing up at her front door with a handful of daisies—her favorite—that I stole out of my mom's flower bed. I asked her on a date, and she said yes. I felt like I was on top of the world."

He could still remember how it felt. A victory a long time

coming. Landing the girl he'd been thinking thoughts about since thirteen or fourteen.

"I took her to dinner at the Italian place. She was sad about Luke, but I worked my charming magic to cheer her up. It was working. We talked and laughed. And I was feeling pretty hopeful. So I suggested that since she didn't have a prom date and I didn't have a prom date, we should go together."

He remembered exactly how she'd looked as he asked. Looking back, he could see the hesitation. But at eighteen, all he noticed was the yes.

"She said yes," he continued. "I was so sure that she was finally seeing me."

Mack leaned back against the brick between dirty windows, listening.

"Garrison and I had it out the next day. He came at me, wanting to know why I was moving on his girl. I wanted to know, if she was his girl, why he'd just let her go like that. We went a few rounds. Nothing serious. Moretta broke it up. And Garrison took off all pissed off. She called me later that night. 'Good news! I don't have to cramp your bachelor style. Luke and I are back together and he's taking me to prom.'"

She winced. "Ouch."

Linc shoved his hands in his pockets. "It was just a crush. I was eighteen. I didn't know anything about life or love."

Sometimes he still felt that way.

"You knew her favorite flower. And you get sad when you talk about her. Feelings are feelings whether you're eighteen or eighty."

"She hadn't even taken me seriously. She said I was a good friend helping her make Luke come to his senses."

"A dick move," she said.

"She was eighteen and in love."

"Oh, so *Karen* could be in love, but you just had a crush?" Mack pointed out.

"Girls are emotionally more mature than boys," he argued.

"A fair point. But that doesn't mean your feelings weren't real."

They'd been real. Real enough that even years later, when he'd arrived on the scene of the accident that had taken her life, he'd frozen in place. She was already gone when they got there. All the dozens of what-ifs running through his mind.

What if he'd fought for her?

What if she'd chosen him instead of Luke?

What if she'd seen beneath his flirty teenage exterior?

But he hadn't. She hadn't.

And at some point, he'd stopped believing there was anything else but the easygoing, serial flirt. He was a good man but never good enough to be someone's partner.

"I was there. On the scene," he said, the memories rising up as they did sometimes late at night when he couldn't sleep. "I remember thinking that it was officially the end. I didn't even know I'd held out hope that someday she'd see me. Choose me. We lived in the same town, ran into each other everywhere. It wasn't like I was hoping she'd get divorced. I'm not that big of an asshole. But I guess I'd always hoped that maybe there was still a chance someday. Someday I'd have that. And then it was all over. No more chances."

Mack didn't say anything as she pushed away from the wall. She just wrapped her arms around his waist and held on tight.

"Sorry for bringing the mood down," Linc whispered against the top of her head.

"Don't be a dumbass," she said. "Ask me how I got this scar."

He went still for a beat. "Are you sure you want me to ask?"

"We're sharing painful shit. You shared. I share."

He nudged her chin up so she'd look at him.

"How did you get your scar, Dreamy?" he asked, tracing a finger over the jagged ivory mark.

She took a breath and let it out slowly. "I was a resident in an emergency department in Texas. A patient was brought in. Car accident. I knew him, but we were short-staffed, and it was life or death. I worked on him, did everything I knew how to do, and it still wasn't enough. He never revived. I called it." Her eyes had a faraway look in them. "I lost the patient. My first. His girlfriend—I knew her too—was...distraught." Her voice was tight. "When I told her he was gone, she broke a glass vase at the nurses' station and came at me with a big shard. It took two orderlies and one really pissed-off nurse to get her off me. I couldn't even fight back. She just kept saying that I killed him. I ended my shift getting stitched up."

"Bad enough to lose one, but to have someone blame you?"

"Loudly. In my workplace, where I was trying so hard to prove myself," Mack recalled. "She was high. Turns out so was he. He overdosed. He might have survived his injuries. I did everything I could. But I still felt responsible. Even now, whenever I learn a new procedure, a new protocol, I wonder if I could have saved him if I'd known more."

"Ghosts," Linc said.

Her gaze returned to him. "Yeah. They're always there, lurking in the background."

"How do we exorcise them?" he joked. Then winced. Ty was right. He was hiding.

"Maybe we just move forward and leave them behind," she mused.

"Sometimes it's a tough choice," he said, tucking a wavy piece of hair behind her ear. "Knowing when to abandon the past and when to build on it."

She slid her hands up his chest, over his shoulders, and linked her fingers behind his neck. "I think you should forget about the past and kiss me right now."

He backed her up slowly until she was pressed against the wall. Her breasts were flattened against his chest. His cock went hard between them, blood pulsing with the need to fuck his way inside her. "How'd you like me to kiss you, Dreamy?"

She wet her lips, and the pink tip of her tongue ignited a want that ached inside him.

"Kiss me like nothing else matters," she whispered. Her green eyes were serious, pleading. And he was helpless to do anything but give her what she wanted.

CHAPTER 41

The kiss changed from soft and sweet to something darker, needier, and Mack reveled in it. Linc crushed his mouth against hers, teeth scraping her lips until she surrendered, opening for him on a thready moan. He pinned her to the wall with his hips. His erection was hot and hard against her belly, and his hands were everywhere at once, tugging at her hair, digging into her hips, and then sliding under her sweatshirt, shoving layers out of the way to get to her electrified skin.

His tongue claimed her mouth like it was a distant mountain peak, something to be conquered victoriously, triumphantly. She wanted him to claim the rest of her. To take it all until she had nothing left to give.

He broke the kiss and yanked her hoodie, then her T-shirt over her head. Burying his face between her breasts, he let out a pained groan. His hips gave a shallow thrust against her that made the throb in her core thrum faster.

He needed this. Needed her. And she wanted to be needed like this.

She pushed him back just far enough to pull his shirt over his head, sank her teeth into the ink over his pec.

"You're so fucking beautiful," she told him, dipping her tongue over his nipple.

"Fuck," he breathed. "If you're not okay with me taking you against this wall right now, I need you to say it, Mackenzie."

The staccato beat of her heart thundered in her ears. A need so fierce, so base, clawed its way through her.

"Fuck me against this wall."

He swore darkly as if she'd unleashed something in him. In one desperate motion, he'd dragged her pants and underwear down her legs. She managed to free one foot before he was boosting her up and wrapping her legs around his hips. The boot made her feel off-balance, but Linc's arms held her tight, and the brick braced her from behind.

"Thank God for sweatpants," she whispered, reaching between them and freeing his cock.

He growled low in his throat when she gripped his shaft. Pressing her against the wall, he yanked her bra down under her breasts and greedily fastened his mouth to one nipple.

It hit her like lightning. Her entire system was alive and on fire. Those decadent, desperate pulls at her breast, the marble-hard dick in her grip that was just an inch away from where she needed it to be.

"We don't have a condom," she breathed.

He let out a litany of curses against her breast and then dragged his teeth over her pebbled nipple.

She let out a little gasp. "I'm good if you're good."

He released her breast with an audible pop. "Yeah?"

There was so much she could see in those blue eyes. So much more than simple, uncomplicated lust. Letting him in, trusting him, meant something. It did to her too. "Yeah."

"I've never—"

"Me neither," she admitted. "But I want you like that. Nothing between us."

He didn't say another word. His jaw clenched, making the cords in his neck stand out as he eased into her inch by perfect inch. Those blue eyes bore into her like he wanted to see inside her, reveal all her secrets.

"Mackenzie." He drew out her name as he sheathed himself in her.

She couldn't speak, couldn't breathe as he invaded her, stretching her to make room. There was a sliver of pain wrapped around the edges of a pleasure so intense she wasn't sure she'd survive it. Then he was filling her completely and going still as she adjusted.

Full. So beautifully full. He was deep and bare, and she reveled in the feel of being possessed. She was nothing but sensation. The rough bite of brick at her back. The hot, hard muscle to her front. And that magnificent cock connecting them both in the most intimate way possible.

She didn't feel empty and sad now. She glowed from the inside out.

He ducked his head and closed his mouth over her other breast, sucking and licking until she writhed against him, desperate for more friction, more motion. She cried out when he gave a shallow thrust with his hips.

"I've dreamed of this, baby," he whispered between masterful laps of his tongue.

"Of what?"

"Being buried inside you, bare. Feeling you come on my dick, those hard, hungry squeezes. That hot flood when I make you let go. Of filling you up when I come inside you. Making you mine."

He was so fucking primal, and so was their need for each

other. Biology. Love and lust tangled up together in unconquerable knots.

Gripping her hips, he withdrew slowly and then thrust back into her, hard. She dug her nails into his shoulders.

"More."

"You like how I fuck you, Dreamy?" His breath was hot on her face and hair as he pulled almost all the way out again. She hated how her body felt without him inside her. Empty. But then he was driving back into her, and everything was right again. Maybe that was the secret rhythm of life. The empty existed to appreciate the full.

"God, yes," she moaned.

His fingers gripped the curves of her hips possessively, thrusting faster now into her. Mack bucked her hips and squeezed him with her thighs. Sweat slicked their skin. She bit him on the jaw. The neck. The flesh of his shoulder.

He was pounding into her now. A wild rhythm that she couldn't keep up with. She could only take. Dizzy with want and need, she clung to him.

He growled and groaned dirty sweet nothings against her skin. Telling her a thousand ways how much he loved her body. How good it felt to be inside her. How right they were for each other. Her orgasm was on a hair trigger, but she wanted to go over the edge with him. Wanted to come as he did.

Her muscles trembled, thighs locked around his hips, inner walls around his cock as he slammed into her over and over again. Her breasts bounced between them with every powerful thrust.

"I feel how close you are, Mackenzie," he whispered in her ear. Grunting every time his cock seated fully in her. "I feel you gripping my dick. I'm gonna make you come, and I'll feel like a goddamn hero when you do."

"I want you to come with me. In me."

His heavy-lidded eyes widened. In wonder, in surprise? She wasn't sure.

"I don't deserve you," he gritted out.

"Yes. You do. Now take what's yours." This time, she kissed him, her teeth latching on to his bottom lip. Their bodies were out of control, racing toward something so powerful, so primal, it was encoded in their DNA. He held her tighter while she carved scratches into his back, arching against him until the head of his cock was hitting her in some magical place.

"That's right, baby," he said. "That's what I want."

Her muscles fluttered around his shaft as he burrowed into her again. She could feel him going impossibly harder, thicker inside her as he chased his own release.

"You're going to make me come, Mackenzie."

She let out a gasp as the flutters changed speed, as she plunged headlong into an abyss of pleasure. Her body contracted and released as the first wave curled her toes and closed her walls around his thick shaft.

His grunt was guttural, wrenching, as he drove into her, pinning her to the wall and holding there. She felt it, that hot flood deep in her core as her muscles clamped down again. He moved, matching her waves and his so every time her walls trembled, he was fully sheathed in her.

They stared into each other's eyes, not wanting to miss a second of the rawness. He was fucking beautiful when he came. Strong. Powerful. Vulnerable. Here. Now.

Right now, there was no past to overcome. No ghosts to chase. Right now, there was only their twin heartbeats and the pleasure they gave and took.

Mack's breath was coming in gasps. Whimpers worked their way out of her throat as they rode each other out. Sweat dotted her chest and trickled down her back. And when it was over, while he was still sheathed inside her, while their pulses thundered victoriously together, he rained soft kisses over her face. Whispered words of praise and gratitude in her ears while their bodies were still connected.

CHAPTER 42

Mack's phone rang for the fifth time under the stack of files on her desk. Insistently. She was in the clinic. That was her excuse for not answering. Sure, the practice had closed an hour ago, but she really wasn't interested in ending her day on a sour note.

She waited an entire minute before pushing Play on the voicemail message.

"Mackenzie, it's your mother. It's very important. Call me." The voice was singsong and had a trademark Texas twang despite the fact that her mother had been born and raised in Delaware and now lived in Illinois.

"Men *love* a southern belle, Mackenzie," she'd always said. Andrea O'Neil Leyva Mann was an expert on what men loved.

Stubbornly, Mack returned her focus to the insurance appeal she was working on. Her patient needed a Tier 4 medication that the insurance company had denied twice. *That* was important. She finished off the letter and attached the necessary documentation. Then she copied all the files into the patient's record and scheduled a note to follow up with the insurance company on Monday.

With all that taken care of, she was officially off duty for the day. And out of excuses to not call her mother back.

Was she being a healthy adult by avoiding unnecessary stress? Or was this an immature defense mechanism left over from a tumultuous childhood?

She picked up the phone and scrolled to her mother's contact. Andrea. Not Mom. Andrea hadn't earned the title.

"Mackenzie!" her mother trilled when she answered, and Mack automatically shifted into carefully listening mode for any signs of alcohol, her mother's favorite hobby.

"Hi, Mom."

"I've been trying to reach you for weeks," Andrea complained.

It had been four hours.

"I've been busy. What do you need?"

"Well, as you know, my birthday is coming up next weekend, and it's been *so long* since you've been home. I would just *love* it if you could come back for a little celebration."

Mack rubbed the dull ache at the back of her neck. Despite her susceptibility to guilt, she hadn't been "home" in two years.

"Is Wendy going to be there?" Mack asked. It was her automatic out where family gatherings were concerned.

"Don't be silly, Mackenzie. I wouldn't ask you if I thought your sister would be around. She moved away ages ago. It'll be just you and me." Her mother gave a shaky, sad sigh. "To be honest, I'm feeling just a little bit lonely these days."

"Aren't you seeing anyone?" Mack's rules where her mother was concerned were simple. One, the rent money continued when Andrea was sober. Two, Mack had no responsibility to ever meet another "Uncle" Anyone or rebuild a relationship with her sister. She hadn't met her mother's last two husbands, holding a firm line when the wedding invitations arrived.

But she'd still sent gifts. And that irked her.

"It's just me all by my lonesome these days." Andrea sighed. "I'm afraid I'm starting to show my age and scaring off all the eligible bachelors."

"Are you drinking, Mom?" Some mothers and daughters talked about work or dinner recipes or books or kids. Mack monitored her mother's sobriety.

"Of *course* not. Sober as a judge, darlin'."

She was too far removed anymore to tell lie from truth over the phone. And in Andrea's mind, sometimes there wasn't a difference.

"In fact, we've got more to celebrate than my little ol' birthday. I got my one-year chip last week," Andrea said, back to chipper.

"Congratulations, Mom," Mack said, calling up the calendar on her desktop.

No new stepfather. No Wendy. And no drunken tantrums.

She could probably get away for a few days. Three max. And then she could put off the next visit for another two years. A reset on the guilt button.

"You can stay here in the guest room. And maybe you could take me out for a nice dinner?" Andrea's voice rose hopefully.

"That sounds nice. I can probably get away." Mack ignored the sick, cold dread that slid into her stomach. Her mother had a disease. Daughters, especially doctors, didn't walk away from a parent because they were sick.

She heard a flurry of barking on her mother's end of the call.

"Hush now, Gigi!"

"Did you get a dog?" Mack asked.

"I did! A couple of months ago. She's a tiny little thing but barks like she's a big dog. Anyway, I took a peek at flights from Philadelphia—"

"I'm not based in Philadelphia anymore," Mack said. "I'm in Maryland."

She'd had no idea her mother had gotten a dog, just like Andrea hadn't known Mack moved.

"Oh well. Isn't that nice?"

And that was the extent of their small talk. Mack promised she'd confirm her travel dates. Andrea gleefully took responsibility for making a dinner reservation for her birthday dinner.

It would be somewhere fancy, with gold-rimmed plates, white linens, and tiny portions. If there was one thing her mother loved more than alcohol, it was appearances. In Andrea's mind, the most important thing in the world was maintaining a certain level of respectability. She was never without makeup, false lashes, and heels. Even when she was shit-faced.

At one time, Mack had thought her mother beautiful. But the ugly truth that no lipstick or pretty dress could conceal never stayed hidden for long.

Mack disconnected, feeling the way she always did after a conversation with her mother: anxious, unsettled, and vaguely ill. She could use a strong hug and maybe a happy dog, she decided and picked up her keys.

————

The fire station's bay doors were wide open as the B shift volunteers buzzed in and out, seeing to routine tasks. Bright lights, shiny trucks, and people doing what they'd promised to do. It was a balm to her irritated spirit.

She parked and got out, now feeling silly.

She should have texted first or, better yet, gone straight home. It wasn't like she was going to tell Linc about her mother. That would open the doors to her childhood. And there was no reason to go digging into that mess. She was a survivor. Not a victim. And looking forward was healthier than looking back.

But there was a joyful bark, and Sunshine was galloping in her direction.

"Hey, buddy," Mack said, kneeling down to give the dog a good scruff. She gave in to her need for comfort and buried her face in the soft, blond fur.

Sunshine snuck in a kiss, and Mack laughed, wondering if her mother had found this kind of joy with her dog.

"I'd like to report a dognapping in progress," Linc called through a bullhorn, strolling out of the garage. "Unhand the dog, lady."

She rose, brushing dirt and dog fur off her pants. He was dressed in tactical pants and a long-sleeved BFD polo that fit him like a second skin. His ball cap was on backward, and there was a smudge of grease on his jaw. That cocky grin was exactly what she needed, as was the hard hug he gave her when she walked into his arms.

"This is a nice surprise," he said, leaning back and lifting her off her feet to the whistles and hoots of appreciation from his crew.

"Hi," she said, feeling the ice in her belly thaw into something molten and warm.

"How was your day, Dreamy?" he asked, setting her back on her feet and slinging an arm around her shoulders.

Before she could answer, the alarm blared.

Everyone around them jumped into action.

"What have we got?" Linc called over the noise as he dragged her inside.

"Car into a structure, possible cardiac arrest," Brody yelled back, shrugging into his gear.

"Feel like taking a ride, Doc?" Linc offered.

A trauma physician on the ground was never a bad thing. "Let's go."

She grabbed her med bag and loaded it into the chief's vehicle. In seconds, Linc was climbing in behind the wheel, wearing the bottom half of his gear. Sunshine watched mournfully from the end of her leash as they pulled away.

"Be a good girl," he called to her through his open window.

Accustomed to lights, sirens, and speed, Mack triple-checked her supplies on the drive while Linc stayed on the radio with dispatch, gathering information. The engine was behind them, and an ambulance was en route too.

They left the town limits and made the turn toward farmland and houses with big yards.

Dusk was falling, and there was a chill in the air.

"Here we go," he said to her. "Command arriving on-scene."

Together they exited the vehicle and jogged toward the wreck.

It was a sedan, or what was left of it, crumpled into the front porch of a tidy white farmhouse that sat up against the road. The driver was still behind the wheel.

"He's not breathing, and I can't find a pulse," a man in jeans and flannel said from his vigil at the open driver's side door.

"Thanks. Let's get him out," Mack said.

"I'm with you," Linc said. He caught the lightweight tarp Brody threw him and spread it on the ground a few feet from the car. "Lighthorse, assume command and get the engineers inside. See if the structure's safe."

"On it, Chief."

The ambulance hadn't arrived yet, and it took Mack, Linc, and another firefighter to ease the man out from behind the wheel and onto the ground. Blood covered his face from the airbag.

"Pop-Pop!" There was a boy crying in the arms of the farmer's wife.

Mack swore ripely.

"What?" Linc asked.

"It's Leroy Mahoney. That's his grandson, Tyrone," she said, cutting Leroy's sweater down the middle. "No pulse. No breath." His lips were already tinged blue.

"Fuck," he hissed.

"Go," she insisted. "Take care of the kid. He trusts you."

"Lighthorse, take over here," he called.

Brody appeared and dropped to his knees. "What have we got, Doc?"

"Sixty-eight-year-old male. Possible STEMI. Starting CPR until we get a defibrillator from the EMTs. Check him for any other injuries." She started compressions while Brody worked his way down Leroy's too-still body. "Get me some light here."

She didn't look up when a floodlight lit up the tarp. She didn't pay attention to the sirens as they approached or the engineer team gearing up to go inside the house. The only thing that existed in her world was Leroy Mahoney's still heart.

She paused after the rescue breath and checked vitals. "No pulse. No breath."

"Possible broken wrist, needs stitches on the forehead. Not sure about any neck or spine injuries," Brody reported as she began the next round of compressions.

"Get the epi in my bag for me," she said, counting compressions internally. "Front pocket right on top."

There was a flurry of activity behind her.

"Ma'am, I'm gonna need you to step back." A paramedic loomed over her.

"That's Dr. O'Neil, not ma'am, and you're in my light," she

snapped. "I need a line in his arm now. And one of your guys needs to check the kid. He was in the back seat."

An EMT hurried off while the "ma'am" man knelt opposite her and shrugged off his bag. "You get any epi in him yet?"

"Nope." Sweat coursed like a river down her back. "Third round of compressions. No breath, no pulse."

Leroy was bagged, and the second the IV port was in, the paramedic delivered the epinephrine. Another EMT slapped EKG sensors in place.

"Charging."

"Go."

"Nothing," he said, reading the portable screen.

"Shock him and call for the chopper," she decided, swiping her forearm over her forehead. Her ankle ached from the awkward position.

She delivered another round of compressions, another shock. Another shot of epinephrine. They pushed fluids into the line. Still nothing.

"Fuck me," she muttered.

She didn't dare look up at Tyrone. But she could hear Linc's soothing voice, the kid's quiet sobs.

"You are not doing this tonight, Leroy," she growled. "Go again."

Again and again, they repeated the process.

"Looks like internal bleeding," the paramedic noted, spotting the violent purple bruising around Leroy's chest.

"Chopper is eight minutes out," Brody reported.

"We don't have eight minutes," Mack said. "Put him on the backboard and get me a scalpel."

"What are you doing?" the paramedic demanded.

"We're opening him up."

CHAPTER 43

Linc had practically grown up on scenes like this. Flashing
lights, fast, coordinated movements by the men and women
who stood between the horror and the crowds of onlookers.
Faces bathed in red and blue. The tension of dozens of human
beings praying, hoping together.

But he also knew when something extraordinary was
happening.

With Tyrone being looked after by an EMT, Linc returned
to Mack's triage area. She was snapping orders, her gloved
hands moving in a concerted blur.

"You can't just open him up out here," the paramedic across
from her warned.

"Argue with me later. When he's open, you treat the bleed
and give me room to massage his heart."

"We don't know if he's on blood thinners," he tried again.
"The guy could bleed out right here."

"The guy's name is Leroy, and I *do* know that he's not on
blood thinners because I'm his goddamn family doctor. And I'm
not letting him die with his grandson watching, so get the fuck
on board."

It hit him. A wave of love and pride so tall, so fierce, it made him weak in the knees.

"On board, Doctor. You ever do this procedure before?"

"Nope," Mack said as she slipped the scalpel into Leroy Mahoney's chest.

"Holy shit. Is she—"

"Yep," Linc told Brody as his captain approached, white-faced.

Brody picked up his radio. "Dispatch, this is Engine 231 on Mulberry Road scene. Doctor is performing open heart massage on-scene."

There was a beat of silence.

"Copy that, Engine 231. I'll tell them to fly faster," was the unfazed reply.

A hush fell over the scene, and Linc imagined dozens of prayers were floating up past the floodlights and into the dusk.

"Get that bleeder," Mack ordered. She was up to her wrists in a human being's chest.

Linc felt a little light-headed, and he wasn't sure if it was from love or the impossibility of watching his girlfriend play God with a man's life.

"Beautiful," she said. Her face was a study in concentration under the floodlights.

Linc could hear the faint approach of the helicopter.

"Bleeding's under control," the paramedic reported gruffly.

"Good. Hang on. I think I've got something," Mack said. Everyone held their breath.

Tyrone appeared at Linc's side, a bandage on his arm, his eyes swollen from tears.

"Pop-Pop?" he whispered brokenly.

Linc put an arm around the kid and hugged him tight.

"I've got a beat!" Mack's face was triumphant.

Breaths expelled in a whoosh.

"Got a radial pulse," an EMT called from Leroy's feet.

"Fuck yes!" Linc whispered.

"BP is stabilizing," the paramedic observed. "I'd high-five you if you weren't elbows-deep inside a patient right now."

"Rain check," Mack whooped. "Strong beats!"

A cheer unlike any celebration Linc had heard before rang out. His guys stuck their heads out the first-floor window and hollered right along with the collection of neighbors and first responders.

There were tears, audible prayers of gratitude. The celebration continued as the chopper touched down in the pasture across the field while Mack quickly stitched her patient back up.

Linc watched her lean in and down, saw Leroy's lips barely moving.

"Tyrone is just fine, Leroy. I promise you," she said. "You hang in there, or I'm gonna be real pissed."

Linc had never been prouder in his entire life than when he saw the professional admiration on the flight doctor's face while she gave him her report.

"Never seen anything like it," he said as EMTs and firefighters transferred Leroy to the spine board.

"I'm not surprised," the hulking flight nurse said with a grin. He offered Mack a gloved hand and helped pull her to her feet. "You're a hell of a doctor, O'Neil."

"Thanks, Bubba," she said. "Take good care of my guy here."

The flight doc glanced down at her footwear and shook his head. "Who knew superheroes wore air casts?" With that, they turned and jogged with the stretcher to the waiting aircraft.

Stripping off her gloves, Mack watched them go. Stood still as the helicopter lifted off. When she turned and stumbled on her walking boot, Linc was there to steady her.

"Dreamy," he said, wrapping her up when she sagged against him.

"I've never been so happy, hungry, and tired in my entire life," she confessed.

"Dr. Mack. Is my grandpa gonna be okay?" Tyrone asked.

Mack pulled him into their hug. "He's got a good chance, buddy. Your Pop-Pop is one tough guy."

"I'm scared," he whispered. "We were talking about what to pack for lunch at school tomorrow. I don't like meatloaf. And Pop-Pop was laughing, and then bang!"

"It wasn't your fault. You didn't distract him or cause this. Your grandpa's heart just picked that moment to stop working right."

Linc gave the kid an extra squeeze. "We called your mom, Tyrone. She's going to meet us at the hospital. So why don't we swing by your house and pick up some things for your grandpa that he can use at the hospital?"

They bundled Tyrone into the chief's vehicle, packed a bag of whatever an eight-year-old considered essential to a grandpa—including corduroy pants, the TV remote, and Tyrone's favorite stuffed bear—and delivered boy and bag to the hospital.

Tyrone's mom, Leroy's daughter, was already there. Mascara running down her cheeks, she hugged each one of them extra hard. They waited with her for an hour.

A nurse popped down with good news from the OR. Minimal damage to the heart muscle. The surgeon was putting in a stent and confident in a full recovery. Tyrone's mom burst into tears, and Mack assured the boy they were happy tears.

This time, it was Linc driving an exhausted, sore Mackenzie home from the hospital.

"Pizza," she said, her eyes closed, head resting against the seat. "Beer. A hot bath."

"TV," Linc added.

"Dog," they said together.

"This was a very good end to what was a questionable day," she sighed, stretching her arms toward the dashboard.

Later that night, after beer, pizza, bath, and dog snuggles, they curled together on Linc's big bed, her back pressed up against his front, his arm anchoring her to him.

He waited until her breaths slowed. And when he was sure she was sound asleep, he nuzzled into her neck.

"I'm so fucking in love with you, Mackenzie O'Neil."

CHAPTER 44

Mack wasn't sure exactly what she was expecting when she opened her back door, but it wasn't seven kids dressed as everything from a robot to a franchise princess to some kind of death-zombie-murderous ghoul. Sunshine was wearing a sparkly tutu and fake pearl necklace. Her cloth tiara was already under her chin.

Linc was in tights. She meant to check out the rest of his costume, but the tights were almost inappropriately highlighting his anatomy.

He cleared his throat, and she reluctantly dragged her gaze away from his crotch. Superman. Of course he was dressed as Superman.

"Happy Halloween," the kids chorused.

"Happy Halloween, guys," she said. "Candy's out front."

"We're not here for candy," Samantha announced, all business.

"Yeah! We're picking you up for twick or tweat!" Griffin said, busting a move in his Darth Vader garb.

Mack felt her mouth fall open to form a perfect O.

"Where are your parents?" she asked finally.

"Our moms are at Uncle Chief Linc's," cloaked vampire

Mikey explained. "Our dads are painting our living room. It's tradition."

"Us guys lost a bet five years ago. So every Halloween, my sisters order pizza and drink too much wine at my place while handing out candy. My brothers-in-law tackle one home improvement project—while drinking too much beer—and I escort these monsters around town," Linc explained. At least, she thought it was Linc, but she was staring at his crotch again and couldn't be sure.

"We're bringing the wagon to pull you if you get tired," robot Brandon promised earnestly.

"You said she'd say yes if we didn't give her any time to think about it," Bryson complained to Linc.

Linc shoved the kid off the step and into a bush. The rest of the kids laughed. "Don't listen to him. And don't think about it. Just say yes and put this on." He tossed a shopping tote at her.

Mack peered inside. "No way. Absolutely not."

"Kids. Deploy sad faces," Linc ordered with a snap of his fingers.

Six pairs of pathetic eyes stared up at her. Seven if she counted Sunshine's. Eight if she counted Bryson's face peering up from the depths of the bush.

"I'm not wearing this," she told Linc.

"It's trick-or-treat. You have to be in costume. It's the law," he insisted.

"Please, Dr. Mack?" Mikey begged, clutching his hands at his chest. "Please?"

"Dammit."

Five minutes later, Mack was shaking her head in front of the mirror. "I'm not wearing this in public."

"You're only saying that because you forgot the bracelets," Linc said from his repose on her bed. He plucked the two plastic cuffs off the bedspread.

"The skirt is completely inappropriate."

"I'm wearing tights. We'll go as Mr. and Dr. Inappropriate," he insisted, sliding the bracelets into place. "Besides, you've got a cape to keep everything covered until later."

"What happens later?" she asked, still eyeing her reflection.

"Superman and Wonder Woman get it on while still in costume," he said, bouncing off her mattress. "In fact, I don't know why we're still standing here talking. Every minute we waste now is one minute longer before I get under Wonder Woman's skirt."

She crossed her wrists and held them in front of her. "Back off, evil Superman. If you start sporting wood in those tights, a kid is bound to lose an eye, and you'll be banned from trick-or-treat forever."

"Your argument is strong, but your skirt is short. I'm having trouble focusing on what's more important."

"Why is it so quiet downstairs?" she asked, adjusting the headband.

"Huh?" His eyes were glued to her legs.

"There are seven kids and a dog downstairs, but it sounds like a library."

"Shit." Linc ran from the room and jogged down the stairs. "Dammit, guys! This isn't your house. You can't just start warming up leftovers!"

———

"I can't believe I'm doing this," Mack hissed to Linc as the kids hauled ass up the walkway to a yellow bungalow decked out with dancing skeletons and hand-carved pumpkins.

"Trick or treat!" the kids yelled in unison when the door opened.

"Hey, Dr. Mack! Hi, Chief Linc," a short ninja with plastic nunchucks called as he or she ran by with a bag of loot.

"That ninja knows my name," Mack said.

"Dreamy, everyone knows your name. You're the talk of the town. 'Doctor saves patient in roadside open heart surgery,'" he said, quoting the local newspaper's headline earlier that week.

"And now I'm dressed as Wonder Woman."

"Relax. Have some candy," he said, producing a mini candy bar from behind his back.

"Did this come from where I think it came from?"

"There's a secret candy holder in my belt, not my well-formed ass."

She unwrapped the candy and laughed as the kids sprinted back to them.

"Homemade caramel corn," Samantha squealed.

Sunshine nosed at the bag of treats Joni Whitwood had handed them at the last stop. Mack restrained herself from asking Linc if he felt strange running into the mother of the girl he'd once loved. Sure, they'd shared things, but most of their relationship centered around great sex and playful banter. It was best not to push too far.

"You really didn't have to bring the wagon," Mack said. "My ankle feels good. And there's no way in hell I would ever willingly ride in that thing."

"Oh, it's not really for you," Linc told her. "It's either for all the candy the kids whine about being too tired to carry, a kid who hits his or her sugar limit and has a meltdown—my money is on Kinley this year—or little Miss Sunshine, who gets too sleepy to walk."

Sunshine, hearing her name, pranced in place.

"I guess trick-or-treat is your favorite night of the year, isn't it?" Mack asked the dog.

Sunshine gave a happy little bark, and Mack obligingly fed her a treat.

"Dr. Mack, what's your favorite candy?" Mikey asked, batting his long lashes at her.

"Get your own girl, Charm School," Linc said, playfully elbowing his nephew out of the way.

"Where to next, Uncle Chief Linc?" Rapunzel Leah wanted to know.

"The Morettas," he decided.

Their motley crew of costumed children cheered.

"What's so great about the Morettas' house on trick-or-treat?" Mack asked as Linc threaded his fingers through hers.

"You'll see," he said, squeezing her hand.

Aldo and Gloria were the king and queen of small-town Halloween. They were dressed as Sonny and Cher, a seemingly adorable inside joke that Mack made a mental note to ask Gloria about later.

Their garage was decked out in not-too-scary haunted house fashion. Aldo manned a grill on the street, handing out hot dogs, hamburgers, juice boxes, and cold beers to costumed visitors. Gloria, her mother, and Aldo's mother ran carnival games from tables in the front yard. There were baked goods and candy and vegetable trays and conversations happening everywhere.

Linc's nieces and nephews dispersed on the lawn, heading for the games, the garage, and the orange-and-black inflatable bouncy house.

"Wow" was all Mack could say.

Her handsome sidekick reached into a cooler and produced two beers. "Wonder Woman?"

"Aren't there open container laws?" she teased.

"We each get one," he explained. "Then you can help me drive my drunk sisters and brothers-in-law home."

"Just what kind of a bet was it?" she asked.

"A really stupid one," he said.

"Dr. Mack! You're right on time!" Ellen, dressed as a cop with a badge that said Fun Police, hurried over. She gave Mack a hard hug and Linc a wink that he returned.

"Ellen, you look great," Mack said. It was true. Her patient-slash-friend was glowing. Her face looked brighter, a little leaner. And there was a definite sparkle in her eyes.

"I feel great," she said. "I had no idea how much I missed swimming, you know? And guess what?"

"What?"

"My husband started coming to the gym with me. He's been lifting weights while I swim, and then we walk the track together for twenty minutes before he goes to work. I haven't had to yell at him about his boxers for two weeks! And my father-in-law and I started cooking dinners together. The man had never used a microwave or loaded a dishwasher in his life. Now he's on Pinterest saving Bolognese recipes."

Mack laughed. "That's great."

"Are we still on for next week?" Ellen asked.

"Yeah. Sure," Mack said. "Ladies' night."

"Great! Do you mind if I bring a couple of my girlfriends? You know, make it a real ladies' night?"

"Uh. No, I don't mind." Maybe she'd invite Gloria and Harper and Sophie, Mack thought. Then wondered who in the hell she was, having girlfriends who she could invite places.

"Awesome. I'll see you next week. I better go get my kids. They're nearing the close-to-vomiting-candy-in-the-bouncy-house phase. Love the tights, Linc!" Ellen jogged off and poked the inflatable wall with her plastic nightstick. "All Kowalskis will now exit the bouncy house."

"Put that beer down right now!" Cher Gloria, wearing her chubby-cheeked baby, hurried toward them.

"Why?" Linc asked. "Is it just for the kids?"

She gave him a playful poke. "No. We have champagne waiting for you two." She gave him a kiss on the cheek and then did the same to Mack.

Gloria Moretta was happy. Down-to-the-bone, swimming-in-the-blood happy. And Mack suddenly, viscerally, wanted to experience that feeling.

"What are we celebrating?" Mack asked.

"You, silly. You saved Leroy Mahoney in front of his sweet grandson, performing open heart surgery on the side of a road. Perfect costume, by the way," Gloria said with a grin. She signaled for Aldo at the grill.

"Oh, I… Well, Linc got me the costume." Mack felt her cheeks flame.

"Come on." Gloria grabbed Mack's hand and towed her toward the front porch of the Craftsman-style house.

There was yet another table and not one, not two, but four bottles of champagne chilling in skull-shaped ice buckets amid a sea of plastic flutes.

Aldo climbed the steps behind them. He gave Linc a punch on the arm and Mack a trademark hug before tickling his baby under the chin. Then, heedless of the audience, he cupped Gloria's chin in his big hands and kissed her gently.

Linc playfully covered Mack's eyes. "If they start taking their clothes off, we're leaving," he said.

Kiss complete, sweet moment shared, Aldo turned to face the yard. "Hey, Fun Police," he called to Ellen. "Give us a whistle, would you?"

Obligingly, Ellen blew her whistle shrilly, and the crowd quieted down.

"Happy Halloween, everyone," Aldo said, slipping his arm around Gloria.

"Happy Halloween!" everyone shouted back.

"We wanted to take a minute to thank someone very special for her good deeds," Aldo said.

"Oh my God," Mack hissed. Linc grinned at her. "You knew?"

"You wouldn't have come if I told you."

Gloria's mother bustled onto the porch and popped open the first bottle of champagne.

"Most of you know Dr. Mackenzie O'Neil," Aldo said, waving an arm in her direction.

The cheer was rousing and completely embarrassing. She wanted to hide under Linc's cape, but he held her firmly in place.

"You deserve this, Dreamy. Soak it up," he whispered.

"You know that Dr. Mack here saved my life. None of this would be here if it weren't for her," Aldo said.

"Oh no," Mack whispered. Her throat was tightening, eyes watering.

"Try not to blink," Linc suggested.

She opened her eyes scary wide and stared blankly at the porch light.

"I wouldn't be here grilling hot dogs with my beautiful wife and two perfect little girls if it weren't for her. And we had a few other people who wanted to say thank you too."

Mrs. Moretta let out a wail and blew her nose in a pumpkin napkin. "Sorry. You can continue," she howled.

Don't blink. Don't blink. Don't blink.

Another bottle of champagne was popped and poured.

"Oh, crap," Mack rasped as Dalton and Mr. and Mrs. McDowell—all dressed as the Incredibles—climbed the steps of the porch. Dalton ran over and handed her a drawing of a gigantic tick biting a stick figure boy and then a stick figure with boobs and a huge scar on her face kicking the tick. Mack laughed.

"Thank you for *everything*," Mrs. McDowell whispered, wrapping her in a hug.

Mack didn't know what to say, didn't know if she could say anything. So she just nodded and let herself be hugged.

"You did good, Doc," Mr. McDowell said, his voice tight with emotion. "Real good."

"Thanks," she managed. She sounded like she'd just swallowed a dozen razor blades. Her eyes burned, and she went back into nonblinking mode.

The McDowells picked up their champagne and Dalton's juice box and stepped aside.

And then there were two more people on the porch. Mack briefly wondered what the weight capacity was, then decided it didn't matter when she realized that Tyrone Mahoney was dressed in a little flight suit and carrying a mini medical bag. His handmade nametag said Dr. Mack. The boy had dressed up as her for Halloween.

"Oh, shit," she whispered. She blinked, and a hot tear spilled out of the corner of her eye.

Linc squeezed her shoulder and cleared his own throat. "Just hang in there."

Tyrone and his mom hugged her hard.

"Pop-Pop is still in the hospital, but he says to tell you thanks," Tyrone told her with a big, beaming grin. "And I'm going to be a doctor just like you someday."

Words failed her. Which was fine because Tyrone's mom, a lovely young woman still in a business suit that Mack felt was probably not a costume but a just-made-it-home-in-time-from-work-for-trick-or-treat, burst into tears while hugging her.

"Thank you," she whispered through tears.

"To Dr. Mack," Aldo said, raising his champagne.

"To Dr. Mack," the crowd in the yard echoed.

The ladder truck that Mack hadn't heard pull up celebrated too, with lights and its horn.

She had never been more uncomfortable in her entire life.

Or happier.

The feeling stuck with her on the way home. On a crisp fall night, in a friendly small town, Linc, her Superman firefighter boyfriend, carried the yawning Griffin on his shoulders. She pulled Kinley and Sunshine in the wagon and listened to Samantha talk about premed courses. Her belly was warm from the champagne, and the twinkle in Linc's eye told her he hadn't forgotten about his quest to discover what Wonder Woman wore under her skirt tonight.

Maybe, just maybe, she could get used to this.

CHAPTER 45

S on of a bitch," Linc grumbled at his reflection in the mirror. Being a fire chief didn't put him in a tie often, which was why he periodically had to google how to tie a fucking tie.

"Need some help?"

Mackenzie appeared in the mirror behind him, a vision in floor-length soft gray that dipped subtly between her breasts.

"Wow." Tie forgotten, he turned around to get a better look. "Wow."

Her red lips stretched into a wide smile, eyes crinkling. She'd done something with her makeup, making her eyes look darker, bigger, her lips delectably fuller.

"I got this when the girls forced me into that shopping trip. Best thing about this outfit?" she said.

"If you tell me it's what you're wearing underneath, I might lose consciousness while walking the bride down the aisle."

Teasingly, she lifted the hem of her dress. "You can barely see the boot."

"You're beautiful, you know that, Dreamy?"

"You're not so bad yourself, Hotshot," she said, fingers slipping up to his tie.

He slid his hands down to cup the curve of her ass while she worked her dexterous magic on his neckwear.

"How'd you learn to do that?" he asked, frowning down as she produced the perfect knot.

She looked embarrassed, shrugged. "I saw my foster parents getting ready for a date night once. She helped him tie his tie. I learned."

He waited a beat. "Foster parents, huh? You know, someday we're gonna be due for a long conversation."

She picked up his wrist and checked his watch. "Yeah, but not today. You've got to get a bride down the aisle."

———

The bride was bubblier than the glasses of champagne that the catering staff doled out to guests as they took their seats in the old barn for the ceremony. The two-hundred-year-old rafters above had been strung with lights. Dozens of white chairs lined an aisle that led to an altar made of braided twigs and more lights. Every flat surface was decked out with a blaze of fall flowers, pumpkins, and pictures of the bride and groom from childhood to present.

The mood was festive as Mindy tucked her arm through Linc's. "You ready for your first trip down the aisle, Chief?" she teased. She was a tiny, blond thing, just as she had been all those years ago. But instead of a nightgown and snarled braids, she wore a lacy, long-sleeved gown, and her hair was curled and coiffed into perfection. Her brown eyes shone with excitement.

"Listen, are we sure that Bill is good enough for you?" Linc asked as the last bridesmaid blew Mindy a kiss before starting down the aisle.

"He's more than good enough," she promised. "He's just

so good and kind and smart and funny. He reminds me of my dad." Her voice broke just a little, and Linc squeezed her hand.

"I'm sorry he's not here, Min."

Her smile was sad. "That's what he used to call me."

"Maybe he's here after all."

"He wouldn't miss it," she said, tears sparkling.

The attendant gave Linc the cue. "You ready to go get married?"

"Let's do this."

It was a big moment. The second Bill caught sight of Mindy, they both let out a sigh of relief. So sure. So happy. After delivering the bride to the altar and her fiancé, Linc took his seat in the second row next to Mackenzie, who beamed at him.

She handed him a glass. "Nice delivery, Hotshot."

Maybe it was the lights, the champagne, or the way the happy couple looked at each other as they made their promises, but he was feeling some feelings.

Mindy's mom sat in the front row, her shoulders shaking as she cried silently. Her daughter was just starting her marriage while she'd lost her partner too soon. The beginning and the end. Everything in between. Linc wanted it all.

Mack reached over the chair and handed the grieving woman a tissue. As she dabbed at her eyes, Linc laid a hand on her shoulder and squeezed.

———

He was still thinking thoughts later with Mackenzie in his arms on the dance floor as the live band played a jazzy number. She glowed. A trick of the lights or maybe something more. She seemed lighter, freer.

"How's your ankle holding up?"

"A little sore but good. The boot comes off soon."

"You look happy," he said, pulling her tighter to him. Never close enough.

"I feel happy," she admitted.

"Is this a good time to pin you down for Thanksgiving plans? Because my sisters have been asking. My parents won't make it. They're coming for a few weeks over Christmas. But the rest of the gang will be there."

She missed a step. "Like a family Thanksgiving?"

"Is there any other kind?"

"Friendsgiving."

"Touché."

"I might have a couple of guests coming in for Thanksgiving," she hedged.

"Bring them. Your place is too small for a big family meal anyway."

She fingered his lapel. "So what you're saying is me and my guests can join your family's celebration, and I don't have to cook the entire meal?"

He grinned. "You'll be lucky if my sisters let you open a bag of rolls."

"This is a very tempting proposition. I'll check with my guests," she told him.

They returned to their table, an interesting collection of Bill's teacher friends and Mindy's office coworkers. Linc looped his arm around the back of her chair, his fingers stroking lazy circles on her arm while the conversations ebbed and flowed.

"Excuse me, if I could have everyone's attention," Mindy said into the band's borrowed microphone.

The crowd quieted.

"I know we've already done our wedding toasts, but there's one more that needs to be made."

Bill approached her with two fresh glasses of champagne.

"Thanks, hubby," she said, making the guests laugh. "Anyway, as many of you know, a long, long time ago, my family's home caught fire."

"Oh boy," Linc whispered.

Mack's hand slid onto his thigh and squeezed. "Ha. Now it's your turn, jerk."

"I almost didn't make it out," Mindy continued. "It was Christmas Eve, and I was trapped in a room with Scratch, the sixteen-pound family cat. The smoke was so thick, I couldn't see a thing. I could barely breathe. And I was losing hope. My daddy wasn't going to come rescue me. I wasn't going to be able to save Scratch. I wasn't going to open that pile of presents my parents wrapped.

"And then out of the smoke came my own personal hero. He was there when I needed him most. Firefighter Lincoln Reed risked his life to save me and Scratch, who lived up to his name during his rescue."

The crowd chuckled warmly.

"Without Chief Reed, none of this beautiful, perfect day would have been possible. I wouldn't be here in a beautiful dress saying yes to the most amazing man. There wouldn't be a reason for all the people I love so much to gather together and drink champagne and dance."

Linc's throat tightened to the point of strangulation. He pawed at his tie, trying to loosen it.

Mackenzie leaned in. "Just try not to blink."

Mindy and Bill raised their glasses to the crowd. "To Chief Reed. My hero. Thank you for every single day since that one."

"To Chief Reed!"

"Good job, Chief," Mack whispered, clinking her glass to his.

"I'm gonna be traumatized by the sound of champagne popping," he grumbled as the applause continued.

Mack's phone vibrated in her clutch. She checked it, frowned.

"What is it?" he asked, leaning in.

"Trish Dunnigan calling. Probably just checking in. I'm going to take this," she said, excusing herself from the table.

He watched her go and felt that longing again.

He wanted to ask her, to push the issue. Things were good. *They* were good. This was a real shot at something. A beginning.

But he didn't. If he asked, if she said no, that was the end of his hope.

He lasted through five minutes of personal thank-yous from the bride, her mother, and a dozen other friends and relatives before he managed to duck out a side door.

It was the first Saturday of November, and the night air held hints of winter coming. The moon above was almost full and painted the fields in a ghostly glow.

He drew in a breath, released it in a silvery cloud.

"You all right?" Mack, rubbing her arms with her hands, stepped out behind him.

She was luminous in the moonlight, a winter queen in silver.

"What is it with people all of the sudden doing these big thank-yous?" he muttered, looking away.

"Let's face it, Hotshot. What you do matters. What we do matters. Other people's lives change because of what we do." She slipped her arms around his waist from behind and pressed her face to his back. "You're a good man, Lincoln Reed."

Then stay. He wanted to say the words that hovered on the tip of his tongue. He wanted to put them out there. But he didn't want to hear what came next.

That he was good for a good time. A good friend. And not much else.

Instead, he turned around, wrapped Mackenzie up in his arms, and breathed her in.

CHAPTER 46

Mack ignored the sinking feeling she had as she pulled up in front of her mother's tidy little town house. It, like every other place her mother had ever lived, would never be home to Mack. But this was one of the nicer neighborhoods that Andrea had settled in. She imagined that her monthly rent check helped considerably as she studied the red brick exterior. The concrete steps were swept, but the planter on the edge of the landing held the skeletal remains of some kind of summer flower.

"It can't be that bad. Just a couple of days," she muttered to herself.

Still stalling, she pulled out her phone and fired off a text.

Mack: Just got to my mom's house. Hope Sunshine keeps you company, Hotshot.

She waited, hoping for a response. But when none arrived immediately, she decided she was being an idiot and stashed her phone in her bag.

He'd offered to come with her when she told him about the impromptu trip. A laughable idea, considering. But it had warmed her heart and made her even more determined to get through the visit.

She eyed her suitcase in the rearview mirror. There was no need to cart it inside right this second. She could easily come out and get it when she needed it. Or drive off without a scene if things got too intense.

"Mackenzie!" Her mother greeted her with an effusive and out-of-character hug. "I'm so glad you made it. Come in. Come in."

Andrea was dressed in a pink jogging suit. Her nails were long and disco-ball silver. Her hair—platinum blond now—was piled and pinned on top of her head. Mack felt guilty at the relief that coursed through her. They no longer looked like each other. Maybe that meant any other similarities had also disappeared.

But the relief didn't last. It never did where her mother was concerned.

The first hint that something was off was the pair of men's loafers on the floor in the foyer.

"Whose are those?" Mack asked, pulling back from the hug and pointing at the shoes.

"Oh, those old things? They're Tony's."

On cue, a man with a big belly and a bowling shirt sauntered down the hallway. His receding hairline was partially disguised by a greasy combover.

"Oh, hey. You must be Kenzie," he said. He sounded more Bronx than Illinois to Mack's ear. "I was beginning to think your mom here was pulling my leg about having two daughters. You don't visit?"

"Mackenzie's a doctor in the military," Andrea cut in.

Mack didn't bother correcting her. It wouldn't stick anyway, she judged by the glass of wine her mother picked up from the coffee table.

"Hi," she said flatly to Tony. "So you two are seeing each other?" She couldn't even pretend to be interested.

"Ha! A little more than that," he scoffed.

Andrea made a show of holding up her left hand and squealing when the big pink diamond that Mack was eighty-five percent sure was fake caught the fluorescent light from above. "We're getting married! Surprise!"

Mack knew the reaction that was expected from her but just couldn't muster it. Her mother wasn't alone. She wasn't sober. She'd just moved on to husband whatever number he was and probably wanted to pressure Mack on a wedding gift. And Mack had been paying his rent for who knows how long.

"So I was thinking, wouldn't it be romantic to go to Mexico for a honeymoon?" Andrea began, clasping her hands under her chin and cocking her head at Mack.

And here was the ask.

It was too warm in this tight space. The light was harsh, accenting the deep lines carved into her mother's face around the eyes, across her forehead. Her skin, once fresh and lovely, now had a sallow tint to it.

"Top you off, honey bear?" Tony offered, wiggling a wine bottle.

"You sure know how to make a girl feel special." Andrea giggled.

Mack felt like she was going to throw up. Once again, it was all just lies. And she'd walked right into it. Not only walked into it but bought a plane ticket, rented an SUV, and showed up on the doorstep. She wasn't sure who she was more disappointed in, herself or her mother.

It was then that she heard the noise on the stairs, saw the bare feet, the familiar tattoo of thorns wrapped around an ankle. Anger, swift and bright, crashed over her.

"What's with the screaming?" Wendy asked with a yawn. She'd obviously just gotten up for the day at four p.m. Her hair was dark like Mack's, but she added bright purple streaks and extensions. Yesterday's eye makeup was smeared under choppy, uneven bangs. She was thinner than Mack remembered. Paler. But Mack wouldn't mistake that for weakness.

"Your sister's here, and we just told her the good news," Andrea announced grandly. "Wendy moved back home! Isn't that wonderful?" she crowed to Mack.

Wendy eyed Mack coolly. She strolled down the steps and brushed past Mack to get to the pink purse hanging on a hook inside the door. She reached inside and pulled out a pack of cigarettes and lit one. "What are you doing here?" she asked.

"Mack's here to help us celebrate my birthday. She's taking us all to dinner tomorrow night," Andrea said brightly. "My girls are always surprising me," she said in an inaccurate aside to Tony.

It was then that Mack noticed the shake in her mother's hand, the unsteadiness of her gate in the four-inch feathered stilettos under the jogging pants.

Andrea had a deep love of alcohol and had always been good at hiding it.

"Are you drunk?" Mack asked.

Andrea hiccupped and clapped a hand over her mouth. "Oopsie!"

Tony laughed adoringly. Wendy blew a cloud of smoke in Mack's face.

"You said you were all alone," Mack said. "You said you were sober, that *she* wouldn't be here, and that you were all alone for your birthday."

Andrea waved the words away, wine sloshing over the rim of her glass and spilling onto her pants. "What in the world are you talking about? I swear, this girl should have been a writer, the *stories* she makes up."

"This is bullshit," Wendy muttered under her breath. "I'm going out," she announced.

"Don't you want to have a big, family dinner?" Andrea pleaded.

"As far as I'm concerned, she's not part of the family," Wendy said, stubbing the cigarette out on Mack's purse.

"Can I talk to you outside?" Mack asked Wendy briskly.

She didn't wait for an answer, simply grabbed her purse and stalked out the front door. She waited on the front steps for a solid minute until the door opened and closed behind her.

"What's your problem now? Kill another patient?" Wendy demanded, drawing her black hoodie closer around her shoulders. She had another cigarette lit and a glass of whatever wine Tony was pouring.

"She's drinking again. She's drunk," Mack said matter-of-factly.

"So?"

"So she said she was sober."

"Oh, come the fuck on, Pollyanna." Wendy scratched idly at a scab on the back of her hand. "Like you even give a shit about this family. You never have. It's always been me and Mom. Since when have you ever cared about this family?"

"Who the fuck do you think pays the rent here, Wendy? Because it sure as hell isn't you or cocktail party Barbie in there."

"What? You expect me to be grateful? You expect me to be happy with a measly six grand and rent? You owe me more than that."

"No, I really don't," Mack shot back. "But I thought you at least cared about Mom."

"Get off your fucking high horse, *Dr.* O'Neil. You're

pathetic. You walked away. I'm the one stuck here dealing with everything."

"Oh? And how are you dealing with anything? You have a job? Are those track marks in your hand? Did your veins wear out?"

"Fuck you, asshole. Why don't you go kill another couple of patients? Maybe then you'll feel special."

Mack laughed, a dry, mirthless sound. "I'm done here. Blood doesn't mean I'm permanently bonded to you. Her either. Good luck paying your own rent."

She was so busy congratulating herself for leaving her suitcase in the car that she didn't see the skinny leg with the thorn tattoo sweep out until it was too late. But Mack was faster than she had been as a kid. As she fell, she grabbed Wendy and took her sister with her.

They tumbled down the six cement steps, landing in a heap at the bottom.

"You killed him! You fucking killed him! Now it's your turn to die," Wendy shrieked. The switch had flipped. Her nails raked over Mack's cheek, over the scar she'd put there ten years ago.

Mack pulled her arm back and fired one beautiful shot to Wendy's nose. The crunch, both the sound and feel, were beyond satisfying. "Stay down. I'm done with you," she said and turned to walk toward the car.

But Wendy had never learned to recognize when a fight was over. She hurled herself at Mack's knees and brought her down to the cold sidewalk.

"Get off me," Mack said with an icy calm as her sister's blood dripped on to her own sweater.

But Wendy had learned a few tricks herself. She locked an arm around Mack's throat and squeezed.

"What the hell is goin' on here?" Tony hollered from the front door. "Is this normal, Andi?"

"Just ignore them," her mother pleaded with him. "Come inside and let's make some drinks."

Mack lurched forward, unsteady on the air cast, and tried to dislodge her sister as her vision tunneled.

"I'm going to be there when you die," Wendy hissed in her ear. "And I'm going to laugh."

Giving up on anything other than survival, Mack lodged her elbow somewhere in Wendy's midsection. Her sister's grip loosened, and Mack dumped her on the ground, dragging in a ragged breath.

"I am done with this family," she rasped.

"She attacked me, Tony," Wendy said, crocodile tears pooling in her eyes. "She threatened me. She's a fucking psycho! She said she was going to kill me and Mom!"

"Now hang on there a minute," Tony said, looking bewildered.

Mack's ankle protested when she turned to get in her rental. "If you rebroke my ankle, I'm suing your ass," she told Wendy. "Make sure you can pay your attorney in hypodermic needles. Oh, and, Tony, get out now before you sign a prenup. She's been married five times so far."

Andrea pretended to fall into a graceful faint at the top of the steps.

Wendy gave up all pretenses of playing the victim and tackled Mack to the ground.

She was a trauma doctor. A retrievalist. A family practitioner. Mackenzie O'Neil did not brawl with ex-family members on the sidewalk.

She rolled, pinning her sister in the gutter. "Now you listen to me. I am done with you. You ever come anywhere near me, you ever even think about asking me for another dime, and you won't like what you find."

Hairy arms locked around her. Tony the idiot lifted her off Wendy and restrained her with big meaty hands just as a squad car with its lights on pulled up.

CHAPTER 47

She could have called Linc from the airport for a ride, but she couldn't stand the thought of him seeing her like this, bruised and battered. Angry. Tired. Disgusted with herself.

She called Russell instead and made him promise he wouldn't ask any questions.

He took one look at her on the sidewalk outside the airport and produced a bottle of extra-strength Tylenol from his bag.

"You're never going back there," he said simply.

"No, I am not," she agreed.

Fifteen hours after she'd flown out, feeling hopeful, Mack was back with no hope. Only pain.

She was an idiot.

And a coward.

She didn't turn on the lights in her house, not wanting to alert Linc to the fact that she was home early.

How in the hell was she going to tell him what had happened? It wasn't like she could avoid him until the bruises faded, until the hurt healed.

But the thought of him knowing what she came from, what she was made of, sickened her.

Wearily, she left her suitcase inside the door and flopped

facedown on the couch. Her phone vibrated in the pocket of her jeans.

She pulled it out and finally checked her messages. Linc had responded to her text earlier that afternoon. Then he'd sent a picture of Sunshine looking happy with a glittery blue tongue with a sign that said, "I ate a bottle of glitter, and now my poop sparkles!"

> **Linc:** How's it going? Miss me? Want me to fly out?
> **Linc:** Did you talk to your guests about Thanksgiving? I mentioned it to my sisters, and they got Chihuahua-on-a-sugar-high excited.
> **Linc:** I'm getting worried, Dreamy. Do you need anything?
> **Linc:** Call me.

And then there was the most recent.

> **Linc:** What the fuck, Mackenzie? Where are you?

She couldn't do it. She couldn't pick up the phone and call him or walk out into the backyard and knock on his door. She couldn't put him in the same conversation as her family. He'd never look at her the same.

Feeling sore and sorry for herself, she powered down her phone and dragged herself upstairs and fell into a fitful sleep.

She woke at dawn, still hurting. But now there was an empty ache gnawing away in her chest. She'd worried Linc needlessly. That was unfair, immature.

Rolling over, she reached for her phone.

There were more than a dozen new messages from Linc.

Still not ready for actual conversation, Mack chickened out with a text.

Mack: Sorry for the radio silence. I'm safe. I'll talk to you later.

Her phone rang in her hand a second after the text was sent.

"Linc," she sighed.

"What the fuck is going on, Mackenzie?" he demanded.

"Look, something came up. I got busy. I'm not required to check in with you constantly," she said defensively. And in that moment, she hated herself.

"That's bullshit. You flying home early from a trip and holing up in your house without telling me is bullshit."

"Russell told you?"

"When I called him ten minutes ago to ask if he'd heard anything from you," he snapped.

Fuck. Fuck. Fuck.

"He said you flew home unexpectedly, and he dropped you off at your house last night."

She knew Russell hadn't completely ratted her out by the fact that Linc wasn't in her bedroom yelling at her and demanding to see her injuries.

"I'm fine."

"I'm coming over."

"No. You're not, Linc," she said, rocketing out of bed. She reached for a sweatshirt and sweatpants. Anything to hide the evidence of what she came from.

"Why the hell not?"

"I don't want you to. I don't want you to come over. I don't want to talk about anything. I just want to be left alone."

There was silence on his end of the call. Part of her hoped, prayed, that he wouldn't listen. That any second now, she'd hear his knock, his demand to be let in. But then he'd see her, and he'd know.

"So that's how you want it?" he asked bitterly.

"Yes," she said desperately. "I need some…time."

"So it's over? Just like that?"

Mack hurried downstairs. She saw him standing there in the dim light of morning on her deck, his phone pressed to his ear, shoulders slumped, a scowl on his beautiful face.

Sunshine was behind him, tail wagging in the morning mist.

"I didn't say that," she said.

He looked up, spotting her through the glass.

"Let me in, Mack," he said softly.

"No. I need to take care of some things myself."

"Let me in, Mack, or this ends now," he said.

No. That wasn't what she wanted. Why should she have to choose? When would she stop losing things to her family?

She shook her head, but she couldn't get the words out.

She couldn't do anything but stand there and watch him hang up and walk away from her.

Sunshine stood there on the deck for a beat, looking back and forth between her humans before wandering off after Linc.

Another knife to her already wounded heart.

This was stupid. So fucking stupid. She'd just explain… vaguely. In a way that didn't make him pity her or realize how damaged she was.

He'd have to listen. To let her back in.

And then she thought about the old fire station. About Karen. About the hurt that had radiated off him at the rejection of the woman he cared about.

The shame, the guilt, took her out at the knees, and she sank to the kitchen floor.

CHAPTER 48

Linc entered the station under a dark cloud. Sunshine, not a fan of Dark Linc, scurried off in search of friendlier people.

"I thought you had the day off, Chief," Zane called out from underneath the carriage of the ladder apparatus. Zane, like the rest of the men, was back to stubble now that the real Movember was in full swing.

Linc didn't bother answering. Instead, he took his mood upstairs and closed the door of his office with a definitive slam.

"Uh-oh," Skyler sang.

"Not good," Zane said.

———

He wasn't *hiding* in his office. He just wasn't opening the door. Or answering the phone. He just wanted to stay in here until he didn't feel a goddamn thing.

He'd called it. He'd known from the beginning that Mackenzie O'Neil was going to pulverize his heart into a thousand shards. And then she'd gone and done it, and he was the idiot who was surprised.

There was a brisk knock at his door.

"Go. Away," he snarled.

It was either an idiot or a very brave person who opened the door. Apparently, it was several of them. Women filed into the room. His sisters, followed by Harper, Gloria, and Sophie, stepped in and closed the door behind them.

"Hey, buddy," Rebecca said.

"How's it going, kiddo?" Christa asked.

"Now is not a good time," he said, glaring at the grant request on his computer monitor that he'd been staring at for the last thirty minutes.

"We heard about the breakup," Sophie said, flopping down in the chair across from him.

Of course they had. This damn town and its damn big mouth.

"We're here for you," Jillian said.

"Do you want to talk?" Harper offered.

He pinched the bridge of his nose. "Look, I appreciate the show of support. But I'm really not interested in talking about anything right now."

"I'm so sorry," Gloria said, sliding a fresh pumpkin pie onto his desk. It smelled like cinnamon and sadness.

"I really thought she was going to be the one," Christa complained.

"Me too," Sophie agreed. "You guys were a match made in hot sex heaven. Plus, firefighter and trauma doc? Who else is going to understand your work better?"

"Don't you all have jobs that you should be at?" Linc asked.

"We're here for you, little brother," Rebecca said, shooting him a look with so much sympathy he briefly considered jumping out his office window to get away from it.

"Did she give you a reason for wanting to break up?" Harper asked.

"She didn't break up with me. I broke up with her," he said.

Several pairs of female eyes snapped to attention.

"You did what now?" Christa demanded.

"She was going to do it. I just beat her to the punch."

Gloria took the pie off the desk.

"Wait, if you're all here, where are the guys?" Linc asked.

Harper and Gloria exchanged a look. "They don't know we're here," Harper said.

"We promised to stay out of it," Gloria added.

"This is you staying out of it?"

"Can we go back to the part where *you* broke up with *her*?" Jillian asked.

"Look, it doesn't matter. It was always going to happen. She was always going to pull away. She was always going to leave. I'm the idiot who got hopeful that she'd change her mind."

Harper pressed the heels of her palms to her eyes and blew out a breath. "Okay. Let's break this down. Soph, man the whiteboard."

As the women diagrammed the timeline of his relationship with Mackenzie, Linc wished desperately that he'd kept a bottle of whiskey in a desk drawer like his predecessor.

"So she flies home unexpectedly from a trip to visit a mother who she never talks about?" Sophie clarified.

"She's mentioned foster parents, but her going to Chicago was for her mother," Christa said.

"Foster parents mean that there's some...at the very least *inconsistency* in her childhood," Harper said. She knew from experience. "It could be worse. A lot worse."

"She was removed from the home at age six for parental neglect," Sophie announced, drawing an arrow behind the timeline and writing the words *shitty childhood* in red.

Everyone froze. Linc came halfway out of his chair. "What?"

Sophie pointed to the Benevolence Police Department

sweatshirt she was wearing. "You guys do know I'm married to Ty, right?"

"Did she ever talk to you about it? About growing up?" Harper asked him.

"Or were you too busy constructing a self-fulfilling time bomb?" Rebecca demanded. "What? Come on. You got yourself all tangled up over Karen Whitwood and then convinced yourself that you were never going to be worth taking a chance on for a long-term relationship."

Linc's sisters nodded in annoying agreement.

"Karen?" Harper's gray eyes widened. "Oh, Linc. I'm so sorry. That must have been awful for you."

He waved it away. Wished they would all just go. "Can you all please get the hell out of my office and leave me alone?"

"Absolutely not," Gloria said firmly. "We're not leaving until you've earned this pie back."

"The point is she didn't trust me to tell me about any of this. She didn't tell me she was home. She didn't need me."

Everyone started speaking at once. The sympathetic vibe in the room was fading and being replaced with the sharp edges of accusations.

"Hang on, ladies. I've got this," Gloria said. "Linc, let me explain to you what shame feels like."

"Gloria, you don't have to—"

"No. I'm talking. You're listening. I wasted a decade of my life on a man who was little more than a monster. I was ashamed. Ashamed that I stayed. That I thought he would change. I felt like his bad tainted me somehow."

"We don't know that Mackenzie has some deep-seated childhood trauma."

"She broke her fucking leg jumping out of a second-story window, you idiot," Christa snapped. "Yeah, Samantha told me.

354

And now we know she was removed from her home around the same time. That's *not* a normal upbringing."

"Something had to happen when she went back," Harper guessed, staring at the whiteboard as if it held the answers to the feminine mystery.

"Something bad enough that she flew back the same day she left and called Dr. Robinson to pick her up instead of Linc," Sophie mused.

"My money is on some kind of emotional falling-out with her mother. Something that shook her up and made her want to shut down. She wouldn't want Linc to see her like that," Gloria said.

Linc couldn't help it. He reached out and laid a hand on Gloria's shoulder. A sign of support.

She reached up and squeezed his hand back.

"Shouldn't we be at the point where we can tell each other about having a fight with a parent?" Linc asked, clinging to the hope that he hadn't just royally fucked up.

"Shouldn't you be at the point where you ask her to consider not leaving?" Rebecca asked, crossing her arms.

"Why should I put myself out there when she's clearly not willing to do the same?" he countered. Why should he open himself up for more scars? More hurt?

He'd just keep doing what he'd always done. Focus on the good times. Having fun. No strings. No expectations. No responsibilities or obligations.

But he wanted those things. Every last damn one of them, and he wanted them with Mackenzie.

"What did she say to you about Dr. Dunnigan asking her to stay on here permanently?" Harper asked.

"What?" He was out of his chair so fast it fell over behind him.

"Oops. Guessing she didn't mention that to you," Harper said guiltily.

"This. This is why we were never going to work," Linc said, pointing at Harper. "She can't even tell me that Dunnigan wanted her to stay."

"And you couldn't tell her that you're in love with her," Christa announced.

There was a beat of silence in the room.

"Actions speak louder than words," he said stubbornly. "She wouldn't even let me in to talk to me this morning."

"Fear makes people act like dumbasses," Gloria said. "It's not an excuse. But it's a reason."

"If neither one of you is willing to be brave enough to say what needs to be said, maybe you're not meant to be," Jillian said sadly.

Linc glared at the whiteboard, the clinical debriefing of his too-brief love affair.

CHAPTER 49

"Open up, Doc," Aldo called through Mackenzie's front door.

Mack pretended not to hear him and continued to stare at the blank TV screen.

"Maybe she's not here?" she heard Luke say. "Never mind. She's in the living room."

"Benevolence PD. Open up!" Ty said in his most authoritative voice.

"Leave me alone," Mack muttered under her breath. Why couldn't she just be left alone here?

"She looks pissed," Luke reported from the window as she stood up.

She slid the chain free on the door and opened it a crack. "What do you want?" she demanded.

"What happened to your face?" Ty demanded. He pushed his way inside and tilted her chin to catch the light on her very impressive shiner.

"Holy shit, Mack." Aldo was practically vibrating with rage. Mack knew it was stirring up old feelings. She understood that irrational sense of powerlessness when some shadow rose up from the ashes of the past.

"It's fine. I'm fine," she insisted.

"Linc didn't do this to you, right? Because if he did, he's a dead man," Luke said.

"Jesus. No! Linc had nothing to do with this. Why are you here?"

"You and Linc broke up. We came to see if you were okay. By the way, if our wives ask you, we were never here," Aldo explained. "Now, back to that shiner."

"Did you have a run-in with the Kershes?" Ty asked, reaching for his radio.

"No! Stop. It happened in Chicago yesterday. It has nothing to do with anyone here, so leave it alone."

"You're pressing charges," Luke decided. "Let's find her a lawyer. We can see if our patent attorney has any pals. Criminal and civil, right, Ty?"

"Did you talk to the authorities in Chicago?" Ty asked, all business.

"Get someone aggressive," Aldo suggested. "Someone who will take the toilet paper out of the fucker's house as part of the settlement."

"Stop." Mack held up her hands. Unfortunately, the movement made the sleeves of her oversize sweater slide up her arm.

"Jesus Christmas," Ty said, pushing one sleeve up higher. "You're beat to hell."

"Oh my God, guys. I appreciate the concern, but I'm handling this on my own. So I need you to get out of my house."

"We're not going anywhere," Aldo said firmly.

"Yes, you are. I'm not pressing charges against anyone. *I* almost got arrested. You can all go home, and we'll never discuss this again. Got it?"

"Have you ever met any of us?" Luke asked. "Because that's the stupidest fucking thing I've ever heard."

"Let me tell you, Mack. Just because you think you can handle something on your own doesn't mean you should," Aldo said. "You can't live your entire life independent from everyone else. Especially not when there are a lot of people who are willing to help. Let us help."

"You can't. No one can," she said. It was *her* problem. And she had to find the solution. "I'm not dragging anyone else down with me."

"I'm gonna go make a few calls," Ty said tersely. "And when I come back, we're gonna have a talk."

Ty walked out the front door.

"Aldo, you remember that time with the boxes?" Luke asked.

"Yeah. Creepy. Two women's lives packed up all nice and neat like you can just hide them away. Fucking weird. Glad you got over that."

"It's my turn to be the voice of reason," Luke told him.

"Got it. I'll go make coffee," Aldo said, heading into the kitchen.

"Just make yourself at home," she called sarcastically after him.

"Sit down," Luke said.

She was tired enough, sore enough, that she complied. He sat down on the sofa next to her, taking up too much space.

"Here's the thing, Mack. You remind me of a stupid motherfucker I used to know."

"I think we're done here," she said, rising.

"Sit," he barked.

She sat.

"That stupid motherfucker was me."

"Okaaaaaay."

"I kicked Harper out of my house, my bed, my life because I was a stupid motherfucking chickenshit. That woman is everything to me. She's given me a life I never thought possible because she was brave enough to go after what she wanted. She was willing to take the lumps and hang in there while I took my dumbass time catching up. I thought that my past determined who I was. I thought it set my course. I thought that trauma defined who I was."

Mack stared at the empty fireplace and tried to pretend she wasn't hurting in body and soul. That his words weren't resonating in her bones like church bells.

"I was too fucking scared to let myself love her, to need her. And here was Harper, this beautiful, kind, stubborn woman who loved me so much she wouldn't let me close down on her. I almost lost her, Mack," he said, looking at her. "You're going to lose Linc, and granted, I don't love the guy, but if you don't work through this shit now, you're never going to have a chance at what I found with Harper. You'll always feel alone."

Well, hell. That hurt.

"And look. If Linc took one look at you like this and walked away or let you walk away, maybe he's not the guy."

"He didn't see me. Not really. I didn't let him in."

He sighed. "Believe me, I'd like to keep hating the guy forever. But maybe you should have let him in. And he definitely should have fought harder," Luke said. "Bottom line, you both fucked up. And now you both need to decide if you're brave enough to give it a real shot."

A real shot. Could she even have that with the way she was raised?

"I don't even know what a healthy relationship looks like," she confessed, slumping back against the couch cushion.

"Open your damn eyes, Mack. Look at Gloria and Aldo.

Look at Soph and Ty. My parents. Hell, me and Harper are doing pretty damn great. Because we love each other. We trust each other to handle the heavy stuff. We know we're always, always going to be there for each other. You didn't give Linc the chance to be there for you. I guarantee if you would have called him and asked him to pick you up from the airport, he would have been there."

"But then he would have seen this, Luke." She gestured at her face. "He'd see a victim who needed saving, not a woman he could maybe spend the rest of his life with."

He sighed heavily. "That's just the stupid motherfucker in you talking. You either trust each other to be there through the bad times or you don't."

"Coffee's ready," Aldo called from the kitchen. "I made some of that green tea crap for you, Dreamy."

The nickname did it.

Mack put her face in her hands, yelped when she bumped bruises. "I hate everything."

Ty came back inside with the slam of the front door. "Cold out there. But I got some interesting news from the PD in your mother's neighborhood," Ty said, leveling her with a cool gaze.

Her story, her past, was leaking out, the poison oozing out and affecting the people near her.

"You're pressing charges," Ty told her. "I will not leave this house until you agree." To prove his point, he toed off his boots and made himself comfortable in the armchair facing the fireplace.

Aldo shoved a mug of coffee at him.

"Pressing charges is just going to make it all worse," she insisted.

"See that?" Luke asked, pointing at Ty. "That's what you do. You stick."

She'd wanted Linc to stick. Wished she could have had the guts to ask him to stick. But neither one of them had tried hard enough. And that said something.

"You sticking around?" Luke asked Ty.

"I've got all the time in the world, till the doc here sees the error in her ways."

"Same," Aldo said.

"I have an errand to run," Luke said, rising.

"Keep your left up," Aldo told him, setting a mug of coffee in front of Ty. "My turn, Dreamy. Let's talk about vulnerability."

"Oh my God. You guys. You're the most masculine girlfriends I've ever had."

"I watched a lot of Oprah when I was recovering from having my leg blown off," Aldo said cheerfully. "And then Ty made me read this book."

"Did you watch the 'standing in her shoes' bit?" Ty interrupted.

"Fuck yeah I did."

Ty pounded a fist to his chest. "Every time. Gets me right here."

"I need a drink," Mack sighed.

CHAPTER 50

Linc's office door burst open. It had taken him over an hour to get rid of the women. He rose, prepared to brush off the next well-meaning busybody. However, he wasn't prepared for Luke Garrison rounding his desk and connecting his fist with Linc's face.

"What the fuck, man?" Linc demanded, holding his jaw.

Luke's fist flew again, and Linc barely managed to dodge it, sending the blow glancing off his jaw.

"You knocked some sense into me once. Now it's my turn, you stupid jackass," Luke said.

Linc blocked the next shot and threw a defensive punch to the gut.

"That's the spirit," Luke grunted, grabbing his arm and dragging Linc over the desk. The computer monitor tumbled to the floor.

"What is your problem?" Linc demanded, shaking free. He delivered a quick jab to the jaw and took satisfaction in watching Luke's head snap back.

"Hey, Chief—Shit."

"Stay out of this, Lighthorse," Luke insisted. "This idiot needs his ass kicked."

"No argument here."

"Whose side are you on, Lighthorse?" Linc complained. Luke took advantage of the distraction and landed two gut punches, knocking the wind out of him.

"You finally have a woman you want to spend the rest of your life with, and you were just looking for an excuse to fuck it up."

"Told you," Brody said to someone else in the hallway.

"I didn't fuck it up! She's the one who shut me out," Linc argued.

They exchanged rapid-fire blows.

"What the hell is going on—oh."

There was a crowd growing in the office doorway.

"Any action on this?"

"Normally I'd go with loyalty and say the chief, but Garrison is pretty pissed."

"There's a difference between shutting out and shutting down, you moron," Luke said as they grappled. He threw an elbow that made Linc's face sing.

"She gave up first," Linc said, grunting as he tried to get Luke in a headlock. They went down in a tangle of legs and unintelligible swearing.

"Did you even *look* at her when you were unleashing a lifetime of bullshit insecurities on her?" Luke demanded.

"Fuck you, asshat."

"Did you see the bruises?"

Linc froze, and his opponent took advantage. Luke rolled, taking the top and hammering his fist into Linc's face twice.

Linc tasted blood and fear. Mackenzie was hurt. "What bruises?" Luke pulled his fist back again, but Linc held up his hands. "Goddammit! What bruises? Is she hurt?"

Luke grabbed him by the shirtfront and shook him. "That's

something you should have figured out for yourself instead of piling onto her like an insecure dumb fuck."

Energized by a new fury directed at some unknown threat, Linc threw Luke off him and jumped to his feet.

"Daaaaaamn," Skyler said when she got a good look at him.

His face felt heavy and swollen. There was a cut on his forehead that was clouding his vision with a steady trickle of blood. He wondered if his nose was broken. He looked back at Luke, who was using a chair to pull himself up to his feet. The man had a cut under his eye and one on his jaw. Bruises were already starting to bloom around his cheek and eye.

"Out of my way," Linc growled at the firefighters in his doorway.

"You better be on your way to her house to grovel," Luke yelled after him.

Linc flashed him a middle finger over his shoulder. "Go fuck yourself, Garrison. Someone watch my dog."

With that, he was sprinting down the stairs to the chief's vehicle. He punched the lights and sirens and tore out of the parking lot without a look back.

"Open the door, Mackenzie," he said, giving the front door of the cottage another pound. "I'm not leaving until you come out. I know you're in there."

"I'm not in there. I'm right here, and now you're free to leave."

He whirled around and found her on the walkway behind him. She was dressed for a run in tights and a long-sleeve shirt. She had a cap pulled down low, but he could still see. Those red lips. Her face was flushed, hair damp with sweat. Her eyes were red, probably from tears that he—the worst asshole human being in the universe—had caused. But what caught his attention now was the blooming black eye she sported.

There were more bruises ringing her neck.

He advanced on her, unable to check the barely restrained need for violence that bubbled up in him. He reached for her but stopped when she flinched.

Goddammit. He felt like a monster.

He wished Luke were here so he could pound him into the ground. "Who the fuck put their hands on you?" he asked, congratulating himself on keeping his tone even.

"Does it even matter?" she asked wearily, giving him a wide berth as she stepped around him.

She unlocked the front door and went inside. He barreled in behind her.

"Mackenzie!"

He found her in the kitchen, guzzling water.

"Go away, Linc. I'm over having visitors today."

He planted his feet wide and crossed his arms. "I'm not leaving. Tell me who the hell did that to you."

She looked at him, really looked at him, and her eyes went wide. "Jesus. What the hell happened to your face?"

"Luke Garrison."

"You're kidding me, right? He said he left here on an errand, not a beatdown."

"Stop trying to change the subject. Who fucking hit you?"

"My sister."

"You don't have a sister," he argued.

"I lied."

He wasn't sure where to go from there, so he planted himself on her kitchen chair.

"I lied. I withheld information about my life. And I didn't come running to you when things went bad at my mother's." She stripped the gloves off her hands and shoved up her sleeves, and Linc lost his damn mind when he saw the bruises on her arms.

He reached for her and shoved her sleeves up higher to examine the marks that looked like meaty handprints.

"That one was from my mom's new boyfriend," she said bitterly.

She had a series of short scratches just under her scar. They looked like fingernails.

"The neighbors rightfully called the cops, and my dear mother and psychotic sister told the police I started it."

He released her arms and whipped out his phone. He dialed blindly, his vision going red with rage. "Jillian? I need you to book me a flight to Chicago. Get me there today."

Mackenzie's eyes went wide and horrified. "Don't you dare!"

"You're not running away from home, are you?" his sister asked.

"I'm going to go tell Mack's family in person if they ever so much as think about sending a text message to her, I will *end* them," he said succinctly.

"Stop it," Mack said. "You can't go there."

"End them. Got it. Can you fit in a middle seat?" Jillian asked.

"You can't ever meet them," Mack whispered. She was shaking so hard her teeth were chattering. She didn't seem aware of the tears that coursed down her cheeks.

"Call you back, Jills," he said and disconnected. He grabbed her harder than he meant to and gathered her against him. "Okay. It's okay, baby. Just hang on to me."

Stubbornly, she stayed stiff in his arms for a beat before slowly wrapping hers around his waist and hanging on for dear life. The feelings. Rage and love and fear and hope pummeled him from the inside out.

"It's okay, Mackenzie," he promised, stroking her hair, her back.

He vowed it would be. Whatever it took. He would make this okay.

"Is Sunshine with you?" she asked softly.

"No, baby. But I can get her here."

She sighed against him, and he buried a hand in her hair, holding her to him.

"I guess you'll do for now."

"You need to talk to me. And then I need to talk to you," he said gruffly. "Or maybe I should go first."

"Can I shower first?"

He moved them both toward the stairs. "What are you doing?"

"I'm showering with you. I'm not letting you out of my sight, Dreamy."

Upstairs, in the tiny bathroom, they both undressed. He kept a tight lid on his anger when he saw the bruising on her ribs. The scrapes on her shoulders.

The handprints, man-sized, on her biceps and forearms made him clench his jaw so tight his head hurt.

She was strong. She wouldn't let this hurt last. But he wanted justice. He wanted to ruin the people who'd done this to her. Who'd so stupidly, selfishly tried to hurt what he loved.

He cranked the water in the shower to just below scalding and pushed her gently under the water. The stall was so tight there was no way to not touch each other. He didn't even try to give her space, running his hands over her body, reassuring himself that she was *okay*. She was *here*.

"Let me," he said, taking the bottle from her. Her shampoo smelled like flowers and herbs when he squirted some into his palm. As gently as he could, he massaged it into her hair, rubbing her scalp in slow circles.

She sighed, bracing her hands on the wall in front of them, her back to his front. His cock had thoughts about her wet, naked body sliding over his. Enthusiastic ones. But Linc wasn't going to let anything derail him from what he needed to do, to say.

Mackenzie turned in his arms. Her nipples puckered as they skimmed his chest. Goose bumps rose on her arms at the contact. "I'll do you," she offered.

Wordlessly, he handed her the shampoo and knelt before her. He rested his face between her breasts while her hands worked gently through his hair. Her touch, the soft curves of her breasts, the steady beat of her heart soothed away some of his rough edges.

He pressed a kiss to her heart and heard her shaky breath.

She tilted his chin to get a better look at his face. "I need my kit," she said, prodding around the cut on his forehead. "I'll fix you up good as new." Then in a gesture so pure, so sweet, it broke his dented heart, she brushed her lips to the cut.

"I love you, Mackenzie."

CHAPTER 51

M ack's heart tripped in her chest.

"I love you," Linc said again, pressing a kiss to her belly, his hands splaying across her back, her ribs, holding her in place, keeping her safe.

She wanted to laugh and cry and settled for a little of both, hugging him to her.

He rose carefully, still holding her, and turned off the water.

"Let's have that talk," she said, reaching for one of the fluffy towels on the hook.

"No matter what you're going to say, Dreamy, I'll still love you," he said, accepting the towel she handed him.

"I guess we'll see," she said quietly.

He followed her into the bedroom and let her push him down on the mattress. "Stay," she said and disappeared downstairs to grab her med bag at the door.

She returned to find him sprawled out against the pillows, taking up most of the bed. Those blue eyes opened when she entered, and she felt the beginnings of a hope so fierce she was afraid of it.

"It takes me a while to process things," she began, settling next to him and opening her bag. "To get comfortable with them."

He closed his fingers around her wrist when she moved in with an antiseptic swab. "It's okay. I'll just keep telling you until you catch up, Dreamy. I love you. I've never said it to anyone outside my family. Well, maybe Brody. But I've never said it to anyone this way. I love you. I've loved you. I will continue to love you, and I really, really need you to stay, or if you don't want to stay, I'll go with you. But I'll keep telling you until you're ready."

She felt her lips curve. "That's not what I mean. I love you, Linc. I've known since—"

But her words were cut off when he surged up and kissed her. His fingers tangled in her wet hair, his lips hard against hers. And then his tongue was sweeping into her mouth, gently, firmly laying his claim. She melted into the kiss. Basking, warming, hoping.

But there was more he needed to know. She drew back. "The cookout."

"The cookout?" he repeated, then hissed when she sneakily pressed the alcohol swab to his cut.

"When you swooped in here with grocery store flowers and ingredients for dip and gave your dog a bath with the hose. I've known since that moment that I loved you, and I'm just now working up the nerve to tell you." She leaned in and blew on the wound.

"Well, how about you work up the nerve to tell me the rest of the story, and then we can spend the rest of the day making up?" he suggested.

"I hope you'll still want that, want me…after." She looked away, organizing her supplies on the comforter.

"Dreamy, have you ever run a puppy mill operation?"

She looked up, shook her head.

"Ever purposely murdered a bunch of my family members?"

"Not to my knowledge." She smiled as she dabbed Neosporin on his wound.

"Have you ever thrown a bag of fast-food trash out your car window because you were too lazy to find a trash can?"

"God! No!" She pressed the butterfly bandage in place.

"Then nothing you say is going to change how I feel about you."

She wanted to believe him but was too afraid to hope.

"Here," she said, handing him two ice packs. "I'm not sure where you'll want these because it looks like you got your entire face punched."

"You should see the other guy," he said, settling one pack on his jaw and the other on his eye.

"Speaking of. I have a sister, and I told you I didn't."

"I hope your sister is wearing some souvenirs from you," Linc said darkly.

"I broke her nose. Yours isn't, by the way."

"That's because my cartilage is much stronger than Luke's pansy-assed fist."

"Your entire face is turning purple."

"Let's get back to this asshole sister of yours."

Mack wanted to curl up against him. To press her face to his chest and let his warmth thaw her out. But this was the kind of conversation that required eye contact.

"She's older by a few years. We've never been close. We've never gotten along. She's always been...not right." She picked at a thread on the comforter. "It's not a surprise. Our mother is an alcoholic who bounced from man to man and dead-end job to dead-end job. We were never in the same place very long. Rent didn't get paid. Electricity got shut off. Or Andrea—my mother—met someone else. Someone who'd take care of her.

"Sometimes she'd just disappear for a day or two, and then

she'd crawl home in dirty clothes and smeared makeup smelling like smoke and men. Once when I was six, she didn't come home from work."

Linc's hand slid around her ankle and squeezed.

"My sister, Wendy, didn't like that I was complaining about being hungry. So she locked me in my room. No food. No water. Storms came through and knocked the power out. It was August in Texas and so hot. No fan. No air-conditioning. No water. I waited and waited and finally I couldn't wait anymore. So I pushed the screen out, and I jumped from the second-story window."

He swore colorfully.

"The next-door neighbor heard me crying. I'd broken my ankle. But I was so happy I was finally free. The hospital had air-conditioning and food and all the water I wanted. The doctor was so nice to me." She smiled, remembering him. "Dr. Vishnu. Thick glasses, no hair. His accent sounded like music to me."

"How long were you locked in your room?"

"Two days."

Linc's free hand fisted at his side.

"When the power went out, Wendy went to a friend's house. She was swimming in their pool while I was in an ambulance."

"She's a fucking monster."

"She was a kid raised by a narcissistic alcoholic."

"Baby, you were too. It's no excuse."

"It is no excuse. She lied to the police and said that Mom had just gone to the store and that I tried to run away."

"But they didn't buy it?"

"My mom didn't come home for another two days. And she didn't have a good enough explanation for why the lock on my bedroom door was on the outside. They took both of us away from her. It wasn't long enough for me. My foster parents—that's who's coming for Thanksgiving—were wonderful. Normal. Kind. Loving. I cried when I had to go back. Andrea showed up in court in a pink suit like she'd just come from the country club or something and cried about how she'd made a mistake, she had an illness. She said she attended AA meetings every day for eight weeks. She brought her sponsor. He told the court that she was sober and contrite and willing to do anything to get her kids back."

"Sponsor meaning her new boyfriend?" he guessed.

"Got it in one. The social worker dropped me off at the house, and within ten minutes, we were packed up and heading north. Left the house, the new boyfriend, and the judge's ruling to check in with a court-appointed social worker," she recalled. "She blamed me. She was *embarrassed* by all the legal fuss. It didn't make her look good. It was just another reason for Wendy to hate me."

"What happened after?"

"More of the same. We bounced around while Andrea looked for the perfect man or job. Wendy was still awful. Not necessarily as bad as locking me up alone for forty-eight hours. But unhealthy. She'd steal money out of Andrea's purse and blame me. She'd hide things in my room like a dead bird or the tennis bracelet a boyfriend gave Andrea. Once, she pushed me down the stairs."

Linc closed his eyes. His jaw was tight.

"Don't feel sorry for me. I'm not some victim," she said sharply.

She wasn't a victim. She was a survivor.

When he opened his eyes, the blue was blazing. "I can feel sorry for the little girl who didn't have a hero," he said. "And I can also struggle with the fact that I'd love to have shoved your sister down the stairs."

Mack smirked.

"When I turned twelve, I was starting to get taller. I hit a growth spurt right around the time we did a self-defense session in gym class. I soaked it up like a sponge. The teacher gave me extra time after school. Looking back, I think she'd seen the bruises, had some suspicions. The next time Wendy tried to mess with me in front of her friends, I threw her on her back. They thought it was hilarious. It made her hate me more, but at least she knew I wasn't going to just take it anymore."

"How did you survive?" he asked. He reached to pull her into his side, but she held back.

"There's more you need to hear first."

"I'm listening." His fingers interlaced with hers.

"Wendy turned from a bad kid into a worse teen. She shoplifted, dabbled in drugs, bullied people, stole things one too many times. She got picked up for I don't even remember what now and was sent to juvenile hall. I still remember watching her leave. It was, to that point, the best day of my life."

"Mackenzie." He hurt for her. She could hear it in his voice. The man who'd grown up knowing nothing but the good of family and love.

"Anyway, when she got out, she was technically an adult and never came home to live again. As soon as I had my high school diploma, I was gone. I worked my way through college—premed, inspired by the nice doctor who fixed my ankle—and then med school. I stayed in Texas when I really wanted distance. But all Andrea had then was me. And I felt responsible for her. I still did until recently."

"You sent her money?" Linc asked.

Mack nodded, embarrassed now. "I did. Every month like clockwork. It's over now. I don't owe her anything anymore."

"Baby, you never did. You didn't ask to be born. You didn't ask her to be your mother."

He tried to pull her down again.

"Oh, there's more," she sighed.

"I don't want to rush you, but there's only so much of you sitting there looking so sad that I can take, Dreamy. I need to hold you."

She took a breath, let it out. "Okay, here goes. I was doing my residency in an emergency department in Dallas. Wendy and our mom had made up again. They were living together in this shitty little apartment where Andrea drank bottles of cheap gin and Wendy did God knows what drugs. Wendy had a boyfriend."

Mack pulled out of Linc's grasp and leaned over the side of the bed. She found the sketch pad in the nightstand and flipped to the last drawing.

"That's him. Powell Coleman III. He had a Mustang and a trust fund. He also had a pretty serious drug problem. My sister, of course, found the whole package very attractive. I never met him. Not until the night he was wheeled into the ED on my shift."

Linc stared hard at the portrait.

"He looks like a dickhead," he said finally.

"Well, the dickhead took his Mustang with my sister in the passenger seat and drove into a concrete barrier at a high rate of speed. He'd also taken what turned out to be a lethal dose of heroin. I did everything I could, but I couldn't save him."

"Some people you can't save, Dreamy," he said, reaching up to tuck her damp hair behind her ear. "And you know that."

"I know that now. And I think I knew it then. But I had to go out to the waiting room and tell her. Tell my sister that Powell Coleman III was never going to take her for a ride again. She attacked me. She was screaming and crying. Shouting that I'd murdered him. I killed her boyfriend, and she was going to kill me."

"Mackenzie?"

"Yeah?"

"I fucking hate your sister."

Mack was surprised when she felt the laugh bubble up. She let it fill up all the empty space inside her, let it carry her over into Linc's warm, solid side. There was something so reassuring to her about the fact that his cock beneath the white terry cloth was still hard. He still wanted her.

"I'm not a fan either. She sued me."

He stiffened against her. "You're shitting me."

She smiled, her mouth curving against his chest. "Nope. Found a shady lawyer. Named me personally and the hospital in a lawsuit."

"She lost," he said confidently.

"She did," she said. "But I still paid her. I gave her everything I had in savings. I'd been hoping to do a stint with a nonprofit that trained trauma doctors in third-world countries. The pay was abysmal, but I figured I could get by on savings for a year."

"And she took that from you."

"Ah, but I found the National Guard. Which brought me to Aldo. Which brought me to you."

He kissed the top of her head.

"I love you, Dr. Mackenzie O'Neil."

"Still?"

"Always. Now tell me what the fuck happened when you went to visit your asshole mother for the very last time ever."

She filled him in on the details, soothed him with gentle strokes across his chest when he vibrated with the need to fight for her.

"You're sure you broke her nose?" he asked.

"Positive. It crunched. Very satisfying."

"Good girl."

"Thanks for listening, Linc," she whispered.

"Thanks for sharing."

They were both silent for a long minute.

"So here's what we're going to do," he began.

She laughed. "What's the plan, boss?"

He levered up on an elbow to gaze down at her. "You've paid enough. The price was never yours in the first place."

"You can't ever meet them," she said earnestly. "I know how that sounds. But I can't stand the idea of tainting you by association."

"Tainting me?" he scoffed.

"I don't want you to ever associate me with them. I look like my mom." It pained her to admit it.

"Dreamy, there is nothing of them in you. You prove that every fucking day. Now, back to what's going to happen. They don't ever get to see you or talk to you or communicate with you in any way. Ever," he said quietly. "You won't send either of them a dime ever again. If they leave you alone, I'll leave them alone."

Mack was suspicious. "You're literally vibrating with rage right now, and you're willing to promise me that you won't do anything?"

"As long as they stay away from you, I'll stay away from them," he promised. "Now, how about you tell me about Dunnigan offering you the job permanently."

Her mouth opened in an O. "Oh. That."

"Yeah. That."

CHAPTER 52

They fell asleep as evening fell outside the curtained windows. Emotionally spent, they wrapped themselves around each other, a tangle of limbs and towels and comfort. He woke to dusk, to the smell of chamomile drifting up from her still-damp hair. To the honeyed heat of her body pressed against his.

His dick, achingly hard, was nestled against the soft curves of her ass. It throbbed with the primal need to claim her, protect her, love her.

She stirred against him, a sleepy sigh escaping her unpainted lips.

He loved her like this. Loved her every way she came.

"We're going to have to talk about what comes next, Dreamy," he whispered, lips brushing her ear. "Because I'm never letting you go."

When she didn't answer, he kissed the nape of her neck, then worked his way down her spine. He paused to pay special attention to every bruise, every scrape. And every time he brushed his lips over a wound, he promised them both: *never again*.

She gave a thready gasp when he got to her hips and sank his teeth into one graceful curve.

"You're so fucking beautiful, Mackenzie. You're so fucking mine."

"I love you, Linc. So much," she whispered against the pillow.

He'd never get tired of hearing those words from that mouth.

"Dreamy, there's no other choice. You're it for me."

"Thank you for still wanting me."

It pulverized his heart for the little girl whose own mother hadn't wanted her, whose sister hated her. But she was here with him now, and he'd spend the rest of his life erasing any doubt those monsters had given her.

He needed a ring. A plan.

She rolled over on her stomach, the smooth hills of her ass greeting him. His cock twitched with the need to conquer.

Testing her, he leaned in and brushed his lips over the curves of one spectacular cheek, then sank his teeth into it.

She let out a breathy little gasp that had his dick going even harder.

"I love every fucking inch of you, Mackenzie," he whispered, moving his lips over her flesh, reveling in the goose bumps that cropped up on her skin. He bit again, lower this time, where the thigh met cheek.

She shivered. "I love how you touch me."

"How do I touch you?"

"Like you love me."

On that soft confession, Linc parted her ass cheeks. His tongue darted out to stroke forbidden fruit. Her head came up off the pillow on a gasp, but the rest of her body remained statue still.

"Is this okay?" he asked her.

"Yes," she breathed. "God, yes. Everything you do to me is magic."

He wanted her, every damn inch of her.

His cock throbbed an incessant SOS even as he took his time, tongue playing, mouth moving. She writhed under him, begging for more.

With his heart in his throat, blood pounding through his veins, Linc slid his way back up her body, covering her back with his chest. His hard-on found its home at the apex of her thighs. He could feel the wet, the heat, the need.

When she rocked her ass against him, his vision began to tunnel.

"Hang on tight, Dreamy," he said, closing her fingers around the spindles of the headboard.

He lined himself up with her opening and, in one swift thrust, buried himself inside her.

He swore. "Your pussy feels so good wrapped around my dick, baby."

She groaned, then cried out when he moved. It was exquisite torture, the friction, the slide.

Cupping her chin in his hand from behind, he whispered dark, dirty praise as he fucked in and out of her.

"You're such a good girl, Mackenzie. I love feeling you get tight on my cock like you're trying to milk the come out of me."

"You're so fucking dirty, Linc," she moaned.

"I can feel how wet it gets you. How wet you get for me."

He gave a harder thrust, pinning her hips to the mattress and holding deep. She bucked against him, and he had to take a breath. Had to fight off the need to ram himself into her over and over again until his come ran out of her and soaked into the mattress.

"Don't hold back on me now," she hissed.

A man only had so much control. He yanked her up onto her hands and knees. "I'll always give you whatever you ask for," he promised darkly. His hips snapped forward, and he buried his throbbing dick inside her. He couldn't catch his breath. Sweat dotted his skin as he continued to thrust into her. She dropped down onto her elbows, rocking back against him.

Those sweet ass cheeks tantalized him. He brought two fingers to his mouth and licked them.

"Hold still," he ordered, feeling her vibrate on the tip of his cock when he pulled out. "Don't move." With his wet fingers, he probed her cleft until he found that tight little rosette of muscle. "Hold tight, baby."

In one motion, he sank his fingers into her ass at the same time that his cock entered her.

The noise that escaped her was fucking beautiful.

He fucked her with his cock and fingers, rocking into her and taking them both right up to the edge. Again and again, he drove into her until they were both panting and trembling. Pulling back and holding still at the last second.

It wasn't enough. He needed so much more from her.

"Baby, I need to see you." He gritted out the words in a voice more gravel than human.

"Make me come, Linc," she begged. "Please!"

"Not until I can see your eyes." As carefully as he could manage, he pushed her down as he withdrew. "Roll over. That's right, baby. Open your legs wide for me."

He settled between her legs as their gazes locked.

"You want to come, baby?"

She nodded, and he could feel the throbbing of her need around the tip of his dick.

He held steady with one inch connecting them. "Look at me, Mackenzie."

Her green eyes flew open.

"You belong to me. I belong to you. This is it. Understand?"

He gave a teasing half thrust, giving her another inch. It drove him crazy not to be fully seated inside her. Not to feel her muscles closing around every fucking vein and ridge of his erection.

"I'm yours, Hotshot. For better or worse, I am all yours."

It was good enough. Until he had a ring on her finger, until she said vows, this was good enough. He flexed his hips, burying himself to the balls in her. She cried out, and he held her closer, tighter. Her nails dug into his shoulders. The pain was a beautiful thing as he pummeled into her.

He could feel her muscles fluttering, knew she was close. His seed burned up from his balls, seeming to climb up his spine. Leaning in, he dipped his head to stroke the flat of his tongue over her nipple. It hardened, peaking and straining toward him.

In and out. Over and over again until there was no rhyme or reason. There was no rhythm or finesse. It was a primal, biological need to feel and see her come. He needed to give her this.

And when she moaned, when those green eyes fluttered open, he knew he was a goner. He could feel his balls pulling up against him, feel the delicious burn of his ejaculation rocket up his shaft.

"Mackenzie," he gritted out.

She was quickening around him, which was a fucking miracle considering he was coming and coming and coming inside her. And she was closing around him, gripping him.

Her hungry squeezes milked his dick, drained his balls, as he emptied himself into her, giving her everything that he had, all that he was.

"Linc," she whispered, arms banding around him as she rode out her world-destroying aftershocks on his still-hard cock. "Linc."

CHAPTER 53

The next morning, Mack's phone rang on the nightstand. Linc had spent the last thirty minutes watching her sleep in his arms. It was almost eight in the morning, and she was still sleeping. Not wanting to disturb her, he reached over her.

Andrea.

It said something that the woman was in her daughter's phone as Andrea, not Mom.

Easing out of the bed, he took the phone with him down the stairs.

Sunshine followed him.

"Hello," he answered sharply.

"Oh, I'm calling for my daughter Kenzie."

"If you mean Mackenzie, she has nothing to say to you," Linc said coldly. He opened the back door and let Sunshine scamper out into the frost-bitten grass.

"Don't be silly. I'm her *mother*. We had a little misunderstanding. That's all. If you put her on the phone, I can straighten it all out."

"Your misunderstanding amounts to assault, Andrea."

"It's Auhn-DREE-uh," she corrected.

"It doesn't matter what your name is because your relationship with Mackenzie is officially over."

"Oh, sweetie, you don't understand. Kenzie and I had a little tiff, and I just need a quick word with her. The rent is due—"

"That's your responsibility. Not hers," he said.

"I'm her *mother*. We're *family*."

The emphasis on the words rang emptily in his ear.

"That's a title you earn, lady, and you haven't earned it. You've done nothing for Mackenzie her entire life. She's no longer obligated to save you."

"Who in the hell do you think you are?" Andrea dropped the sugary-sweet southern accent.

"I'm the man who's going to convince Mackenzie to marry me someday."

"She didn't say anything about you while she was here."

"You mean while your other daughter assaulted her on the street? Why would she? Why would she share anything important with you?"

"We're family." Andrea was back to wheedling.

He thought of his own parents, of his sisters, of his nieces and nephews. *That* was family.

"You don't know the meaning of the word. You and your other daughter are no longer welcome anywhere near Mackenzie. No more money. No more guilt trips. She's mine, and I protect what's mine."

"You don't understand. I *need* to talk to her! The police were here looking for Wendy, and I accidentally forgot to pay the light bill—"

"Don't call her. Don't email her. Don't even think about showing your face here. Ever. As far as you're concerned, Mackenzie is an orphan. You never deserved her."

"Oh, and you do?" she snapped back.

"No, but I'm sure as hell going to try."

He hung up.

"What are you doing?" Mack asked.

He turned around and found her in the kitchen doorway. Sleepy and sexy. She was wearing his discarded T-shirt from the night before. Even with the bloodstains on the cotton, the bruises on her face, she was breathtaking.

"Taking out the trash," he said innocently.

"You yelled at my mother. You threatened her."

"Yep. And now I'm figuring out how to block her number from your phone. You're done with her. Forever, Mackenzie. She's no longer a concern of yours."

"Did you mean what you said?" she asked.

"The part about you being an orphan?"

"The part about you convincing me to marry you," she said.

Oops. She had been there a while.

Linc dropped her phone on the counter and casually started pawing through her refrigerator. "Maybe," he said.

"Because if you did mean it, I wouldn't have a problem with it."

He poked his head over the fridge door.

"Are you saying what I think you're saying?"

"I'm saying if we're both in this, then why not? I wouldn't mind a nice barn wedding."

He crossed the room in two swift steps and lifted her up.

"Just so you know, I'm not officially asking yet. I wouldn't do that without a ring, and I want to meet your parents. Your *real* parents," he said. "When they come here for Thanksgiving."

Her eyes went watery. "And I'm not officially saying yes yet."

"But it's on the table?" he clarified, almost afraid to breathe in case this delicate truce would shatter or pop like a bubble.

She nodded. "It's on the table."

"So we're staying here, or we're moving away when you're done at the clinic?" he asked, cocking his head, holding his breath.

"We're staying here."

He kissed her and swung her around until they both groaned.

"That Garrison can throw a punch," Linc muttered.

Mack reached for the ibuprofen. "We are quite the pair. What's Georgia Rae going to say when she gets a load of our faces?"

"One of a kind, Dreamy. You and me."

"Thank you for standing up for me even though I didn't need you to."

"Thanks for letting me take a few hits for you."

"I love you, Linc."

He took the caplets she handed him and leaned in close.

"Love you too, Dreamy. You're never gonna be alone again," he promised.

"It's going to take some getting used to. I'll probably screw up again once or twice."

"I won't," he joked. "By the way, Andrea said the police were there looking for your sister."

She sighed. "It's time she was the one to pay."

CHAPTER 54

O h! You got your boot off! But daaaaaamn, girl. What happened to your face?" Ellen looked both fascinated and horrified when she opened the door to her split-level house. There were balloons on the mailbox like it was signaling the destination for a kid's birthday party and a dozen cars parked in the driveway and on the street.

"Uh, hey. Did I get the date wrong?" Mack asked.

Raucous laughter exploded behind Ellen.

"No! You're right on time," she said, grabbing Mack's arm and towing her inside.

The house looked like it had been designed in the late seventies and haphazardly updated over the ensuing decades. The carpet on the stairs was pea-soup green, and there was a birdhouse-themed wallpaper border peeling from beneath the popcorn ceiling in the foyer.

"Barry, say hello to Dr. Mack."

A hairy arm shot up from the big brown leather sectional visible through the white metal spindles of the railing that cordoned off the second-floor living room.

"'Lo!"

"Keep the kids out of the basement, you know?" Ellen

yelled, then turned back to Mack. "Come on downstairs," she said gleefully. "We're all hanging out in the family room."

"All?"

But Mack's question was drowned out by another round of laughter.

"Ladies, look who's here!" Ellen made a grand ta-da gesture in Mack's direction.

There was spontaneous applause that cut off abruptly as guest after guest noticed the bruising on Mack's face.

I should have been much more generous with my makeup application, Mack realized.

"What happened to you?"

"You didn't have another run-in with the Kershes, did you?"

"I'd hate to see what the other guy looks like after Linc got done with him."

"Come on. Dr. Mack probably fights her own fights."

"It's fine. I'm fine," Mack insisted. "It was nothing."

"She's so modest. I heard the last 'nothing' involved her being thrown down a twenty-foot ravine on an accident call. She climbed back up, gave the guy a poke in some secret pain point, and now his peep don't work."

Small damn towns.

"You really should start taking better care of yourself, walking around all banged up all the time," Mariana Brewster suggested.

The greetings blurred together in a sea of faces and names that Mack would never remember.

"This is my sister-in-law Tiffany. My neighbor from two houses down Marie. My coworkers Sandra and Ellen. Two Ellens! Madison's son is on my son's soccer team and runs car pool on Tuesdays and Thursdays…"

Harper and Gloria were there. And Mack recognized Beth,

from the offices of Garrison Construction, perusing the snacks on the sawhorse and plywood table.

There were women everywhere—on the worn couches, the upholstered rocking chair, two even sharing a yellow vinyl bean bag. Plates of appetizers and bowls of snacks hogged every flat surface. If there was music playing, she couldn't hear it over the hum of female conversation.

The mood was festive, light.

"Do you see the appetizers?" Ellen asked. "We've got a veggie tray, a fruit tray, grilled chicken skewers that my father-in-law made. The water is cucumber lemon, just like at a spa!"

"Very nice," Mack said, feeling just a little overwhelmed.

"And healthy!" Ellen elbowed her. "I'm down six pounds. Six! Can you believe it?"

"That's fantastic," Mack agreed. "How's the swimming?"

"Amazing!" Ellen drew the word out to three full syllables. "Which is what I wanted to talk to you about. I guess I should have talked to you about it before I sprung a dozen extra ladies on you for ladies' night. But when I started telling people about what I was doing, they had questions."

Questions about eating right and exercising? Wasn't that what the internet was for?

Mack felt a flicker of concern. If this was about to turn into a Q and A with the doctor, she was going to fake an emergency call. She could clamp an artery and save a limb when necessary, but giving a lecture on nutrition was a bit out of her area of expertise.

"We got to talking, and we had a crazy idea that we wanted to run by you, you know?"

"Okay."

Ellen clapped her hands. "Ladies, let's tell Dr. Mack our idea."

The crowd hushed. Someone turned on the TV mounted on the wall under a creepy, stuffed ram head.

"We made a PowerPoint," announced a woman with curly hair somewhere between the shade of strawberries and wheat.

"Cue it up, Roberta!"

"Here, you can sit here," Harper said, patting the cushion next to her.

Mack crammed herself between Harper and another woman she recognized as Peggy Ann Marsico from the grocery store and the Little League national anthem.

"We, the overworked, underexercised, convenience food–dependent women of Benevolence, Maryland, would like to propose a social solution to our problems," Ellen began.

Mack wouldn't be able to send an SOS text to Linc without the women on either side reading it. She was good and stuck.

"Dang it. This thing isn't working," the woman with the slide remote said, shaking it vigorously. Her generous breasts bounced in a bra that clearly didn't fit.

"Gimme the clicker thing," Peggy Ann demanded.

They fought with the technology, at one point fast-forwarding through the entire presentation upside down.

Harper coughed. "Uh, how many slides are there?" she asked.

"Forty-eight," Ellen said cheerfully. "We even made pie charts."

Sweet baby Jesus.

"Maybe we should just summarize it?" Harper offered helpfully.

"Yes!" Mack said, unwedging herself from the couch and its occupants. "How about a summary?"

"Gosh. I don't know if we can summarize this easily." Ellen frowned.

"We want to start an activity club that combines a social event with some kind of physical fitness or healthy eating theme," Harper announced.

"Well, that does about summarize it."

"We don't spend enough time with our friends, and when we do, it centers entirely on food and/or alcohol," Beth complained. "We want to start something that changes that. With some professional guidance, of course."

Realization started to sink in. "And you want me to organize this?"

A dozen heads nodded enthusiastically.

"You have the background obviously," Ellen began. "And you're also not bogged down with kids, sports, pets, oil-leaking minivans, and five loads of laundry a day in addition to your job—not saying that you're not very, very busy or that your time isn't important, you know?"

Mack nodded. "I know."

"We'll understand if you say no," Harper said to her. "Mack does have a very demanding job and boyfriend," she pointed out to the rest of the women.

A purr of feminine satisfaction rose up.

"Lord, if Harry looked at me the way Chief Reed looks at Dr. Mack, I wouldn't survive the night," Georgia Rae said, fanning herself with a paper plate.

"She's obviously got stamina," another woman, this one in a misbuttoned red cardigan and orthopedic shoes, mused.

"Which is why we need this club. If I don't start doing something, I'm going to continue to do nothing, and I won't need stamina for a hot boyfriend with excessive sexual needs because I'll be too tired to go out looking for one."

An activity club. With events like group walks or maybe a couch-to-5K program. Winter hikes or workouts in the park.

Maybe she could borrow a nutritionist from the hospital for a monthly healthy cooking demonstration or a grocery store tour.

The idea wasn't terrible. In fact, it was kind of exciting.

"We saw how much happier Ellen is with just a couple of lifestyle changes. What if we all made some changes?" Beth asked. "What if all our lives improved?"

"This is a really interesting proposal," Mack said. "I'm going to think about it for a bit, if that's okay?"

There were a few smug smiles in the room, and Mack knew that they knew they'd hooked her.

———

Later, on her way home with a belly full of carrot sticks and baked spring rolls, she dialed Linc.

"Dreamy. Are you on your way home?" His voice pooled like warm honey in her belly. Apparently, her delicious boyfriend wasn't the only one with excessive sexual needs.

"I am. What do you think of hosting a monthly health and wellness screening at the fire department?" Mack asked him. "Maybe blood pressure and cholesterol checks, flu shots? Throw in some first aid training? We could do it by donation and have the proceeds benefit the fire department."

"What kind of ladies' night did you go to, Dreamy?"

"One with a PowerPoint and a lot of really convincing ladies."

CHAPTER 55

The mid-November morning air was a refreshing shock to her system as Mack sucked in a lungful. She'd gotten the all clear from her doctor earlier in the week, and the second thing she thought of when she woke up was lacing up her running shoes.

The first thing was how much she missed waking up with Linc's arm locked around her waist. She'd slept at her place when he pulled B shift. And it made her think about their living arrangements.

As comfortable as she was in his refurbished gas station dude den, she realized they were going to have to make some decisions. Her rental was too small for a family. And Linc's place wasn't much bigger. There were no real bedrooms. Just a sleeping loft.

Now, her feet drummed the pavement in a steady beat next to Aldo's and Harper's, and she felt free.

"Is that some kind of bionic leg?" she gasped as they crested a hill on a sleepy residential street. Aldo took pity on her and slowed to a stop.

"It is. It has magic powers," Harper insisted, drawing in a breath.

"Maybe cut yourself a little break. You've been out of commission for two months," he suggested.

"I'm just saying I've got two good legs. I should be kicking your ass."

"Woman, please." Aldo snorted.

"It's Moretta power." Harper sighed, rolling her eyes. "He's superhuman."

Even at a slow jog, Mack felt a bit superhuman herself. Her physical aches and pains were fading. More importantly, her heart was healing.

They got to the lake where Aldo and Harper peeled off for a trail run. Mack headed back toward home, slowing her pace through quiet neighborhoods.

She wondered what kind of house she and Linc would end up in. Neither of them was the farmhouse with a garden type. And a beige town house that looked just like its neighbors didn't fit either.

She'd figure it out. *They'd* figure it out. She adjusted the thought with a little thrill. She'd told Linc everything, and he'd still stood for her. He still loved her. He still wanted her. The miracle of it hadn't lost its shine yet.

Mack turned onto another street. One mile to go, and she felt warm and loose in the early morning cold.

She felt a tingle between her shoulder blades. A little niggling of warning. Danger.

Carefully, she plucked the earbuds from her ears and made a show of stopping to stretch her calves at the curb. She didn't see anyone. There weren't any suspicious cars. No masked criminals looking to cause harm. But still, she felt the familiar tingle.

Was it the other Kersh? Things had been quiet on that front since the vandalism.

She'd check in with the sheriff when she got home. Just to be sure.

She wasn't in peak physical condition. Not after weeks in an air cast and her most recent bruises and scrapes. But she would never be an easy mark.

Her internal warning system formed out of necessity when she was a child. She learned when her mother was safe to approach and when it was smarter to stay hidden in her room. As she got older, it evolved. It warned her of sketchy guys in dirty bars, and it had signaled a red alert seconds before the chopper carrying her and a patient experienced engine failure, forcing an emergency landing in the desert.

Protocol. Training. Those were what made her a survivor instead of a victim.

She couldn't be in real danger. Not here in the midst of families waking up, getting ready for school and work. She wasn't in a war zone anymore. Her life didn't have to be a delicate balance of life, death, and adrenaline.

She jogged casually toward the tiny park half a block from the middle school. Trees and playground equipment meant cover. A place to hide and observe.

She'd nearly made it to the cedar-chipped playground when she heard a whistle.

"There's my girl!"

Mack whirled around and bent at the waist in relief as Linc, in jogging pants and a long-sleeve tee, grinned at her.

"What are you doing here?"

He held up his watch. "Got off a couple minutes early and thought I'd catch up with my girl."

"Hi," she said when he picked her up off her feet and spun her around.

"Hi yourself, Dreamy." He let her slide down his body in a

sinfully decadent move that was not safe for public consumption. She kissed him lightly on the lips.

"You can be my running buddy," she told him.

"I'm all for that as long as it doesn't jeopardize my position as your naked orgasm buddy," he teased.

"You know, if we run fast enough," she mused, "we could have dirty shower sex before you go to bed and I go into the office."

"I knew I loved you for a reason."

"So Thanksgiving…" Mack began.

"Here's the plan. We'll host at my place, which is a little tight, but then I'll be on my turf when your foster dad is like, 'What are your intentions toward Mackenzie?'" Linc mimicked.

She laughed as they turned the corner. "You're insane."

"My sisters are already primed to sing my praises. I compiled a top ten list of my best rescues, and they're under orders to deploy them if anything starts to go south."

"Nothing is going to go south, you weirdo." Mack laughed. "You'll love Dottie and Win, also Violet. They're good people, and they want me to be happy. And you and your gigantic cock, heroic personality, and sweet, beautiful dog will win them over in seconds."

"I approve the order of my virtues."

They turned down another street, closing in on home and that shower.

"Do you think Sunshine would like a little brother or sister?" she mused.

"Human or canine?"

"Canine. For now."

"We should involve her in the decision, but yeah. I think she'd love another dog."

"And if we get another dog, we might have to talk about living arrangements," she said, biting her lip.

He loved his gas station. It suited him to the ground.

"Race you to the stop sign," he said, nodding toward the end of the block.

Mack took off. Even two months stale, she beat him by two paces.

He slung an arm around her shoulder, and they walked toward home. "About these living arrangements."

"My place isn't *mine*."

"Plus, it's a shoebox."

"There is that. And your place is an ode to the bachelor lifestyle," she pointed out. "Not that I don't absolutely love your gas station."

"Of course you do," Linc said amicably. He dropped a kiss on the top of her head. "But we're going to need more room for dogs."

"And maybe other things…small people type things." Mack felt her heart catch in her throat. She was expressing a desire—poorly—but she was still attempting it.

Progress.

He beamed down at her. "We'll find the right place for our menagerie of dogs and small people type things," he promised.

"And a big shower made for after-run shower sex?"

He stopped her on the sidewalk. "Dreamy, anything you want. All you have to do is ask. I'll do anything in my power to give you everything you want."

CHAPTER 56

"Yes, you can have dinner in five seconds. Geez. Just let me unlock the door," Mack said to Sunshine as the dog whimpered and tap-danced next to her at the front door.

It was three days to Thanksgiving. Linc was still working B shifts at the station, and Mack had taken over primary parent duties where Sunshine was concerned. She'd taken the dog to the clinic today. Sunshine had whiled away her day snoozing on a pet bed in Mack's office and entertaining patients in the waiting room.

She pulled the keys out of her bag and frowned in the dark at the knob. The brass finish was scraped and scratched. It struck her as odd. She didn't remember it being that way.

The dog bolted inside as soon as the door was open, and Mack followed her. The lights were off, and the living room had a chill consistent with an empty house on a winter day. But still… There was something off. It nagged at her.

She hadn't left that book on the floor, had she?

And the pillows on the couch looked different.

Sunshine was busy nosing around the perimeter of the room, some mystery scent catching her attention.

Mack put her bag down inside the door and flicked on the lights.

It had been a long day thanks to flu season. Dehydrated patients and exhausted caregivers had kept them hopping all day long. She was probably just imagining things.

In the kitchen, things looked the same. Except for that coffee mug in the sink. Mack hadn't had time for tea that morning. She'd gone through a drive-thru on her way to the clinic.

Maybe Linc had been here on some boyfriend mission. Maybe he'd helped himself to a cup of coffee.

Sunshine's snuffling at the back door caught her attention. The worn sliding door was unlocked and askew on its track. There was a tiny pile of wood shavings on the floor.

"Shit," Mack muttered.

She dialed Linc.

"Hey, beautiful," he answered.

"Hey. Were you in my house today?"

He shifted gears from playful to serious. "No. I slept at my place, worked out, and then came straight to the station."

"I think someone's been here."

"Mackenzie, go to my place and wait there," he said.

"I don't think they're still here," she complained.

"My place. I'll be there in five minutes. Go now and stay on the phone."

"You're overreacting."

"And you're underreacting."

"Fine. Sunny, come on." The dog trotted into the kitchen, a dust bunny stuck to her nose. "We're going to Daddy's house."

She could hear Linc saying something to someone on his end and then the slam of a car door. "I think we're overreacting," she insisted, opening the garden gate and stepping into his backyard.

"Better safe than sorry," he said.

400

She heard a faraway siren. "You better not be coming in hot. I'm fine. I'm walking into your house right now," she said, opening his back door.

"Are you in? Is the door locked?"

Mack rolled her eyes at the dog and mouthed "overreacting." She flipped the dead bolt. "I am officially locked inside."

The sirens cut off.

Linc arrived two minutes later and found Mack sipping tea on his couch, her feet pulled up under her, Sunshine wriggling on her back on the floor.

"Don't you feel silly now?" she said as he barreled in through the door.

"Nope."

A police cruiser pulled up in front of Linc's place.

"Oh, come on, Linc. The police?"

Deputy Hiya Tahir climbed out and adjusted her belt.

"You are overreacting," Mack said in exasperation.

"We'll see about that," he said mildly as he gave her a hard, reassuring hug.

————

A search of Mack's house revealed several missing items. A bottle of wine, a pair of small diamond studs that her foster parents got her for her graduation from med school, and two hundred dollars in cash that she kept in an empty box of K-Cups in the kitchen cabinet.

The weak lock on the back door had been jimmied open, and Mack could see Linc's wheels turning.

"No other damage that I can see," she said as she perused her bedroom under Deputy Tahir's watchful eye.

"Where's your sketchbook, Dreamy?" Linc asked, peering into the drawer of her nightstand.

"It's right...it should be right there," she said, frowning. The charcoal pencils were there, the eraser. But no book.

"Is it missing?" the deputy asked.

"Why would someone take that?" Mack asked half to herself. She peered under the bed in case she'd mislaid it.

That tickle between her shoulder blades was back. Something was wrong.

"Dr. O'Neil, do you know anyone who would mean you any harm?" Deputy Tahir asked.

"You mean besides the Kershes?" Linc put in.

"We'll ask any questions that need asking, Chief," Deputy Tahir said.

"Someone broke in here," Linc said succinctly. "You think asking questions is going to keep Mackenzie safe?"

"Linc." Mack laid a hand on his arm. "I am safe."

"I want you to stay at the station with me tonight," he said, his jaw hard.

"I'm not staying in a firefighter fart factory."

"You're not staying here alone."

"Sunshine and I will stay at your place. Final offer."

"I want drive-bys," he insisted.

"We'll have patrol come by every hour," the deputy offered. "It's probably just kids being stupid. But it doesn't hurt to be careful."

Mack waited until Linc walked Deputy Tahir to her cruiser before pulling out her phone.

"Well, look who it is. The daughter who disowned me," Andrea sniped when she answered the call.

"Where's Wendy?" Mack said flatly.

"What does it matter? Are you going to try having her arrested again?"

"Where is she, Andrea?"

402

"Andrea? I'm your *mother*. You will show me the respect I deserve!"

"When you've earned my respect, I'll be happy to give it to you. Where is Wendy?"

"She's in the shower getting ready for work."

"She has a job?"

"Don't pretend you know us, Kenzie."

"Don't call me Kenzie."

"I need money, Ken—Mackenzie."

"That's no longer my problem. You've done nothing but lie to me and use me. Those checks weren't for you to support a boyfriend and the sister who has meant me nothing but harm."

"Wendy has had a rough time since Powell died."

"She locked me in a room for two days when she was ten years old."

"That's just sisters being sisters. You've always been too sensitive, Kenzie."

"And you've always been a lying alcoholic with no intention of changing."

Mack hung up as her mother sputtered more lies, more excuses into the phone.

She didn't have to listen anymore.

A minute later, Linc stalked back inside. "Come on," he said.

"Where are we going?"

"To buy that goddamn video surveillance system I shouldn't have let you talk me out of."

CHAPTER 57

The day before Thanksgiving, Mack sat gingerly on her office chair and quickly transcribed her notes from her last patient appointment into the portal.

Her lips quirked when she added the note, "Keep up the great work!" Seventy-four-year-old Jimmy McGuire had come in for a long-overdue physical after a come-to-Jesus talk from his pal Leroy Mahoney. Together, the two fishing buddies had decided to start walking and take a stab at a pescatarian diet. Jimmy had already lost five pounds in two weeks, and Mack was betting his inflammatory markers and cholesterol would be drastically different when he repeated the blood work in three months.

With a few minutes to herself, she opened her new handy-dandy home security app on her phone and snickered while she rewatched the backyard camera's recording of the middle of the night backyard patrol by Linc and Sunshine. Both security officers paused to take a piss synchronized on the lawn before they returned to her bed.

Men.

Her desk phone buzzed. When she reached for it, the chair lurched under her in warning.

She steadied it—and herself—before answering the phone. "What's up?"

"You have a couple of walk-ins out here," Tuesday announced chipperly.

"As in plural? Flu or pink eye?"

Tuesday laughed. "Neither, but you're definitely going to want to see this."

Mack eased out of the chair, then gave it a quick kick for good measure.

She was just tucking a sticky note that said "Order a new fucking chair" into her coat pocket when she rounded the corner at the front desk.

"Surprise!"

Mack gaped at Dottie, Win, and Violet Nguyen, who were grinning at her like a JCPenney family portrait. "You guys are early," she exclaimed even as she was wrapped in Dottie's strong hug. It always lasted a beat longer than Mack expected, and it always made her feel...safe.

"You look so official," Dottie squealed. She was an inch or two shorter than Mack and wore her hair in a short, curly, face-framing do. The woman loved turtlenecks and themed earrings. She was rocking both today.

Win, dressed in podiatrist casual Dockers and a check-ered button-down shirt with Nikes, nudged Mack. "You hear about the podiatrist who was having a bad day?" He wiggled his eyebrows over his silver-rimmed glasses.

Mack pinched her lips together. The man took dad jokes to a new low, combining them with lousy podiatry jokes. "I did not."

"He started the day on the wrong foot."

"Dad!" Violet rolled her eyes. She was shorter than Mack and had the slump-shoulder posture and amused smirk of a teenager. She was going through a cute Nirvana/ Seattle-grunge phase and experimenting with eye makeup and flannel.

Mack laughed. She couldn't help it. "That's terrible."

Win pulled her in for a hug. "You look good, Dr. O'Neil."

Her bruises had finally faded enough to be hidden under a coat of makeup—thankfully. She had no real need to walk the Nguyens through the latest and final ordeal with her family. They'd witnessed enough of that history. It felt like it was finally time for them all to focus on the future.

She slung an arm around Violet's shoulders and gave the girl a squeeze.

"Nose stud, huh?" Mack asked, tapping the tiny heart-shaped stud in Violet's nose.

"Awesome, right?" It kinda was.

"It suits you."

"Tuesday, would you mind taking a picture of us together?" Dottie asked, pulling a hefty, practically antique digital camera out of her purse and handing it over.

Tuesday eyed the dinosaur with apprehension and fascination. Dottie was big on pictures. Some of the kids she and Win had fostered didn't have a photographic history of their child-hoods, so the Nguyens made sure to document every moment they could for the kids who came into their lives.

The first time Mack had seen the Nguyens as an adult, Dottie had presented her with a photo album of her ten weeks with them. To this day, it was the only photo album Mack owned. Her mother had left behind Mack's baby pictures somewhere along the way, either in a half-empty apartment or in the home of one of the long line of "uncles."

"I can take a bunch on my phone, do some fun filters. I can text them to you," Tuesday offered. She'd spent fifteen minutes of her lunch break explaining photo editing apps to Mack earlier in the week.

Violet snorted, then hugged her mother, who probably had only understood every other word in that sentence. "You can text them to me or Mack. We'll get them to Mom," the girl offered.

"Get over here, Mack," Dottie insisted, putting an arm around her and Violet. Win squished in next to Mack.

"Everyone say 'duck lips,'" Tuesday sang.

"Duck lips!"

Mack mentally added "Get Dottie a smartphone for Christmas" to the sticky note in her pocket.

They smiled cheesy smiles and let Tuesday play Annie Leibovitz before Dottie invited Tuesday, Freida, and Russell to join them for "one of those selfies."

While Dottie oohed and aahed over Tuesday's photographic expertise, Win stuffed his hands in his pockets, rocked back on his heels, and made some wistful comments about lunch. Next up would be jokes about hypoglycemia as well as twenty questions about local restaurants and their signature dishes.

"Go," Russell said when Mack looked at him. "We're closing early anyway. Take your family to lunch."

Family. The word used to stick in her throat. They weren't hers. Not legally or biologically. But damn it, in her heart, in the place that it counted the most, Dottie and Win were the best parents she could have asked for.

"Why don't you see if your man friend can join us?" Dottie suggested brightly.

"Linc? Oh, he might be busy." The plan had been for Mack to have a fun takeout dinner with the Nguyens tonight while Linc worked the night shift. They'd meet him officially tomorrow.

"It sounds like you're scared to introduce him to us," Violet mused. "So does that mean you're ashamed of us or him?"

"It has to be him," Dottie said, playing along. "We're amazing."

They were.

"You can call him on the way to the diner," Win suggested as he peered over Freida's shoulder while she walked him through the local dining options. "What kind of specials do they have on Wednesdays? Oh, lookie here. They've got their specials online."

Mack was starting to sweat. This wasn't the plan. But had she bothered adhering to the plan since she got here? Sighing, she pulled her cell phone out of her coat pocket and texted Linc.

Mack: Short notice, but my foster fam showed up early. We're going to lunch at the diner. Want to meet them? It's no problem if you can't.

It would be more casual than having them all over to her place for dinner. That felt too official. Casual was good. Casual meant she wouldn't have to answer questions about futures.

Linc: I can't wait to meet them. Finishing up a call, but I'll swing by after. PS. I promise not to tell them how beautiful you are when you're naked.

Mack's face turned six shades of scarlet.

"Uh-oh. What's that face?" Dottie demanded, her motherly instincts not missing a beat.

"Nothing!" Mack coughed. "Uh, how about I drive us? Linc is on a call."

Yes, she felt silly for being nervous about her ex-foster

parents meeting her adult boyfriend. And yes, she knew it was stupid. But sometimes facts didn't change feelings.

———

Thirty minutes later, over hot open-faced roast beef sandwiches, crispy fries, and, okay, a boring salad for Mack, they and the rest of the diner patrons watched as the command vehicle rolled up in front of the diner, lights flashing.

"Oh, God. No," Mack whispered.

Linc, looking dashing in his turnout pants with dirt streaked over his face and a fresh bandage on the back of his left hand, climbed out of the truck, waved to a handful of onlookers, and strolled to the door of the diner.

He looked like a firefighting Ken doll. And Mack couldn't decide if she was more proud or embarrassed.

"Is *that* him?" Dottie hissed. "Oh, good job, honey."

"O-M-G, Mack. If that is him, I promise I'm going to stop calling you a sad single lady," Violet said. She left a makeup smear on the window.

"Big deal. So he puts out fires and saves lives for a living. Can he identify all the metatarsal bones?" Win wanted to know.

And then Linc was in the diner, strolling toward them. "Hey there, Dreamy." He dropped a kiss on her cheek and presented her, Dottie, and Violet each with a single rose from behind his back. The women swooned.

"Little freezer fire at the florist's," he said. "Gloria says hi. You must be Mackenzie's parents. I'm Linc." He offered his hand to Win.

He was showing off. For her family. And she loved him for it.

CHAPTER 58

Mack woke to the silence of the middle of the night. Something had jolted her out of sleep. It wasn't the gradual awakening in the space between dreams. Something had dragged her from sleep into awake.

In the dim light, she saw Sunshine sit up on the bed next to her and cock her head.

Three a.m. That meant it was officially Thanksgiving Day.

"What's the matter, buddy?" she rasped. Her throat tickled as if it was irritated.

Then her senses caught up. There was a tang in the air, something bitter, acrid. Something wrong.

There was a noise downstairs. A shuffling, a soft thump.

It could be Linc. He could be coming home early from his shift. But that wasn't his tread.

Her gun was in a lockbox in the coat closet on the first floor. A really stupid place for it, she realized too late.

She snapped on the bedside light, grabbed her phone with shaking fingers, and sent off a text to Linc.

The room looked hazy, and she blinked her eyes, trying to clear them.

Mack: Are you here at my place?

There were footsteps on the stairs now.

She knew before the door opened that it wasn't him. The figure in her doorway was framed in a ghostly orange flicker of light. It wasn't Linc. And it wasn't the sunrise lighting the interior of her home.

It was fire.

Sunshine let out a low, threatening growl, her body stiffening into a defensive posture between Mack and the figure.

Black smoke billowed lazily in, clinging to the ceiling.

Blindly, she hit what she hoped to God was the emergency call button on her phone.

"What have you done?" she gasped, pulling the sheet over her face as smoke stung her throat and lungs.

The figure stepped across the threshold, an arm extended toward Mack.

A gun pointed at her heart.

Sunshine snarled, and the hand that held the gun wavered toward the dog.

"No!" Mack said, yanking Sunshine back. The figure closed the door, grinning maniacally.

"Guess who finally wins, Kenzie?"

"Jesus. What have you done, Wendy?"

Wendy stood between Mack and the door, the stairs, the way out.

"You took everything from me. You couldn't stand to see me happy. Now, it's my turn to take from you."

Logically, Mack knew there was no reason to argue with unhinged. There would be no making her sister see the reality. But in the moment, with adrenaline pumping through her system, with the need to live to see Thanksgiving

411

morning when the people she loved most would gather, she was fearless.

"I did everything I could to save him, Wendy. Everything. He was already gone before he got to the hospital."

"You killed him," she shrieked.

"I swear I didn't, Wendy. I tried so hard to save him. I tried to save him for you." Keep her talking. Keep her engaged until either the authorities arrived or the smoke got too thick to see. She'd get Sunshine out on the roof, and they'd escape. Somehow.

"You don't get to have what you took from me."

"I didn't take anything from you!"

"You killed him. You did it just to hurt me. And now I'm going to watch you burn, and I'm going to kill your firefighter when he comes through that door to save you!"

"Where did you start the fire, Wendy?" Mack demanded, slipping off the bed and hoping to God the call had connected. Hoped that someone in dispatch could hear what was happening. In case she didn't make it. She wanted them to know the truth.

Wendy giggled. "The garage. I figured it would give us time to talk, give your man time to get here before you both die."

"I love Linc," Mack said. Not for Wendy's benefit but for him. If she didn't make it, there would be a record of her saying it. "Put the gun down, Wendy. You don't really want to shoot first responders. You just want to hurt me." She took a step toward her sister.

"Stay where you are!" The gun was pointed at her again. "Don't make me shoot you before the smoke gets you. Your boyfriend will find you," Wendy said, gleeful now. "He'll find your body and know he couldn't save you."

"You're really going to kill us both?"

"I'll watch you burn," she said, her smile a terrifying machination. She laughed.

Sunshine whimpered.

It was getting hotter and darker in the room. The layer of smoke on the ceiling was thickening.

Mack's phone screen glowed dimly, half under the pillow. *Please be listening.*

It was eerily quiet except for the pops and bangs from the fire as it consumed the cottage beneath them.

Wendy coughed into her arm, the gun pointing at the floor for just a second.

"I didn't kill Powell," Mack said.

"Yes. You did. He was yelling. That night in the car. I couldn't see. It was dark, foggy. Powell was singing or maybe yelling," Wendy murmured, coughing again.

If Mack could get to her and disarm her, there was a chance she and Sunshine could make it out.

Sunshine wiggled closer to the edge of the bed. The roof was steep, but maybe they could get down the stairs or out the window, onto the roof.

God. Once again, Wendy had her trapped in a second-floor bedroom. But Mack wasn't six years old anymore. And she had a hell of a lot to live for.

It was so damn hot. And Linc did this for a living, walking into the flames. *Linc.* The smoke was so thick now. Someone would notice the flames. Someone would call. Someone would come.

Sweat ran freely down Mack's back. Her hair hung limply in her face.

"Powell overdosed. He had too much heroin in his system," Mack said.

"I had the methadone. We did it for fun. But I didn't see the barrier." Wendy sighed dreamily, sinking onto the edge of the bed. "But I saw his head hit the dashboard."

413

Mack pulled Sunshine off the bed, pushed her to the floor out of the smoke. "Stay, girl."

Understanding hit her. Sick recognition.

"You were driving that night. It wasn't Powell. It was you."

Her sister had killed Powell. Her sister and his bad decisions.

"Shut up! Shut the fuck up!" Wendy shot back up off the mattress. Her hand trembled as she pulled the hammer back on the revolver.

It was so dark in the room. Like the smoke was extinguishing everything.

"You *know* it wasn't my fault. You blame yourself. But it's easier to blame me."

There were sirens, Mack thought. She hoped it wasn't a delusion, a hallucination.

They were getting louder and louder now. It wasn't her imagination.

Help. Linc.

She needed to get out. Needed to get Sunshine out. They had a future. The three of them. There were kisses to be kissed. Vows to be made. Babies to have.

And she was going to fight for him, for their future.

She launched herself at her sister.

The sound of a gunshot rang in her ears.

CHAPTER 59

I literally can't taste the difference," Linc announced, dragging the blindfold off to stare at the two bowls of chili in front of him.

"Seriously? I use chipotle seasoning and jalapeños," Al complained.

"Pfft. Please, amateur. This is chorizo sausage," Lucille insisted, pointing at the bowl on the right.

"Both taste like Chef Boyardee to me," Linc said.

Their jaws dropped in abject horror.

"Oh my God. I'm just kidding, guys." Linc laughed, wiping his mouth with a napkin.

The alarm rang out.

"Let's get to work," he said as they hurried out of the room and down the stairs.

He was shrugging into his gear when his cell rang.

"Shit." He had a text from Mackenzie. "Yeah, Linc."

"Chief, this is Cheryl at dispatch. Mike's got an open line on an emergency call. It's coming from Dr. O'Neil's address."

His fingers froze on his coat. "Mackenzie."

"It's her house. Voices are garbled. She's not alone. Sounds like whoever set the fire is still in there? Neighbors are calling in now. Structure fire."

"Fuck. Brody, it's Mack's house," Linc called.

Their gazes locked. "Go," Brody said.

"I'm on my way," Linc told the operator as he climbed behind the wheel of his chief's vehicle and tore out of the parking lot, lights and sirens blaring.

Fear was a living creature trying to claw its way out of his chest as his tires squealed around a corner.

"Hang on, Dreamy," he whispered. "Just hang on."

"Chief, Mike's saying it sounds like the doc is saying something about a gun."

He could see the flames from the end of the street. Neighbors were gathered on the sidewalk, clumps of people in pajamas and winter coats.

He heard the faint pop.

"Shots fired," the call came across the radio. "All units to 214 Rosebud Lane. Shots fired. Structure fire."

He stopped on the street, leaving the truck on, door open. He could hear the sirens coming. A quarter mile out. But he couldn't wait. He grabbed his helmet, threw on his bottle, and sprinted across the yard.

He could hear a barking dog, and his blood boiled. His girlfriend and his dog were in there, and he wasn't waiting.

"Chief to dispatch. I'm on-scene. Going in."

"Good luck, Chief," dispatch replied.

"Engine 231, one minute out."

"Get her out, Chief," one of the neighbors called.

"Be safe!"

With the well wishes ringing in his ear, Linc affixed his mask and kicked in the cottage door.

If it were any other firefighter and any other house, Linc

would have made them wait for backup. For command. For a plan. But it was Mackenzie.

The flames had engulfed the living room and dining room completely. He dropped to the floor as smoke billowed in hypnotic waves, blinding him.

His gloved hand found something that shouldn't have been there. A gas can. Accelerant. Jesus.

He crawled forward into the inferno, the ceiling raining down on him in slow motion as the fire fueled itself. Flames and insulation, ceiling tiles. A macabre storm.

He couldn't even see the stairs.

"Mackenzie!" He shouted her name. But there was no response.

He tried uselessly to knock back some of the flames licking at the drywall, the floor, as he made his way forward.

The stairs. He found them with his hands. They were on fire, almost melting in front of him. He had to get upstairs. He crawled up one, then another. The carpet on them was on fire. Everything was on fire.

Something hit him on the shoulder, then gripped.

It was Brody and Stairmaster. And they were dragging him away from the stairs. Away from his woman. Away from his future.

"No!" Linc roared. He fought them, but they didn't let him go.

They were almost to the door when the stairs gave, collapsing, sending a cloud of dust to mix with the toxic fog bank of smoke.

They dragged him out.

"Chief and search and rescue are out of the structure," Command announced in a relieved breath.

Linc yanked off his helmet, his mask. "I'm going back in there."

Brody stopped him with a hand to his chest. "There were shots fired."

"Do I look like I fucking care? Mackenzie is in there. Sunshine is in there, and I'm getting them out."

"The stairs are out," Stairmaster said.

"I don't care if I have to climb my way up with an ax. I'm not letting her go."

"It's too tight. We can't get the ladder truck any closer, and we can't go over the roof," one of the volunteers reported breathlessly.

"Then we'll take a ladder around back to the bedroom."

"Let's get it off the truck," Brody said. "Where is it?"

"Staging at the end of the road. Units are stacked up like Tupperware out there."

But Linc couldn't wait for the volunteer to return with it.

"I have an idea," he said and sprinted for the fence, for home.

Less than a minute later, he aimed Betsy at his backyard fence. He didn't stop to think. He simply mashed the gas pedal and sent the antique truck smashing through the fence.

He slammed on the brakes as a half-dozen firefighters threw themselves over the locked front gate into the side yard. Together, they braced Betsy's ladder against the side of the house.

His heart was in his fucking throat as he started to climb.

He needed to be careful. To be smart. If the arsonist was in there, if they were still conscious, he'd be a sitting duck. The bedroom window was closed. No ventilation. Trapping all that poison in that tiny room.

It could be a trap, but it didn't fucking matter. He was going in.

He felt the ladder shake beneath him. One of his crew climbed behind him.

"Please," Linc whispered. There was a tug on his pant leg.

He stopped, ready to kick whoever the fuck it was in the face.

"Chief, you don't have your mask," Skyler said, holding out her own. "Take it. Go."

He slipped it over his head, took her helmet too, and then took the last two rungs and shattered the fucking glass.

"Mackenzie!" he roared.

But the gunshot was louder.

He threw himself into the room, disoriented, fell to his hands and knees. There was something there. A lump. Jesus Christ. Sunshine. His Sunshine.

"Mackenzie," he shouted again, his throat burning up.

"I'm here. Get Sunny!"

She was alive. She was alive. She was alive.

He couldn't see her, but Mackenzie was alive.

"Come toward me if you can," he yelled. "Follow the sound of my voice."

He shoved his hands under Sunshine's limp form and lifted her to the window.

Gloved hands were ready and waiting to take his girl. He waited until they had her and then turned back. It was black as pitch in the room. He hurried forward on his hands and knees, pacing off the room in his mind. The flames were here now, licking under the door, flashes of orange through choking smoke.

"Mackenzie!"

"Here!"

A hand reached out and gripped his coat. He grabbed her and pulled, but she didn't move.

"Are you stuck?"

There was a steady stream of requests for CAN reports blaring through Linc's radio.

"I'm trying to drag my sister with me."

"Your sister?"

"She's unconscious. I think she hit her head when I hit her!"

"Let go of your sister, Mackenzie."

"Promise me you'll get her out."

"I swear to you, I will personally carry her out of this house, but you need to move now!"

He dragged her forcefully, not even giving her the option to decide.

"Take my girl," he shouted as he shoved the coughing Mackenzie's head and shoulders out the window. He waited until she disappeared into the night onto the ladder before crawling back into the room. In such a tiny room, it wasn't hard to find the sister.

Her form was limp on the floor at the foot of the bed. Something small and metal beside her. The gun. She'd stood between Mackenzie and the door with a gun. He pocketed it, shoving it into one of the exterior pockets on his gear.

He refused to think. Refused to acknowledge the rage that boiled hotter beneath his gear than the flames that were smothering him.

"Chief Reed, exiting the structure with third victim," he growled into the radio.

The angle of the ladder was too steep for a two-man team to take her. He hefted her up and over his shoulder and swung onto Betsy's ladder.

"Linc, hurry!" he could hear Mackenzie shouting from the ground.

Carefully, he descended, as the world above him wavered in the flames. The ceiling came down halfway between the second and first floor. By the time his feet were on the ground, part of the roof had caved in over the bedroom.

He handed the sister over to a team of EMTs and opened his arms.

Mack fell into them and buried her face in his chest.

"Mackenzie. Baby." He shoved his mask off, stroked her face. "Open your eyes."

When she did, when he saw that bottle green and the curve of her lips, his heart started again.

"You came," she whispered.

"You're damn right I did. I'm so sorry I wasn't here."

"You're here now." A coughing fit racked her body.

Khalil, the paramedic, knelt down. "We've got your blond on oxygen," he said. "Now let's take a look at your brunette."

"I'm fine," Mack insisted. "Is my sister alive?"

"No breath. No beat," Khalil said.

Mack dropped to her knees next to the spine board they'd placed Wendy on and waved away the EMT. She listened for breath.

Linc shrugged out of his coat and draped it over her shoulders, then stepped back and watched her begin chest compressions on the woman who tried to end her life.

"You all right, Chief Idiot Who Can't Follow Protocol?" Ty demanded, approaching.

Linc ran two shaking hands through his hair.

"I may never be all right again for as long as I live," he predicted, swiping an arm under his nose.

Ty pulled him in for a hard, one-armed hug. "Scared the shit out of us when you fell through the window on that gunshot."

Linc patted down his body. Nothing felt holey. "She must have hit the wall or the window frame," he guessed. "You got gloves?"

"I can get a pair."

"I've got a weapon in my pants," Linc said.

"I'm not falling for that one again," Ty said.

The laugh felt good and loosened some of the fear that still had his heart in a death grip.

Once Ty fished the gun out of Linc's pants and into an evidence envelope, Linc went for his first girl.

Sunshine watched him from a blanket where one of his firefighters and an EMT were keeping her company. Her tail thumped, the mask over her nose fogged as his sweet girl breathed.

He lay down on the cold ground next to her. "Hey, pretty girl."

Her tail thumped a little harder, and she wriggled closer to him. Linc stroked his hand from head to tail. She nudged him.

There was a commotion behind him.

Everyone seemed to be talking at once.

"Got a pulse!" Mackenzie said. She'd shrugged out of his coat, out of the blanket someone had given her.

"Got blood," Khalil yelled, but he wasn't looking at Wendy.

People were converging around them, but not before Linc spotted the red stain spreading on the white of Mackenzie's tank.

Then he was running again.

"What is everyone's problem?" she demanded as a paramedic tried to shove her down on a stretcher. "Get off me!"

Linc slid to a stop at her side. "Mackenzie, why the hell are you bleeding?"

She pulled up her tank and looked down at the small hole in her abdomen. "Oh, shit."

"Jesus, Dreamy, you got shot."

"Huh," she said, looking bewildered. "Sunshine lunged at her when you broke the window. I tried to get in the way. Guess it worked." Her hair was a snarled mess, her face streaked with soot and dirt, and she was fighting with the

EMT who was trying to cut her tank open. She slapped her hands away. "You're not showing my boobs to my coworkers! Not when I have cornbread to make in four hours for Thanksgiving! Oh, shit! Linc, can you go to the store? All the ingredients were in there." She pointed toward the smoking inferno.

Her home was burning to the ground. Firefighters had hacked through the garden gate with hatchets to get to the backyard. Her sister had tried to murder them both. And she was worrying about Thanksgiving.

"Dreamy?" Linc cupped her face in his hands. He could feel the steam of sweat evaporating from his head and neck rising into the ether.

"Yeah?" She winced as someone put pressure on the fucking bullet hole her sister had put in her.

He was going to marry this woman. And he was going to tell their kids every Thanksgiving just how lucky they were to have a hero for a mom. He needed to seal the deal now. Not another second wasted on separate lives or separate houses.

"Don't you dare do it, Lincoln Reed," Mackenzie snapped, pointing a finger in his face.

"Do what?"

"You have that proposal look on your face. If you propose to me right now with no ring while this very insistent lady is trying to flash my tits to all the first responders of Benevolence, I will say no, and I will mean it."

"You riding with us, Chief?" Khalil asked as they started to wheel Mack toward the smashed gate and one of the waiting ambulances.

"You're damn right I am."

"You guys are overreacting. It's a freaking flesh wound. Jeez, I could patch myself up," she complained.

"You better get yourself a ring," Brody said, slapping a hand on Linc's shoulder.

Linc pulled him in for a hard hug. "Thanks for having my back, bro. You'll take Sunshine?"

"Already called the wife. She's making your baby girl a steak as we speak."

"Thanks, man."

"Happy Thanksgiving!"

Linc climbed into the back of the ambulance and leaned over Mackenzie. They'd slipped an oxygen mask over her face and given her something for the pain. *She'd hate that*, he thought with a grin.

"Dreamy, if you ever again have a single doubt about what kind of person you are, I'm slapping you upside the head and reminding you that you saved the life of the woman who tried to kill you."

"All in a day's work," Mack sighed sleepily.

"You're my hero, Dreamy."

"You're mine, Hotshot."

CHAPTER 60

The hospital was a zoo. It felt like half the damn town, including Mack's foster parents and their daughter, showed up just to make sure she was okay. By the time they were all reassured that Mack was alive and she was finally discharged, it was nine in the morning, and she and Linc were exhausted and starving.

To Mack, it felt like a lot of fuss for a bullet wound that hadn't hit anything vital.

Skyler and Zane had dropped off Linc's truck at the hospital and thoughtfully included a change of clothes for them both. They changed into their matching BFD sweats, and then Linc carted Mack out of the hospital like she was precious cargo.

She yawned mightily from the passenger seat. "This is *not* the Thanksgiving I imagined," she sighed.

"Dreamy, any day with you is a gift," he said, interlacing his fingers with hers. "A bullet-riddled, arson-fueled gift during which all my coworkers caught a glimpse of my girlfriend's perfect breasts."

"Yay them," she said sarcastically.

"Old time's sake?" he asked, pointing ahead of them through the windshield.

"Hell. Yes."

They stopped at the diner, sat at "their" table, and sat on the same side of the booth.

The server, the same woman they had their first time there, paused mid special retelling to take them in. The bruises, some fresh and some fading, on both their faces. The layers of grime. Linc had some of Mack's dried blood on his neck and chin. The server grunted. "Holidays sure are hard on some people."

Mack snorted tea through her nose, and Linc put his head down on the table and laughed until he couldn't breathe.

When they got home—to the residence that hadn't burned to the ground—they stripped down and fell into Linc's bed, exhausted both physically and mentally. She woke, hours later, dizzy and disoriented but warm and safe, anchored by Linc's arm. Her side hurt like a few dozen hornets had taken a shot at her, but other than that, Mack felt remarkably chipper.

He stirred against her and buried his face in her hair. "We smell," he sighed but made no attempt to release her.

"Shower?" she suggested.

"Shower."

They showered carefully, gently, and then spent a very long time staring out Linc's gym window at the charred carcass of the cottage Mack had called home for the last three months, the mangled remains of the fence.

"Guess I'm moving in," she mused over her green tea.

"Damn right you are," he said.

"Poor Betsy."

"She'd be proud to give her life this way," he said. Though Mack thought his eyes looked a little glassy as he stared out at the wrecked truck. Someone had thoughtfully pushed it back into his yard. Betsy's front end was crunched in, her pristine paint scraped, her fenders dented. It would take another five years for him to restore her again, Mack bet.

"You know, I came here to start a calmer life," she said.

"You came here for a new adventure," he corrected her. "And you found me."

"Maybe I'll learn to make jelly."

"I'll take up competitive corn hole," he decided.

She glanced out at the ruins again. "I just keep thinking about all those doilies that went up in flames."

Linc snorted. "Maybe that can be your new hobby. Flame-retardant doilies."

She put her mug down and ran her hands up his chest. "Or—and I'm just throwing this out here—we could just have a lot of sex all the time."

"Uh-uh, Dreamy. No sex until you've had your wound care follow-up. Doctor's orders."

"You asked Dr. Ling that?" Mack was horrified.

"Yep. And double-checked with Russell. He confirmed. I had a feeling you'd try to seduce me."

There was a knock at the door, and she groaned. "I guess we can't just hole up here for the rest of the weekend. Can we?"

"Baby, you got shot in a house fire saving my dog from your whack-job sister. We're lucky they left us alone this long."

"I feel bad that we ruined everyone's holiday," she said. "I had a really good cornbread recipe too. It involved beer and cheese."

"I'm sure they're all fine. They probably got pizza or takeout, and everyone is napping in front of someone's TV. I heard my sister talking to your foster parents about oven space in the hospital waiting room."

They found one Sheriff Ty Adler in a fresh uniform on

Linc's doorstep. His cruiser was parked up against the front of the building.

"Soph sent these for you," he said, holding out a bag with a change of clothes. Comfortable leggings, a soft sweater, an actual bra, and a tube of red, red lipstick.

"Thanks," Mack said, clutching the bag to her chest in gratitude. "Are you here to catch us up?"

"I can do that on the way."

"On the way where?" Linc asked.

"We've got some business to take care of is all," Ty explained vaguely.

"She can give her statement to you tomorrow," Linc growled.

"It's fine." Mack sighed. "Let's just get this over with."

"I'll drive y'all," Ty volunteered.

They changed first and then let the sheriff whisk them off. Linc, playing the overprotective hero, refused to leave Mack's side and insisted they both ride in the back seat.

"So quick recap," Ty said, glancing their way in the rearview mirror. "Wendy is alive thanks to Doc O'Neil here. She suffered some smoke inhalation and burns. But we got her prints on the gas cans and video footage from your own security system, before it melted, that shows her rolling up into your garage. She stole the extra garage door opener out of the kitchen drawer when she broke into your house a week ago. She's being belligerent, and I'm told she'll be meeting with a staff psychiatrist for an evaluation before her ass is carted off to jail for a very, very, very long time."

"Are you sure he's not arresting us for something?" Mack whispered, leaning into Linc's side.

"You never know with Benevolence. But I think we can take him if he tries anything funny." He kissed her on the head and snuggled her closer. "This isn't the police department,

Sheriff Numb Nuts," Linc pointed out when the cruiser rolled up in front of the fire station. Ty gave the sirens a chirp, and the middle garage door rolled up.

"Oh. My. God," Mack said, sitting up straighter.

"Looks like you're getting a Thanksgiving after all," Linc observed.

"I swear to God, if someone so much as pops a bottle of champagne, I am out," she whispered to him as they slid out of the back seat.

They were all there. Dottie, Win, and Violet. Linc's sisters and their families. The firefighters and EMS crews and their families. Harper and Luke. Gloria and Aldo. Sophie and all the kids. *So many kids.* Mrs. Moretta and her football boyfriend were chatting it up with Gloria's mother and Claire and Charlie Garrison. Russell and Denise were there with Skyler. Freida and her husband. Tuesday and her boyfriend. Joni was there too, with half of the ladies' night ladies.

Sunshine, looking spiffy in a turkey and pumpkin neckerchief, sprinted over to them. Someone had given her a bath.

"Hey, sweet girl! You were so brave," Mack said, burying her face in the dog's fur.

The station smelled like home cooking and happiness.

Someone had wheeled a big screen into the garage, and a football game was on.

"Imagine that. We finally used that extension cord," Linc said.

Tables were set up and covered with tarps. Stacks of paper plates and cups and utensils sat ready to be put into service.

The Nguyens practically tackled her and didn't back off until Mack winced when a hug got too tight. She was passed around, more carefully, until someone yelled, "Time to eat!"

Ellen and her father-in-law wheeled in a rolling mechanic's

rack with trays of turkey meat, stuffing, mashed potatoes, and all the sides. The gravy boat was a repurposed oil drip pan. "Who's ready for a little Thanksgiving?"

"This is amazing. I don't know what to say," Mack said, finding Linc's hand and holding on tight.

He brought her knuckles to his lips and kissed them lightly. "We're going to have to invite all these people to the wedding."

"We're going to need a bigger barn," she predicted.

"Linc, Mom and Dad are FaceTiming," Christa said, holding up her phone.

"Go," Mack said, nudging him toward his family.

"Yoo-hoo, Dr. Mack!" Freida wiggled her fingers in Mack's face and giggled.

"We got you a little something. Since you're sticking around," Russell said with a wink. He looked dapper as always in a charcoal button-down. But his tie had cartoon turkeys on it. He gestured toward the tarp-covered mound behind him.

With a flourish, Tuesday yanked the tarp away to reveal a new desk chair in sleek white leather.

"You guys," Mack said, pressing her fingers to her mouth.

"Glad you decided to stay. We're going to do good work here," Russell predicted.

"Yes, we are."

She sat in her new chair and ate a full Thanksgiving meal, slipping Sunshine bits of turkey under the table. She caught up on all the news with the Nguyens and made plans for a visit in the spring.

Linc's hand stayed on her knee under the table.

"This is the *best* Thanksgiving ever."

"You got shot, and your house burned down," he reminded her.

"Well, you've met my sister. The bar wasn't set very high."

"Dreamy, I promise you, there are more good times ahead. More love. More laughs. More of all this. And way fewer fires and GSWs."

She believed him. She trusted him to deliver on that promise.

"You showed up for me when I needed you. I'll never take that for granted."

"And I'll always be there for you, Dreamy."

EPILOGUE

I t was one of those crisp, cold nights that made sure everyone knew it was winter. The Christmas lights seemed to sparkle extra bright in the cold, reflecting off the two inches of snow Benevolence had gotten earlier that day. Not enough to snarl traffic or ruin holiday travel plans, but just enough for a real, white Christmas.

"Okay, people. It's on to the next house," Mack said through the bullhorn she'd borrowed from Linc. The Christmas Light Walking Tour was the first official event of the Benevolence Wellness Club.

She hadn't been sure what kind of a turnout to expect and had been overjoyed when seventy-five people, bundled up in winter gear, showed up at the fire station.

"This is pretty great, Dreamy," Linc said, holding her hand as they led the way down the sidewalk toward the glowing spectacle on the next block.

Everything had been pretty great since Thanksgiving.

Bruises healed. Bullet wounds too. Though maybe a bit more slowly. Mack sat behind her desk in her office on her new desk chair. And every evening, she met Linc at home. Moving in together had been a necessity but one they both adapted to quickly. Sunshine—who was currently chewing on her reindeer antlers—was happy to finally come from a two-parent household.

Wellness Club members started to ooh and aah the closer they got to the Garrisons.

"Damn," Mack said. "You did good, Hotshot. It was nice of you to help Luke."

Linc grinned. "Yeah. I did it to learn all his secrets. Next year, I'm gonna kick his ass in decorating. He won't know what hit him."

Mack laughed and took Sunshine as Linc headed off to go find Luke.

Harper hurried down the porch steps, bundled up in a bright red parka.

"Your house looks stunning," Mack told her.

It did. There were thousands of lights. Every window, every door, was framed in white Christmas lights. The porch columns and railings were wrapped so tightly the wood wasn't even visible. The roof was lit up like a runway. Wreaths hung from every window. Candy canes lit the walkway from sidewalk to front porch.

"Thank you," Harper said, beaming. "Luke goes bigger and bigger every year."

"I think he does it for you," Mack guessed.

Harper's eyes filled with tears, reflecting the dancing lights that covered just about every inch of her home. "I can't believe I could have missed this. I could have left. I *was* going to leave. Move on. Start over again. And I would've missed out on the greatest things in my life."

Lola the pit bull in her Santa sweater and tiny Max in his bow tie barked playfully at an inflatable snowman in the front yard.

The kids ran in and out of the crowd, playing keep-away with a reindeer mitten. Luke and Linc stood side by side, arms crossed, feet wide on the sidewalk as they admired their handiwork.

Tears rolled down Harper's face. Tears of joy and gratitude, of a happiness that filled her to the point of overflowing.

"I'm glad you stayed," Mack said, clearing her throat.

"I'm glad you stayed," Harper said, leaning in to give her a hard hug.

Mack swiped her sleeve under her nose. It wouldn't do to have the town's family practitioner sobbing on the sidewalk on Christmas Eve.

———

"Dreamy, we need to go back home and get naked together soon or I'm going to go hypothermic," he groused as she led him somewhere. He wasn't sure where because she'd insisted he close his eyes. He just knew that as soon as the Wellness Club's Christmas Light Walking Tour wrapped up, she was dragging him off.

"Yeah, yeah. Soon. I promise."

"It's Christmas Eve. I want to unwrap my Christmas present."

"Almost there," she promised breathlessly.

"And by 'Christmas present,' I mean you, and by 'unwrap,' I mean take your clothes off."

"Okay. You can open your eyes now." Mack sounded practically giddy.

Linc opened his eyes. She was bouncing on her toes, hands clasped under her chin, in front of the old fire station. Sunshine danced excitedly next to her.

He glanced up to the second-floor windows, the exact spot where, only a few weeks ago, they'd fucked themselves senseless.

"Since your place is too small and mine burned down, I thought we'd need a more permanent option," she said gleefully.

"Another option?" he parroted.

"To live in."

"You want to live here? With me?" He was leveled. Absolutely fucking leveled.

She nodded. "That's kind of the plan. I mean, if you're smart enough to recognize what a good deal this is."

He was having trouble comprehending what she was saying.

"Run this by me again one more time?" he demanded gruffly.

"I'm picking you. I'm choosing you. And I'm asking you if you'll…" Her voice got tight, her words stalling.

Dreamy was never without her nerve.

"Are you okay?" He reached for her, but she took a step back.

She shook her head impatiently and took a breath. "I'm asking you, Lincoln Reed, if you'll marry me. If you'll move into this fire station with me. If you'll help me plant roots here."

Sunshine let out a happy little bark as if she understood everything Linc was having trouble grasping.

"What? Wait. What?" This time when he reached for her, she let him.

"Oh, come on! I'm asking you if you'll make an honest woman out of me, Hotshot." She grinned up at him and threw her arms around his neck. "Say yes."

He was the luckiest son of a bitch in the world.

"You're damn right I'll marry you," he said, lifting her feet clear off the ground and spinning her around. Sunshine ran in delirious circles.

"I knew you were beautiful *and* smart." Mack laughed. Her arms tightened around him, and he saw the glisten of tears in those beautiful, bottle-green eyes.

"Are you sure about this?"

She shook her head. "I'm scared shitless. That's how I know it's going to be good."

"I won't let you down, Dreamy," he promised her earnestly.

She smirked. "I know *you* won't. And I'll do my best to return the favor. This is going to be one hell of an adventure."

"I'll make sure it is," he promised fervently.

"It's a wreck," she warned him. "I've already walked the building with Luke. It's gonna be a lot of work to make it livable."

"A hell of an adventure," Linc repeated, feeling his heart swelling in his chest.

She'd chosen him. Mackenzie O'Neil had picked him to spend the rest of her life with. He wasn't just lucky. He was golden.

"You must really like this idea," she whispered, cuddling against the hardness in his pocket.

And that was when he remembered what he'd put in there.

"About that, Dreamy," he said, sliding a hand into his pocket.

"Don't you dare get your dick out yet," she hissed.

"I'm not getting my dick out."

But his complaint was drowned out by the creaky ascent of the fire station's garage door. He saw feet. A lot of them. And tires. And a gleaming chrome grill.

"What did you do?" he asked her. Sunshine darted under the door and disappeared.

Mack grinned at him and pressed her face into his chest. "Happy engagement present."

His crew, all of them grinning maniacally, surrounded his beloved Betsy. His 1954 Mack B85 antique fire engine. But it wasn't the wreck it had been. It was pristine, perfect.

"How?" It was the only word he could get out.

"Abner Kersh and Shorty's garage helped out with the bodywork, but your guys did the rest," Mackenzie told him.

"You do a lot for us, Chief," Brody, in a Santa beard, told him. "This is a thank-you."

"Shut the fuck up," Linc said, feeling his throat tighten.

"You shut the fuck up," Brody countered, pulling him in for a hug.

"Thanks, Chief," Kelly said, elbowing her way into the hug.

There were hugs, a few manly tears, and a lot of appreciative nodding as they circled Betsy with him.

"Who wants a beer?" someone yelled.

"Me!" they all responded.

Linc found his way back to Mackenzie. He always would.

"Pretty confident that I was gonna say yes," he teased, slipping his hands around her waist and bringing his forehead to hers.

She pinched his ass. "It was incentive. I mean, I already bought the station."

"Doc Dreamy owns real estate?" he teased.

"Doc Dreamy and Chief Dreamy own real estate," she corrected.

"About that," he said, once again slipping his hand into his pocket. "Sunny, come here."

Sunshine trotted up to them and plopped her butt on the cold concrete.

"Mackenzie O'Neil, let's make this official," Linc said, producing the box from his pocket.

"Shut the fuck up," she said, bringing her gloved hands to her mouth.

"I will once you put this damn diamond on your finger," he promised.

She tore off her glove and threw it on the floor.

437

Sunshine helpfully picked it up and watched dopey-eyed while her mommy and daddy made things official with a bit of sparkle and a long, sweet kiss.

BONUS EPILOGUE

A few years down the road…

T hat's quite the equipment you're packing, Dreamy," Linc said, eyeing his wife as she crammed an SLR camera with a zoom lens into her bag.

She shot him a look. "Need I remind you that this is Casey's first Christmas assembly and Hadley is lead reindeer? We're not missing a second of it." She paused and straightened to tickle the baby he was bouncing. "You're doing video, right?"

"No, I'm not. And you're not taking pictures either." He held up a hand when Mackenzie opened her mouth to tell him exactly what kind of an idiot he was being. "I paid Skyler and Zane fifty bucks each to get front row seats and document the entire thing for us so we can sit there being present and amazed and possibly appalled—because Hadley was *not* committing to practicing the footwork for the dance number until I got the guys involved—by our girls."

Those green eyes went smoky on him, taking his breath away like they always did.

"You, Chief Reed, are a damn genius."

The baby on the blanket next to them waved his chubby arms and blew a spit bubble in approval.

"See? Lucas agrees," she said, beaming at their youngest. Six months old, and he'd officially wrestled the title of Biggest Flirt away from his father. Grown women swooned over his baby blues and round cheeks.

His big sisters found him charming, except when he was in meltdown mode, which wasn't quite as often as his first few months. And now they were settling into being a family of five.

Seven actually.

Sunshine, still spry at age twelve, tip-tapped into the room with Muttski on her heels. Muttski was a nondescript mix of seven different breeds—according to the genetic test Mackenzie had insisted on—with one ear up and one ear down. He'd developed a crush on Sunshine three years ago when the fire department and Wellness Club had cohosted an animal rescue event.

And the rest of them had fallen hard for his barrel-like body and little doggy grin.

It was a really good fucking life. They worked hard and played harder, juggling work schedules, kid activities, and naked time. In between it all, Mack learned to make jelly, and Linc tried his hand at gardening and corn hole.

"I don't suppose we have half an hour—"

"No," she said firmly. "But Dottie and Win are picking up all three hellions in approximately four hours and keeping them overnight."

Linc swooped Lucas into his carrier and pulled Mackenzie into his arms.

"Have I mentioned how much I love you?"

She slipped her arms around his neck. "Only once since breakfast."

"Take a look around us. Look what we've built, Dr. Reed."

The firehouse was home now. Its concrete floors and brick walls were softened by comfortable furniture, cozy rugs. A never-ending deluge of kids' toys that were picked up every night somehow always seemed to spill forth in the daylight hours.

The kitchen was a bright, airy room where their girls perched on stools for their breakfast and in the afternoons to tell Linc every single thing that happened in their days at Benevolence Elementary School while he made them snacks.

Their dining table was big and beefy and expanded to fit both families for a monthly brunch.

They'd hosted cookouts on the rooftop deck. Read stories to their babies in bedrooms where firefighters had once caught Zs between calls. Their bedroom was a haven of heavy drapes, big furniture, and a bed that they were both happy to spend as much time in as possible.

The firehouse that he'd once thought of as his second home was now truly home. It was filled with love and laughter...and, given the ages of everyone, an overabundance of tears on any given day. But he wouldn't change a damn thing.

Every night, when he crawled into bed exhausted and wrung out, he buried his face in Mackenzie's hair and breathed her in. They both knew what a delicate balance it was between life and death. Between well and unwell. Between busy and burnout. And they worked hard to maintain that balance.

———

Linc watched his tough, beautiful doctor wipe away a tear as the first reindeer pranced out on stage. Hadley had dark, wavy hair like her mother and his blue eyes that she used to defraud them of snacks and extra screen time. She'd also inherited her stubborn streak from both sides.

Casey was a rough-and-tumble pixie whose independence

was under constant expression. Her blond hair was cut short after an unfortunate yet hilarious gum incident that she tried to fix herself with safety scissors…the day before kindergarten picture day.

A word to parents everywhere, those things can still cut hair.

He wondered what kind of personality Lucas would have as the little boy bounced happily in his lap, making eyes and belly laughing at Grandma Dottie.

"Oh, I can't take it another second," Dottie said, shoving her camera into Win's hands. "Give me that beautiful baby boy!"

Linc unloaded Lucas and wrapped an arm around his wife's shoulder.

His mom half rose out of her seat next to him, phone trained on the stage. His dad put down his crossword and watched his granddaughters with pride.

Mack leaned in. "Did you ever think in a million years you'd be taking a half day off work to watch your kids butcher a school Christmas production?" she asked as Casey turned the wrong way during the very simple kindergarten choreography of "We Wish You a Merry Christmas."

Apparently the song wasn't doing it for her because she belted out a line from *Frozen*. The rest of the kids must have thought it was a way better option and joined in. The music director shrugged at the audience and tossed her baton over her shoulder. Mack stifled her laughter by burying her face in Linc's chest.

"Baby, I think I've been dreaming about this for a long, long time."

"Softie. I just assumed I'd be medevacing patients into my seventies and then retiring to the Caribbean. Elementary school Christmas assemblies were not on my radar."

Plans changed. Dreams grew. And happiness sometimes just snuck up on a person when they were least expecting it.

"Speaking of," he said. "I booked it. You and me. An entire week in January. A tropical island."

"First of all, you're the most amazing husband in the universe. Second, we're going to drink too many umbrella drinks, have all the sex, and take lazy naps by the pool." She sighed dreamily.

"We should definitely work on our endurance for all those things. Don't want to go into this vacation as amateurs."

"Agreed. Are you sure your parents are up for dealing with three little, beautiful, evil kids?" she asked.

"They're trading off with your parents for the weekend, and then my sisters, who owe me two and a half years of free child care—I did the math—have them the rest of the week. The kids stay at our place, and the babysitters are rotating out. Harper and Luke are the backup backups."

"You've thought of everything."

"Dreamy, nothing is going to keep me from you on a beach in the very small, very red bikini I ordered you last night."

"Damn. The Speedo I got you is red too," she teased. "We'll be twinsies."

He grinned and squeezed her hand.

The number came to a welcome and out-of-tune ending on stage.

"Remind me to talk to Ellen about the New Year's Throw Down," Mack whispered.

Thanks to Mackenzie's persistence and Linc's grant-writing skills, Benevolence had acquired a grant to expand their Wellness Club. It had grown to include weekly social events that included fitness and wellness and nutrition, like step contests and weight loss challenges. Hell, Abner Kersh had organized an entire trick-or-treat route for kids with allergies at Halloween. The whole damn town's cholesterol was down, blood pressure falling. So were things like loneliness and feelings of isolation.

All because Mackenzie O'Neil came to town.

He reached over to toy with her wedding band. He'd had it engraved with the words he wore on his heart. *I'll always be there.*

Lucas clapped in his grandmother's lap.

Linc noted a couple of his crew from the station standing along the wall, their feet moving in unison with the kids onstage. They'd all learned the choreography to help Hadley practice. His daughter danced with what they'd dubbed her fierce face. Intent and serious, just like her beautiful mom.

Luke and Harper were there a few rows back, Gloria and Aldo too, even though most of their kids were older and had moved well beyond elementary school. James and his husband, Manny, were there recording second-grade Oliver's one-liner in the play and daughter Tate's kindergarten dance number.

Time marched on, families grew, love deepened. And Linc wouldn't have it any other way.

The assembly mercifully ended with an out-of-tune, tuba-heavy performance of "Rudolph the Red-Nosed Reindeer" by the fourth graders. The kids got a standing ovation. Not so much because of their performance but because it was over.

"Daddy!"

Hadley launched herself at him, and he caught her, just like he always would. "Great footwork, kiddo!"

Joyfully, she squished his cheeks between her little seven-year-old hands. He'd painted her fingernails red and green for the occasion while Mack had reinforced her floppy antlers with a metal clothes hanger. Both had held up well.

"Did you see me? I nailed that three-sixty."

"I saw it! Zane and Skyler recorded the whole thing."

"Mommy's gonna make us watch it a hundred million times, isn't she?" Hadley groaned.

"She sure is."

"She's so funny."

"Daaaaaaaaaaaaad!" Casey came running, and Linc scooped her up, his arms full of giggling girls arguing about what they should have for dinner. And then Dreamy was walking toward them through the crowd, her cheeks flushed, her smile bright.

Linc knew without a doubt that he'd never feel more love than he did in that moment.

He also knew that he'd be proven wrong tomorrow. Because every damn day was a new happily ever after.

The Story of the Real Sunshine

Sunshine was a real dog. My real dog. And she taught me the greatest life lesson.

For a few years, Mr. Lucy and I fostered rescue dogs in our home. We'd helped make several serendipitous dog-human matches. There was Archer, the puppy that my social worker friend found tied to a client's porch with no food. Maddie Mae, the puppy mill Jack Russell terrier that never learned not to pee on the carpet. Sam, the pit bull-mastiff mix that now paddleboards with his human and carries puppies in his saddlebag.

And then there was Sunshine.

A rescue we hadn't worked with before posted an emergency SOS. They'd liberated her from an Amish puppy mill in Lancaster County. She was a six-year-old, overbred yellow Lab with the softest fur I'd ever had the privilege of petting.

Turns out she also had raging separation anxiety.

I was at a low point when little miss Sunshine pranced into my life. I'd been laid off from a job with a newspaper, a place I'd dreamed of working since I was a kid watching Lois Lane chase down stories on TV.

My savings were running out and the novella I'd written

and thrown at Amazon like overcooked spaghetti at a wall had flopped.

I felt depressed and adrift and unnecessary.

Enter Sunshine on September 4, 2013. Somehow, she didn't see the sad, unemployable, replaceable Lucy. She looked at me and saw a radiant beacon of peanut butter...or cheese. Or whatever dogs value the most.

It took us a few days to catch on to the depth of Sunshine's separation anxiety. The claw marks in the doorframes and giant puddles of pee on the carpet were hints. But it wasn't until we came home from dinner and found the couch moved two feet backward with dog toenail marks carved into it that we realized we had a big problem.

Turns out, Miss Sunshine had bonded her little blond self to me. And any time I wasn't right in front of her, she was convinced the world was going to end.

So we made concessions. We tried rarely leaving the house. We held rather one-sided conversations with her about the concept of objects and people existing even though she couldn't see them. We tried crating her. Calming treats. Thunder jackets.

But apparently nothing compared to my company. Ego boost!

We'd had our disaster dog for a few weeks when Mr. Lucy and I started having the "No one is going to adopt this dog" conversation. Which evolved into the "So this is what foster failure feels like."

We loved her. Despite her disastrous crazy-pants fears, she was a super good girl (read in human to doggy tone). She slept at our feet and every morning would belly crawl her way up the bed between us to shove her big wet nose in our faces, her tail thumping maniacally because, for the first time in her life, she had humans who didn't leave and a soft, squishy bed. She had endless green grass outside, daily walks, and all the food and water she could ever want. She also had a weird four-legged pillow that didn't like her very much.

To this day, Sunshine is the only other living organism that Cleo the cat learned to tolerate. Somewhere in the archives, a picture of Sunshine using Cleo as a reluctant pillow exists.

Leashes were purely decorative because our fluffy little girl never left my side. Even in a dog park, I couldn't get her to do anything but sit in front of me and stare at me like her own personal cheese goddess. Toys held no interest for her. Other dogs didn't exist. She would tolerate love from other humans, but always with her brown eyes on me or Mr. Lucy.

It was around this time that Mr. Lucy noticed that one of Sunshine's doggy boobs was swollen and seemed painful to the touch.

The rescue that had originally liberated Sunshine was no longer involved in her care, but Central Pennsylvania Animal Alliance hooked us up with a vet appointment. After an intense surgery and a visit with a specialist, we had our diagnosis.

Our little girl had cancer and it was everywhere.

Our little family didn't have much time together.

The vet was an incredible woman—her patients include wolves at a local sanctuary—and she gave us a very explicit list of symptoms to watch for so we would know when it was time. She explained that dogs hide their pain so well, their humans often don't realize how much they hurt until it's too late.

Since Sunshine was a foodie, we were instructed to watch her appetite, because as soon as that went, it meant her situation was dire. In the meantime, we were to give her anything her puppy dog heart desired.

On the way home, we stopped at Wendy's and got her her own chicken nuggets.

From that day on, Sunshine was never alone. She had scrambled eggs for breakfast and ground turkey and vegetables for dinner. She went to yoga with me and to work with Mr. Lucy. She would wait in the car when I went grocery shopping…and then eat entire loaves of bread if I left her alone for two minutes with the bags.

We snuggled with her and scheduled our days around her without worrying about spoiling her. Our friends brought her gourmet treats and fancy toys. And she basked in the attention of loving humans. And Cleo's disdain.

On December 23, 2013, Sunshine went to sleep one last time with her head in my lap in our living room while a kindhearted vet recited a poem and told her she was a good, beautiful girl.

My best friend was gone. But she wasn't in pain anymore. She wasn't scared anymore.

And I had done my best by her.

That was the lesson Sunshine taught me.

With the end always in mind, we made the best of the present. And when the time came to say goodbye, we had already said everything else. Because not a minute of Sunshine's time with us had been wasted.

Sunshine revealed the very best in us. Our patience, our uncomplicated, unconditional loving hearts. Our ability to be present and do our very best. And in the end, she showed us how beautiful a goodbye with no regrets can be.

She also taught me that even unemployed and vaguely depressed, I still deserved to be loved unconditionally.

Yeah, so. I'm basically geysering salt water out of my eyeballs right now remembering the pretty little girl who didn't have enough time on this planet with good people who loved her.

We'll never forget Sunshine, destroyer of carpets and

furniture, stealer of peanut butter and jelly sandwiches, our bread-loving bed hog.

We'll also never forget the kind folks at Central Pennsylvania Animal Alliance who set up vet appointments, paid for surgeries and meds, and cried for us when Sunshine—a dog they hadn't even rescued—pranced across the Rainbow Bridge.

Mr. Lucy and I don't foster anymore. But we do write checks. If you are ever looking for a cause that deserves your dollars, CPAA's Hounds of Prison Education program is amazing. They pair carefully vetted prisoners with rescue dogs that need special training. Magic happens for the human wards and the canines that come to love them unconditionally.

https://www.hopedogs.org/

After everything Sunshine gave me, I'd always wished I could have given her more time. The best I could do was give her Lincoln Reed and her own happily ever after. I hope you loved my fictional girl as much as I loved the real thing.

Remember, all we have is right now and it's up to us to make the best of it. So live life Sunshine style. Love someone so much it hurts when they're not there. Steal a PB&J. Make a memory. Keep those regrets out of your goodbyes.

Author's Note

Dear Reader,

How was that for a five-alarm happily ever after? Whew! *smears sweat around on face with third wear taco T-shirt*

I hope you loved Linc and Mack and your revisit to Benevolence. This was one of those books that just flowed like queso through my fingers and onto the screen. It felt like Linc had been marinating in the back of my mind for a very long time! And I had the best time catching up with Luke and Harper and Gloria and Aldo. All the heart eyes!

I delved pretty deeply into research for this book and came away obsessed with *Air Ambulance ER* episodes. Plus, I got to fictionalize some real-life events. That opening scene with Linc on his way to buy an extension cord? That actually happened. And so did the roadside open heart surgery.

I couldn't have written this book without the help of Brooke Kell Morgan and her reluctant brother Christopher Kell, along with the rest of the Help a Lucy Out: First Responder Research Group. Thank you from the bottom of my heart for helping me write this book!

Loved Linc and want to leave a review? Thank you! You're the sweetest and you clearly have phenomenal taste! Don't want to ever miss a word I write? Sign up for my rarely annoying, always entertaining newsletter. Thank you for spending your reading time on this book. You're the bestest!

Xoxo,
Lucy

Acknowledgments

- Brooke Kell Morgan and Christopher Kell for making sure I didn't write a super inaccurate fire department.
- All the members of Help a Lucy Out: First Responder Research Group.
- Author Jamie Schlosser for hunting down and tackling real-life fire chiefs to get answers to my random questions.
- Joyce and Tammy for being so pretty and fun and not letting me linger in the "this book might be garbage" phase.
- My eagle-eyed proofers and editors: Jessica Snyder, Dawn Harer, Amanda Edens, and Sabrina Baskey.
- Mr. Lucy for being so Mr. Lucy-y. You're my real-life bearded hero!
- My readers. Loves of my life. You guys are too tacorific for words. Thanks for always showing up for me!
- First responders everywhere. You are the heroes of everyday life and we thank you from the bottom of our hearts. Stay safe out there.

About the Author

Lucy Score is a #1 *New York Times, USA Today,* and *Wall Street Journal* bestselling author. She grew up in a literary family who insisted that the dinner table was for reading and earned a degree in journalism. She writes full-time from the Pennsylvania home she and Mr. Lucy share with their obnoxious cat, Cleo. When not spending hours crafting heartbreaker heroes and kick-ass heroines, Lucy can be found on the couch, in the kitchen, or at the gym. She hopes to someday write from a sailboat, ocean-front condo, or tropical island with reliable Wi-Fi.

Sign up for her newsletter and stay up on all the latest Lucy book news.

And follow her on:

Website: lucyscore.net

Facebook: lucyscorewrites

Instagram: @scorelucy

TikTok: @lucyferscore

Binge Books: bingebooks.com/author/lucy-score

Readers Group: facebook.com/groups/BingeReaders Anonymous

Newsletter signup: